Tiny Hector Glum snuck into Billie's lab and got stuck in her hair. Let's get him out of there!

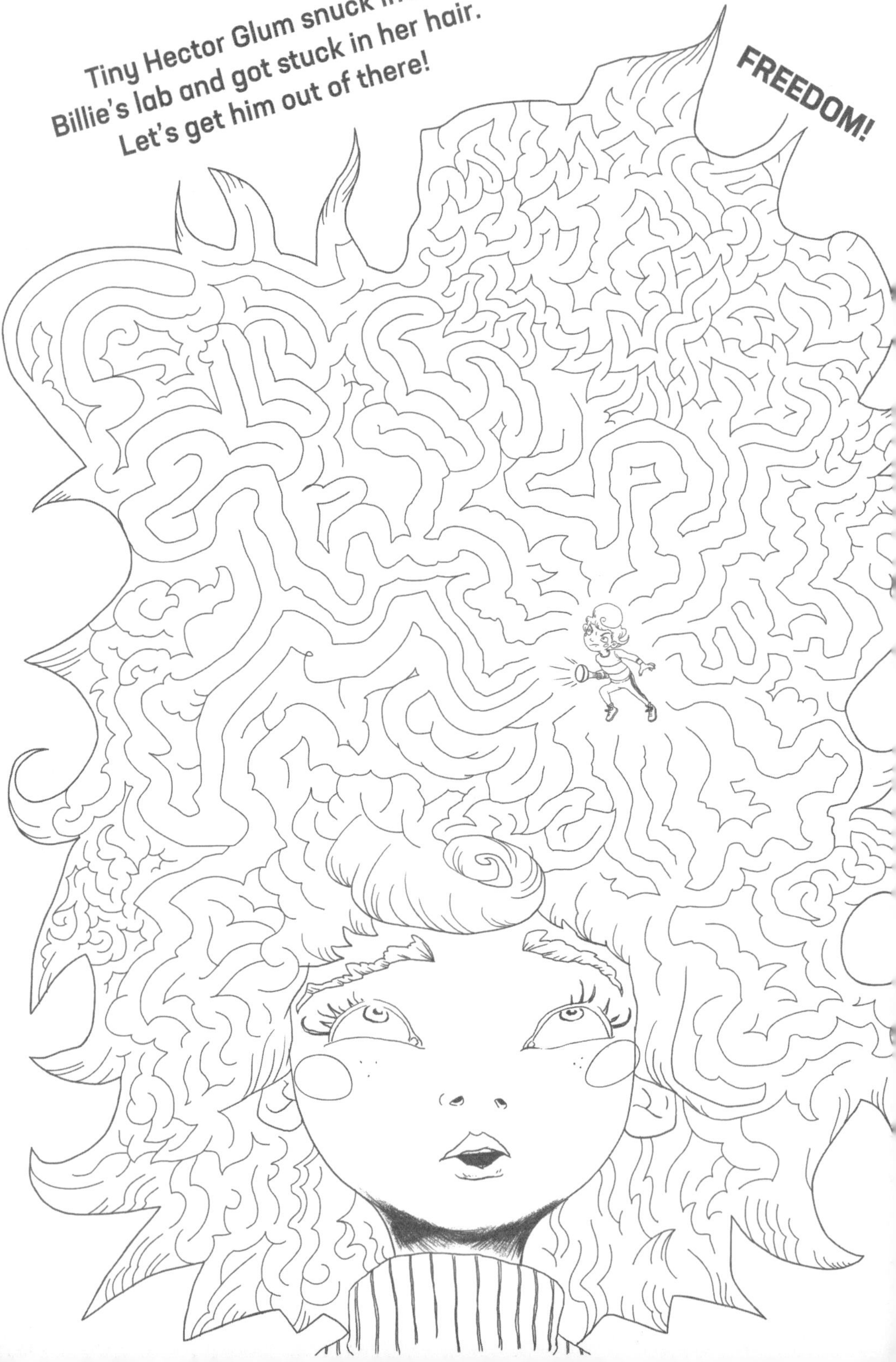
FREEDOM!

BILLIE BLASTER

AND THE ROBOT ARMY
FROM OUTER SPACE

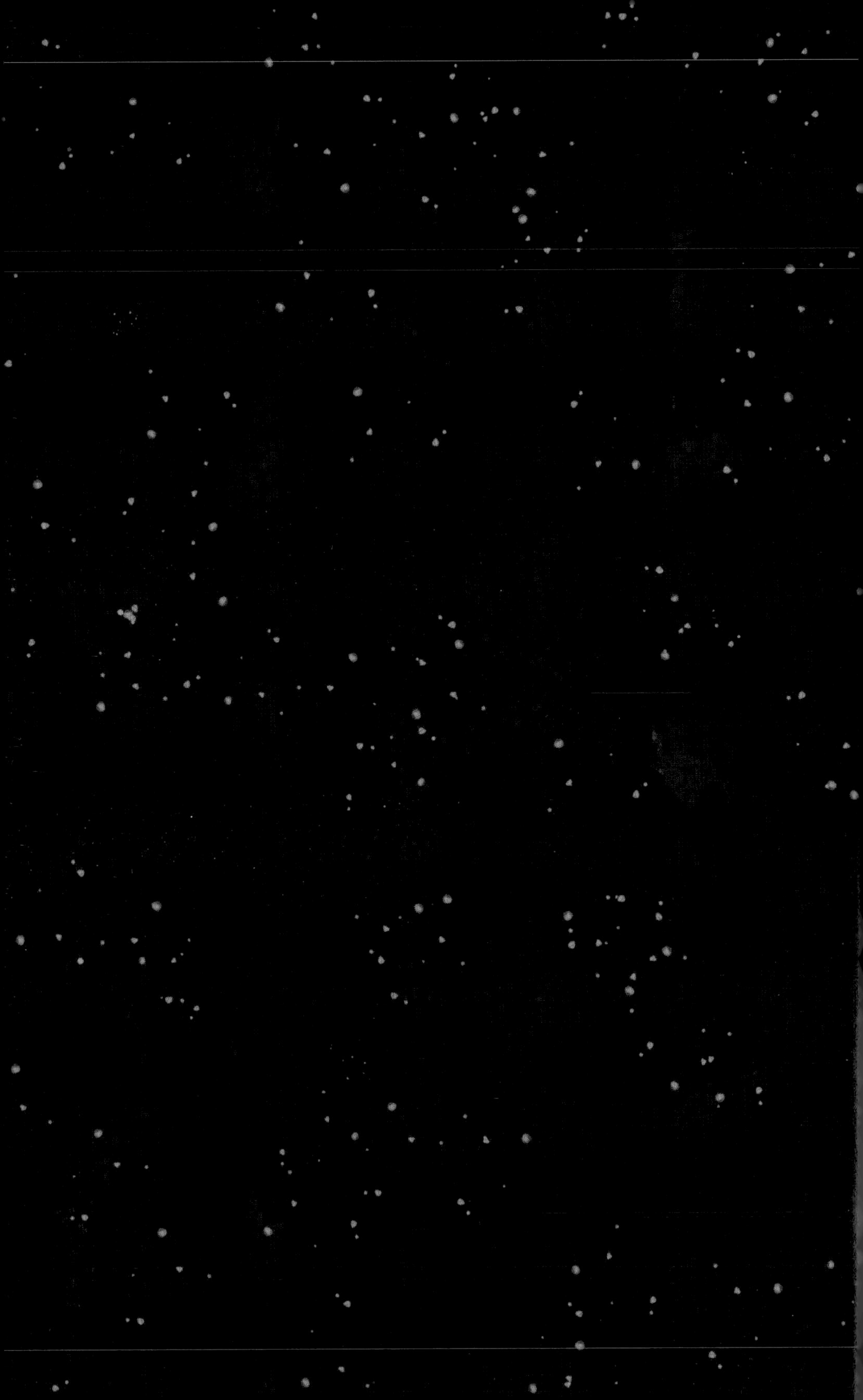

BILLIE BLASTER

AND THE ROBOT ARMY FROM OUTER SPACE

BY LAINI TAYLOR
& JIM DI BARTOLO

AMULET BOOKS ★ NEW YORK

Library of Congress Control Number 2022952145

ISBN 978-1-4197-5384-8

Text © 2023 Laini Taylor and Jim Di Bartolo
Illustrations and colored cover art © 2023 Jim Di Bartolo
Book design by Andrea Miller
Interior colors by WK Sahadewa
Lettering by Dave Sharpe

Published in 2023 by Amulet Books, an imprint of ABRAMS.

Printed and bound in China
10 9 8 7 6 5 4 3 2 1

Amulet Books are available at special discounts when purchased in quantity for premiums and promotions as well as fundraising or educational use. Special editions can also be created to specification. For details, contact specialsales@abramsbooks.com or the address below.

Amulet Books® is a registered trademark of Harry N. Abrams, Inc.

ABRAMS The Art of Books
195 Broadway, New York, NY 10007
abramsbooks.com

FOR OUR DARLING
CLEMENTINE

BILLIE BLASTER

AND THE ROBOT ARMY FROM OUTER SPACE

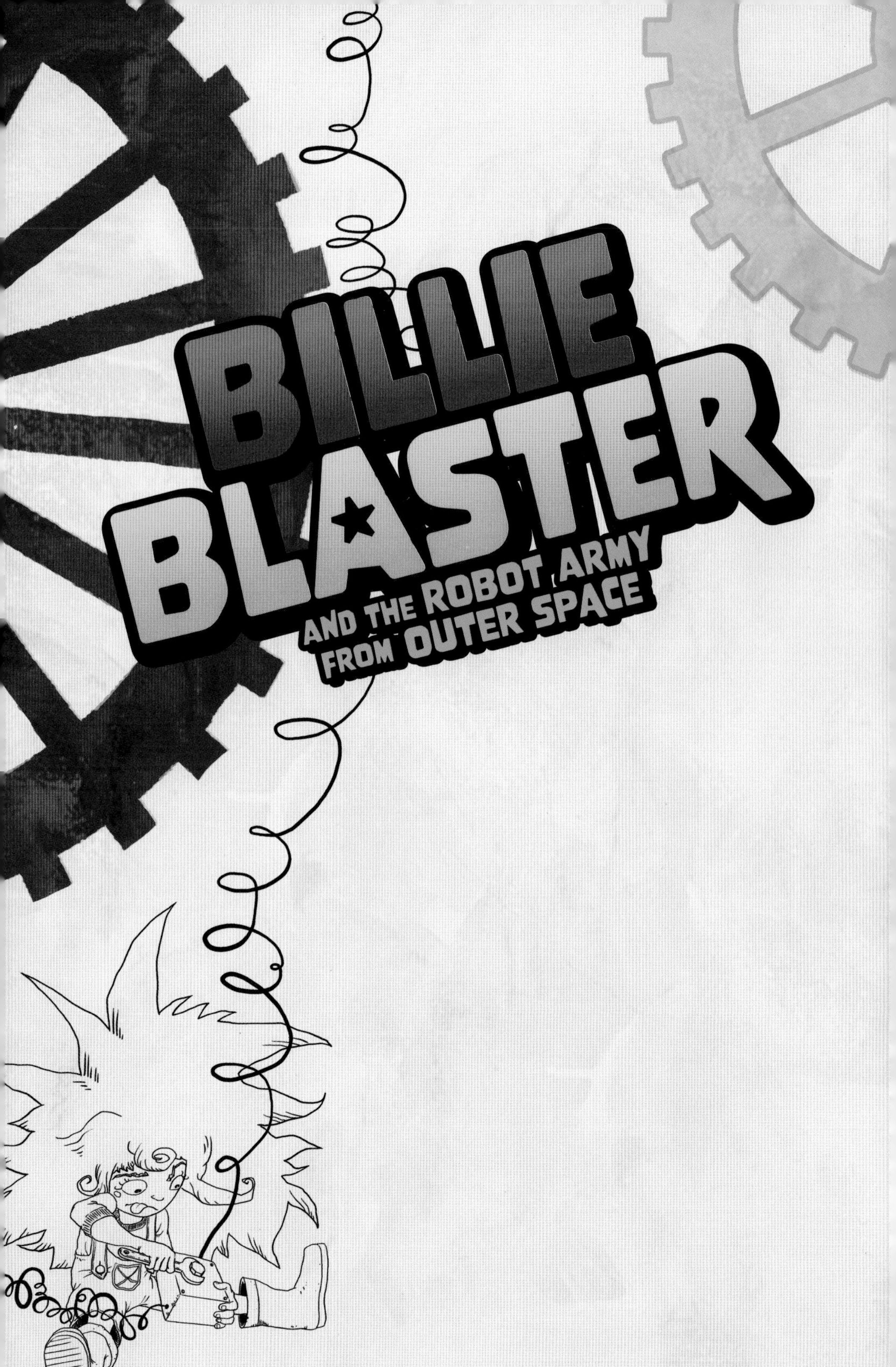

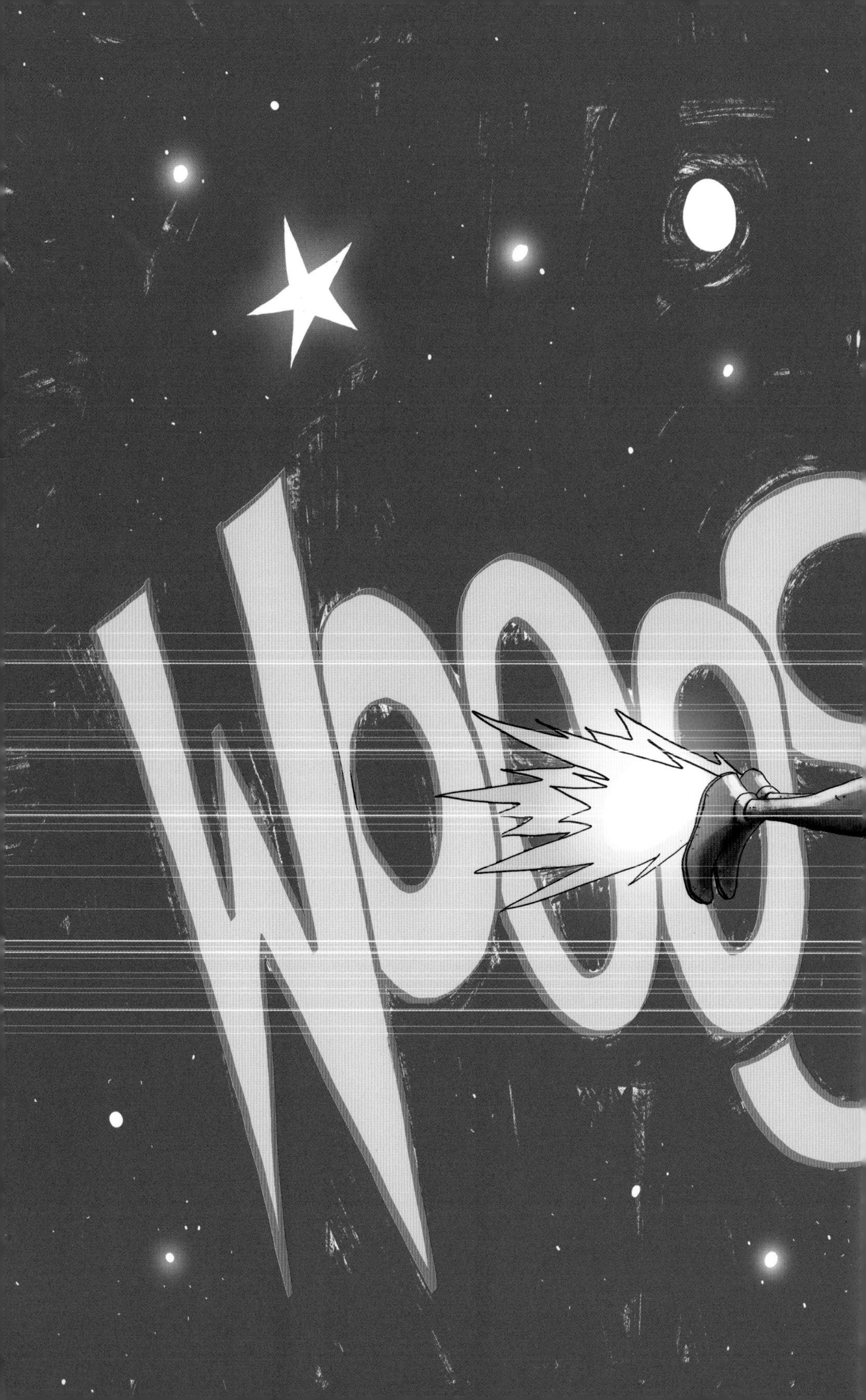
WOOOS

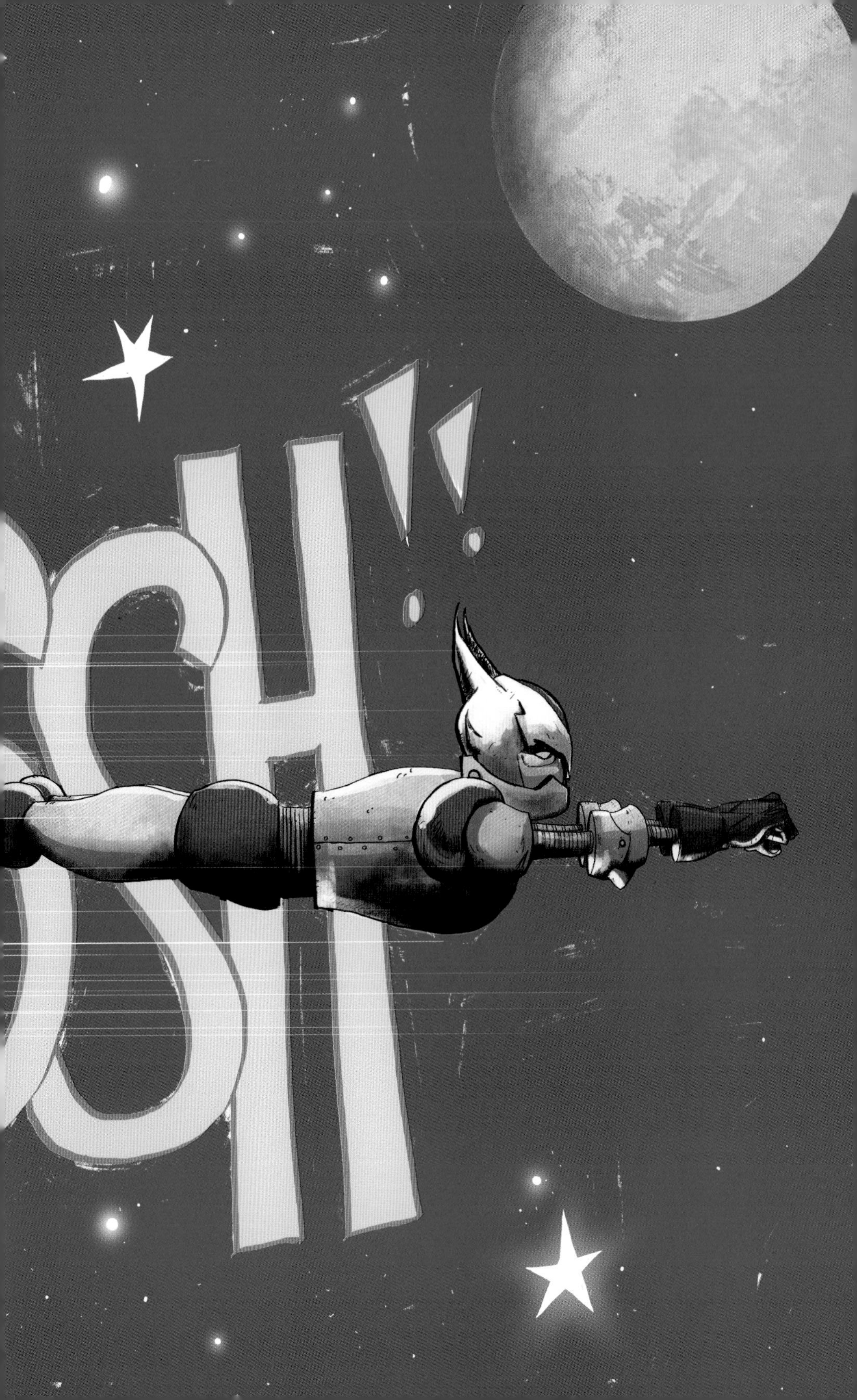
SH!!

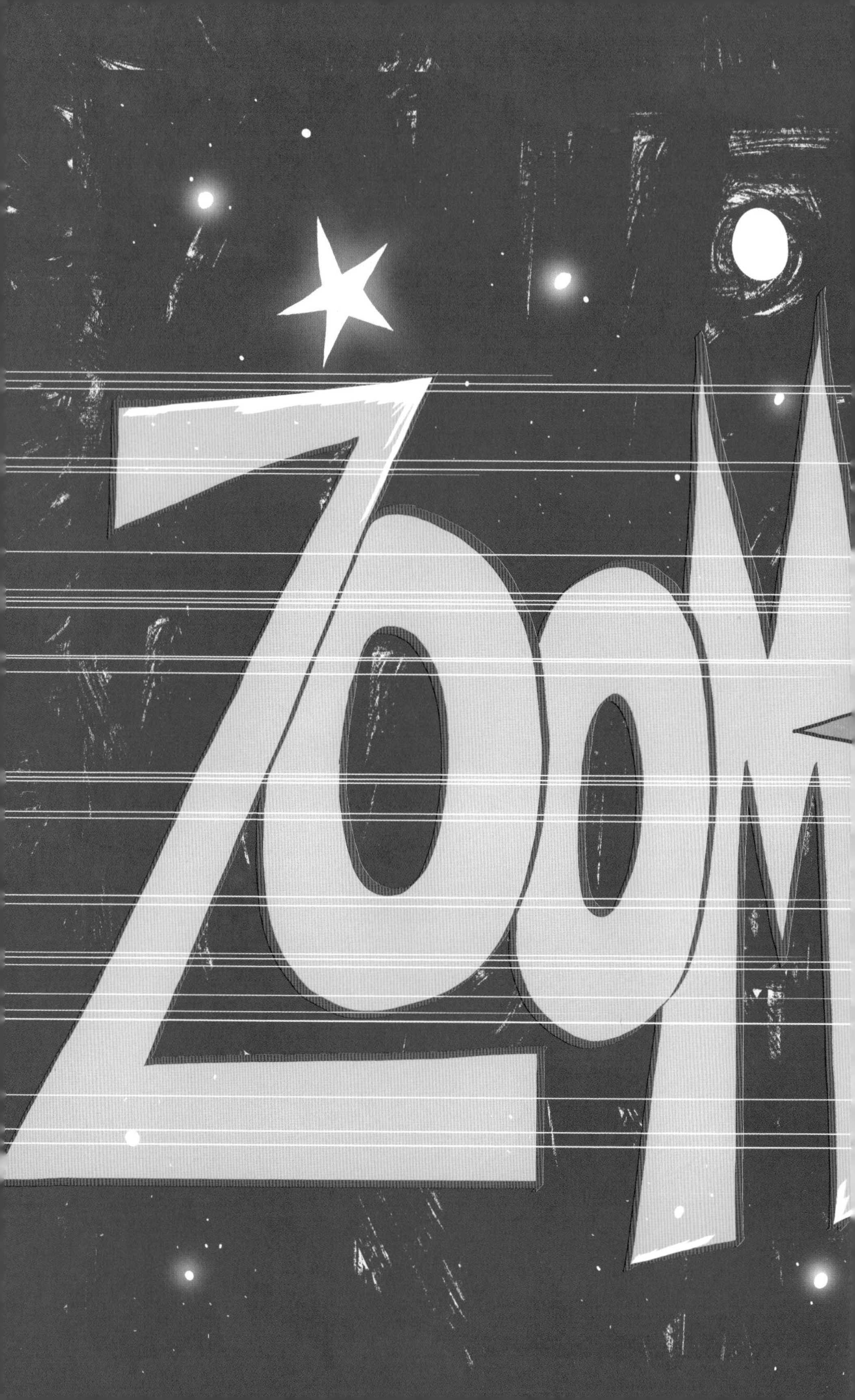
ZOOM

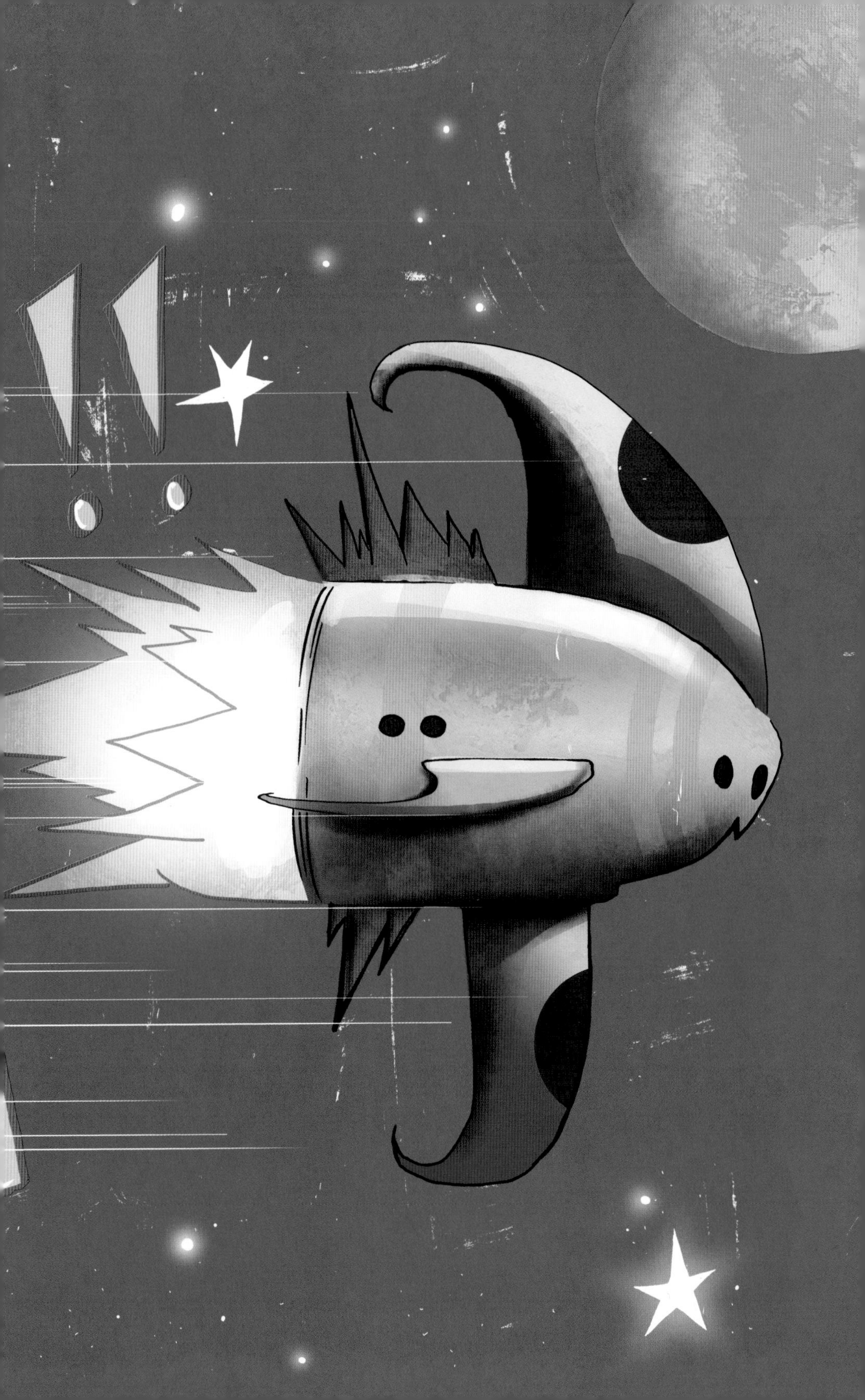
!!

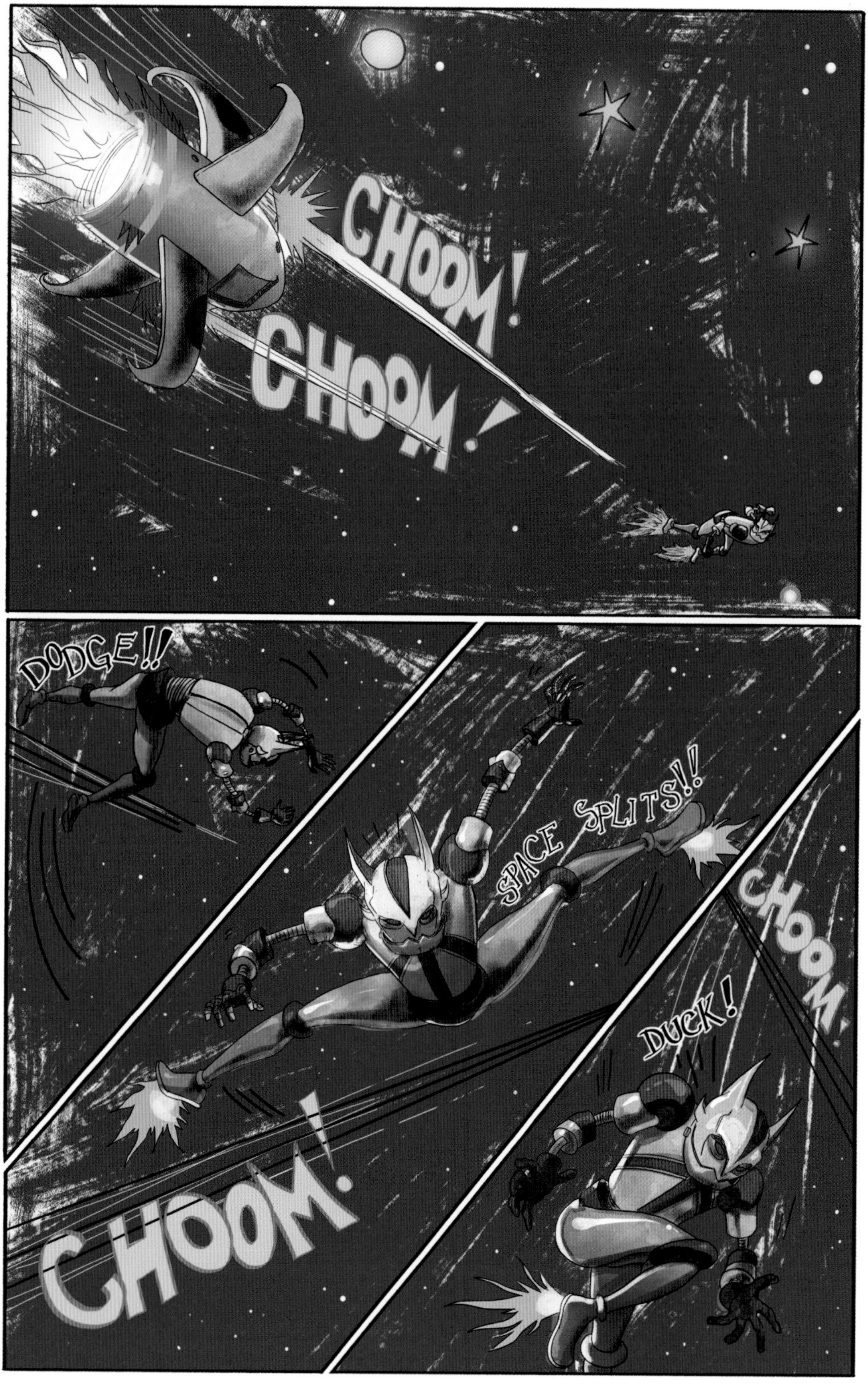
CHOOM!
CHOOM!
DODGE!!
SPACE SPLITS!!
CHOOM!
DUCK!
CHOOM!

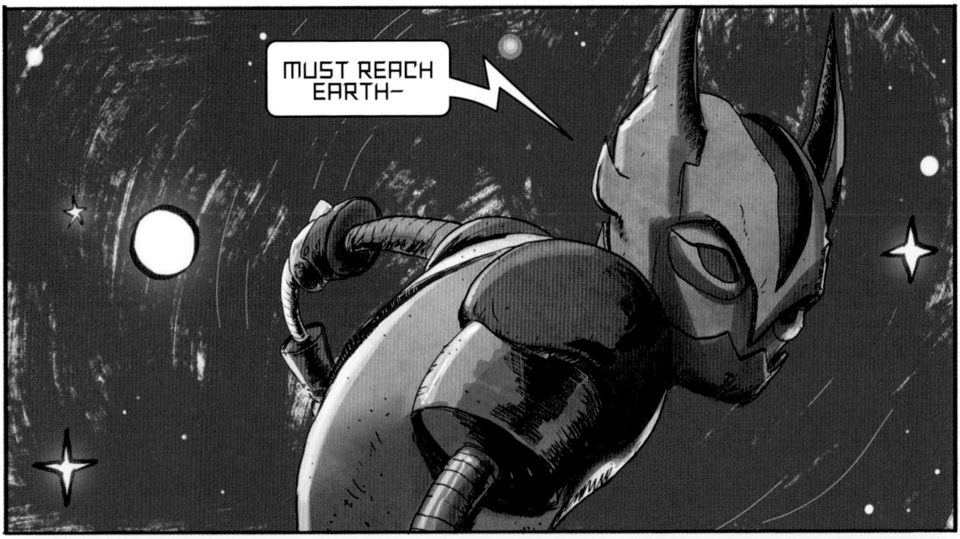
MUST REACH EARTH-

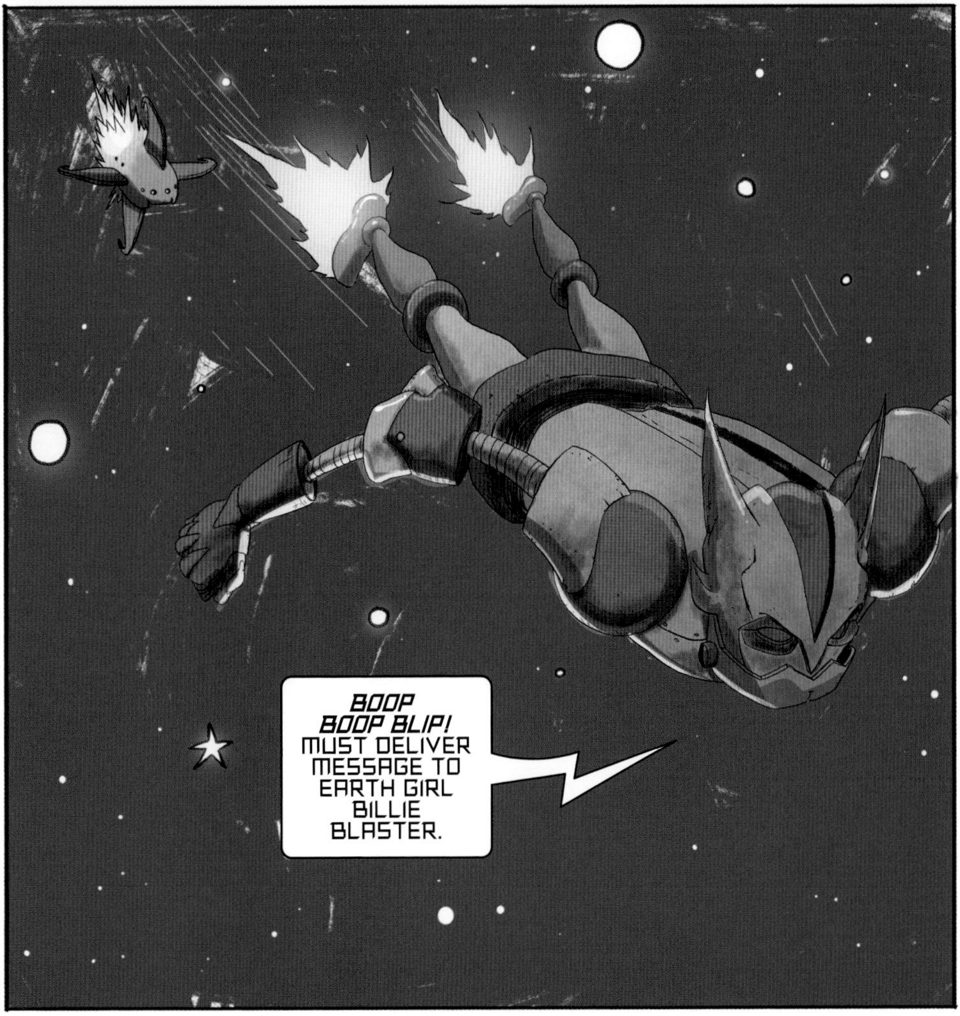
BOOP BOOP BLIP! MUST DELIVER MESSAGE TO EARTH GIRL BILLIE BLASTER.

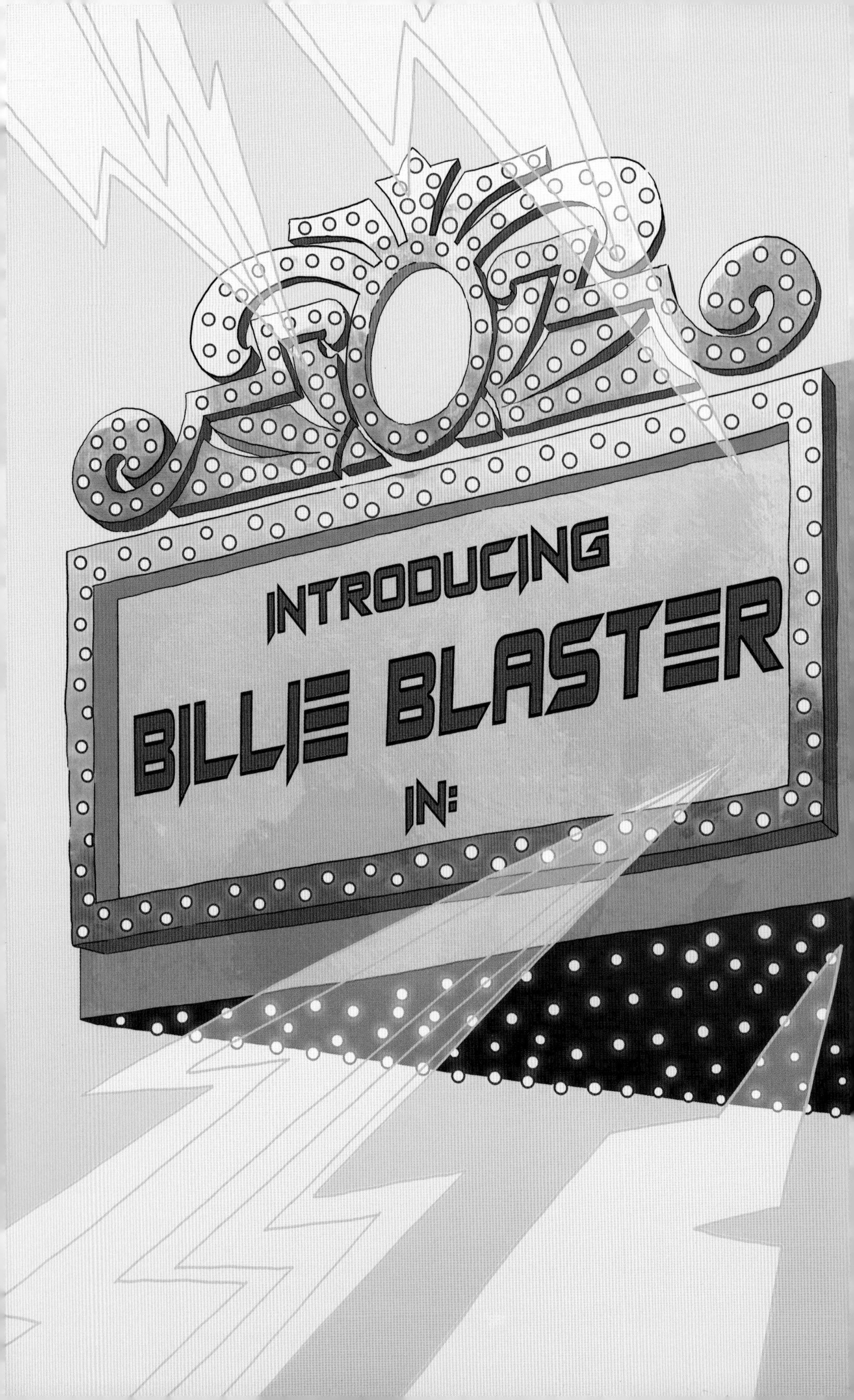
INTRODUCING
BILLIE BLASTER
IN:

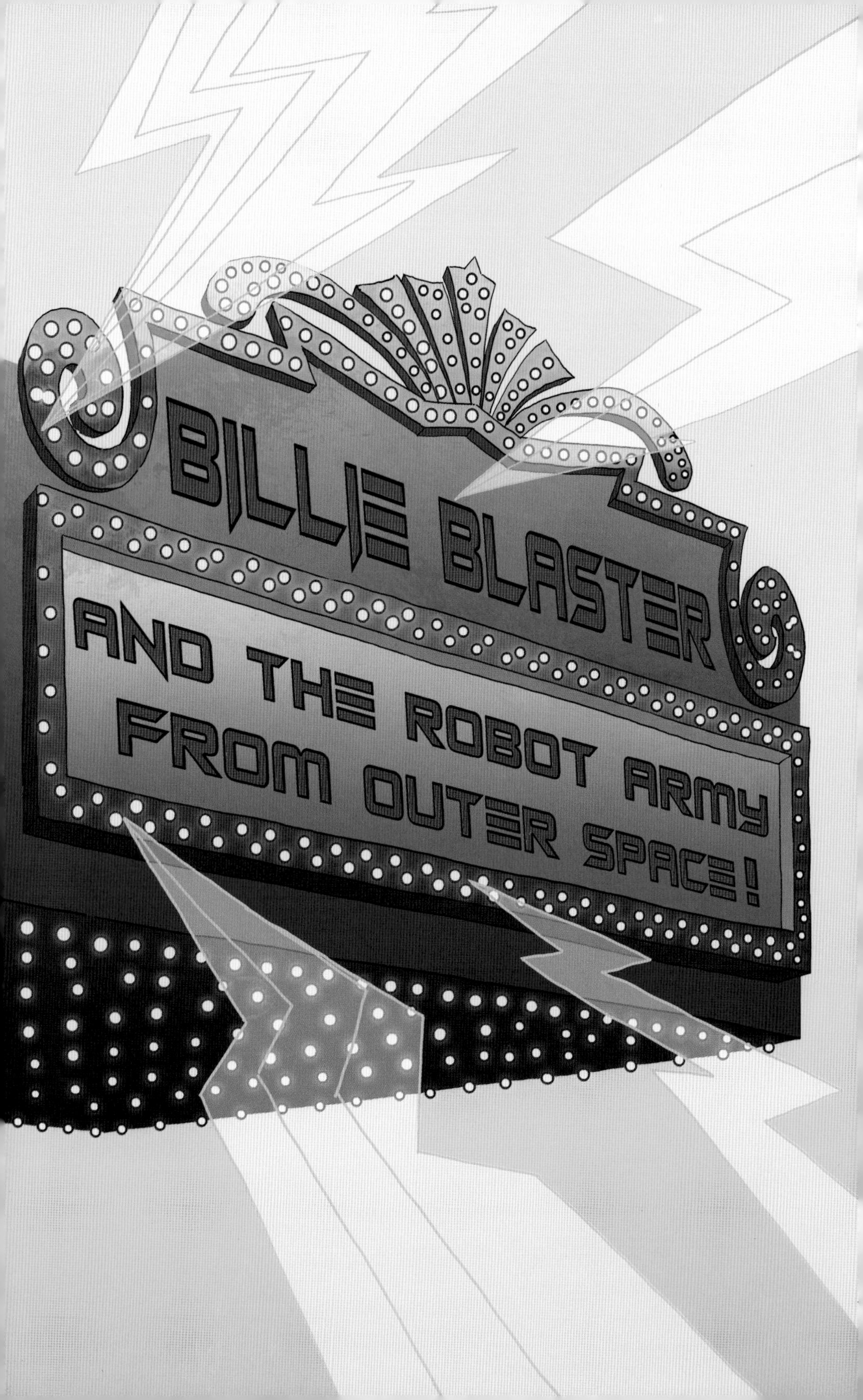
BILLIE BLASTER
AND THE ROBOT ARMY
FROM OUTER SPACE!

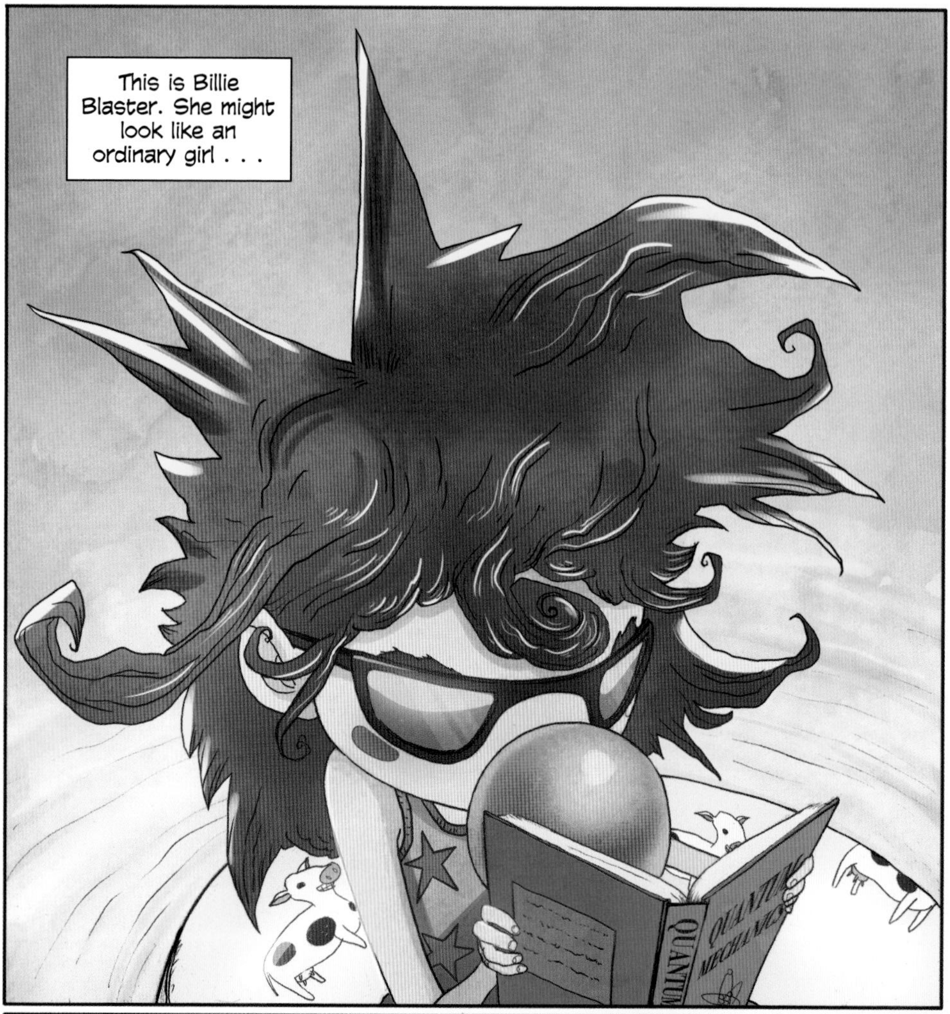
This is Billie Blaster. She might look like an ordinary girl . . .
QUANTUM

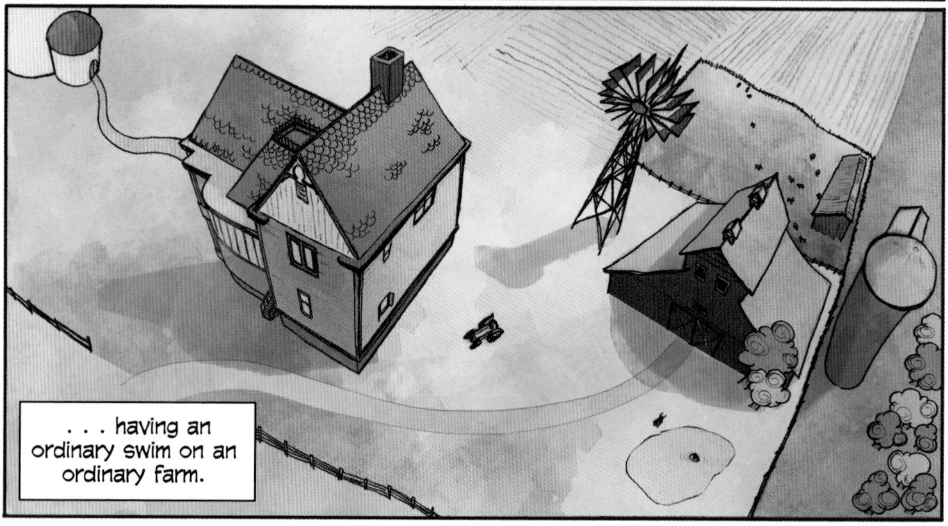
. . . having an ordinary swim on an ordinary farm.

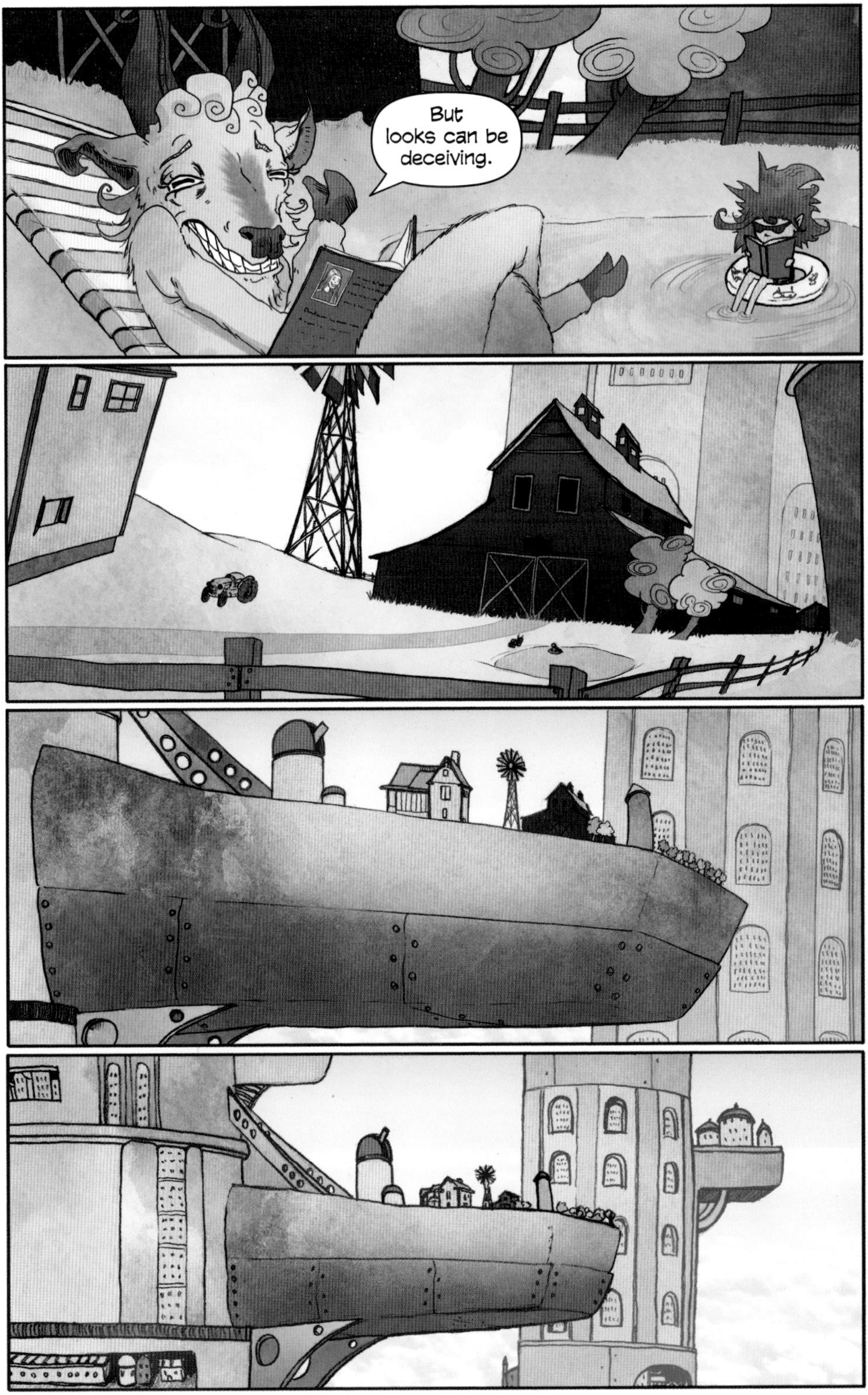
But looks can be deceiving.

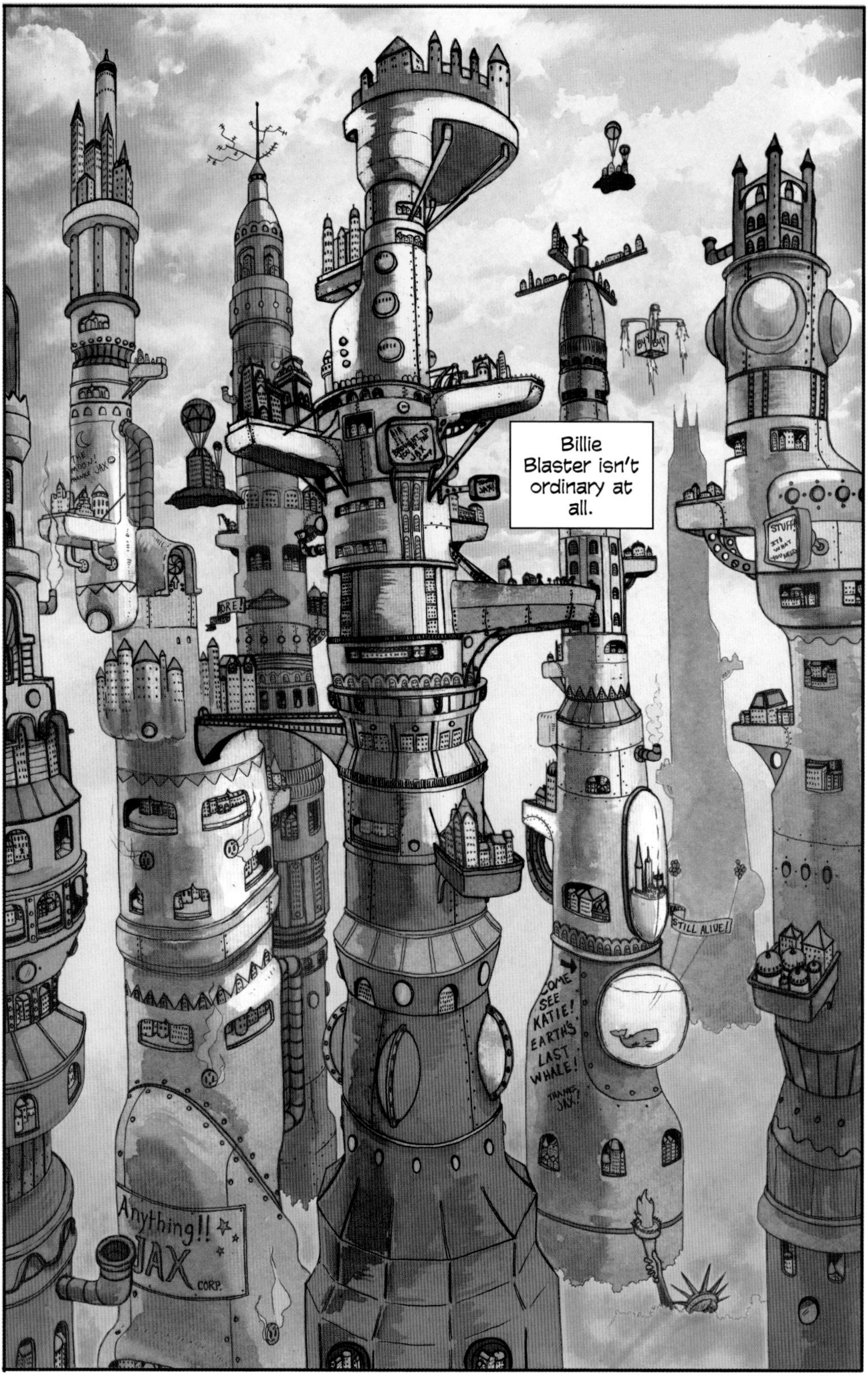
Billie Blaster isn't ordinary at all.
THE MOON! THANKS JAX
AIR BROUGHT TO YOU BY THE JAX CORP.
MORE!
BUY BUY
STILL ALIVE!
COME SEE KATIE! EARTH'S LAST WHALE!
THANKS, JAX!
Anything!! JAX CORP.

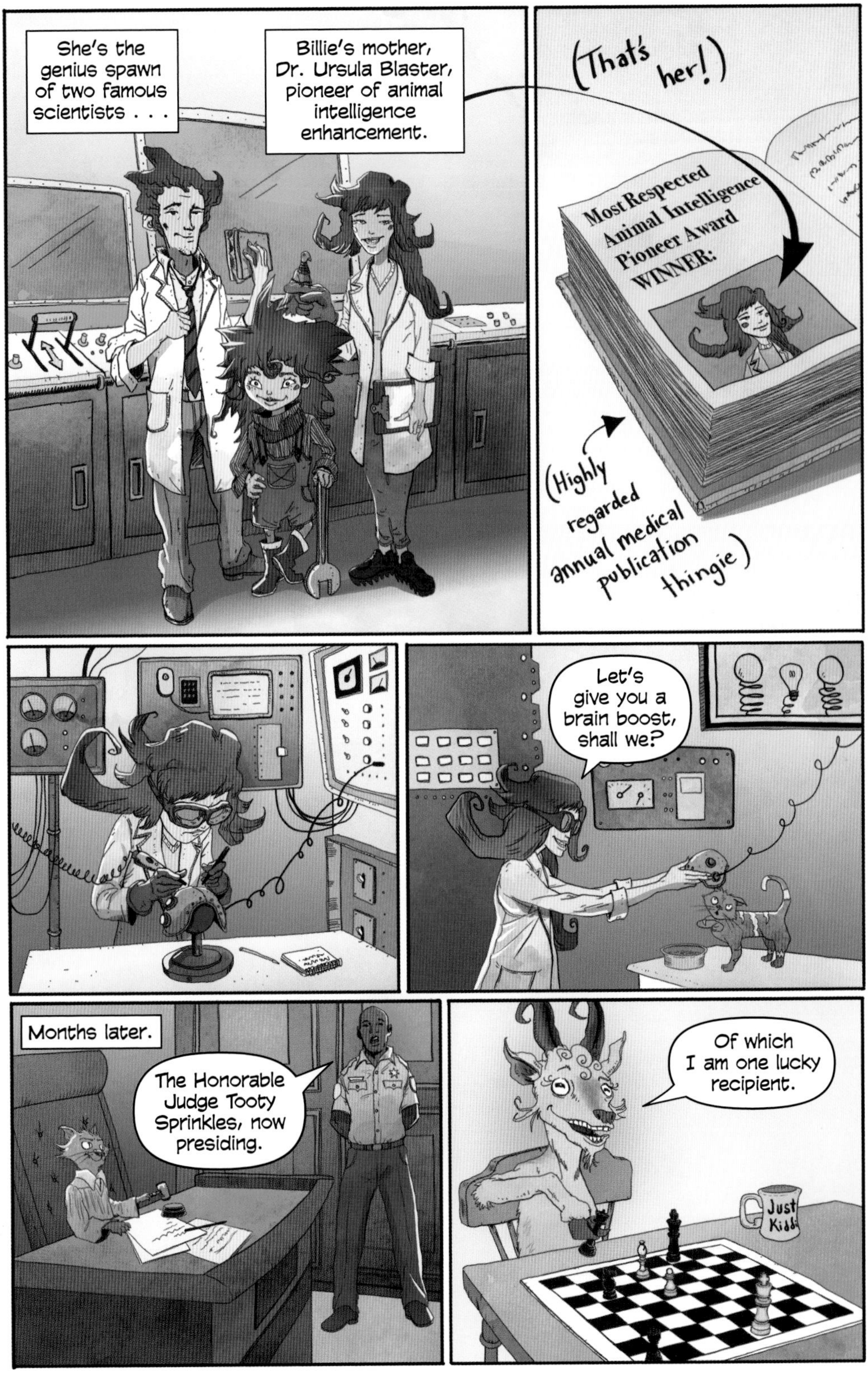
She's the genius spawn of two famous scientists . . .
Billie's mother, Dr. Ursula Blaster, pioneer of animal intelligence enhancement.
(That's her!)
Most Respected Animal Intelligence Pioneer Award WINNER:
(Highly regarded annual medical publication thingie)
Let's give you a brain boost, shall we?
Months later.
The Honorable Judge Tooty Sprinkles, now presiding.
Of which I am one lucky recipient.

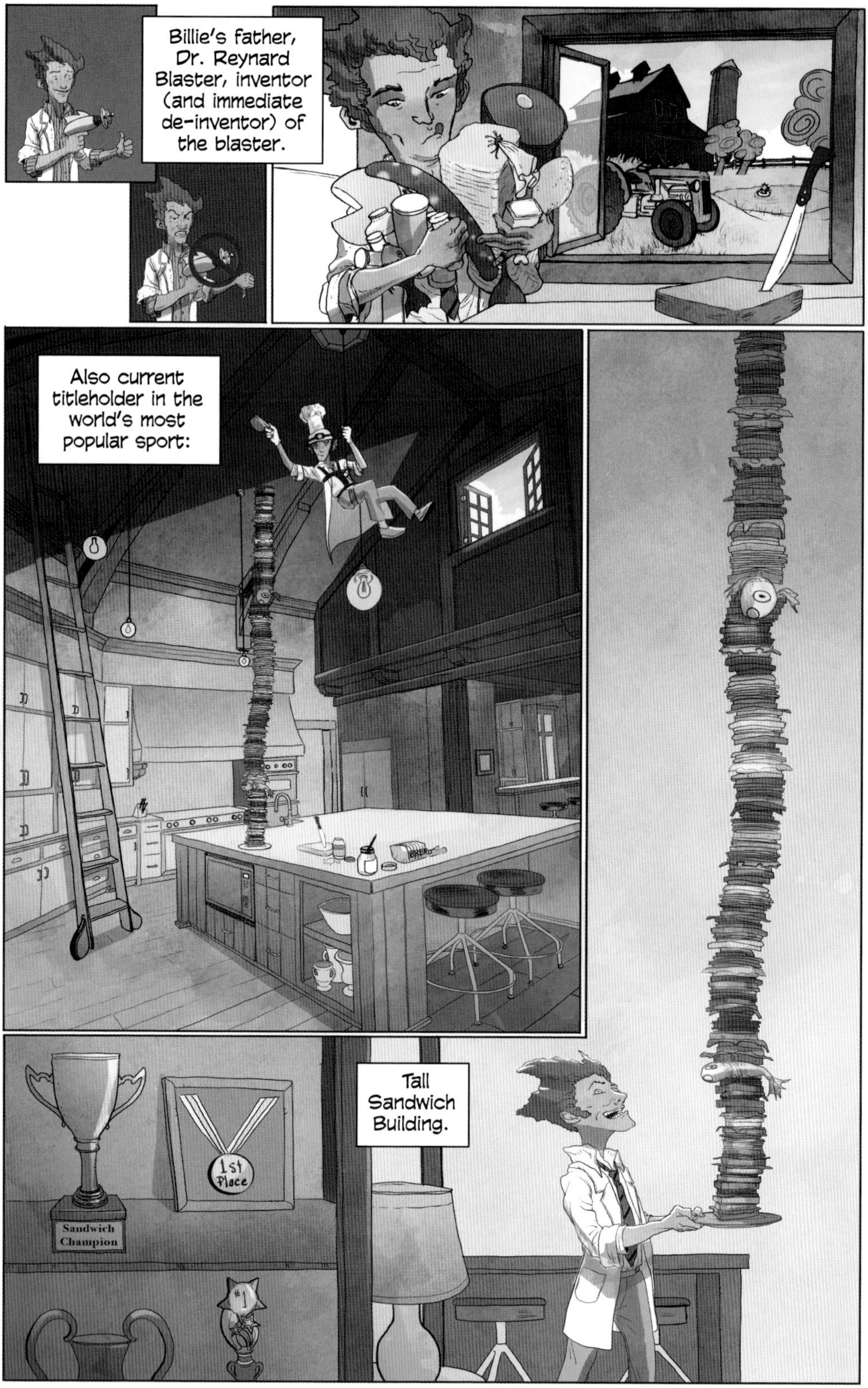
Billie's father, Dr. Reynard Blaster, inventor (and immediate de-inventor) of the blaster.
Also current titleholder in the world's most popular sport:
Tall Sandwich Building.
1st Place
Sandwich Champion
#1

. . . and Billie is quite the scientist herself.

By the age of five, she had invented jet skates . . .

. . . glow-in-the-dark toothpaste . . .

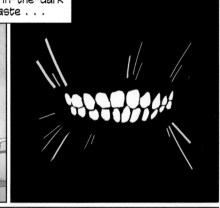

. . . and lap dinosaurs . . .

(though lap dinosaurs weren't as brilliant an idea as you might imagine).

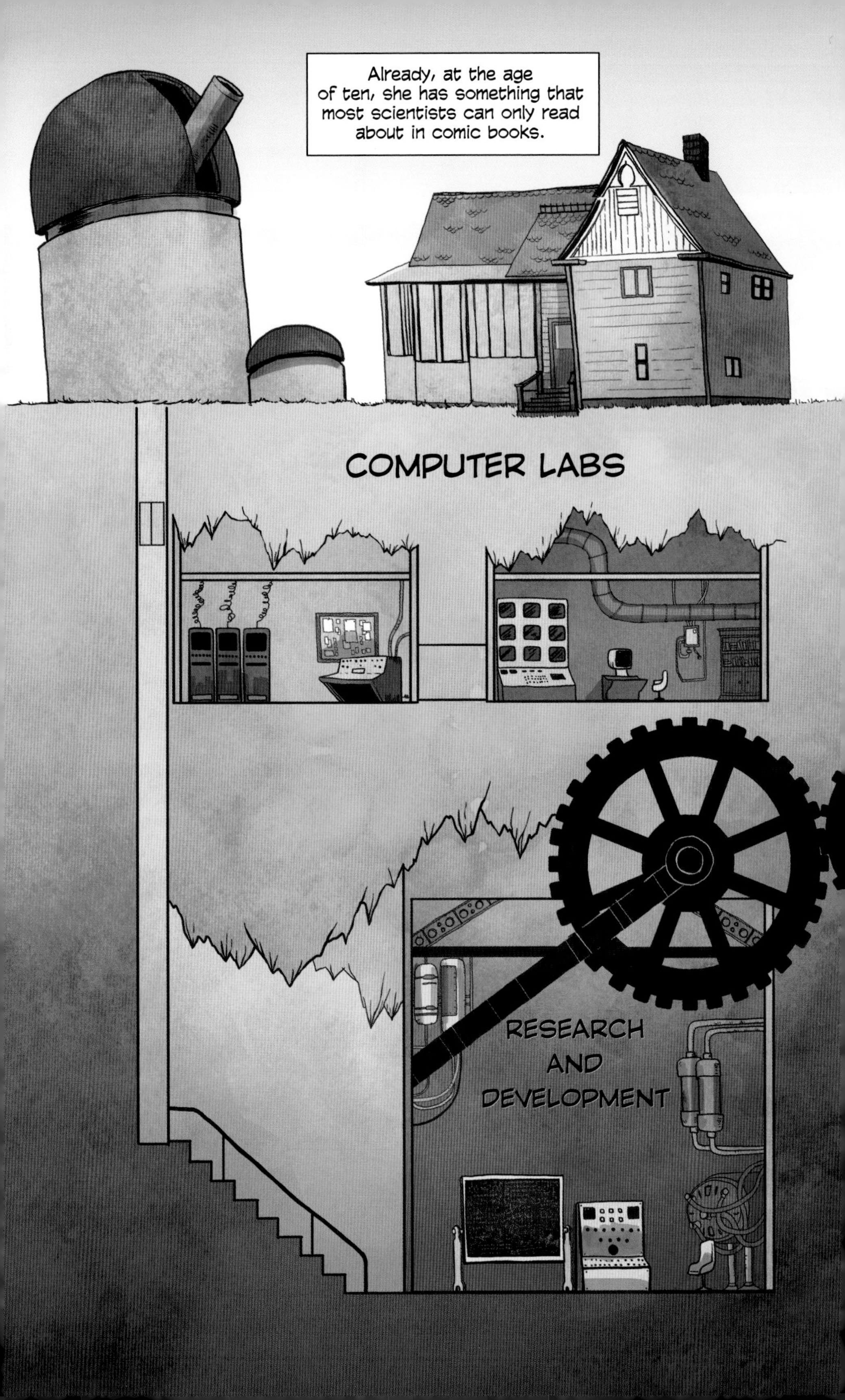
Already, at the age of ten, she has something that most scientists can only read about in comic books.
COMPUTER LABS
RESEARCH AND DEVELOPMENT

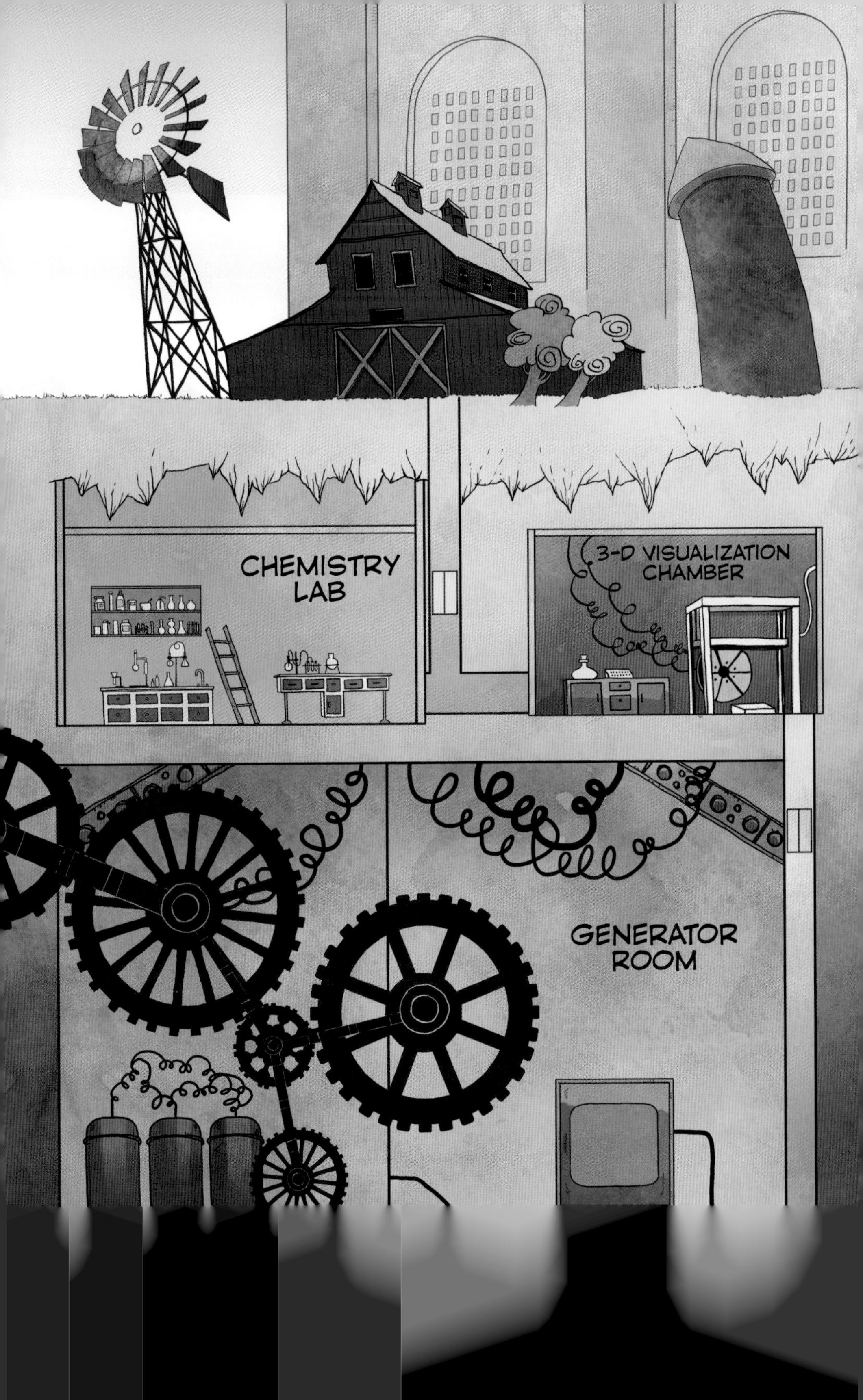
CHEMISTRY LAB
3-D VISUALIZATION CHAMBER
GENERATOR ROOM

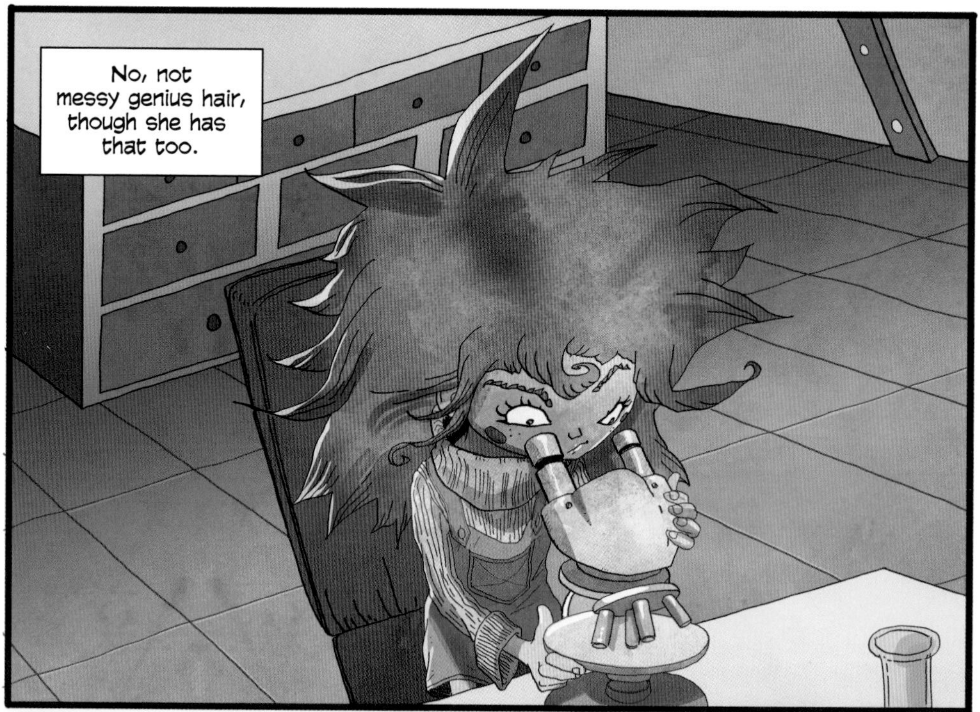
No, not messy genius hair, though she has that too.

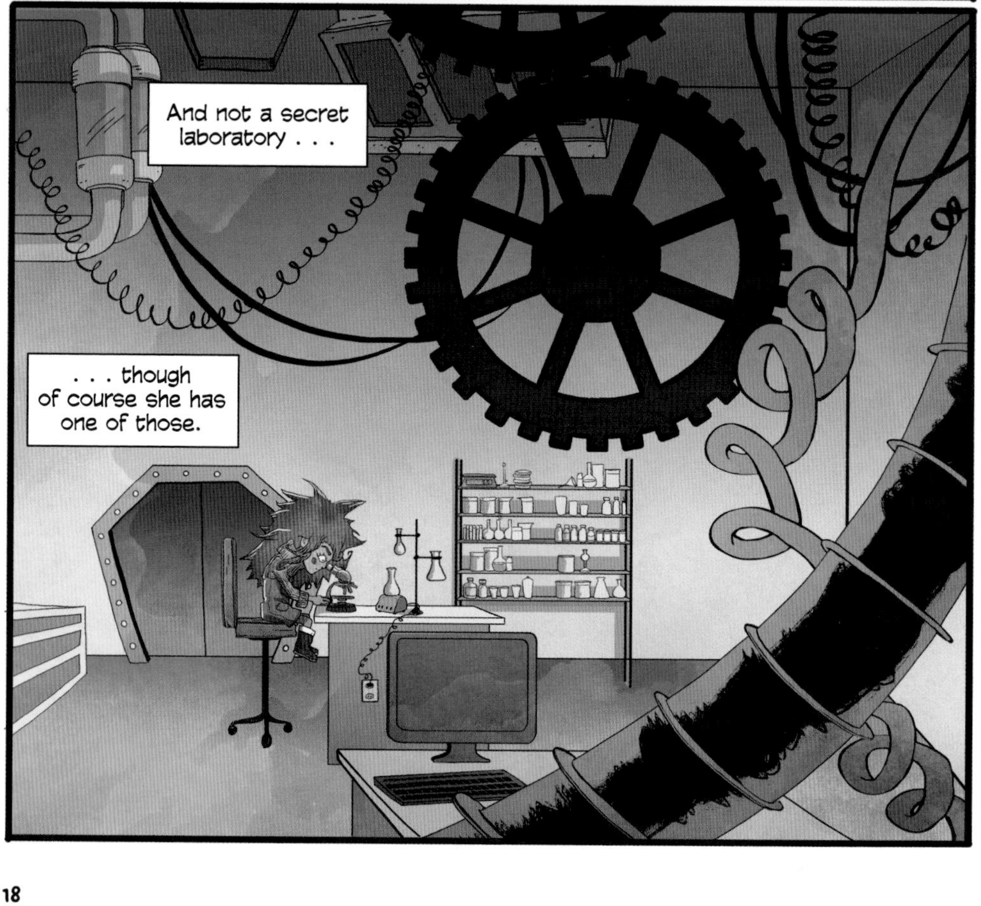
And not a secret laboratory . . .
. . . though of course she has one of those.

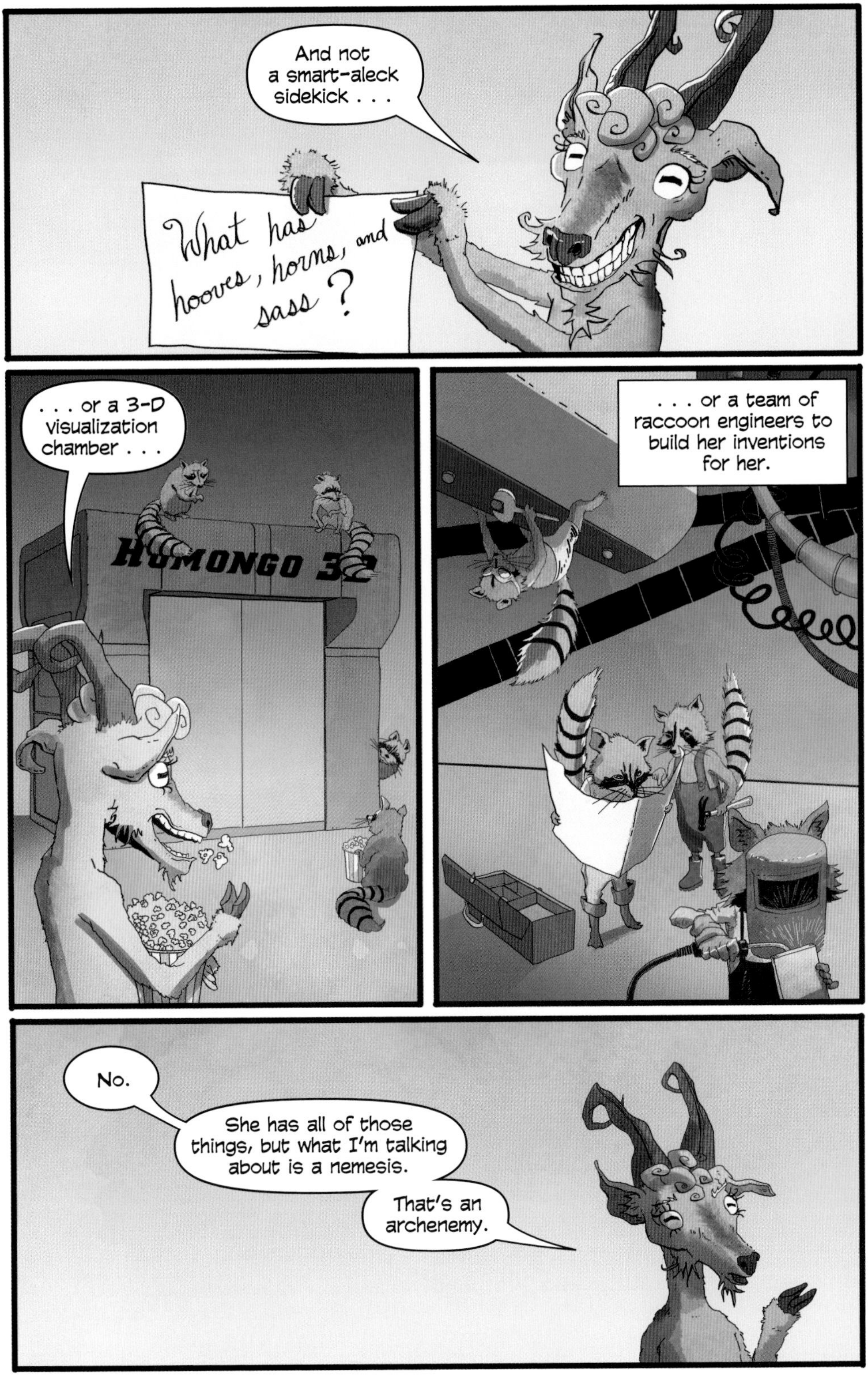
And not a smart-aleck sidekick . . .
What has hooves, horns, and sass?
. . . or a 3-D visualization chamber . . .
HUMONGO 32
. . . or a team of raccoon engineers to build her inventions for her.
No.
She has all of those things, but what I'm talking about is a nemesis.
That's an archenemy.

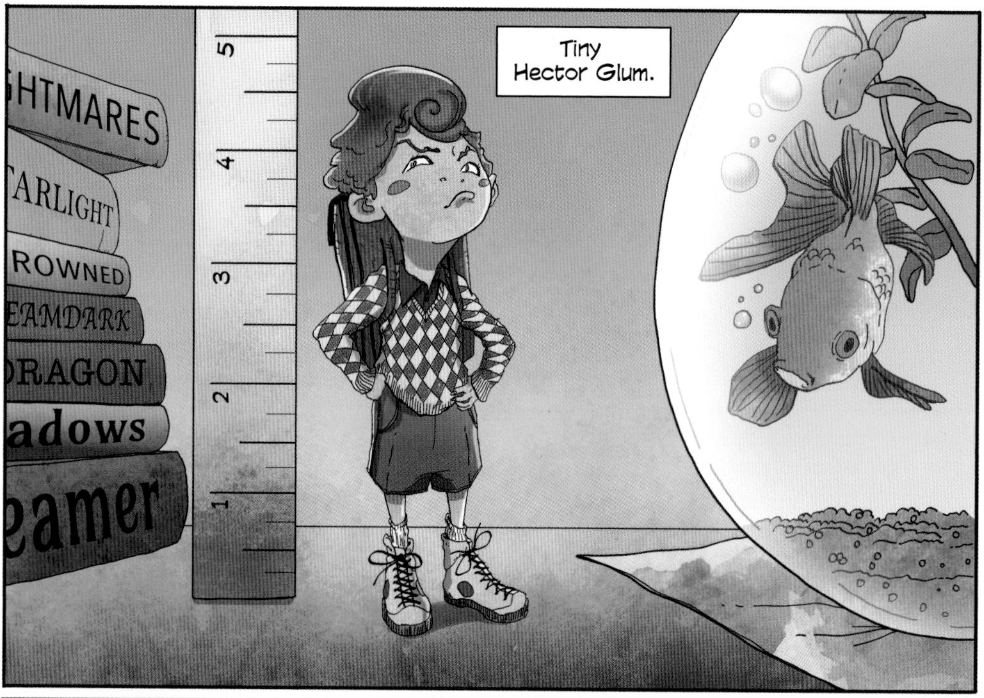
Tiny
Hector Glum.

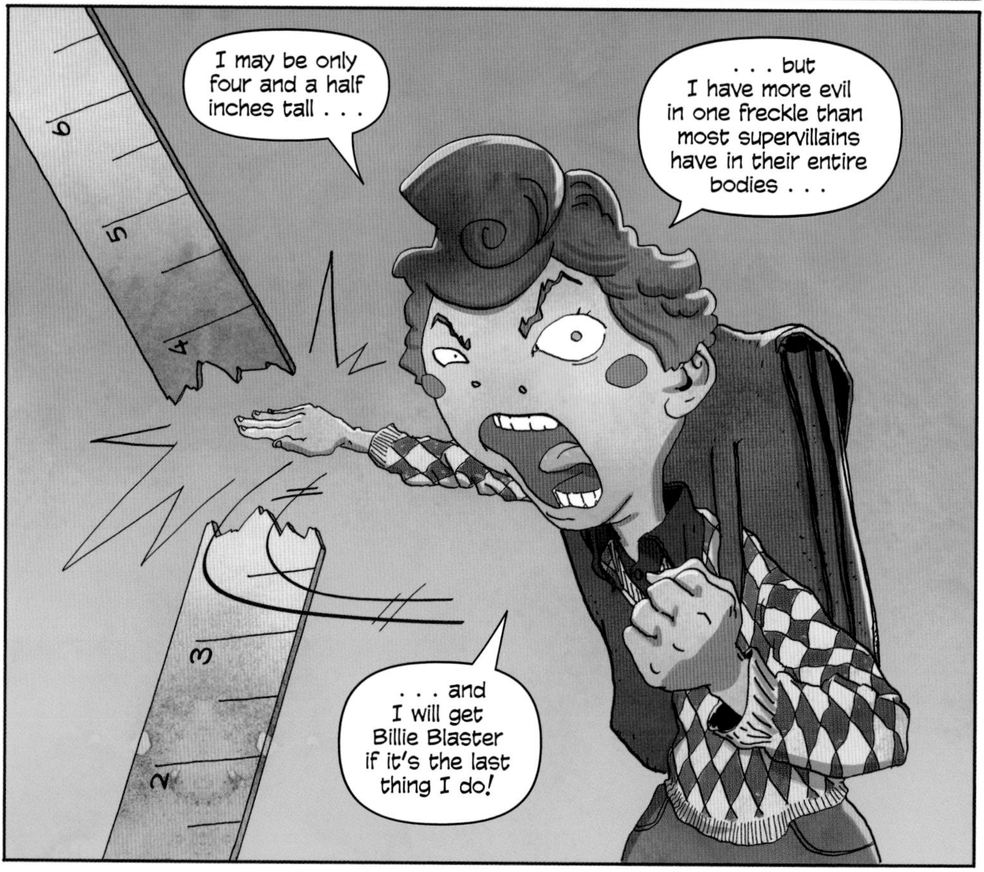
I may be only four and a half inches tall . . .
. . . but I have more evil in one freckle than most supervillains have in their entire bodies . . .
. . . and I will get Billie Blaster if it's the last thing I do!

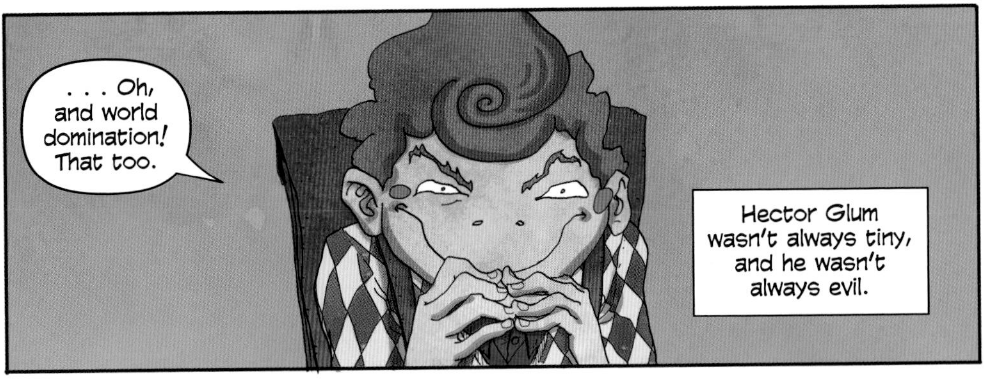
. . . Oh, and world domination! That too.
Hector Glum wasn't always tiny, and he wasn't always evil.

FLASHBACK INTERLUDE

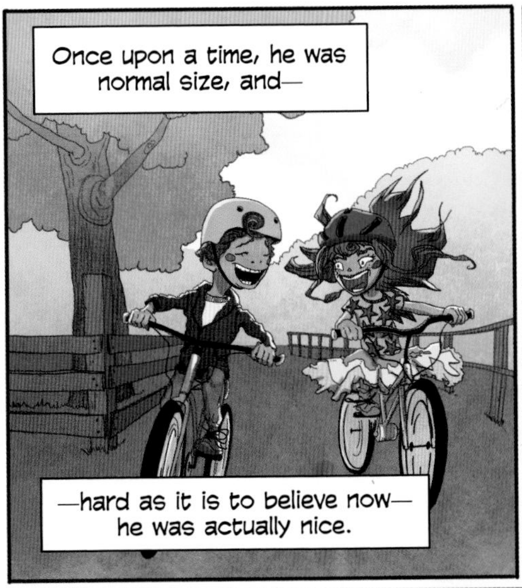
Once upon a time, he was normal size, and—
—hard as it is to believe now—he was actually nice.

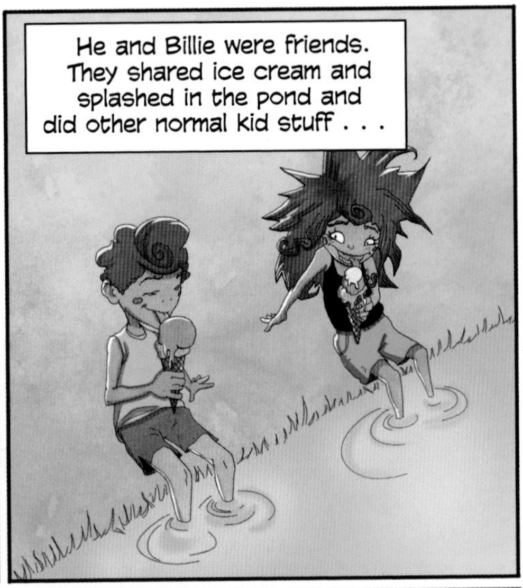
He and Billie were friends. They shared ice cream and splashed in the pond and did other normal kid stuff . . .

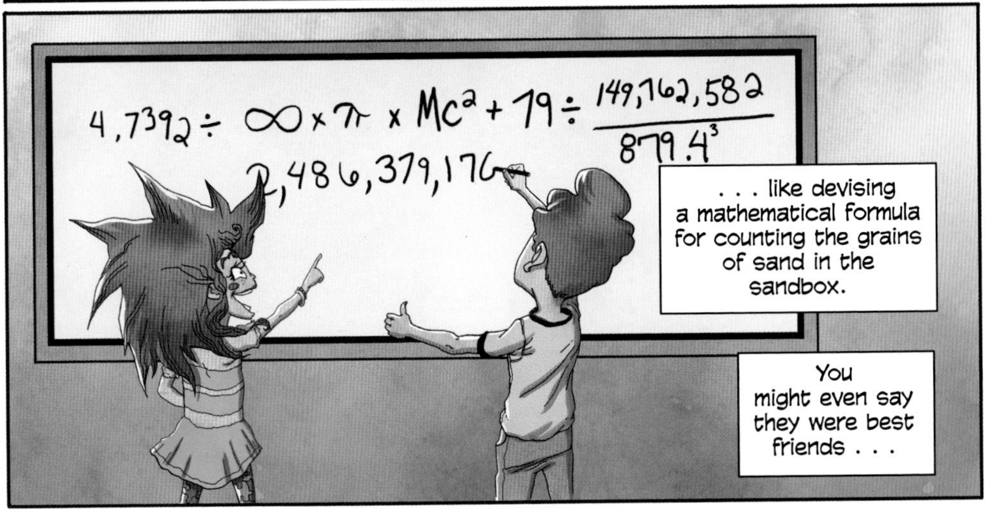
$4{,}739_2 \div \infty \times \pi \times Mc^2 + 79 \div \frac{149{,}762{,}582}{879.4^3}$
2,486,379,176
. . . like devising a mathematical formula for counting the grains of sand in the sandbox.
You might even say they were best friends . . .

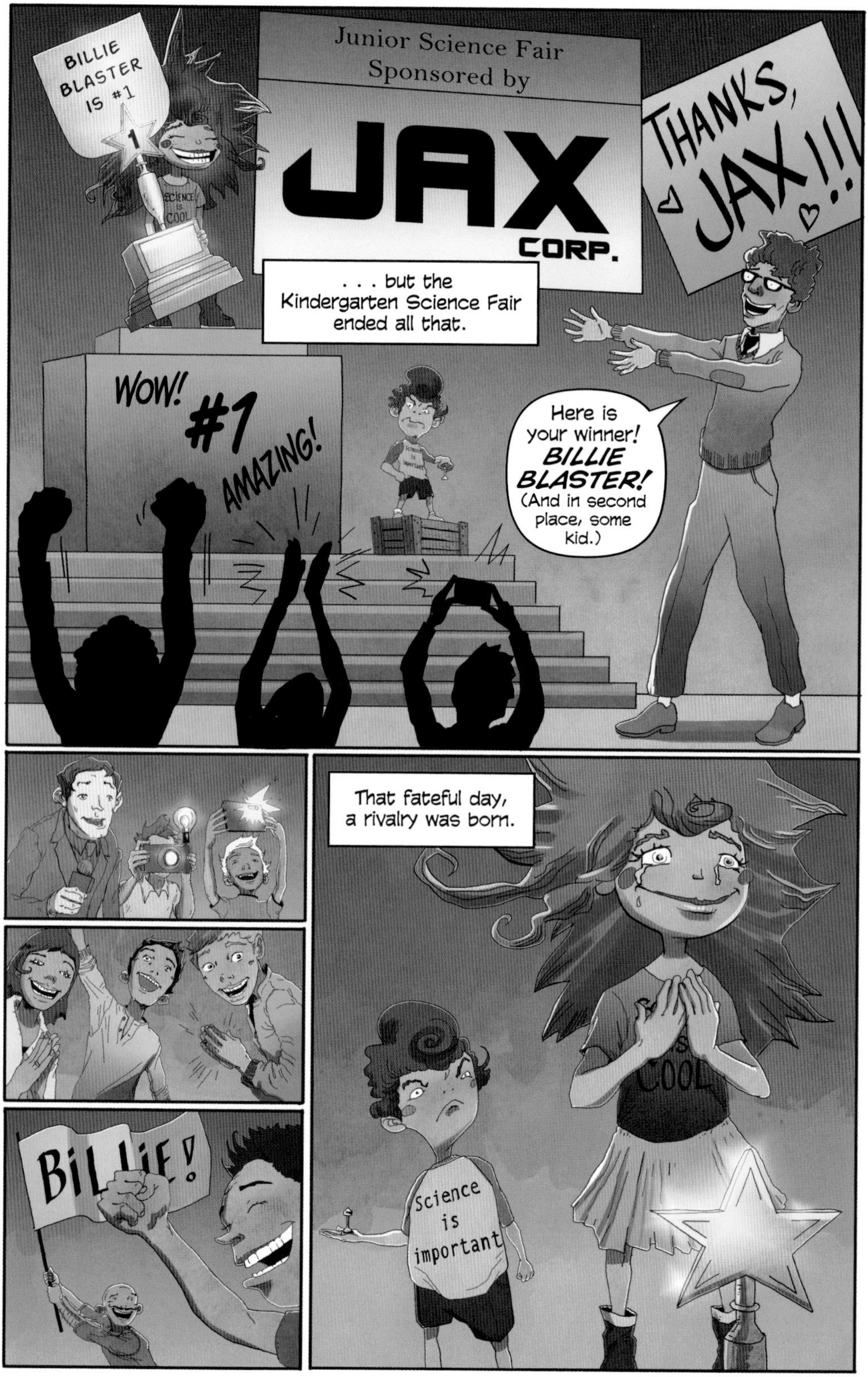

BILLIE BLASTER IS #1
Junior Science Fair Sponsored by
JAX CORP.
THANKS, JAX!!!
. . . but the Kindergarten Science Fair ended all that.
SCIENCE IS COOL
WOW!
#1
AMAZING!
Here is your winner! BILLIE BLASTER! (And in second place, some kid.)
BiL LiE!
That fateful day, a rivalry was born.
Science is important

When the First Grade Science Fair rolled around, Hector was sure he would win. He'd worked on his project all year.

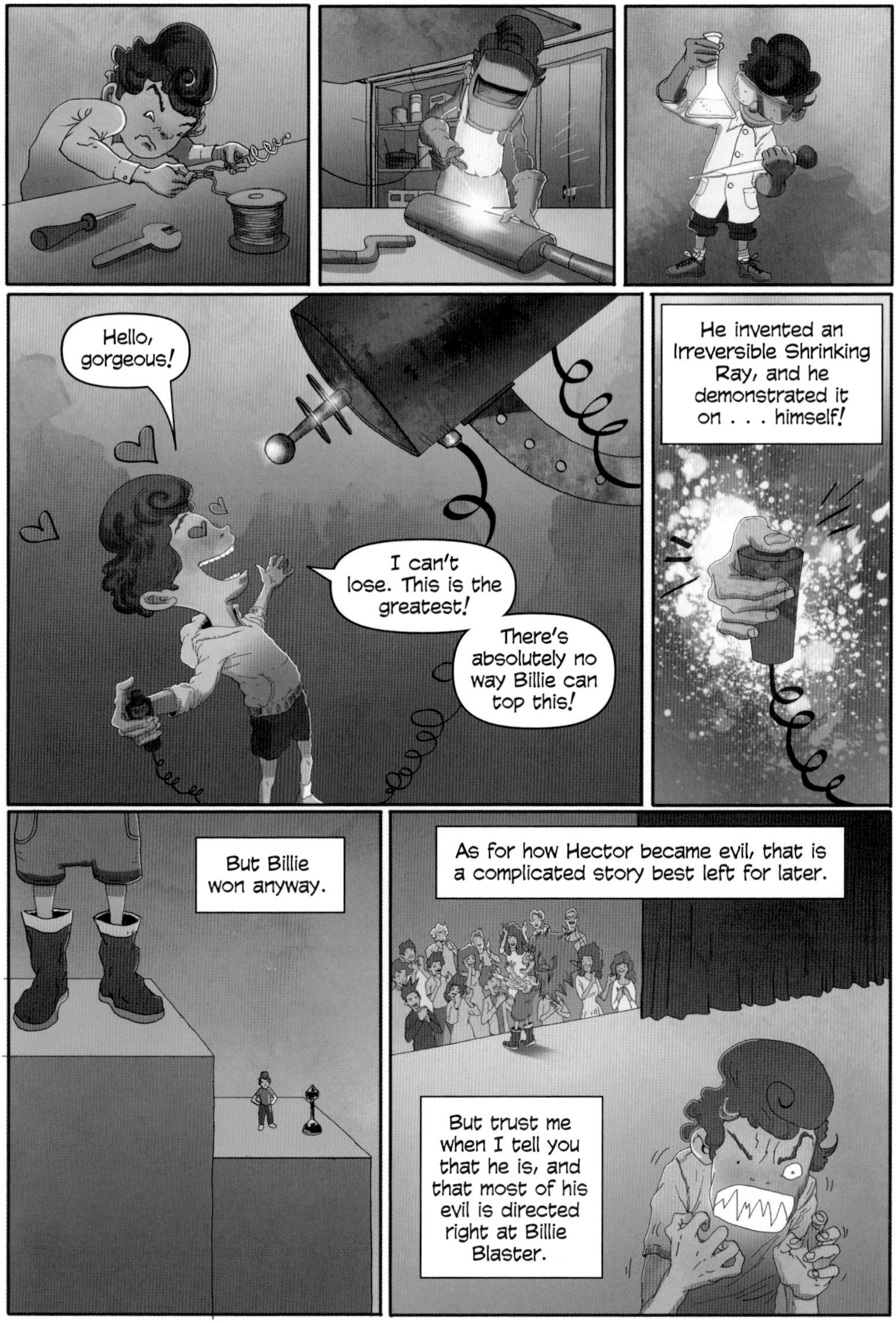
Hello, gorgeous!
I can't lose. This is the greatest!
There's absolutely no way Billie can top this!
He invented an Irreversible Shrinking Ray, and he demonstrated it on . . . himself!
But Billie won anyway.
As for how Hector became evil, that is a complicated story best left for later.
But trust me when I tell you that he is, and that most of his evil is directed right at Billie Blaster.

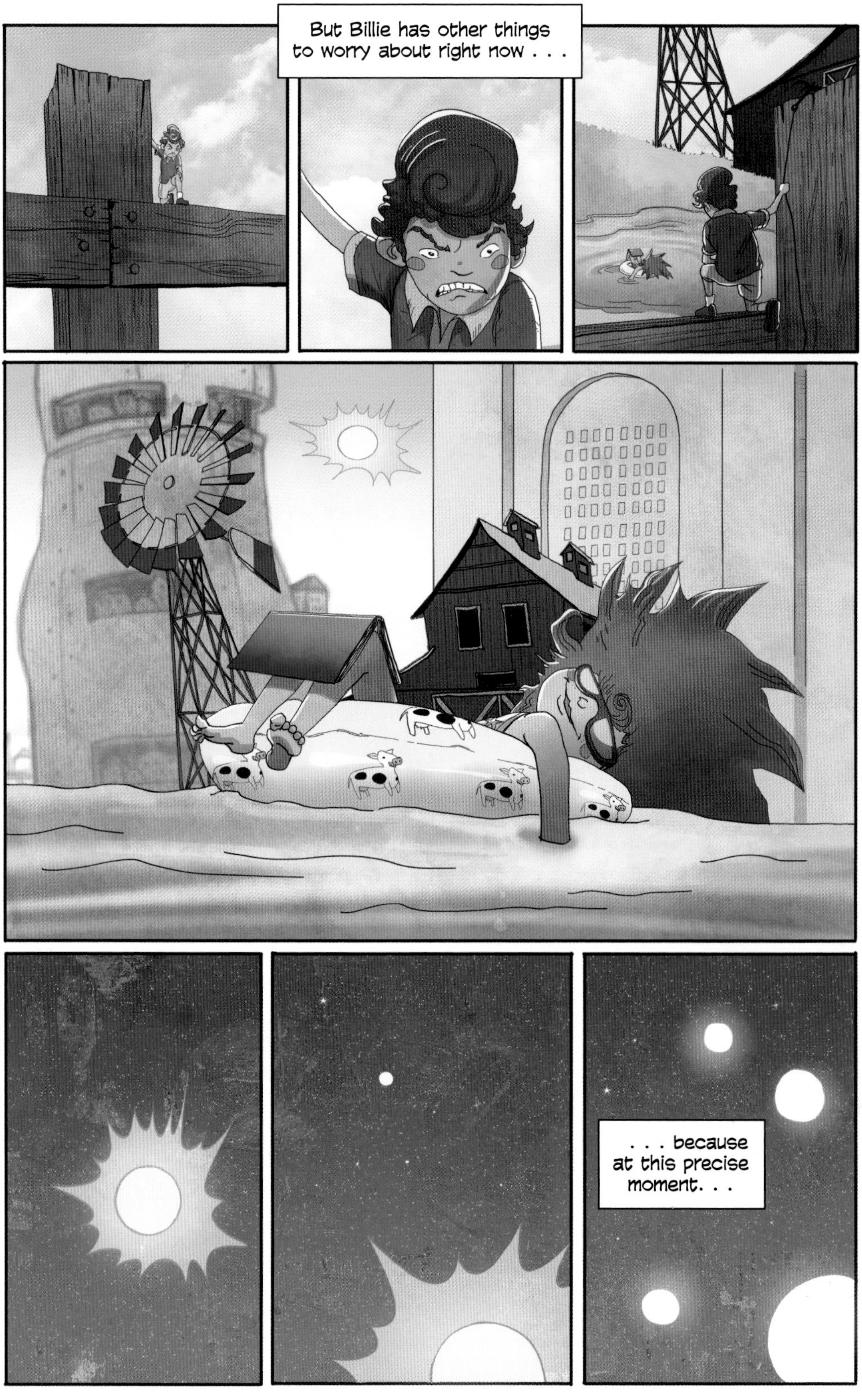
But Billie has other things to worry about right now . . .
. . . because at this precise moment. . .

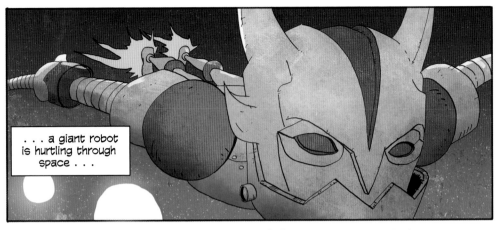

. . . a giant robot is hurtling through space . . .

. . . pursued by aliens, intent on fulfilling its desperate mission and delivering a dire message of warning to her before—

FIRE!

KAZAAM!

Oh. Dang. Too late.

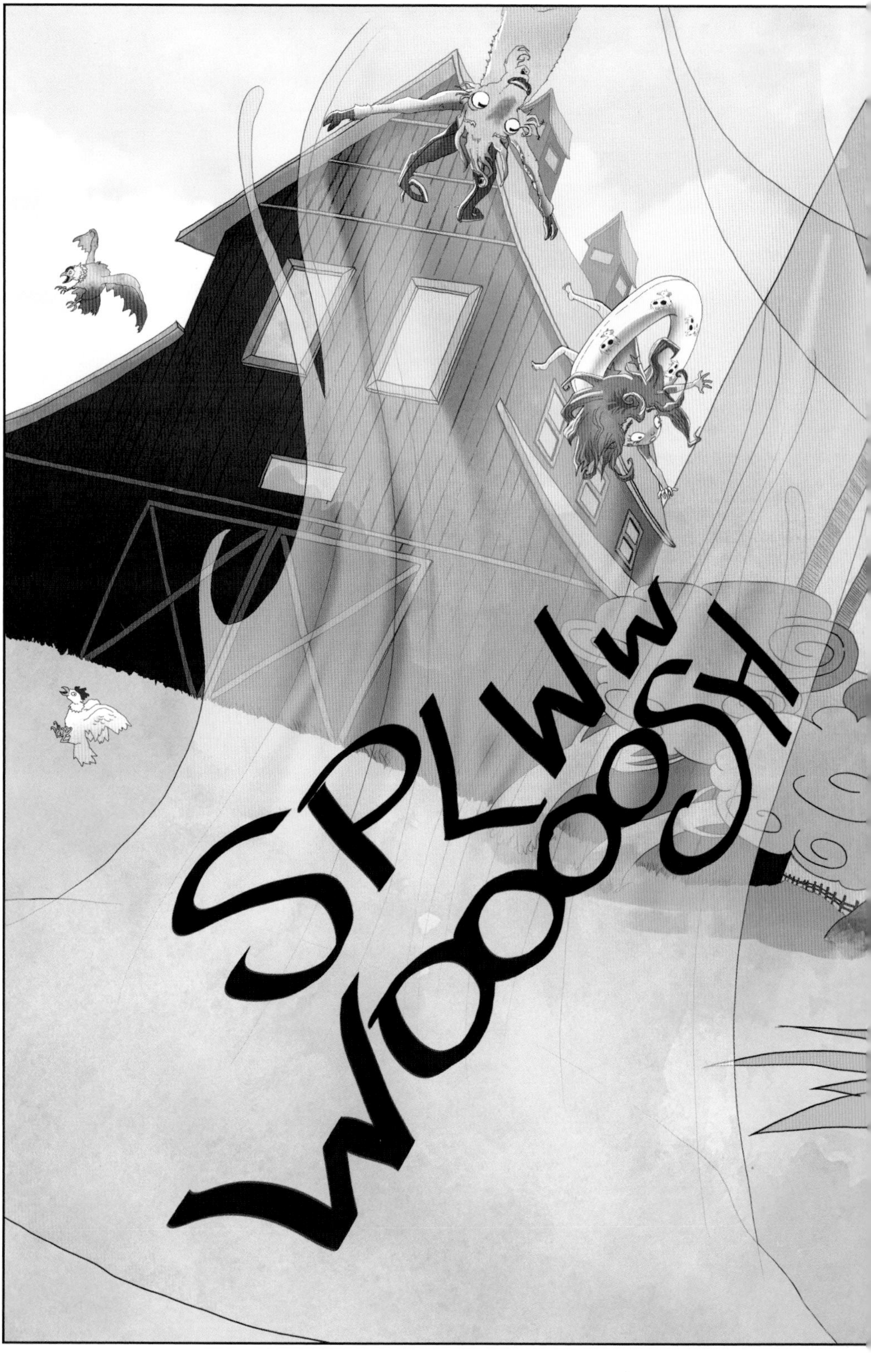
SPLWWWOOOOSH

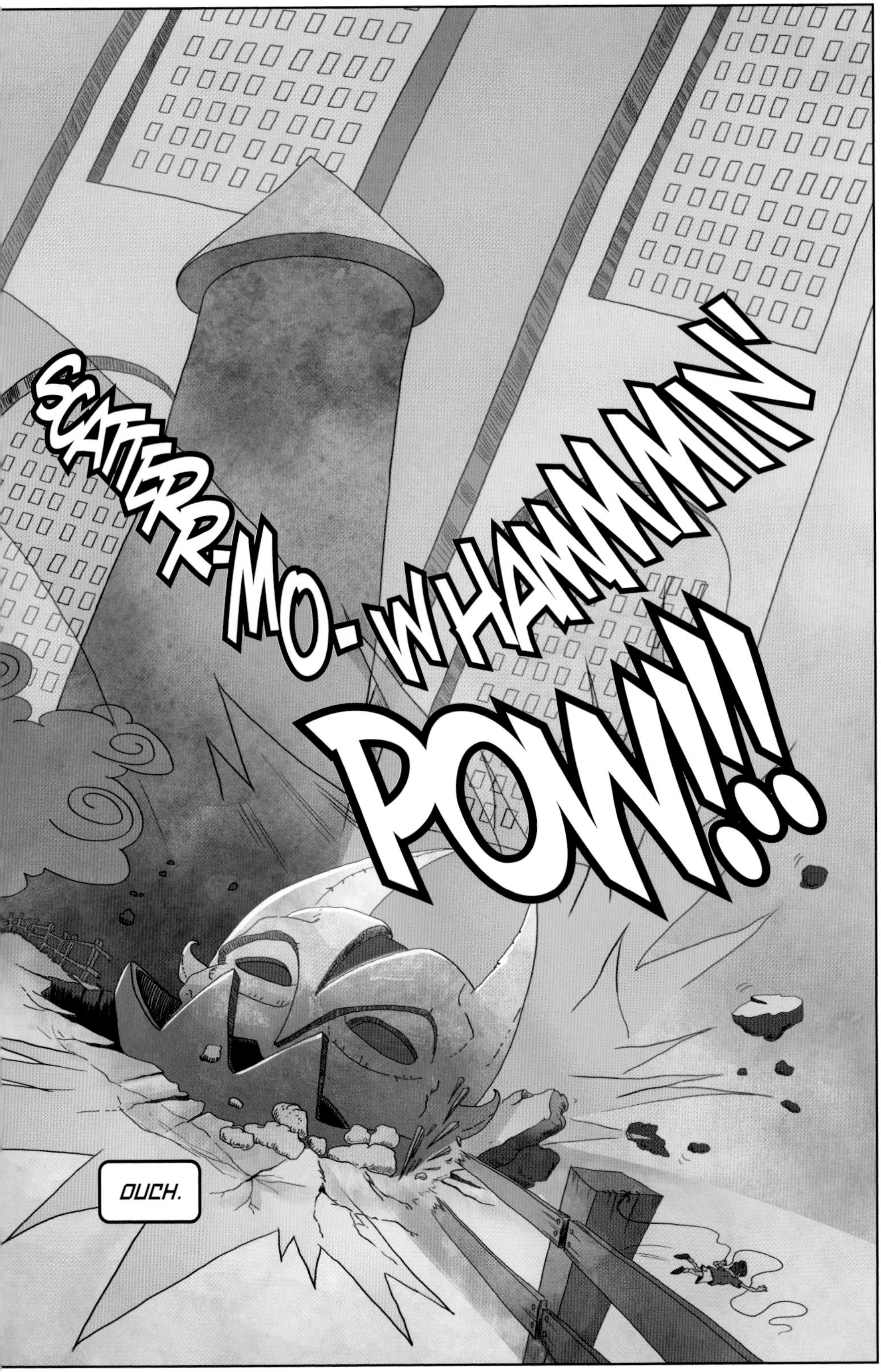
SCATTER-R-MO-WHAMMMIN' POW!!!
OUCH.

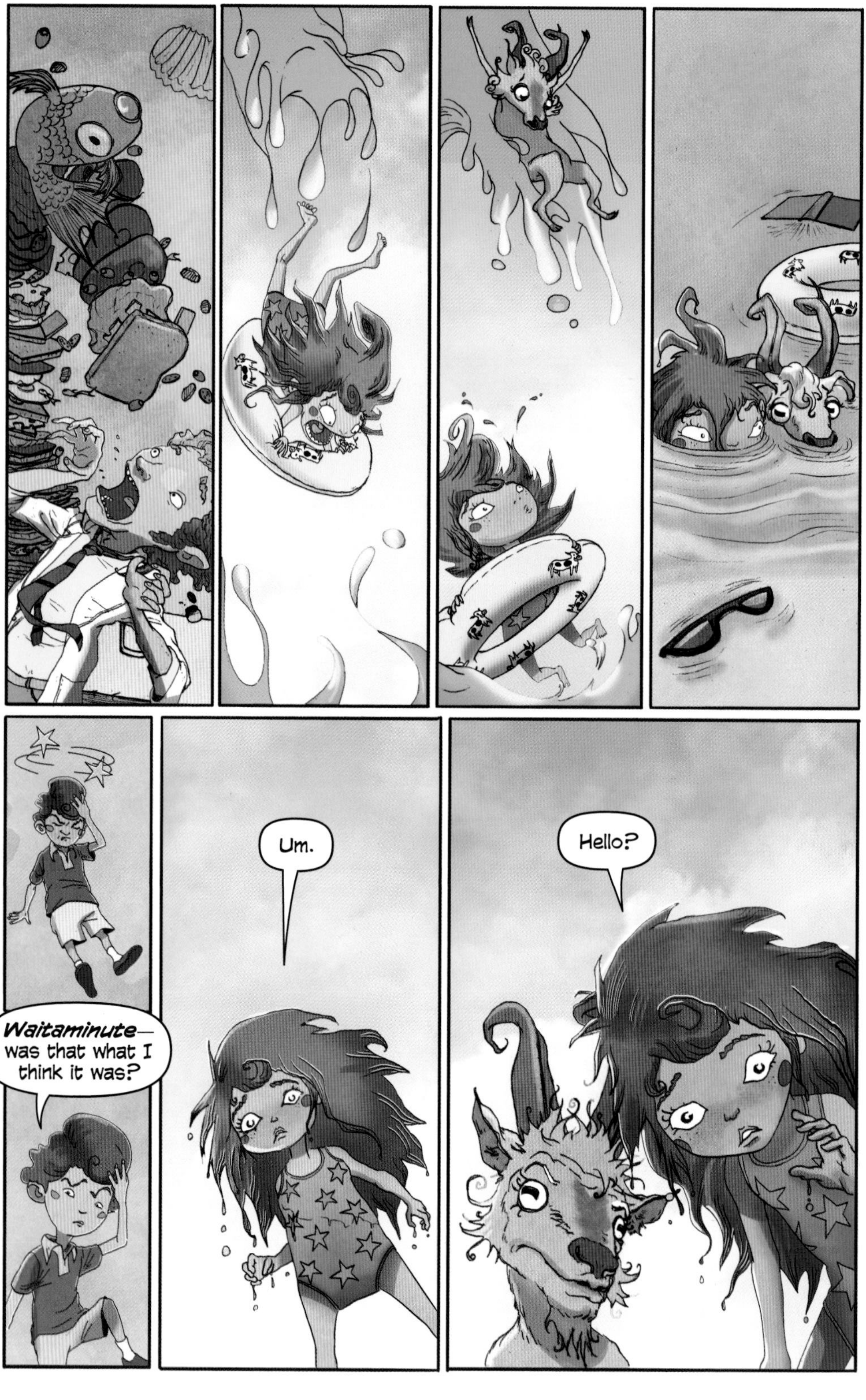
Waitaminute—
was that what I
think it was?
Um.
Hello?

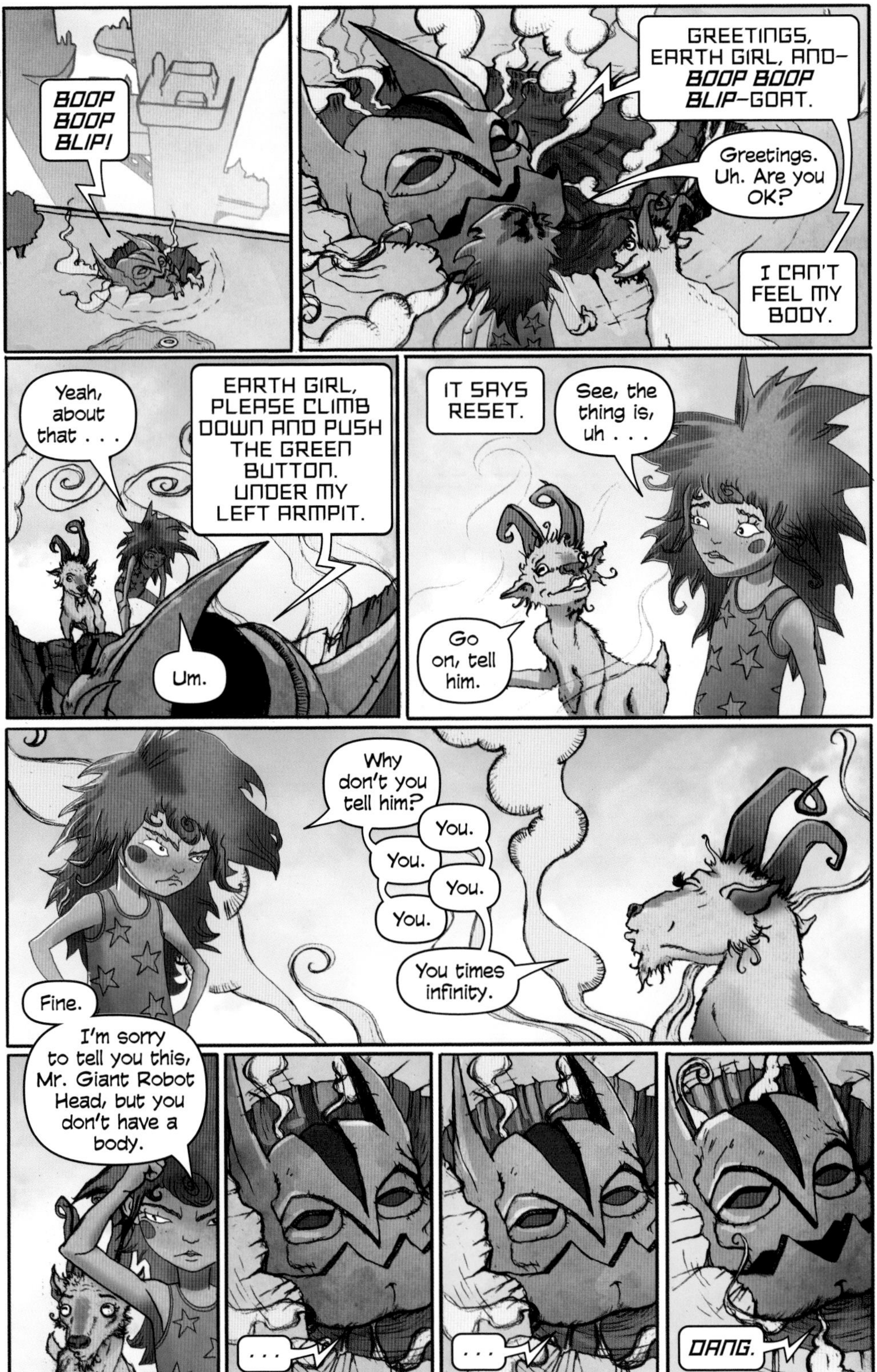
BOOP BOOP BLIP!
GREETINGS, EARTH GIRL, AND—BOOP BOOP BLIP—GOAT.
Greetings. Uh. Are you OK?
I CAN'T FEEL MY BODY.
Yeah, about that . . .
EARTH GIRL, PLEASE CLIMB DOWN AND PUSH THE GREEN BUTTON. UNDER MY LEFT ARMPIT.
Um.
IT SAYS RESET.
See, the thing is, uh . . .
Go on, tell him.
Why don't you tell him?
You.
You.
You.
You.
You times infinity.
Fine.
I'm sorry to tell you this, Mr. Giant Robot Head, but you don't have a body.
. . .
. . .
DANG.

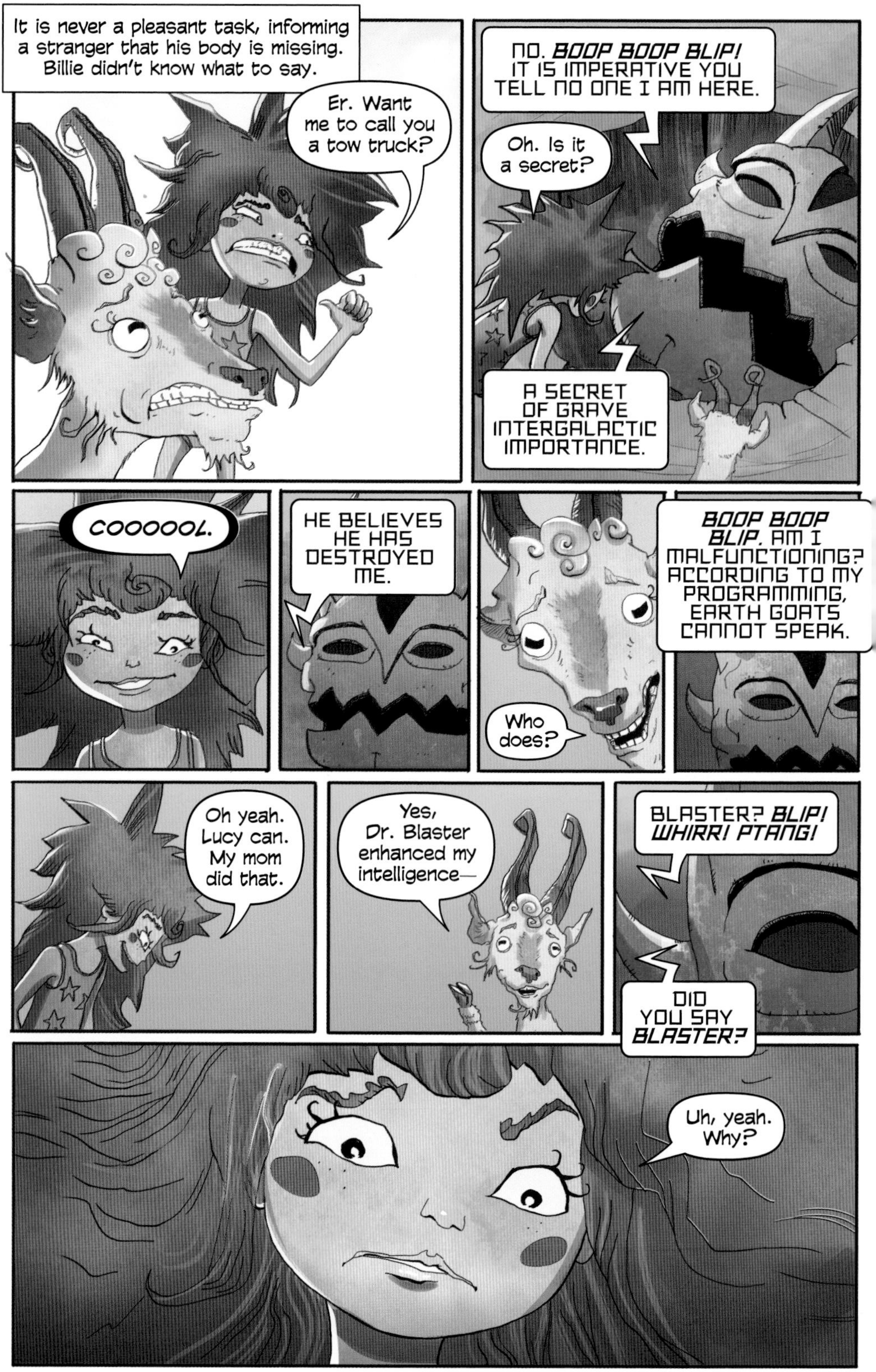
It is never a pleasant task, informing a stranger that his body is missing. Billie didn't know what to say.
Er. Want me to call you a tow truck?
NO. BOOP BOOP BLIP! IT IS IMPERATIVE YOU TELL NO ONE I AM HERE.
Oh. Is it a secret?
A SECRET OF GRAVE INTERGALACTIC IMPORTANCE.
COOOOOL.
HE BELIEVES HE HAS DESTROYED ME.
Who does?
BOOP BOOP BLIP. AM I MALFUNCTIONING? ACCORDING TO MY PROGRAMMING, EARTH GOATS CANNOT SPEAK.
Oh yeah. Lucy can. My mom did that.
Yes, Dr. Blaster enhanced my intelligence—
BLASTER? BLIP! WHIRR! PTANG!
DID YOU SAY BLASTER?
Uh, yeah. Why?

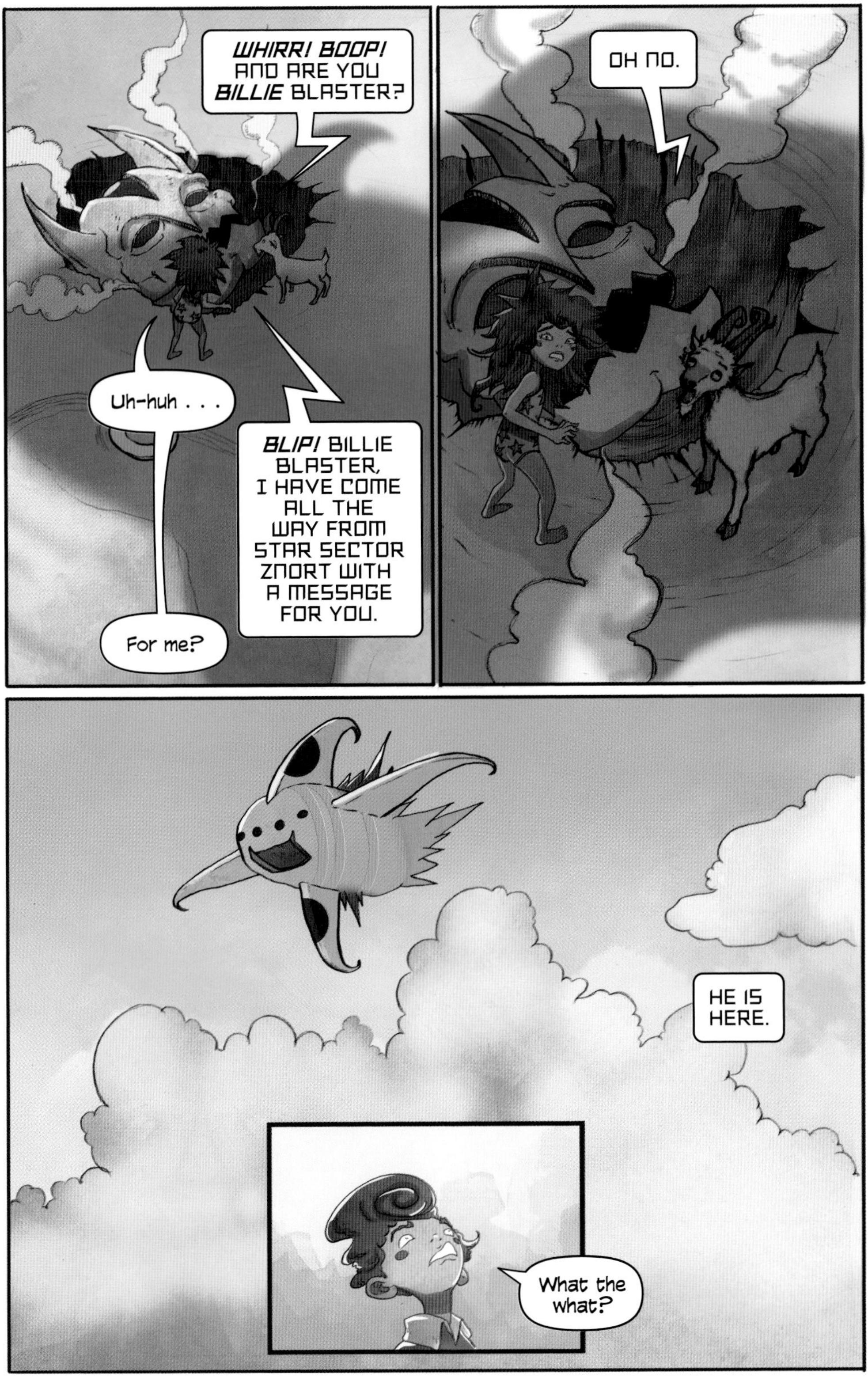
WHIRR! BOOP! AND ARE YOU BILLIE BLASTER?
Uh-huh . . .
For me?
BLIP! BILLIE BLASTER, I HAVE COME ALL THE WAY FROM STAR SECTOR ZNORT WITH A MESSAGE FOR YOU.
OH NO.
HE IS HERE.
What the what?

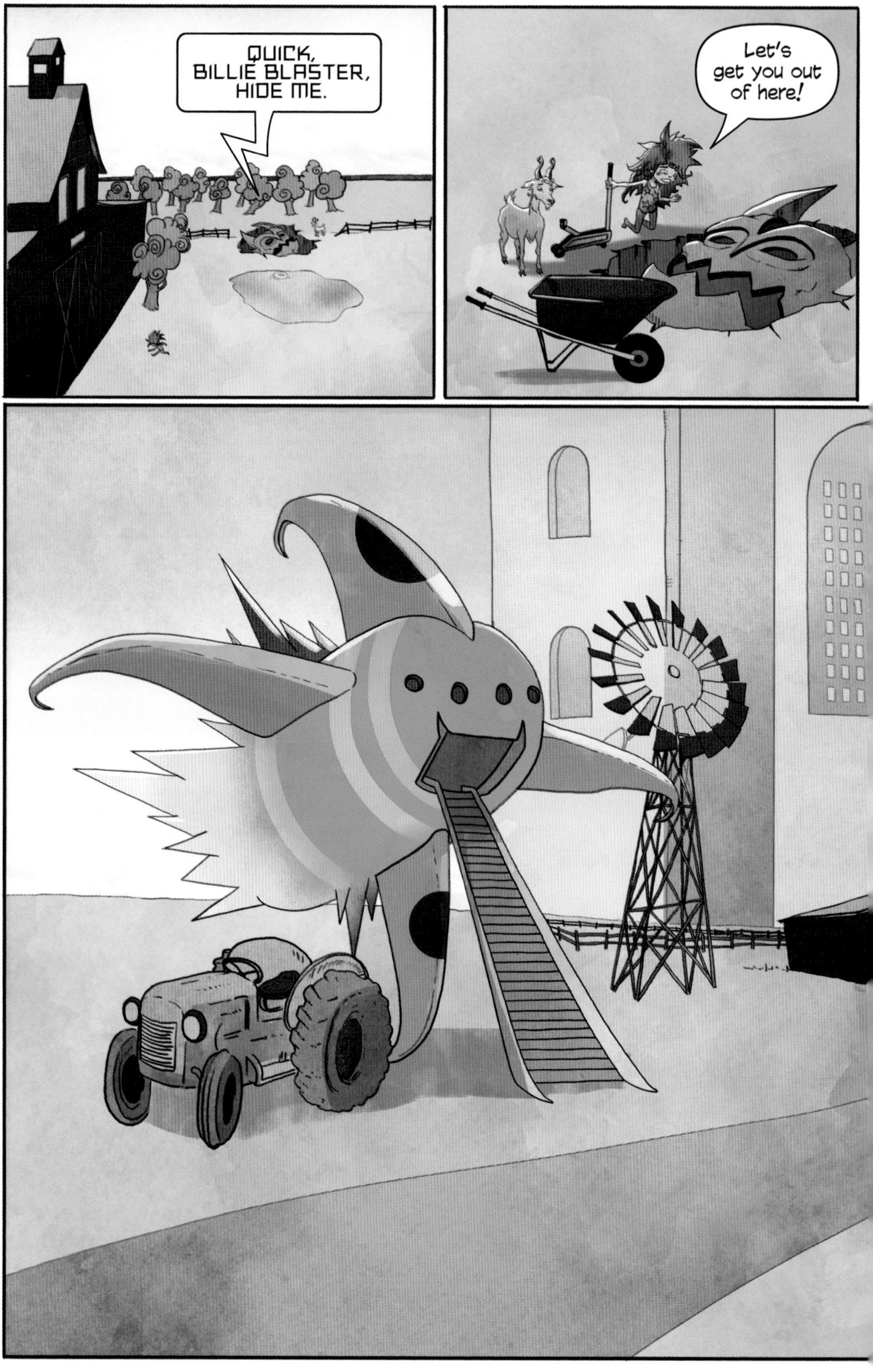
QUICK, BILLIE BLASTER, HIDE ME.
Let's get you out of here!

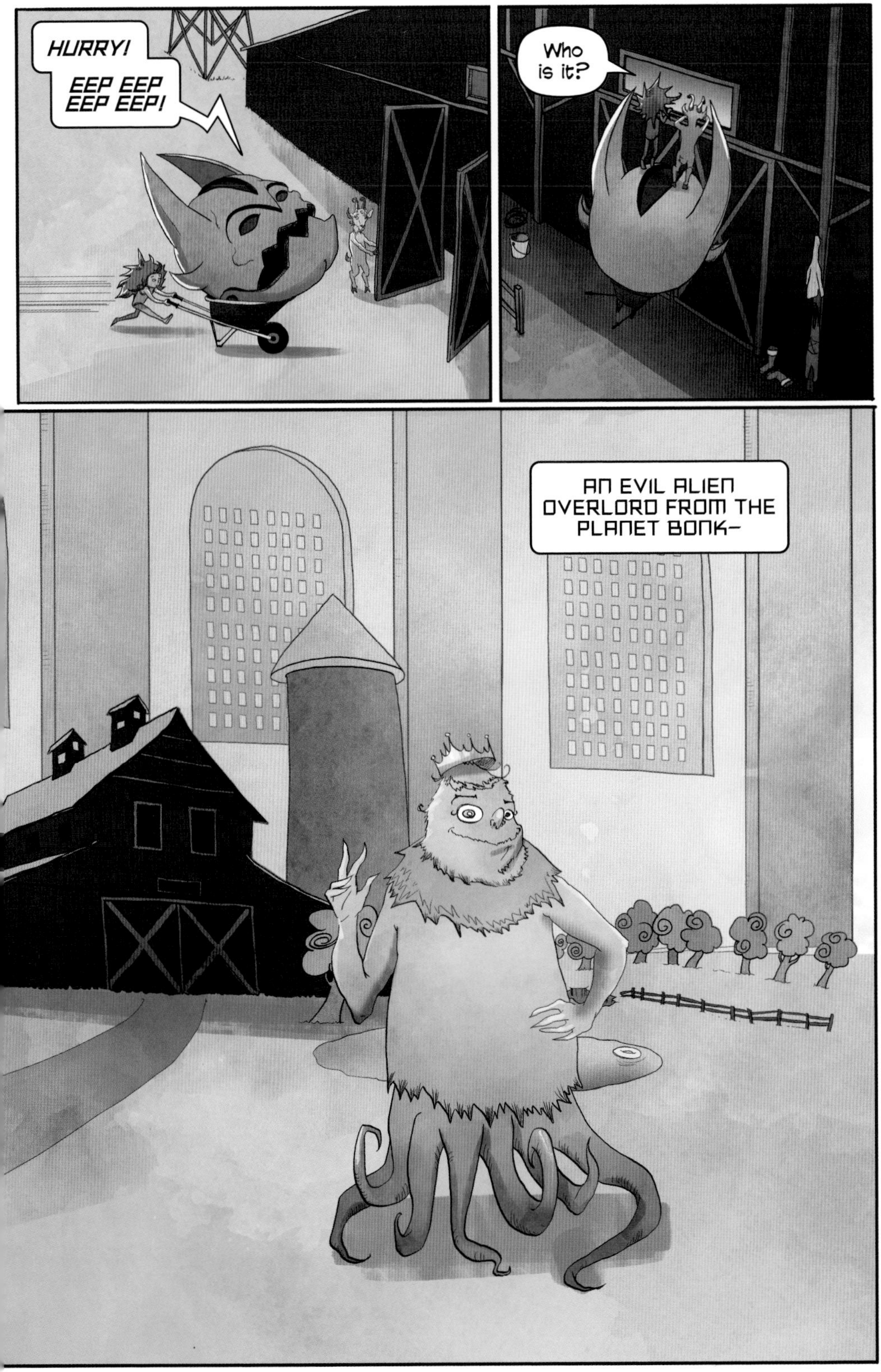
HURRY!
EEP EEP EEP EEP!
Who is it?
AN EVIL ALIEN OVERLORD FROM THE PLANET BONK-

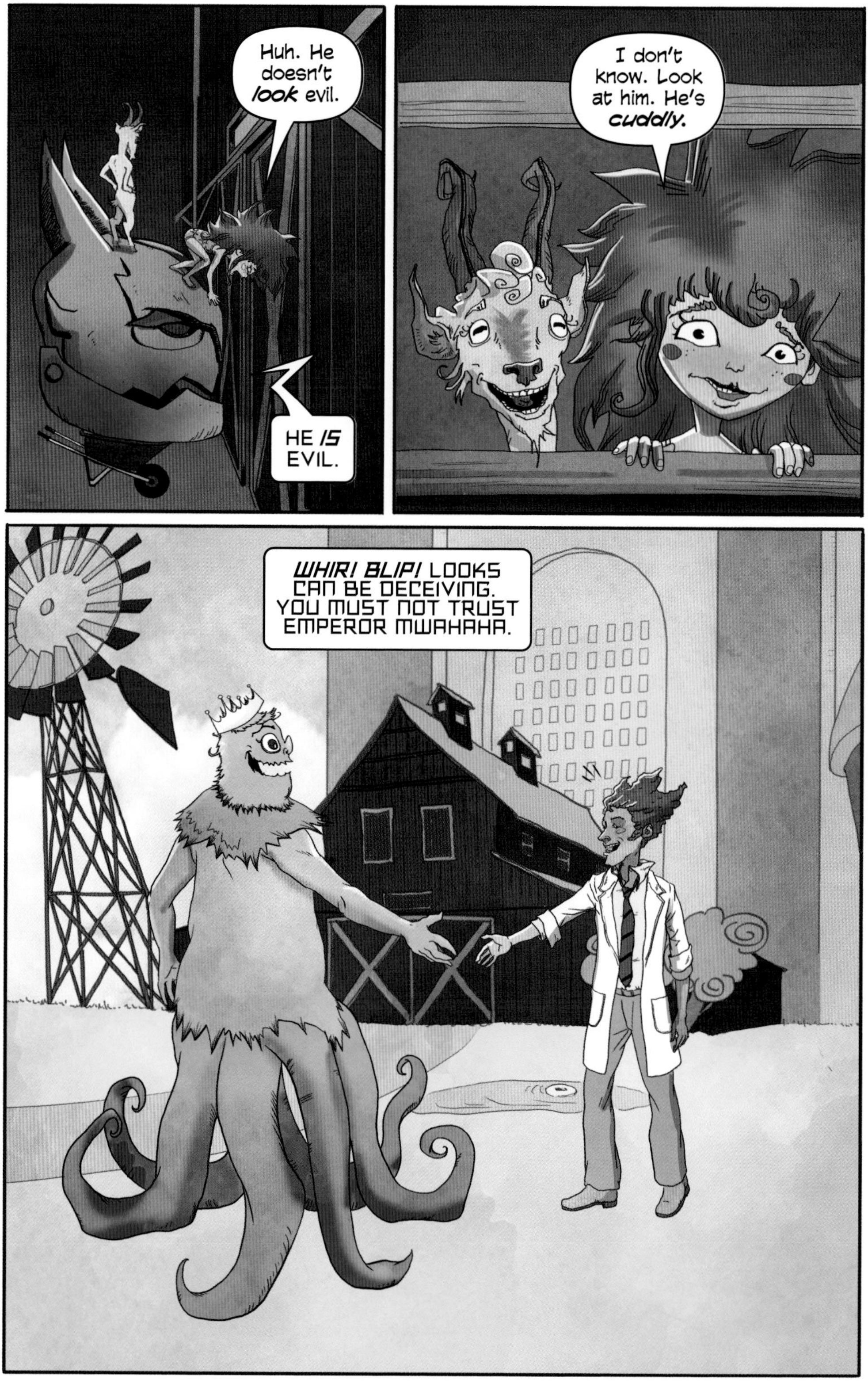
Huh. He doesn't *look* evil.
HE *IS* EVIL.
I don't know. Look at him. He's *cuddly.*
WHIR! BLIP! LOOKS CAN BE DECEIVING. YOU MUST NOT TRUST EMPEROR MWAHAHA.

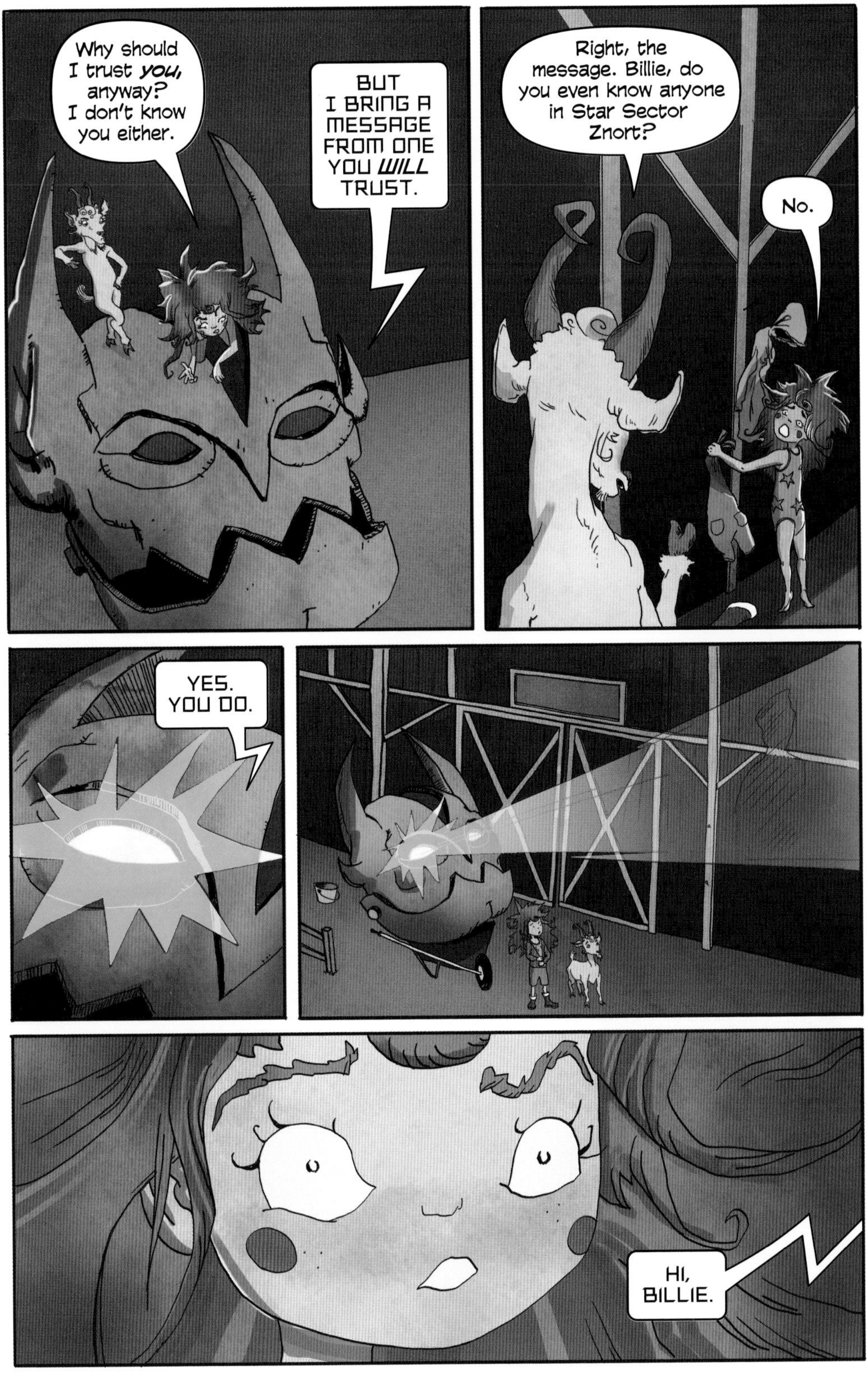
Why should I trust *you,* anyway? I don't know you either.
BUT I BRING A MESSAGE FROM ONE YOU *WILL* TRUST.
Right, the message. Billie, do you even know anyone in Star Sector Znort?
No.
YES. YOU DO.
HI, BILLIE.

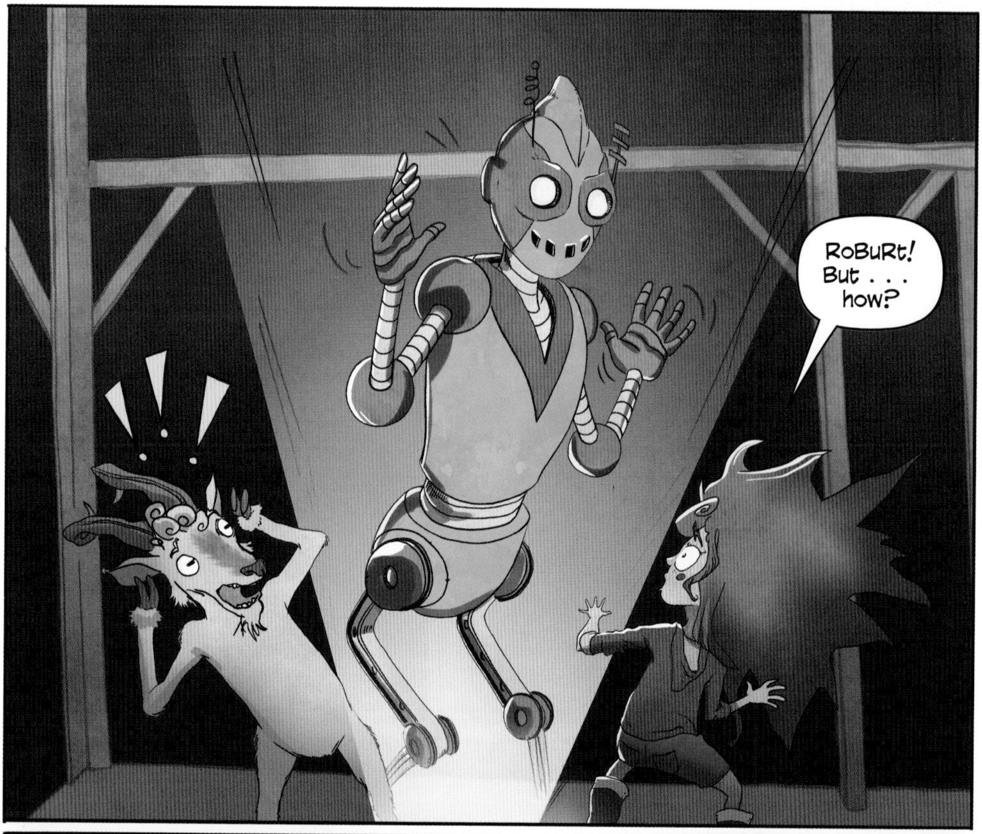
RoBuRt! But . . . how?

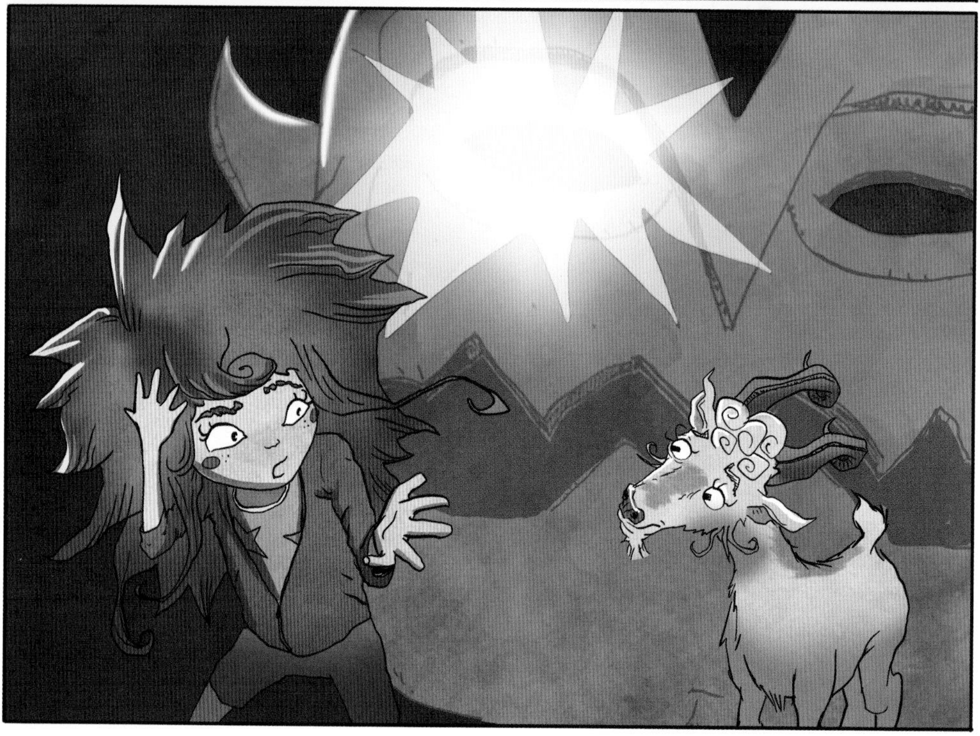

FLINGS VS. BOTS

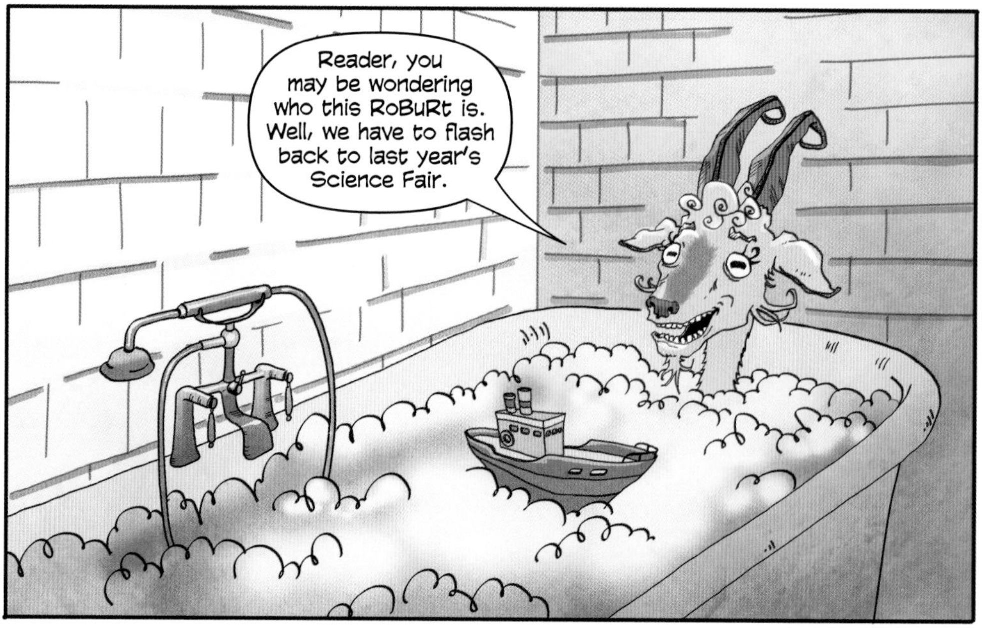
Reader, you may be wondering who this RoBuRt is. Well, we have to flash back to last year's Science Fair.

FLASHBACK SEQUENCE

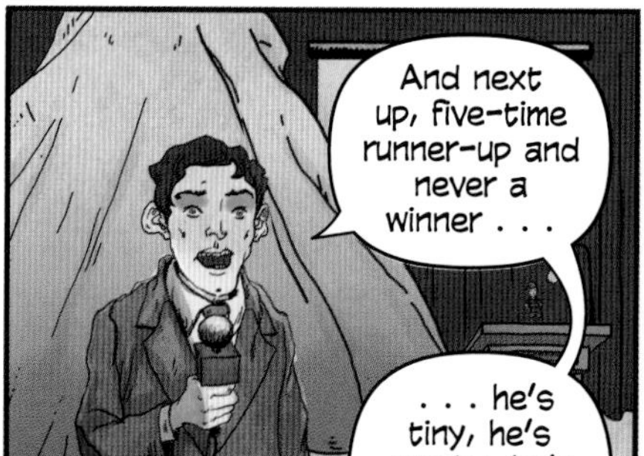
And next up, five-time runner-up and never a winner . . .
. . . he's tiny, he's cranky, he's kind of hard to like, he's . . .

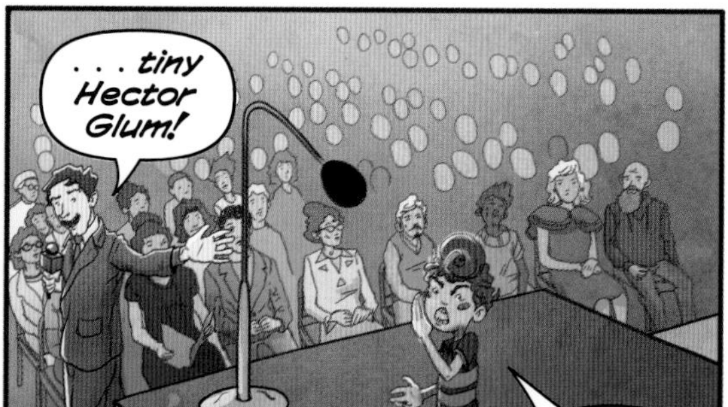
. . . *tiny Hector Glum!*
This year I'm sure to win!

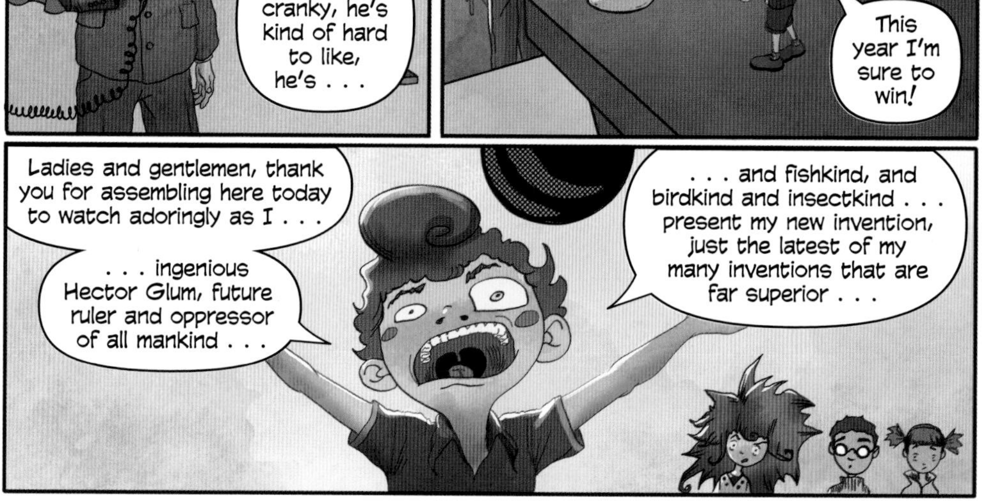
Ladies and gentlemen, thank you for assembling here today to watch adoringly as I . . .
. . . ingenious Hector Glum, future ruler and oppressor of all mankind . . .
. . . and fishkind, and birdkind and insectkind . . . present my new invention, just the latest of my many inventions that are far superior . . .

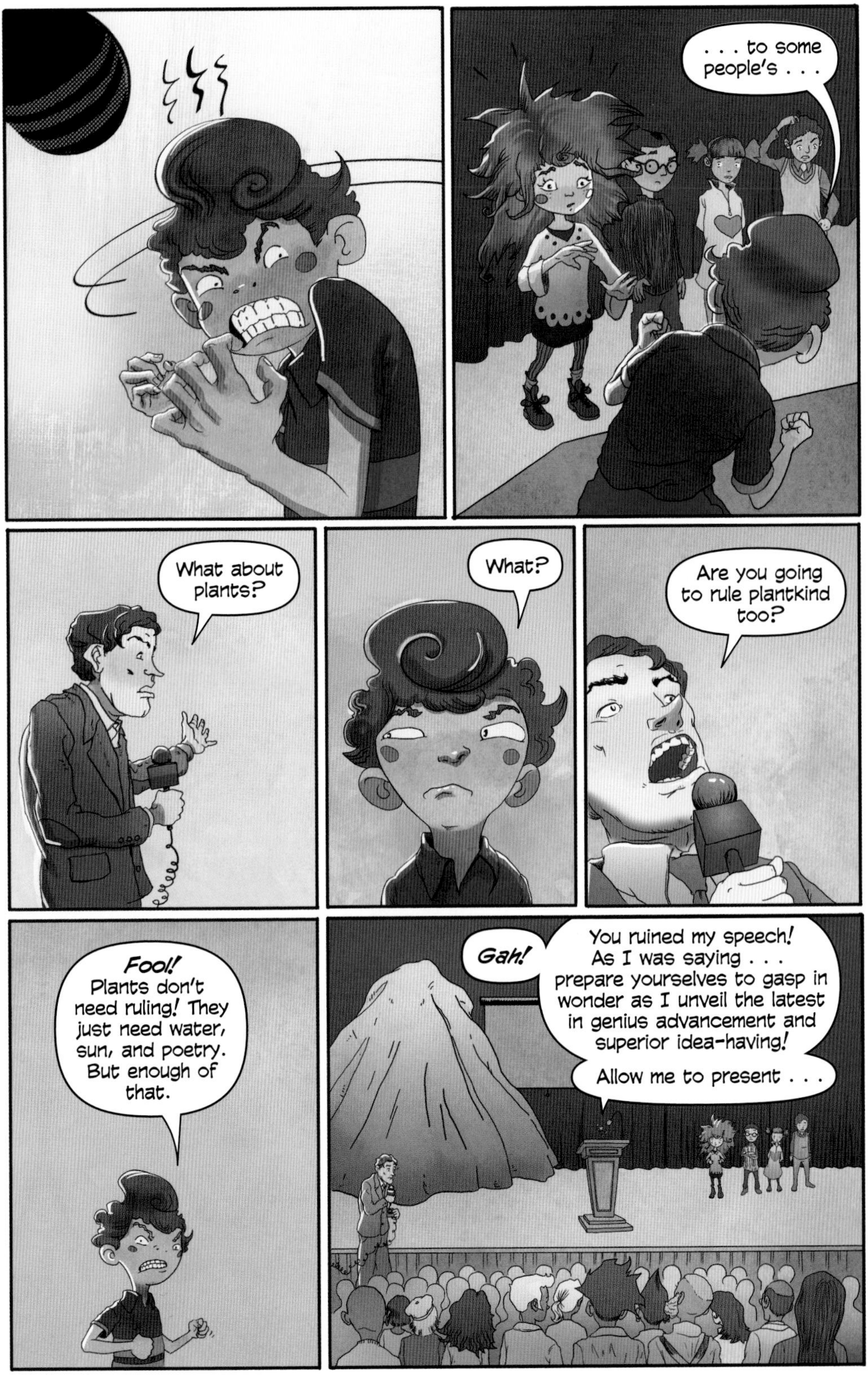
. . . to some people's . . .
What about plants?
What?
Are you going to rule plantkind too?
Fool! Plants don't need ruling! They just need water, sun, and poetry. But enough of that.
Gah!
You ruined my speech! As I was saying . . . prepare yourselves to gasp in wonder as I unveil the latest in genius advancement and superior idea-having!
Allow me to present . . .

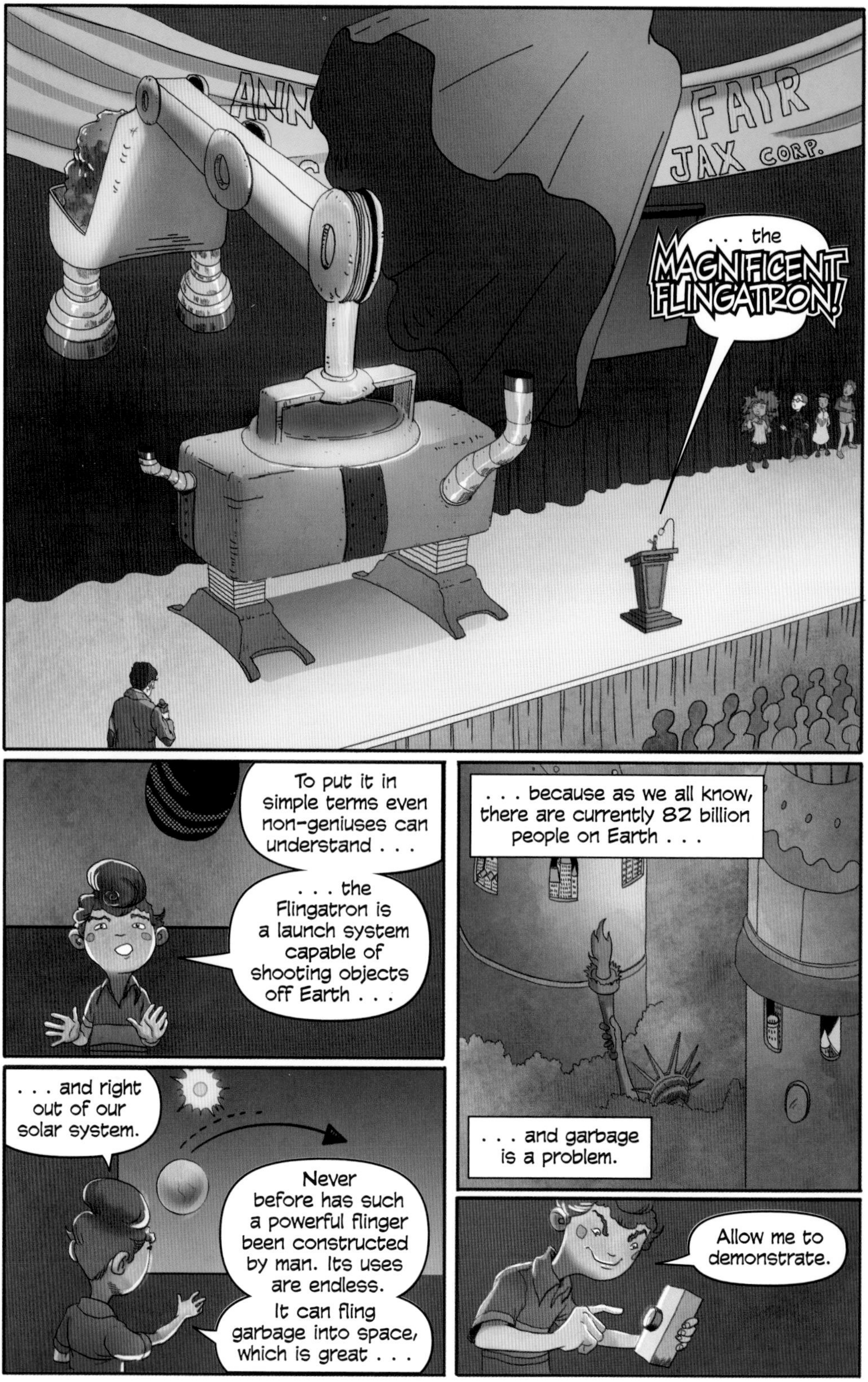

ANN
FAIR
JAX CORP.
. . . the MAGNIFICENT FLINGATRON!
To put it in simple terms even non-geniuses can understand . . .
. . . the Flingatron is a launch system capable of shooting objects off Earth . . .
. . . because as we all know, there are currently 82 billion people on Earth . . .
. . . and garbage is a problem.
. . . and right out of our solar system.
Never before has such a powerful flinger been constructed by man. Its uses are endless.
It can fling garbage into space, which is great . . .
Allow me to demonstrate.

CHOOM!

WOW!

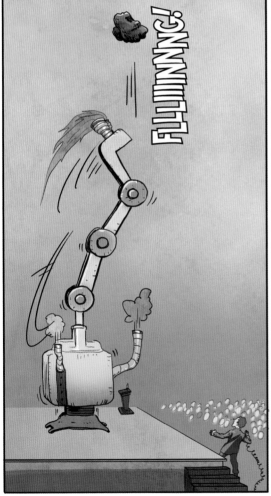

FLLIIINNNG!

AUDITORIUM

I think it's clear who the rightful winner is this year.

Up next, a certain someone who's not even worthy of breaking in my shoes—

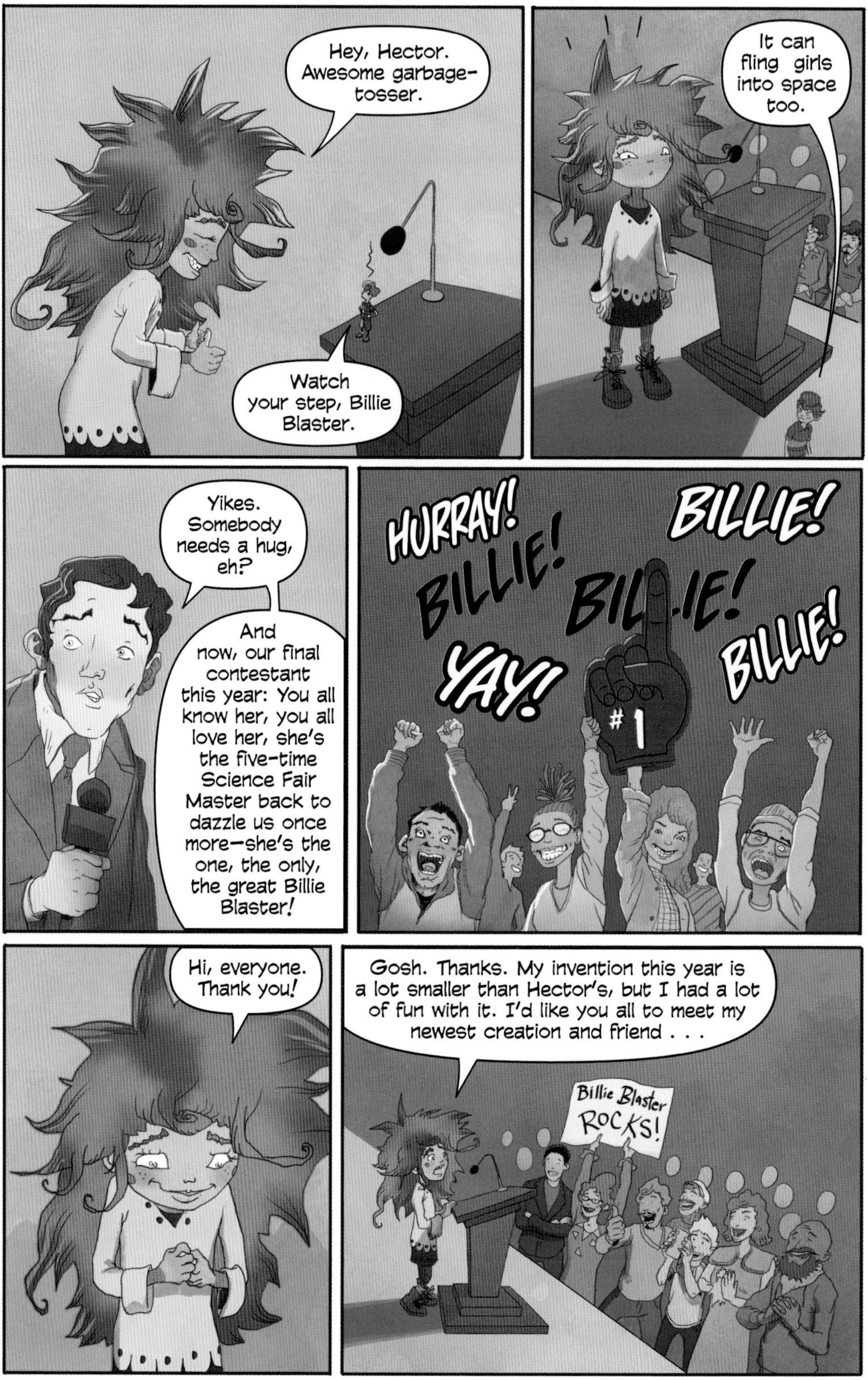
Hey, Hector. Awesome garbage-tosser.
Watch your step, Billie Blaster.
It can fling girls into space too.
Yikes. Somebody needs a hug, eh?
And now, our final contestant this year: You all know her, you all love her, she's the five-time Science Fair Master back to dazzle us once more—she's the one, the only, the great Billie Blaster!
HURRAY!
BILLIE!
BILLIE!
BILLIE!
YAY!
BILLIE!
#1
Hi, everyone. Thank you!
Gosh. Thanks. My invention this year is a lot smaller than Hector's, but I had a lot of fun with it. I'd like you all to meet my newest creation and friend . . .
Billie Blaster ROCKS!

. . . RoBuRt the Robot.

He can do most things ordinary people can do. Pet the cat, tap dance, perform brain surgery . . .

HAHAHA!

But his specialty, the thing he's going to demonstrate today, is this:

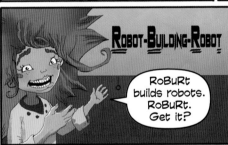
ROBOT·BUILDING·ROBOT

RoBuRt builds robots. RoBuRt. Get it?

Thanks to a special new Creativity Engine I thought up during recess . . .

. . . RoBuRt is the first robot in history to have an imagination, and each robot he builds will be entirely his own design, complete with its own Creativity Engine so it too can build robots.

I can't even predict what RoBuRt is going to make right now! We'll all just have to watch and see.

OK, show us what you can do!

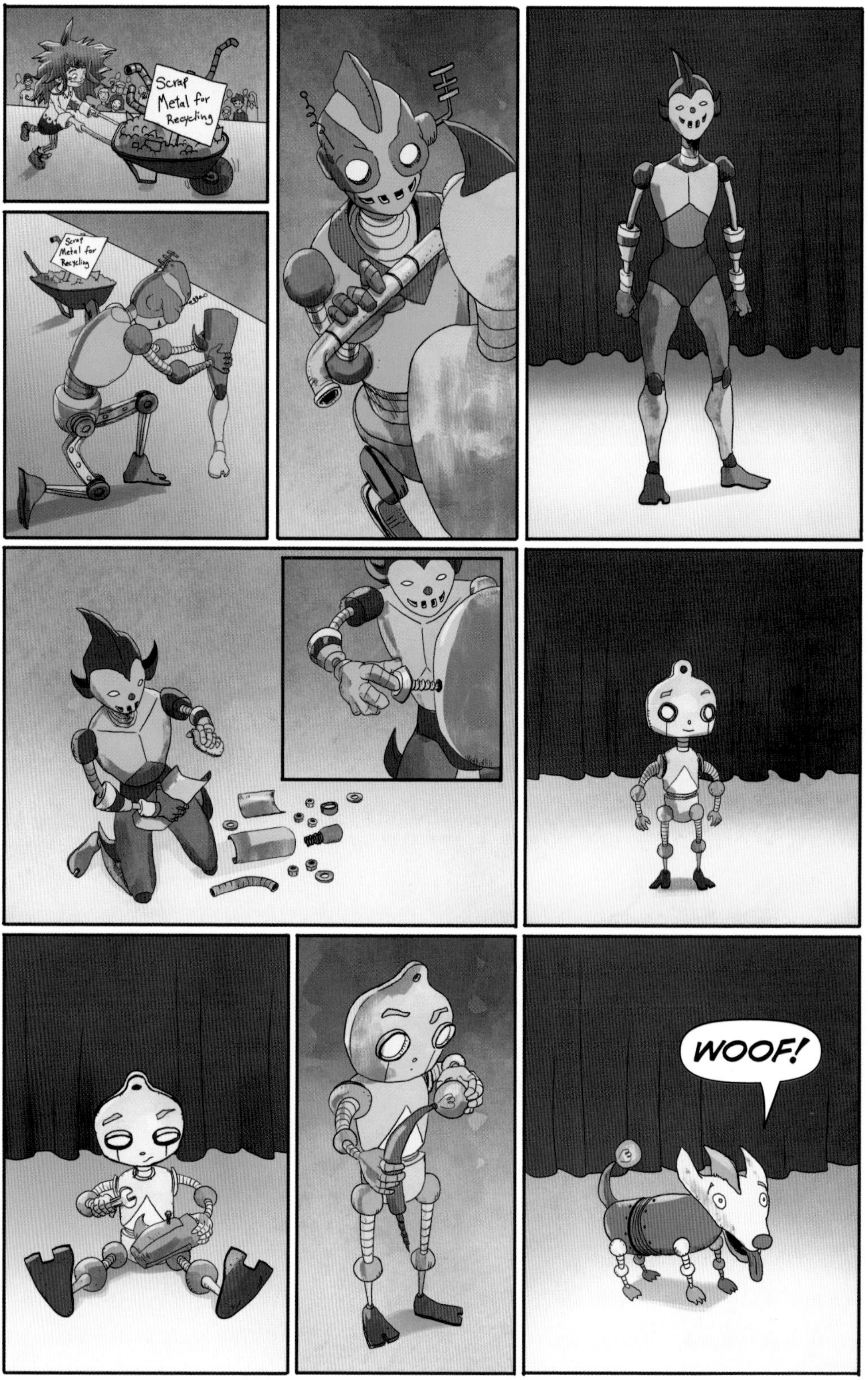
Scrap Metal for Recycling
Scrap Metal for Recycling
WOOF!

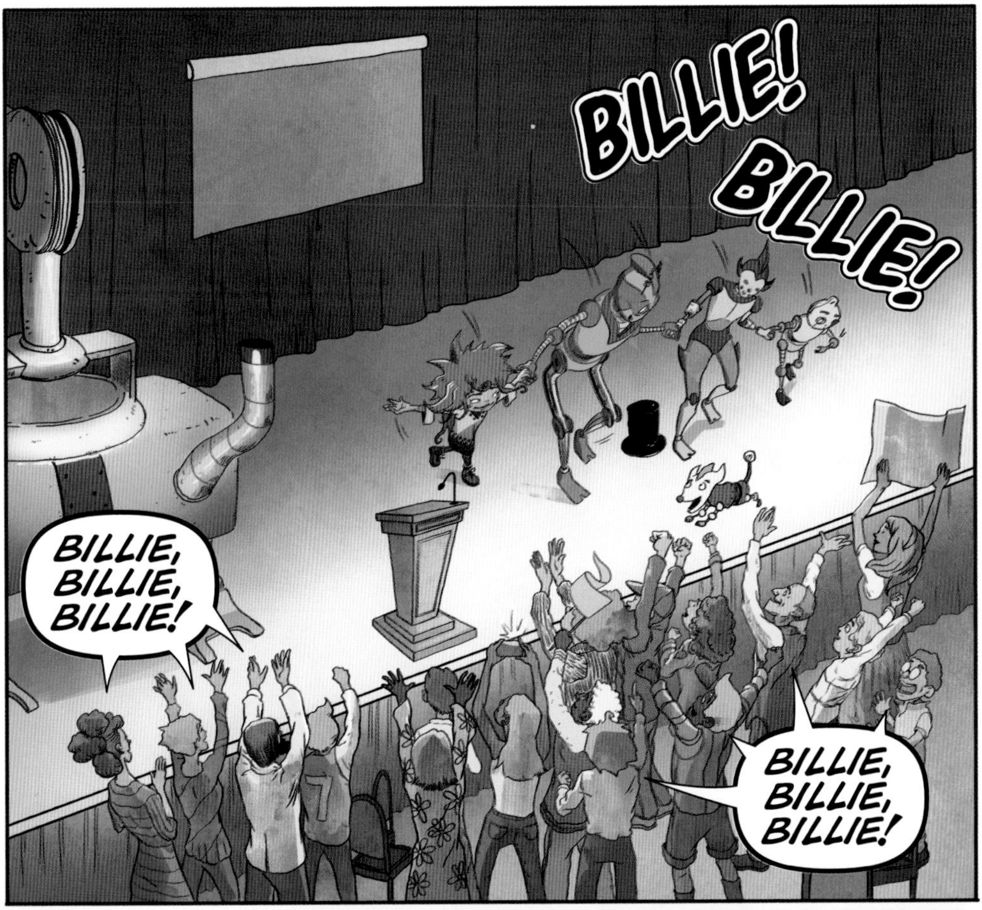
BILLIE!
BILLIE!
BILLIE, BILLIE, BILLIE!
BILLIE, BILLIE, BILLIE!

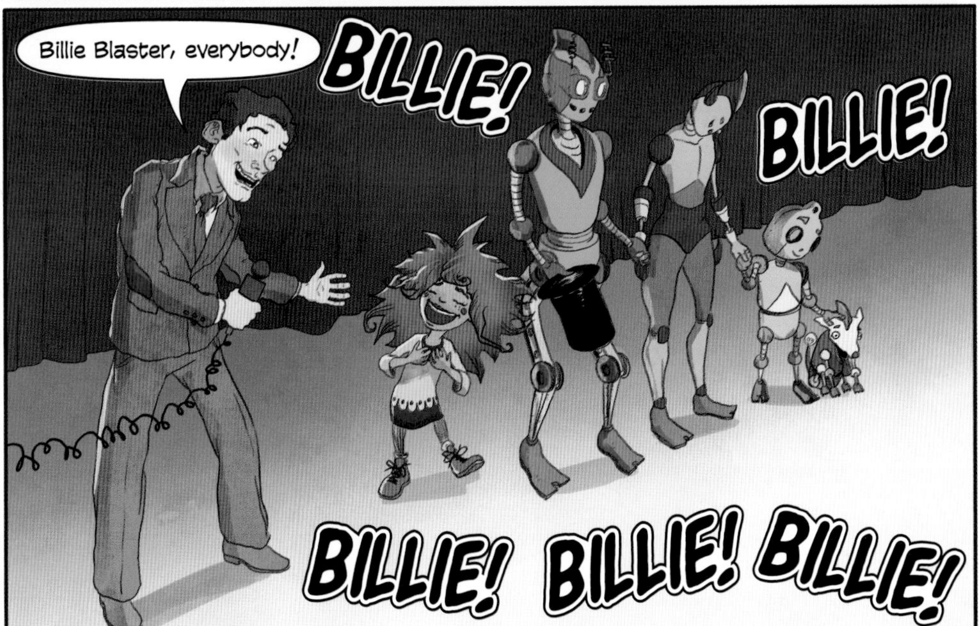
Billie Blaster, everybody!
BILLIE!
BILLIE!
BILLIE! BILLIE! BILLIE!

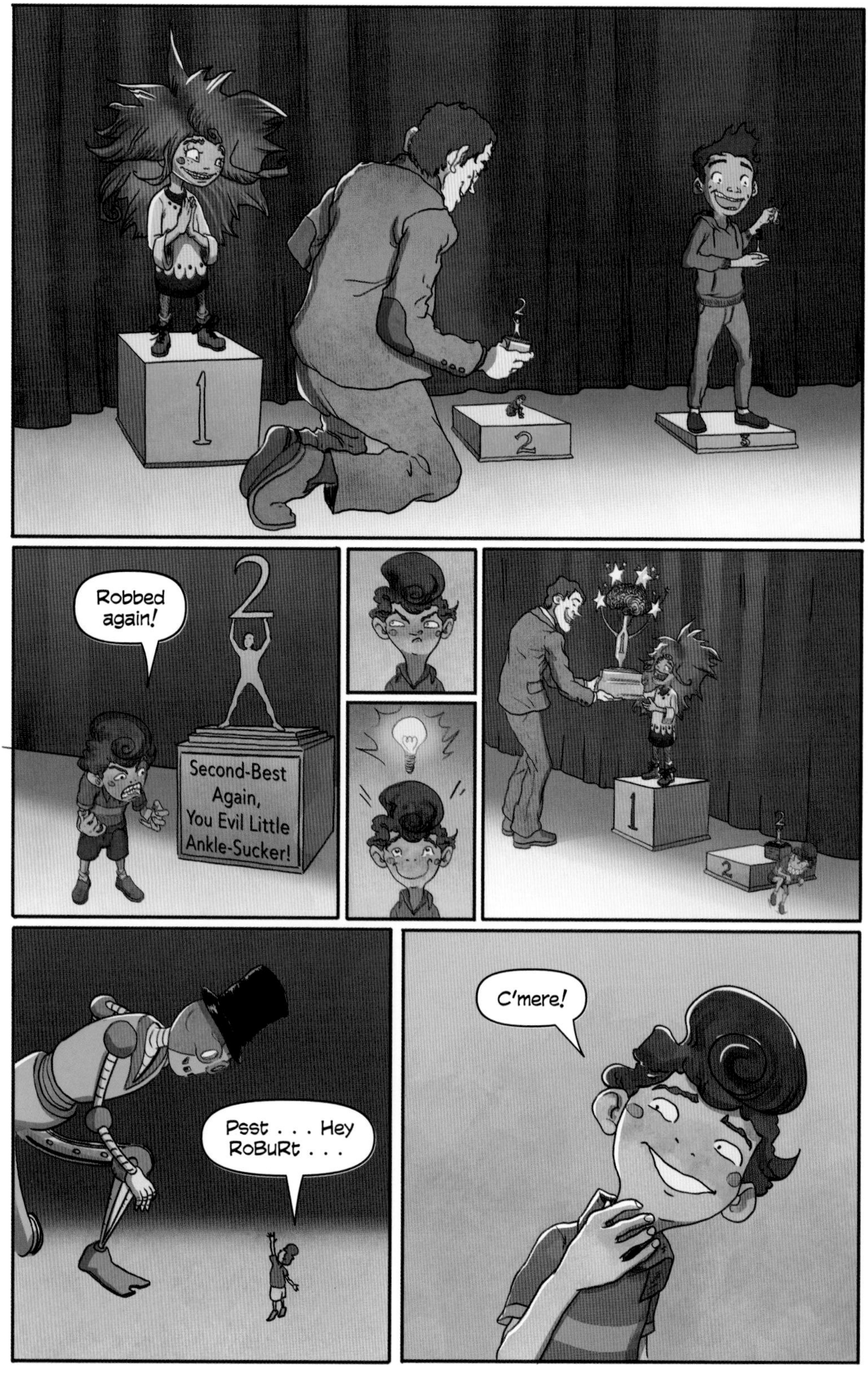

1
2
3
Robbed again!
2
Second-Best Again, You Evil Little Ankle-Sucker!
1
2
Psst . . . Hey RoBuRt . . .
C'mere!

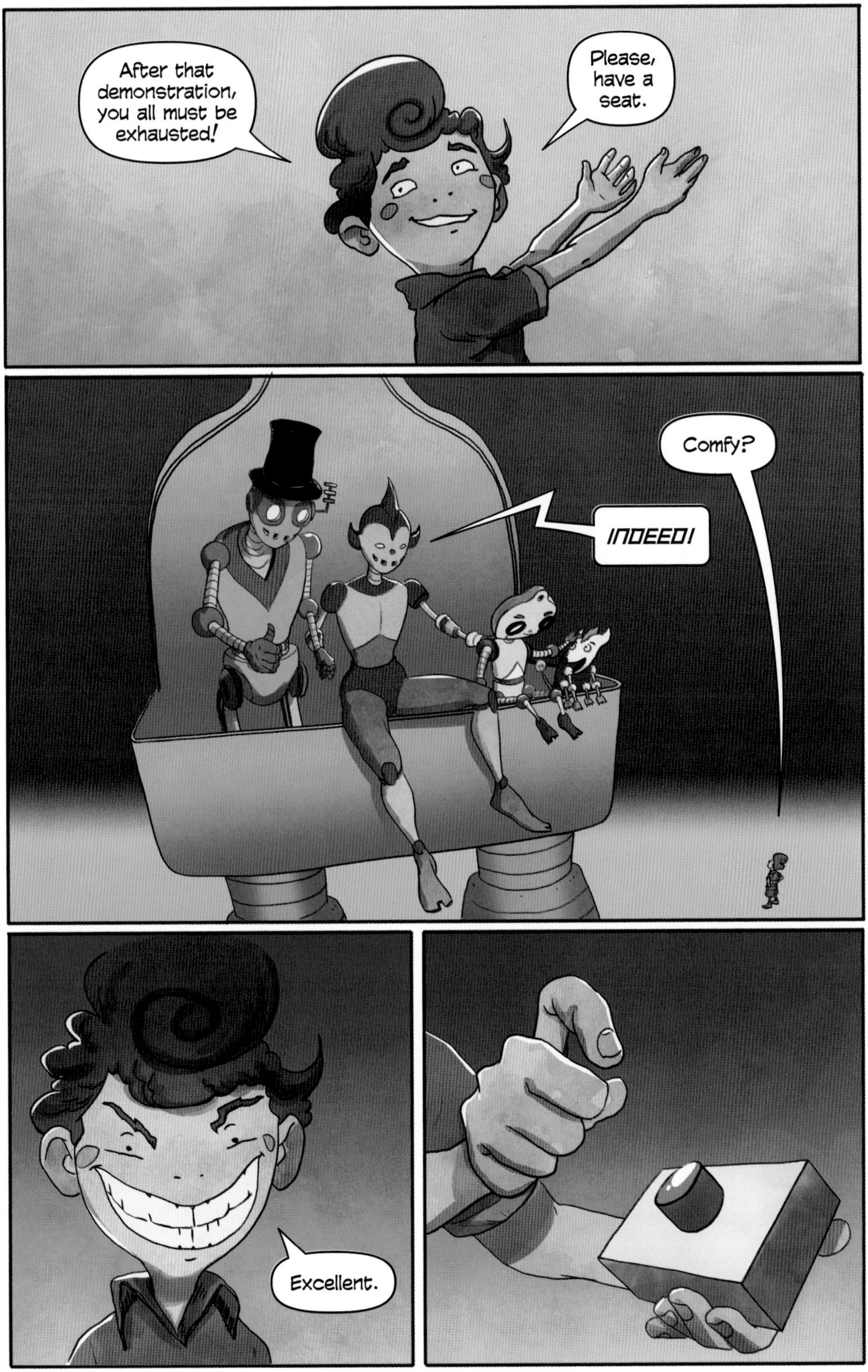
After that demonstration, you all must be exhausted!
Please, have a seat.
Comfy?
INDEED!
Excellent.

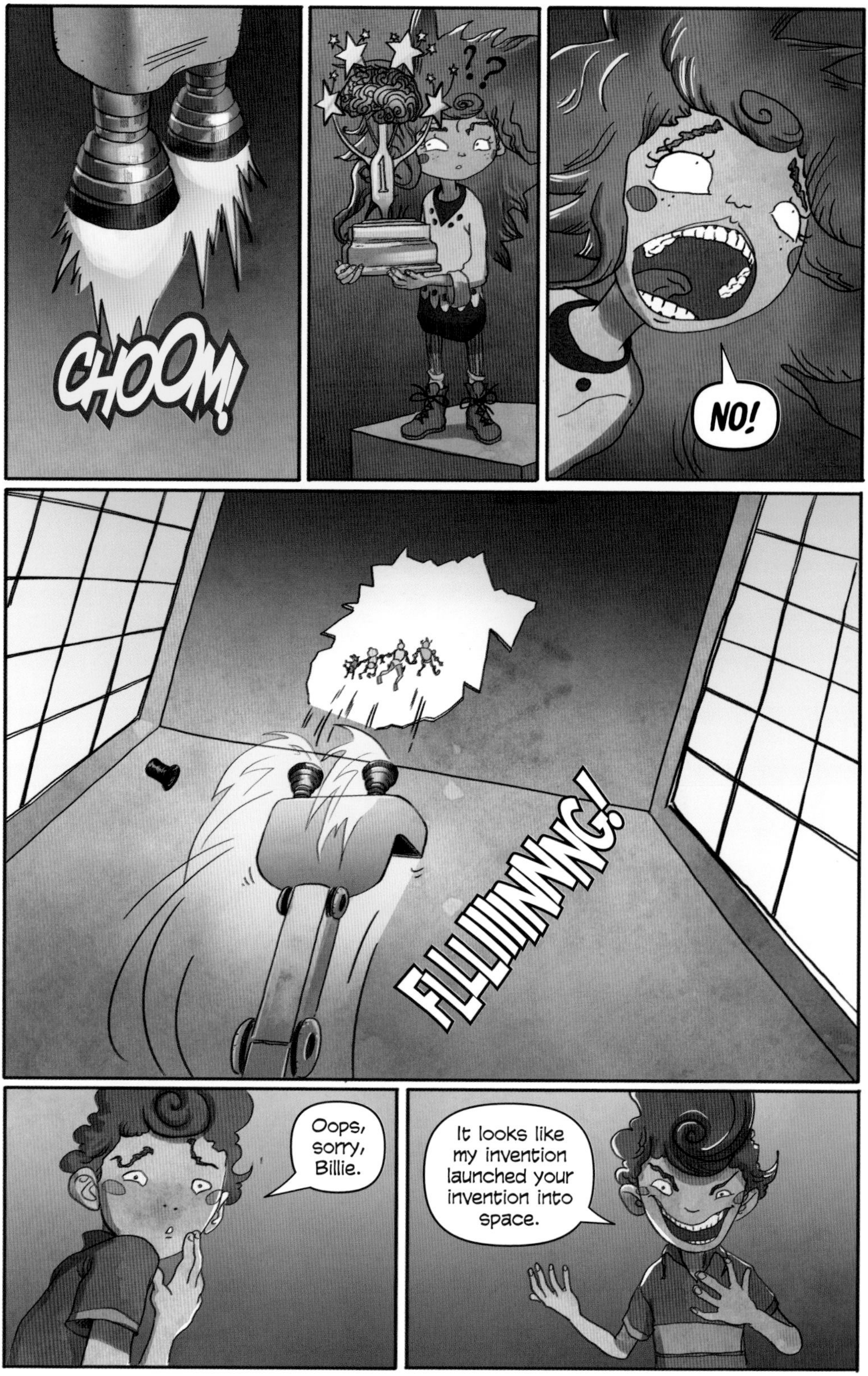
CHOOM!
NO!
FLLIIIINNNG!
Oops, sorry, Billie.
It looks like my invention launched your invention into space.

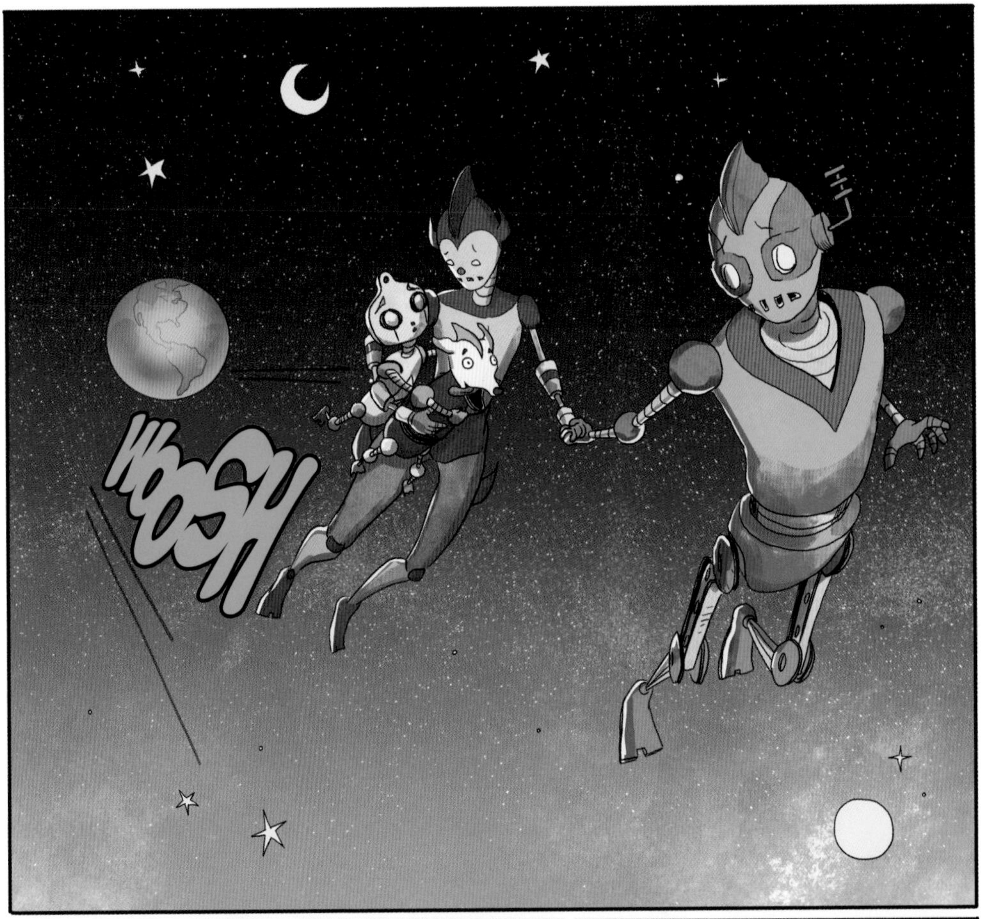
WOOSH

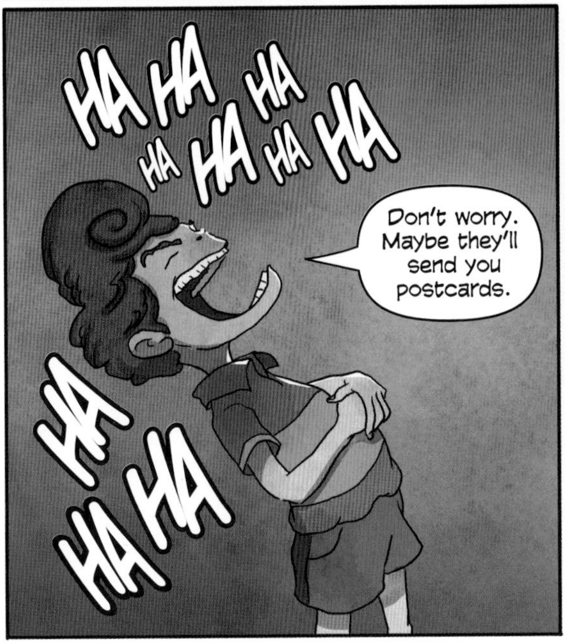
HA HA HA
HA HA HA HA
Don't worry. Maybe they'll send you postcards.
HA
HA HA

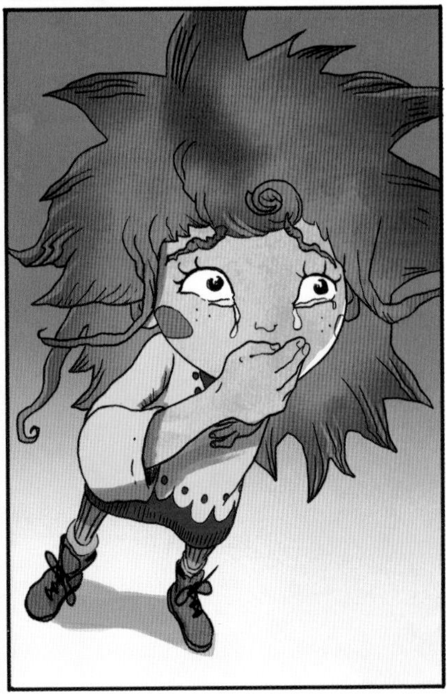

RoBuRt's MESSAGE

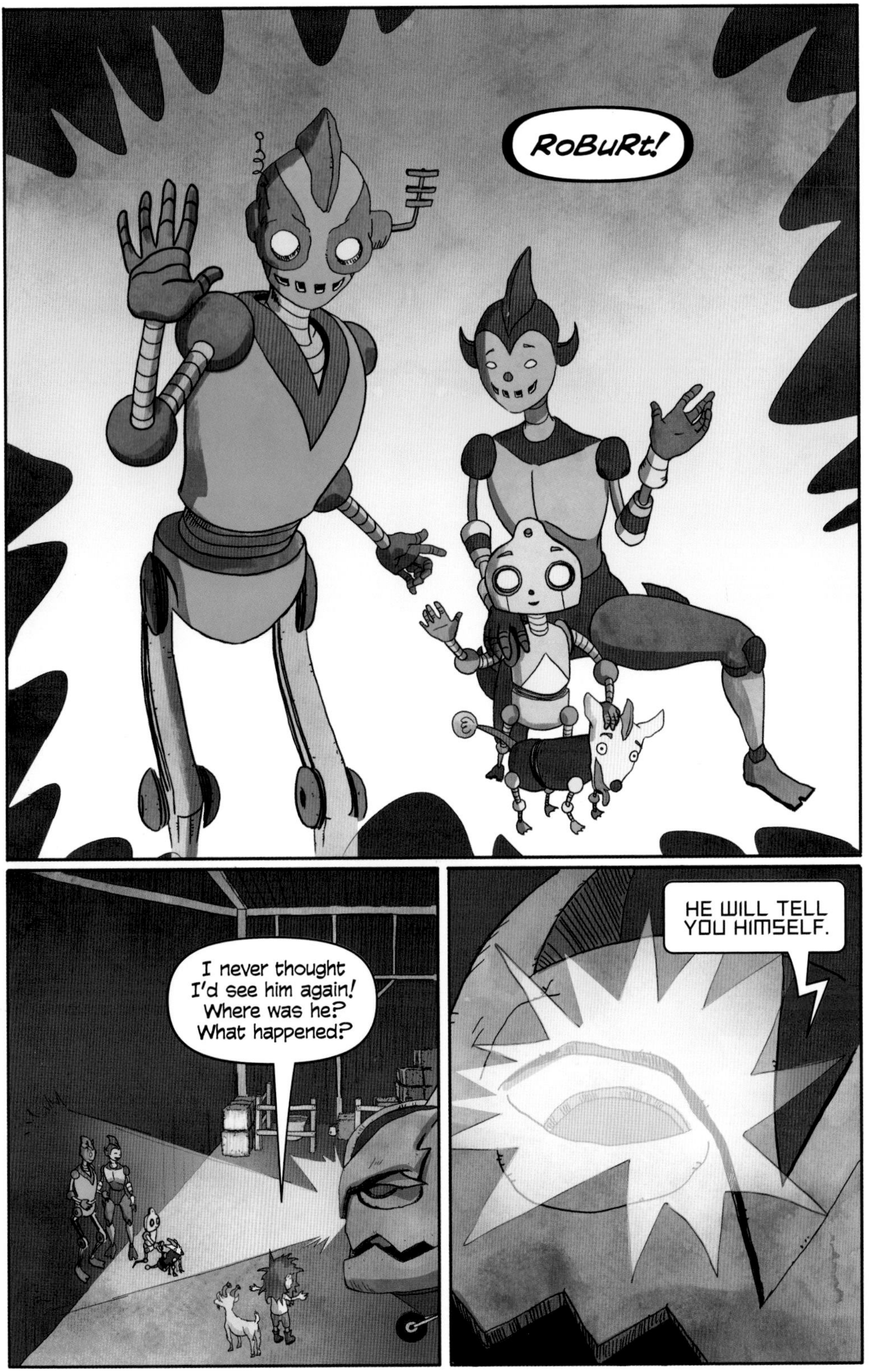
RoBuRt!
I never thought I'd see him again! Where was he? What happened?
HE WILL TELL YOU HIMSELF.

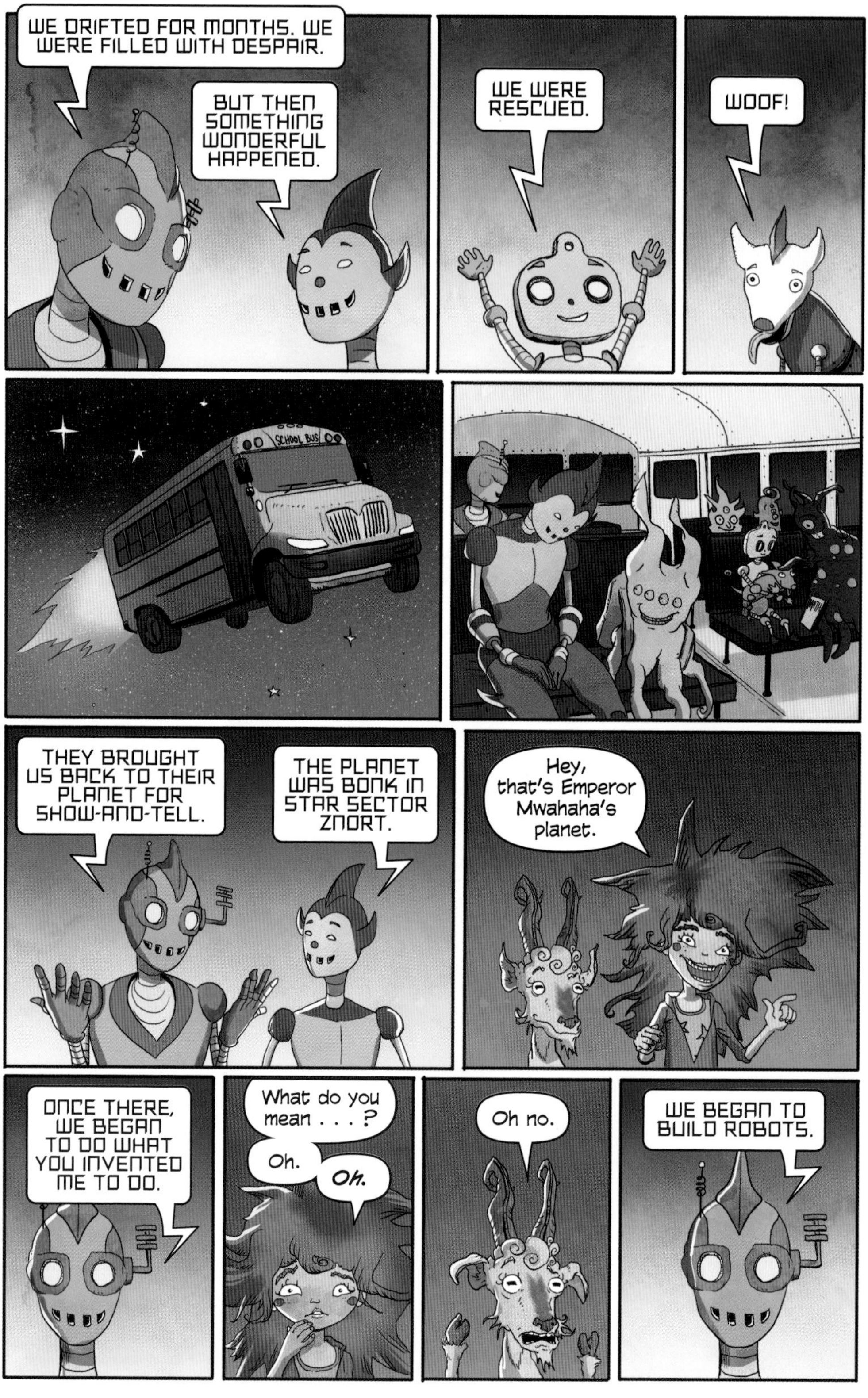
WE DRIFTED FOR MONTHS. WE WERE FILLED WITH DESPAIR.
BUT THEN SOMETHING WONDERFUL HAPPENED.
WE WERE RESCUED.
WOOF!
SCHOOL BUS
THEY BROUGHT US BACK TO THEIR PLANET FOR SHOW-AND-TELL.
THE PLANET WAS BONK IN STAR SECTOR ZNORT.
Hey, that's Emperor Mwahaha's planet.
ONCE THERE, WE BEGAN TO DO WHAT YOU INVENTED ME TO DO.
What do you mean . . . ?
Oh.
Oh.
Oh no.
WE BEGAN TO BUILD ROBOTS.

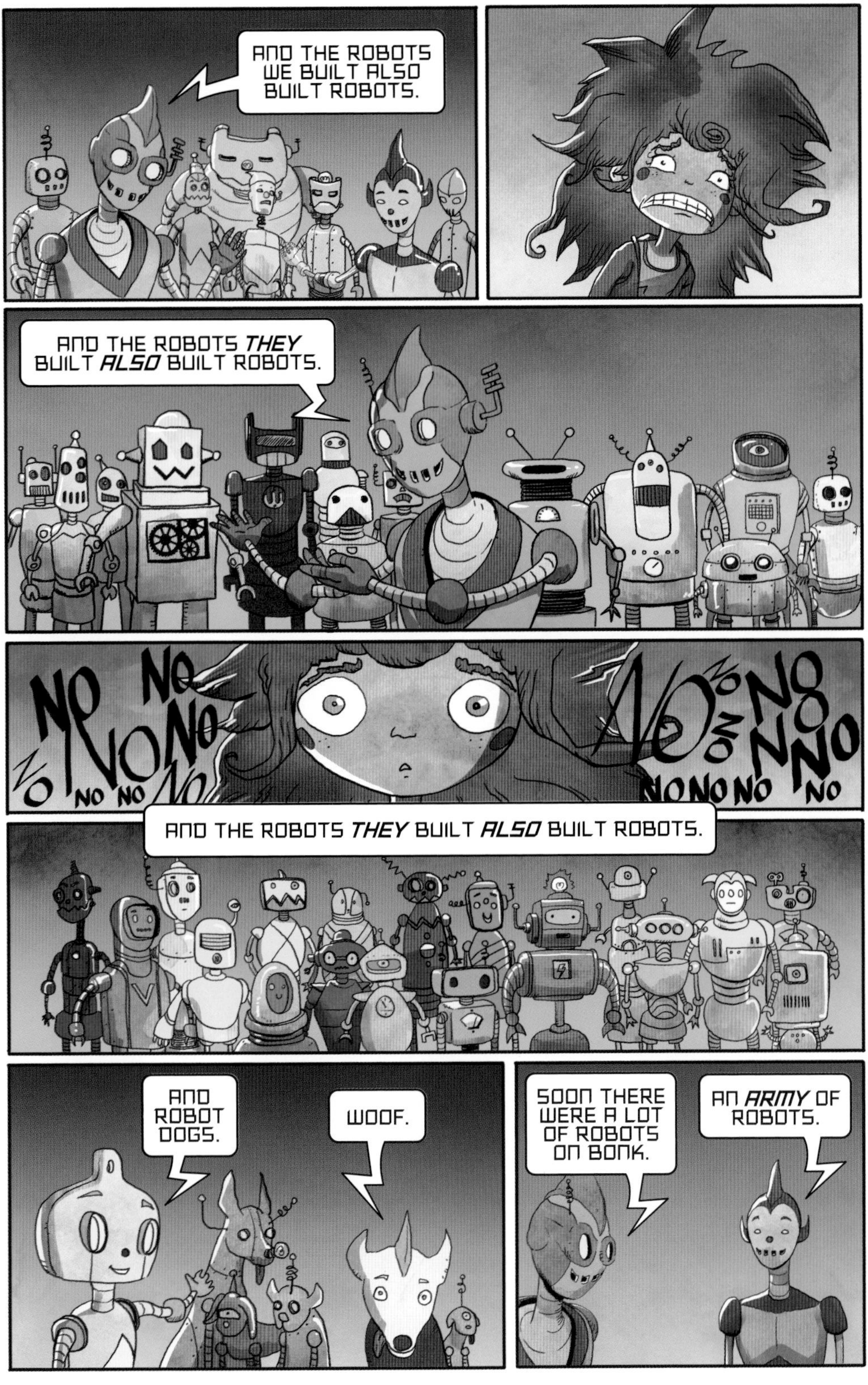
AND THE ROBOTS WE BUILT ALSO BUILT ROBOTS.
AND THE ROBOTS *THEY* BUILT *ALSO* BUILT ROBOTS.
NO NO NO NO NO NO NO NO NO NO NO NO NO NO NO NO NO NO NO NO NO
AND THE ROBOTS *THEY* BUILT *ALSO* BUILT ROBOTS.
AND ROBOT DOGS.
WOOF.
SOON THERE WERE A LOT OF ROBOTS ON BONK.
AN *ARMY* OF ROBOTS.

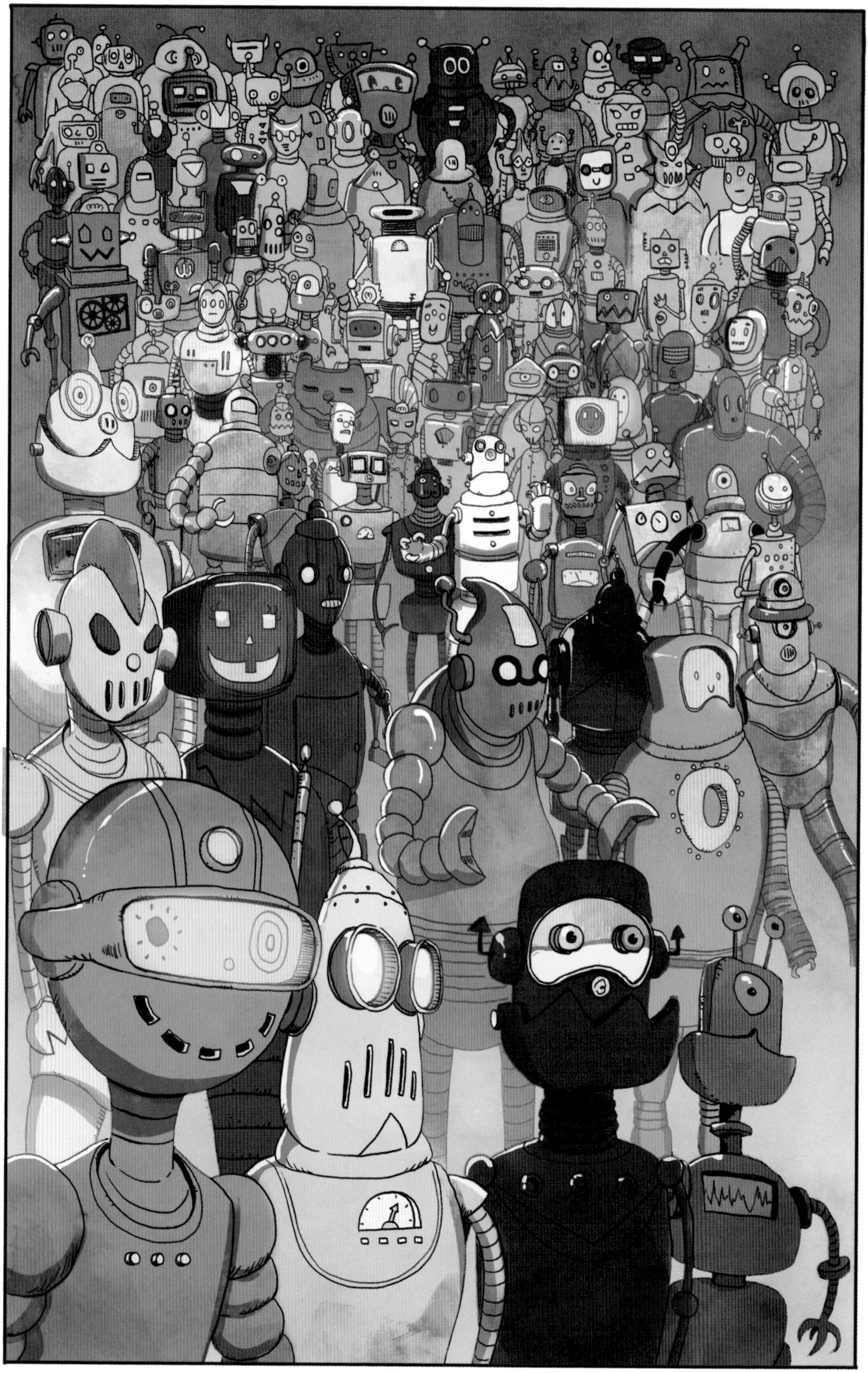

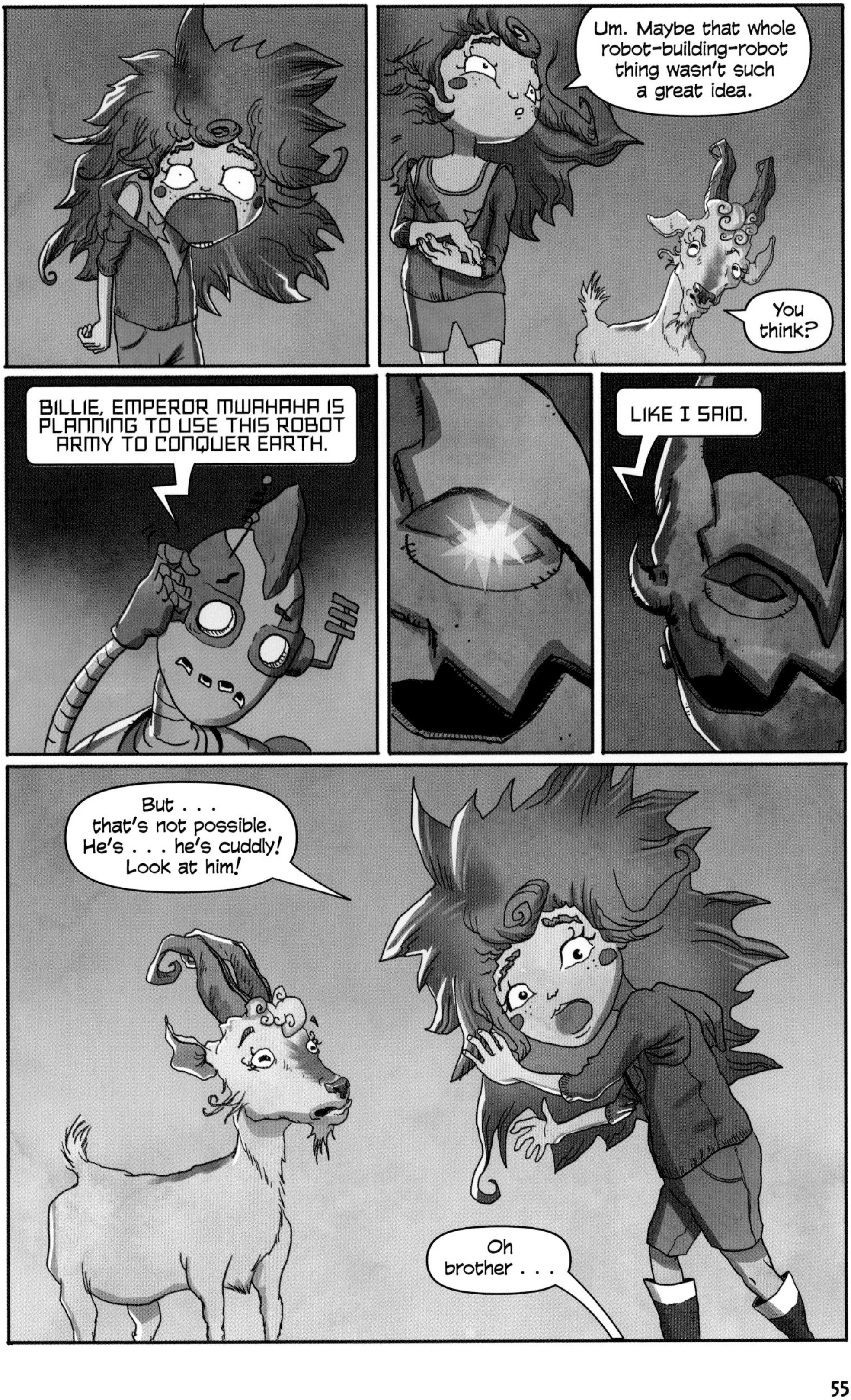
Um. Maybe that whole robot-building-robot thing wasn't such a great idea.
You think?
BILLIE, EMPEROR MWAHAHA IS PLANNING TO USE THIS ROBOT ARMY TO CONQUER EARTH.
LIKE I SAID.
But . . . that's not possible. He's . . . he's cuddly! Look at him!
Oh brother . . .

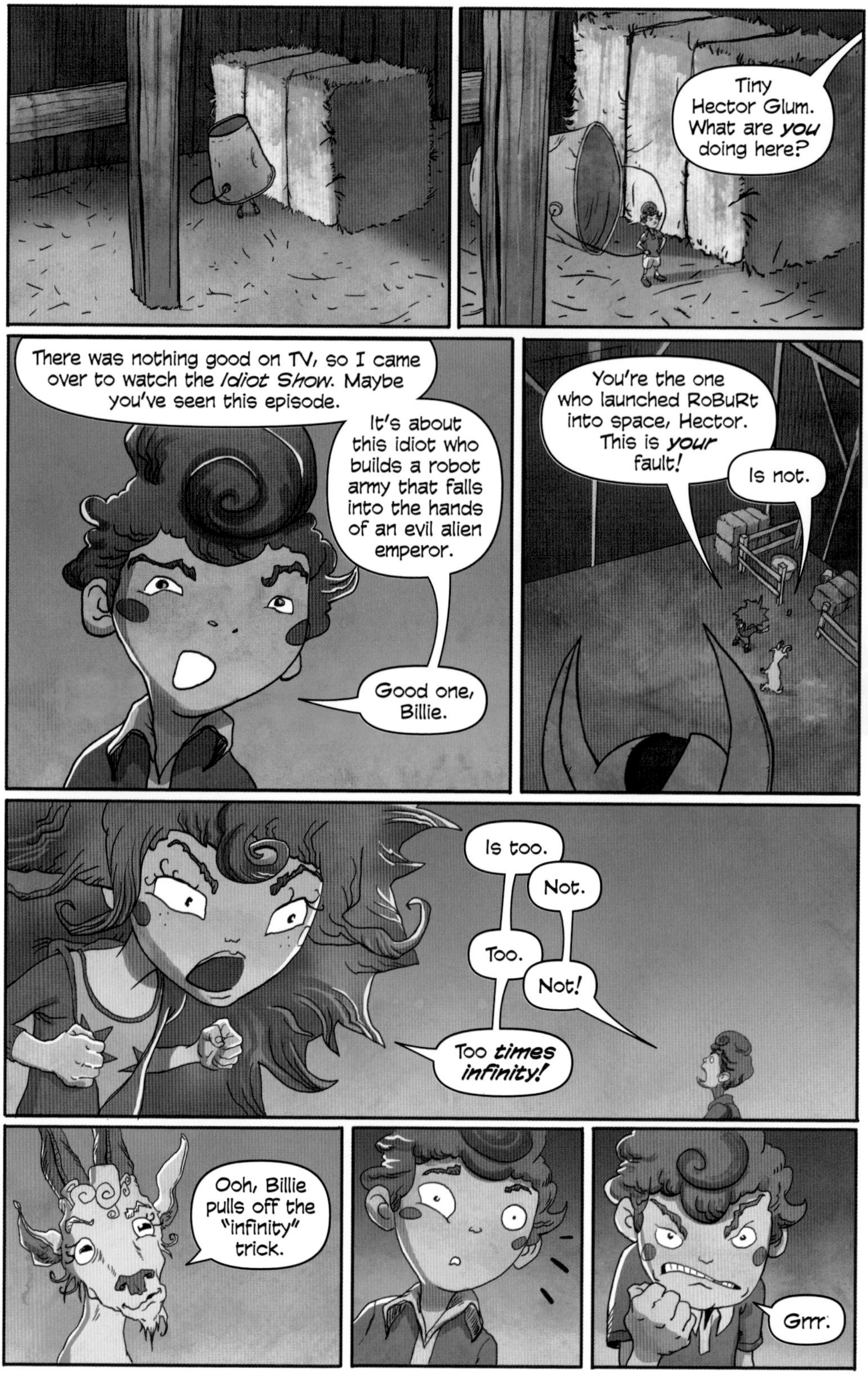
Tiny Hector Glum. What are *you* doing here?
There was nothing good on TV, so I came over to watch the *Idiot Show*. Maybe you've seen this episode.
It's about this idiot who builds a robot army that falls into the hands of an evil alien emperor.
Good one, Billie.
You're the one who launched RoBuRt into space, Hector. This is *your* fault!
Is not.
Is too.
Not.
Too.
Not!
Too *times infinity!*
Ooh, Billie pulls off the "infinity" trick.
Grrr.

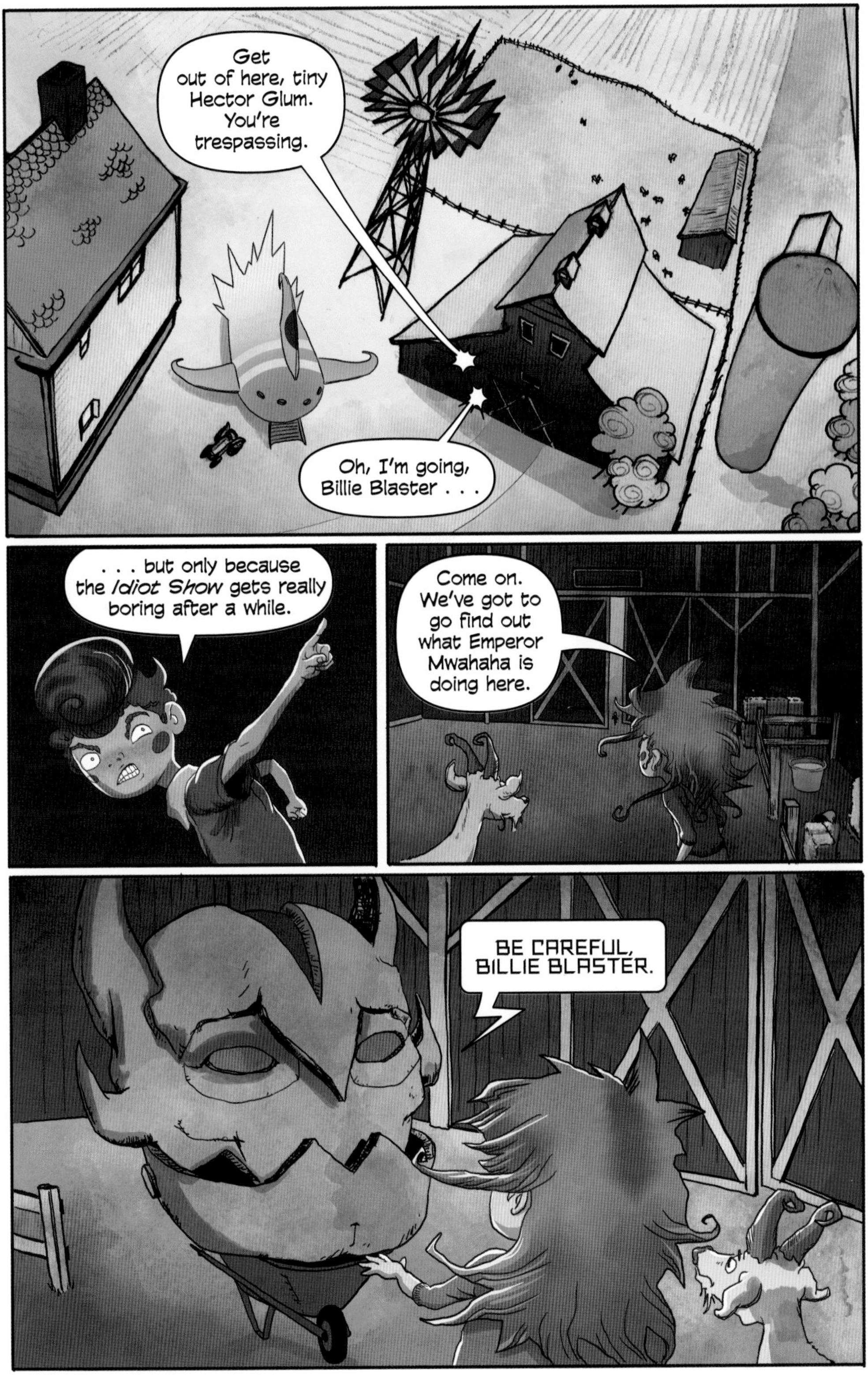
Get out of here, tiny Hector Glum. You're trespassing.
Oh, I'm going, Billie Blaster . . .
. . . but only because the *Idiot Show* gets really boring after a while.
Come on. We've got to go find out what Emperor Mwahaha is doing here.
BE CAREFUL, BILLIE BLASTER.

THE ALIEN OVERLORD

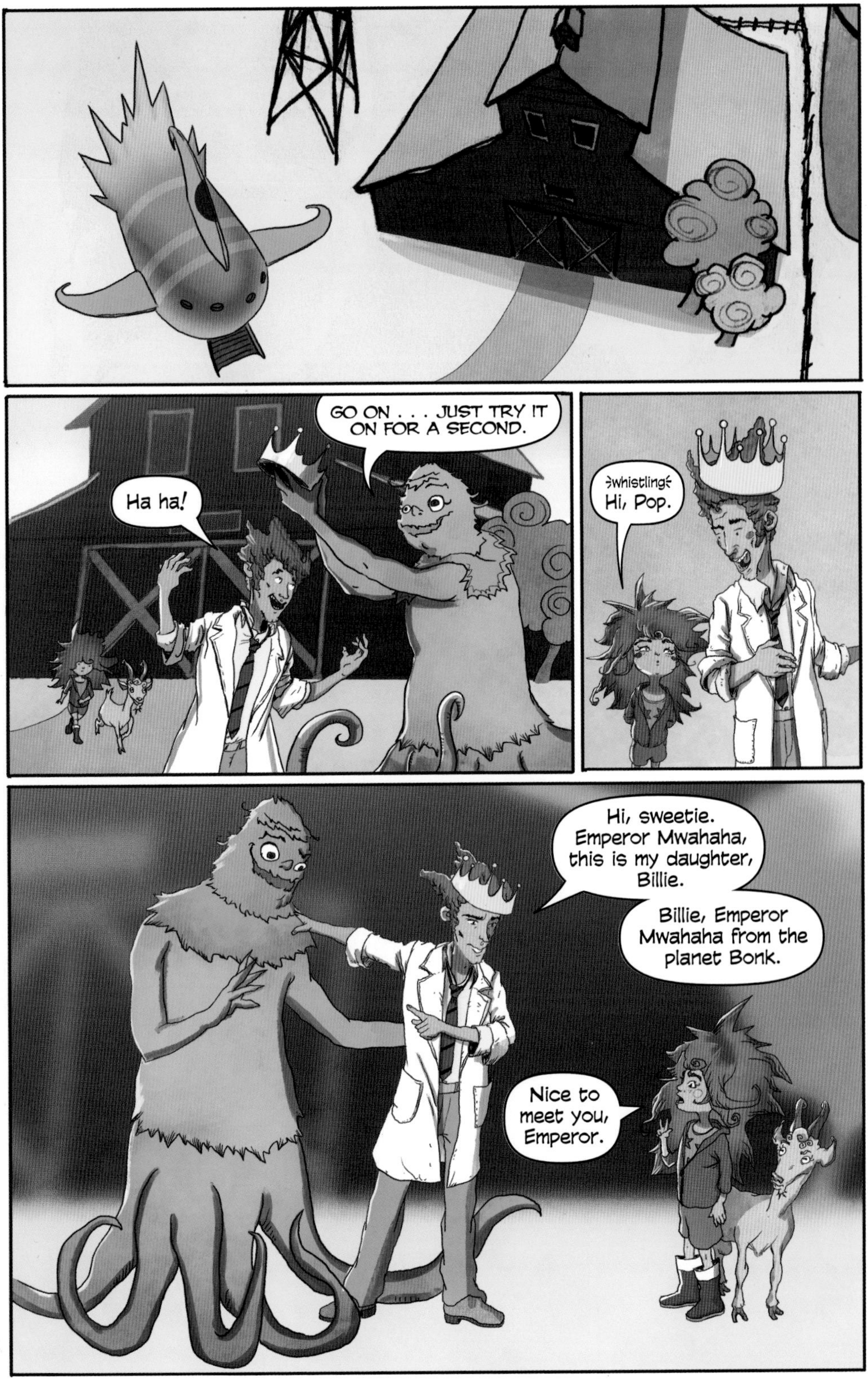
GO ON . . . JUST TRY IT ON FOR A SECOND.
Ha ha!
whistling
Hi, Pop.
Hi, sweetie. Emperor Mwahaha, this is my daughter, Billie.
Billie, Emperor Mwahaha from the planet Bonk.
Nice to meet you, Emperor.

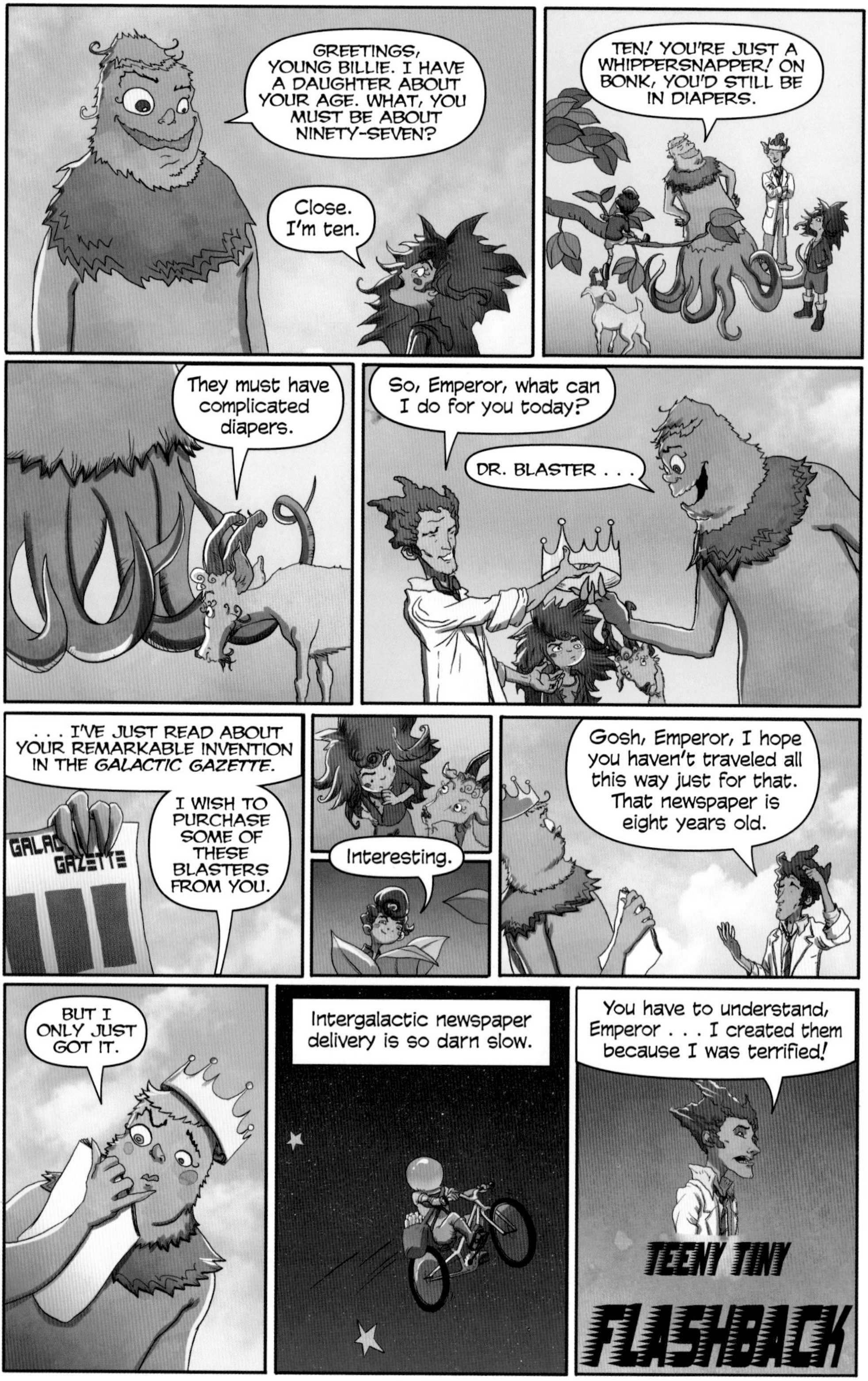
GREETINGS, YOUNG BILLIE. I HAVE A DAUGHTER ABOUT YOUR AGE. WHAT, YOU MUST BE ABOUT NINETY-SEVEN?
Close. I'm ten.
TEN! YOU'RE JUST A WHIPPERSNAPPER! ON BONK, YOU'D STILL BE IN DIAPERS.
They must have complicated diapers.
So, Emperor, what can I do for you today?
DR. BLASTER . . .
. . . I'VE JUST READ ABOUT YOUR REMARKABLE INVENTION IN THE *GALACTIC GAZETTE*.
I WISH TO PURCHASE SOME OF THESE BLASTERS FROM YOU.
GAZETTE
Interesting.
Gosh, Emperor, I hope you haven't traveled all this way just for that. That newspaper is eight years old.
BUT I ONLY JUST GOT IT.
Intergalactic newspaper delivery is so darn slow.
You have to understand, Emperor . . . I created them because I was terrified!
TEENY TINY
FLASHBACK

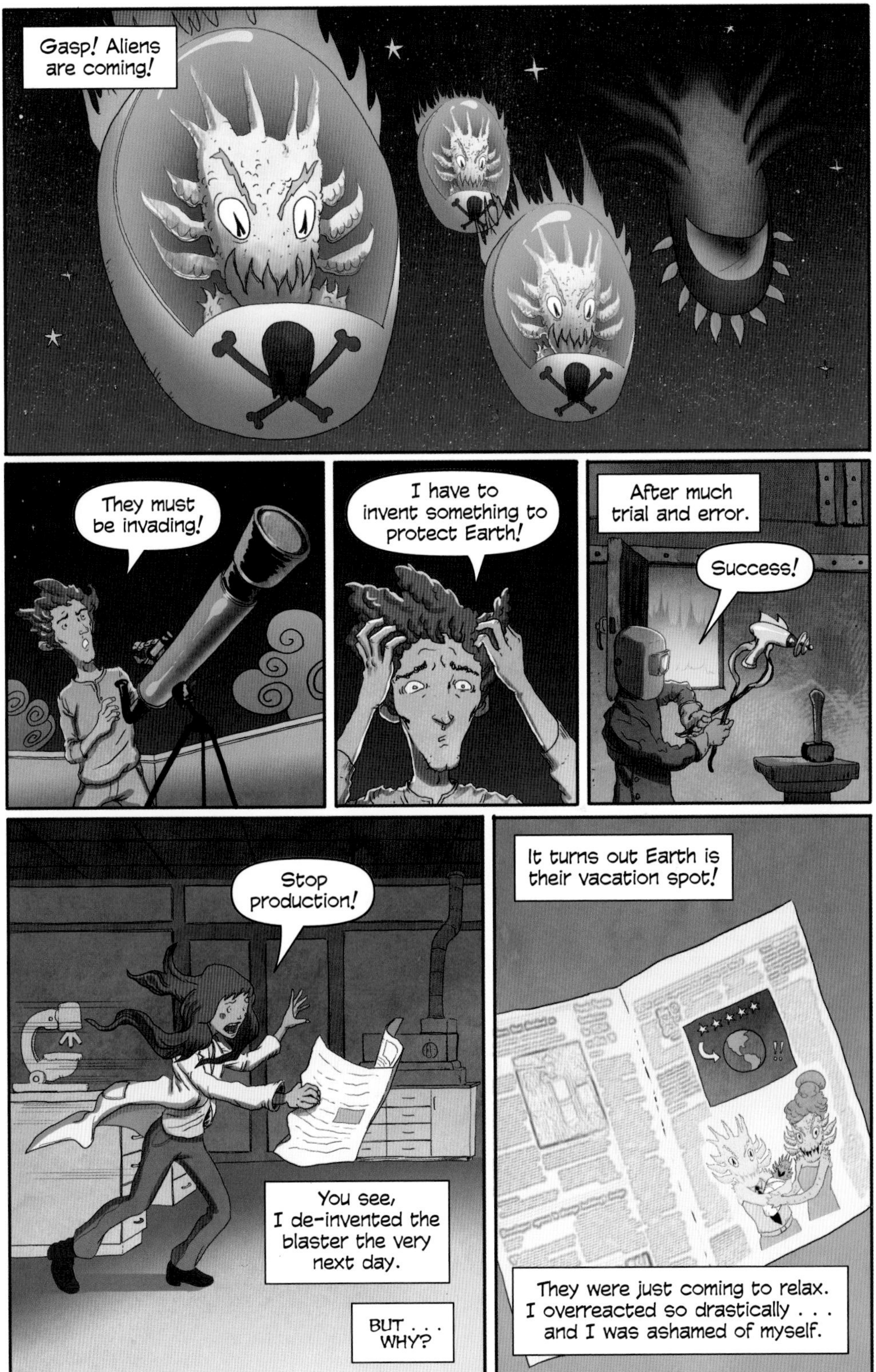
Gasp! Aliens are coming!
They must be invading!
I have to invent something to protect Earth!
After much trial and error.
Success!
Stop production!
You see, I de-invented the blaster the very next day.
BUT . . . WHY?
It turns out Earth is their vacation spot!
They were just coming to relax. I overreacted so drastically . . . and I was ashamed of myself.

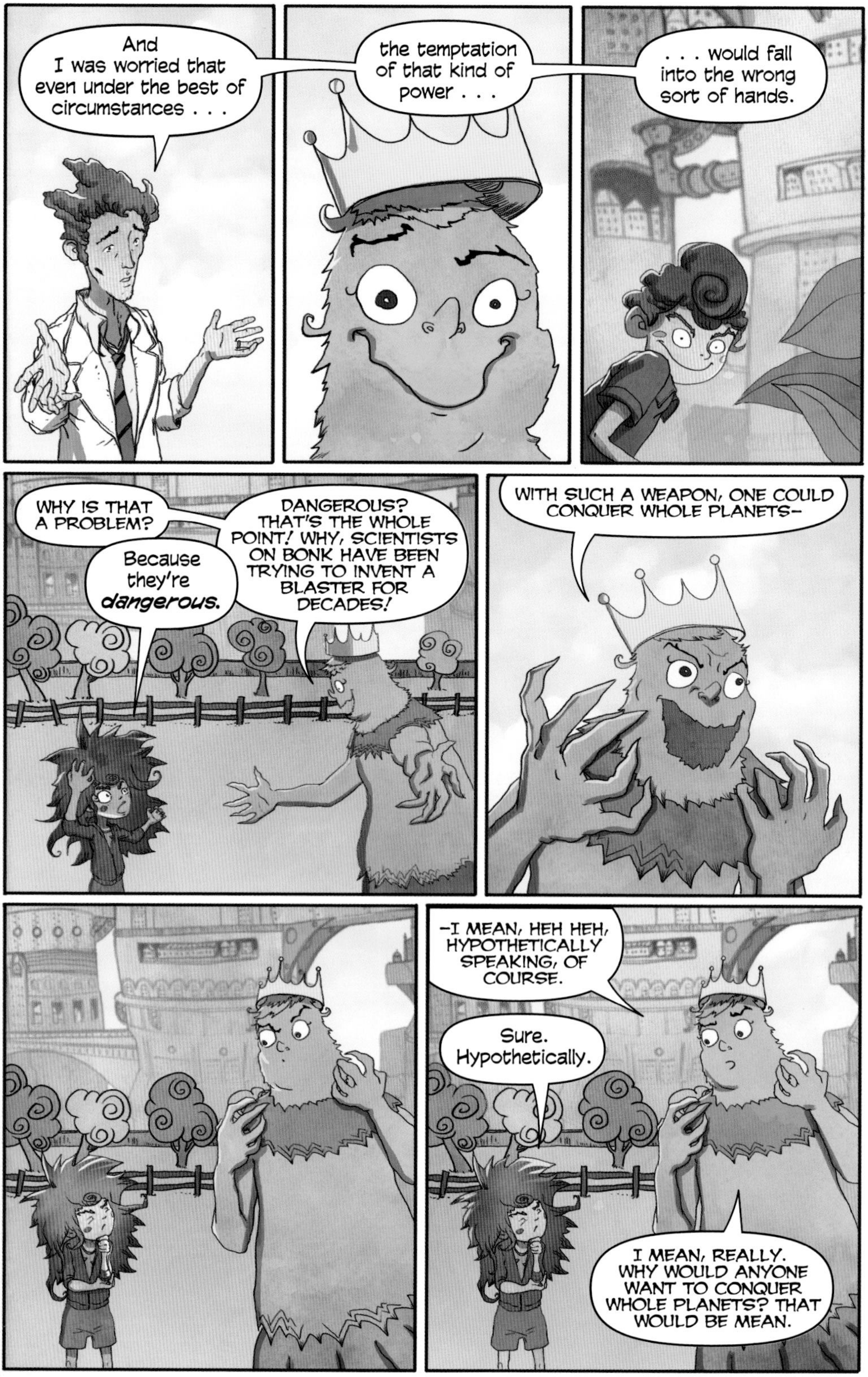
And I was worried that even under the best of circumstances . . .
the temptation of that kind of power . . .
. . . would fall into the wrong sort of hands.
WHY IS THAT A PROBLEM?
Because they're *dangerous.*
DANGEROUS? THAT'S THE WHOLE POINT! WHY, SCIENTISTS ON BONK HAVE BEEN TRYING TO INVENT A BLASTER FOR DECADES!
WITH SUCH A WEAPON, ONE COULD CONQUER WHOLE PLANETS–
–I MEAN, HEH HEH, HYPOTHETICALLY SPEAKING, OF COURSE.
Sure. Hypothetically.
I MEAN, REALLY. WHY WOULD ANYONE WANT TO CONQUER WHOLE PLANETS? THAT WOULD BE MEAN.

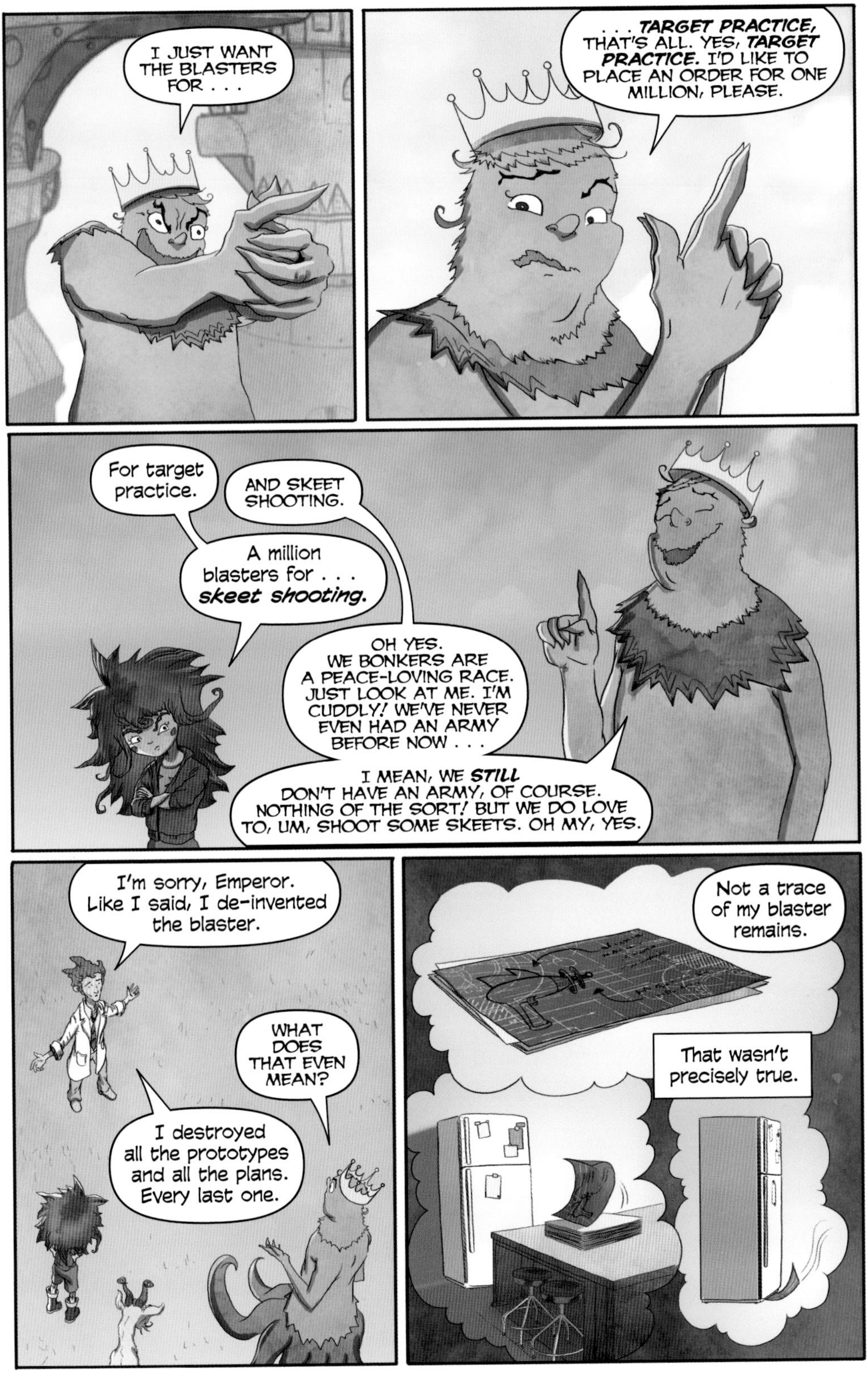
I JUST WANT THE BLASTERS FOR . . .
. . . TARGET PRACTICE, THAT'S ALL. YES, TARGET PRACTICE. I'D LIKE TO PLACE AN ORDER FOR ONE MILLION, PLEASE.
For target practice.
AND SKEET SHOOTING.
A million blasters for . . . skeet shooting.
OH YES. WE BONKERS ARE A PEACE-LOVING RACE. JUST LOOK AT ME. I'M CUDDLY! WE'VE NEVER EVEN HAD AN ARMY BEFORE NOW . . .
I MEAN, WE STILL DON'T HAVE AN ARMY, OF COURSE. NOTHING OF THE SORT! BUT WE DO LOVE TO, UM, SHOOT SOME SKEETS. OH MY, YES.
I'm sorry, Emperor. Like I said, I de-invented the blaster.
WHAT DOES THAT EVEN MEAN?
I destroyed all the prototypes and all the plans. Every last one.
Not a trace of my blaster remains.
That wasn't precisely true.

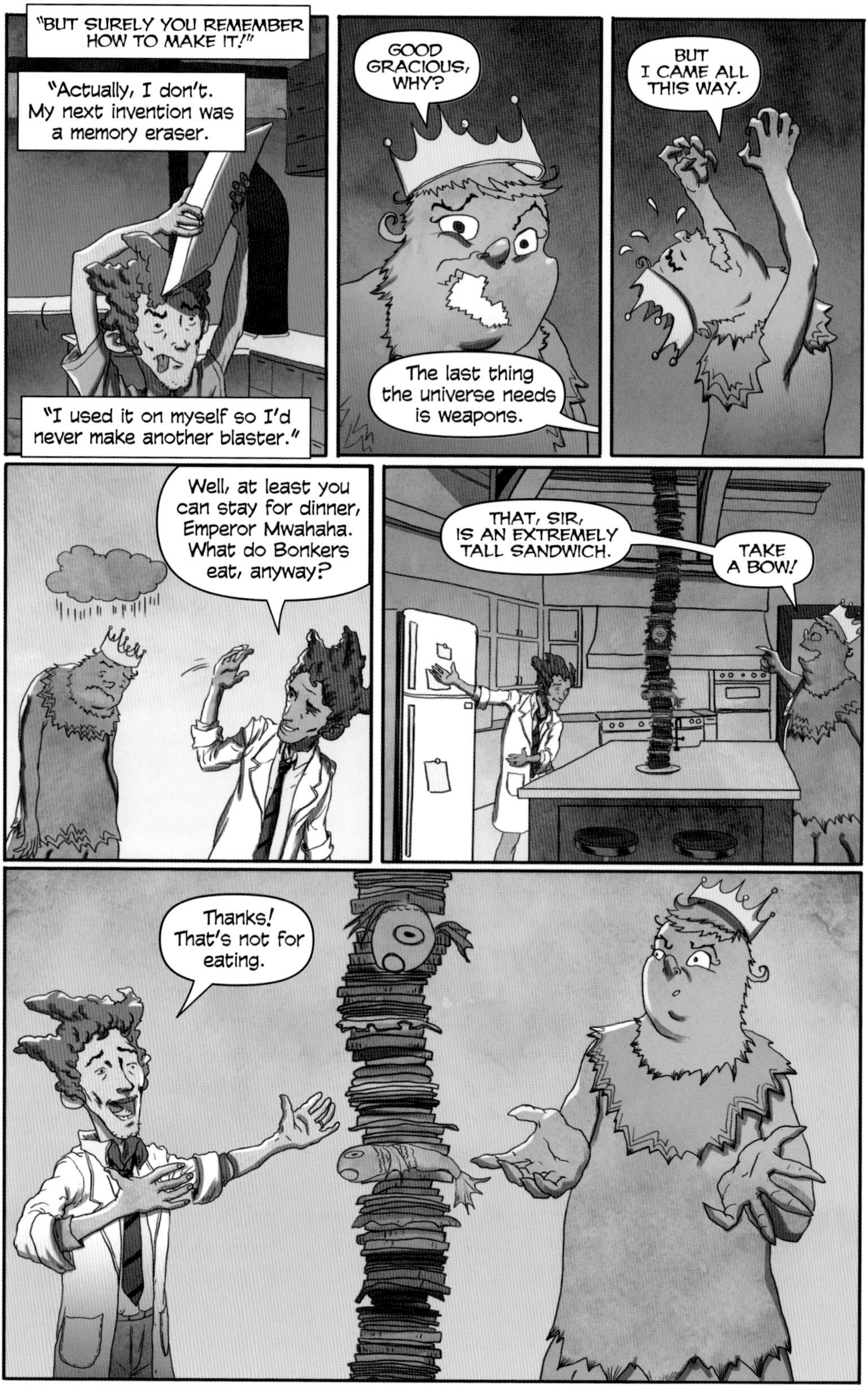
"BUT SURELY YOU REMEMBER HOW TO MAKE IT!"
"Actually, I don't. My next invention was a memory eraser.
"I used it on myself so I'd never make another blaster."
GOOD GRACIOUS, WHY?
The last thing the universe needs is weapons.
BUT I CAME ALL THIS WAY.
Well, at least you can stay for dinner, Emperor Mwahaha. What do Bonkers eat, anyway?
THAT, SIR, IS AN EXTREMELY TALL SANDWICH.
TAKE A BOW!
Thanks! That's not for eating.

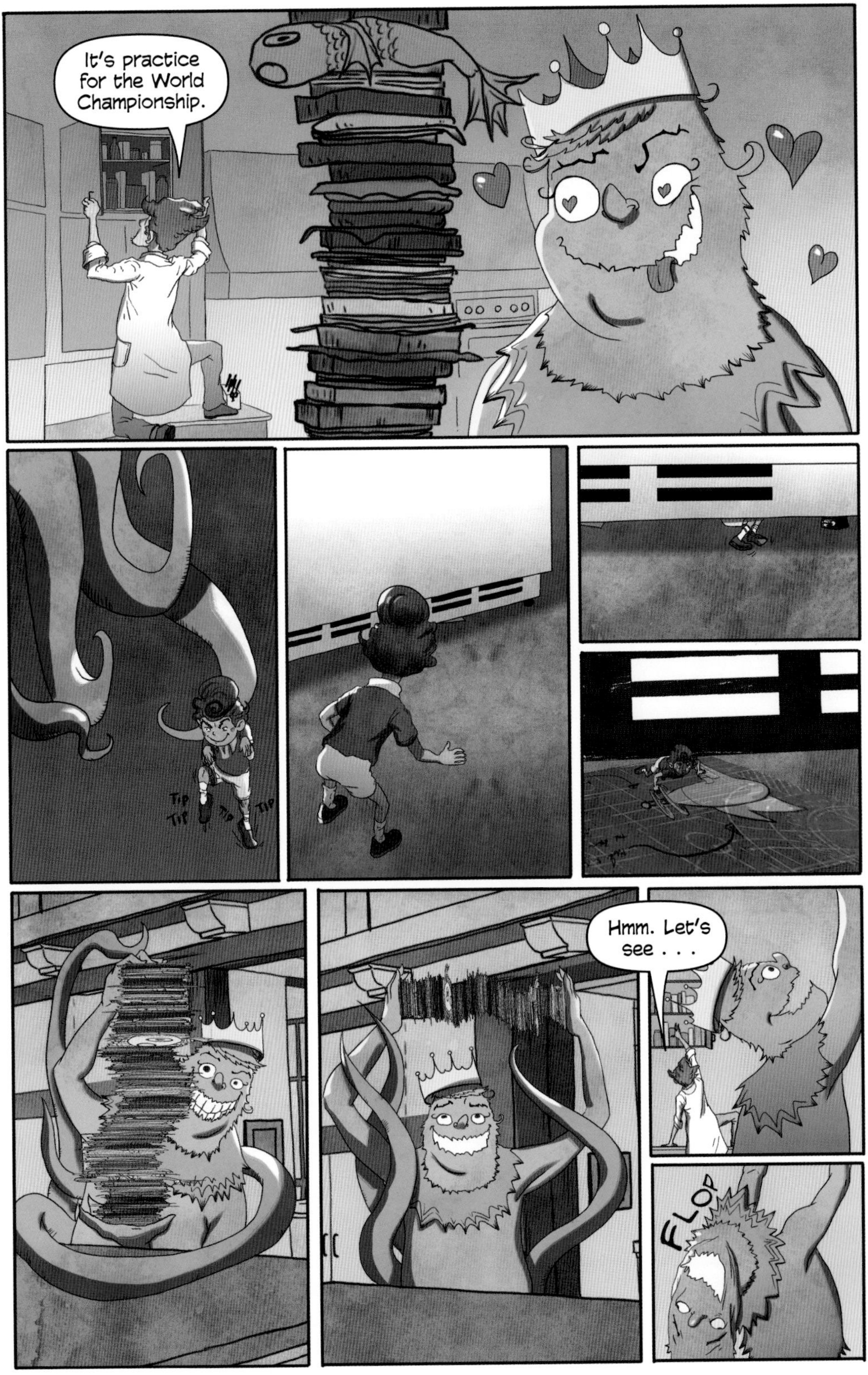
It's practice for the World Championship.
TIP TIP TIP TIP
Hmm. Let's see . . .
FLOP

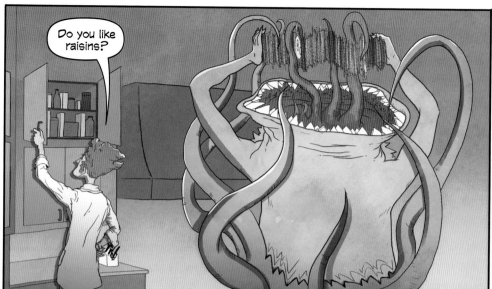

Do you like raisins?

Well, that's one disaster averted.

Yeah. Whew.

"There's no way Emperor Mwahaha is getting his hands on blaster technology."

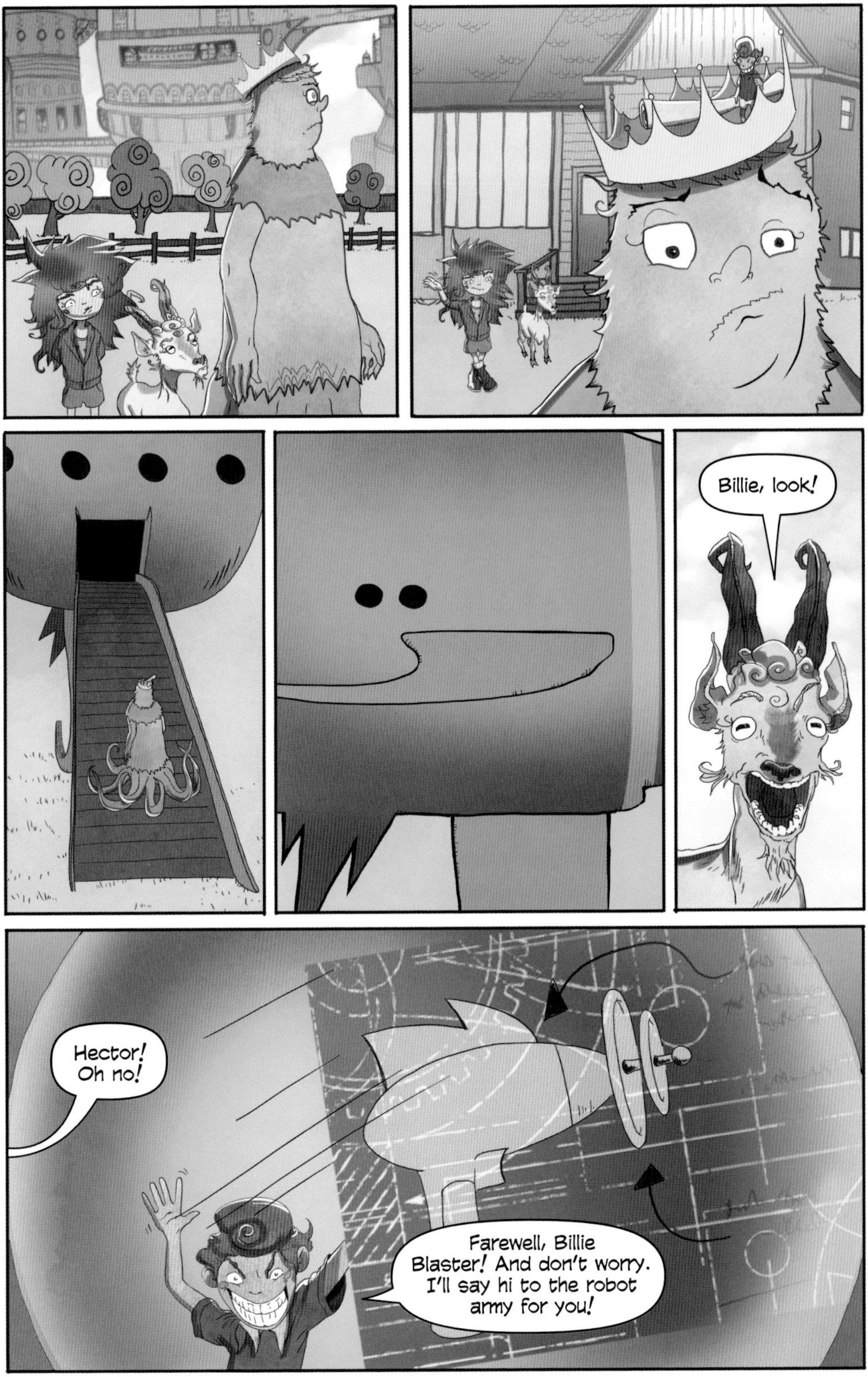
Billie, look!
Hector! Oh no!
Farewell, Billie Blaster! And don't worry. I'll say hi to the robot army for you!

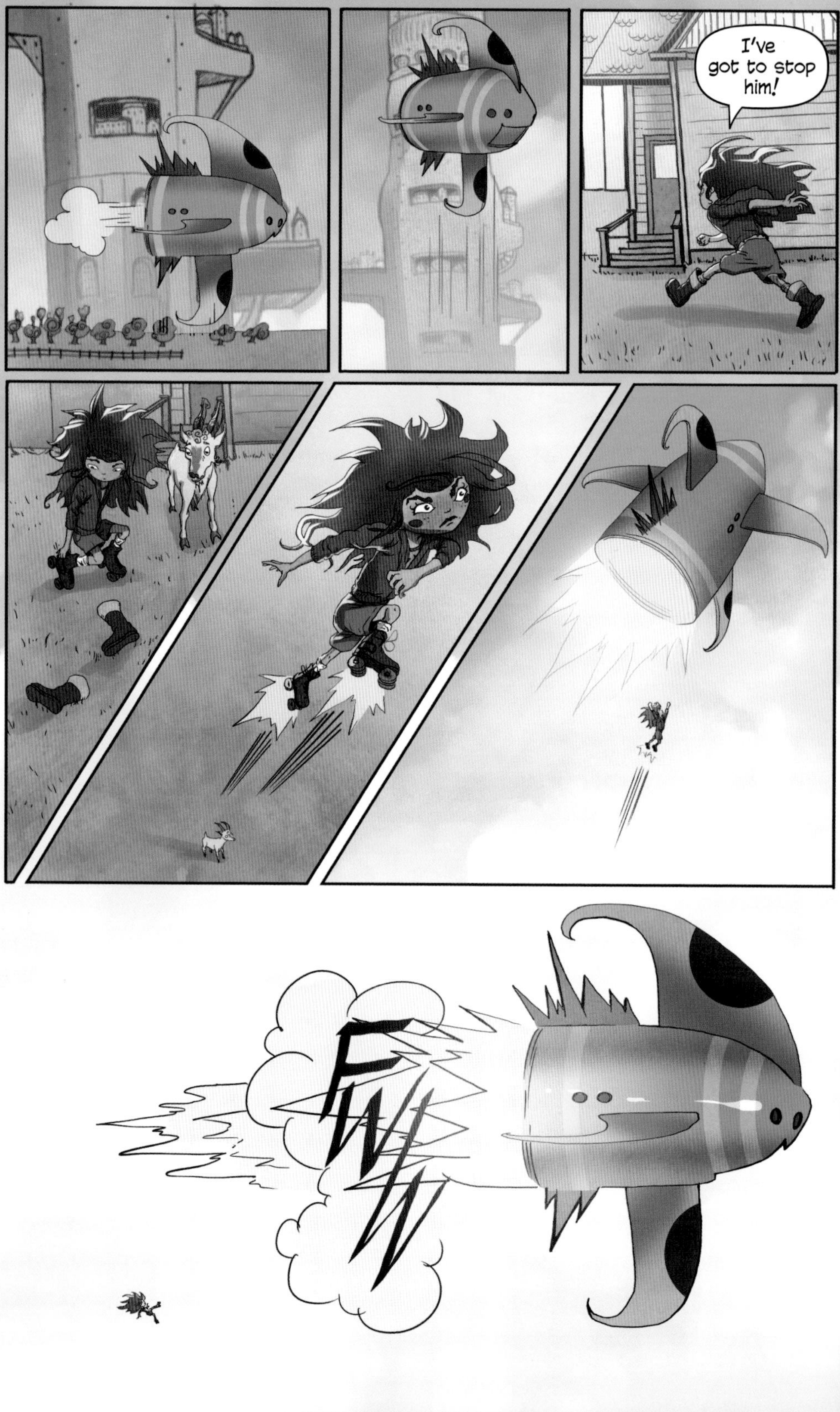
I've got to stop him!
FWSH

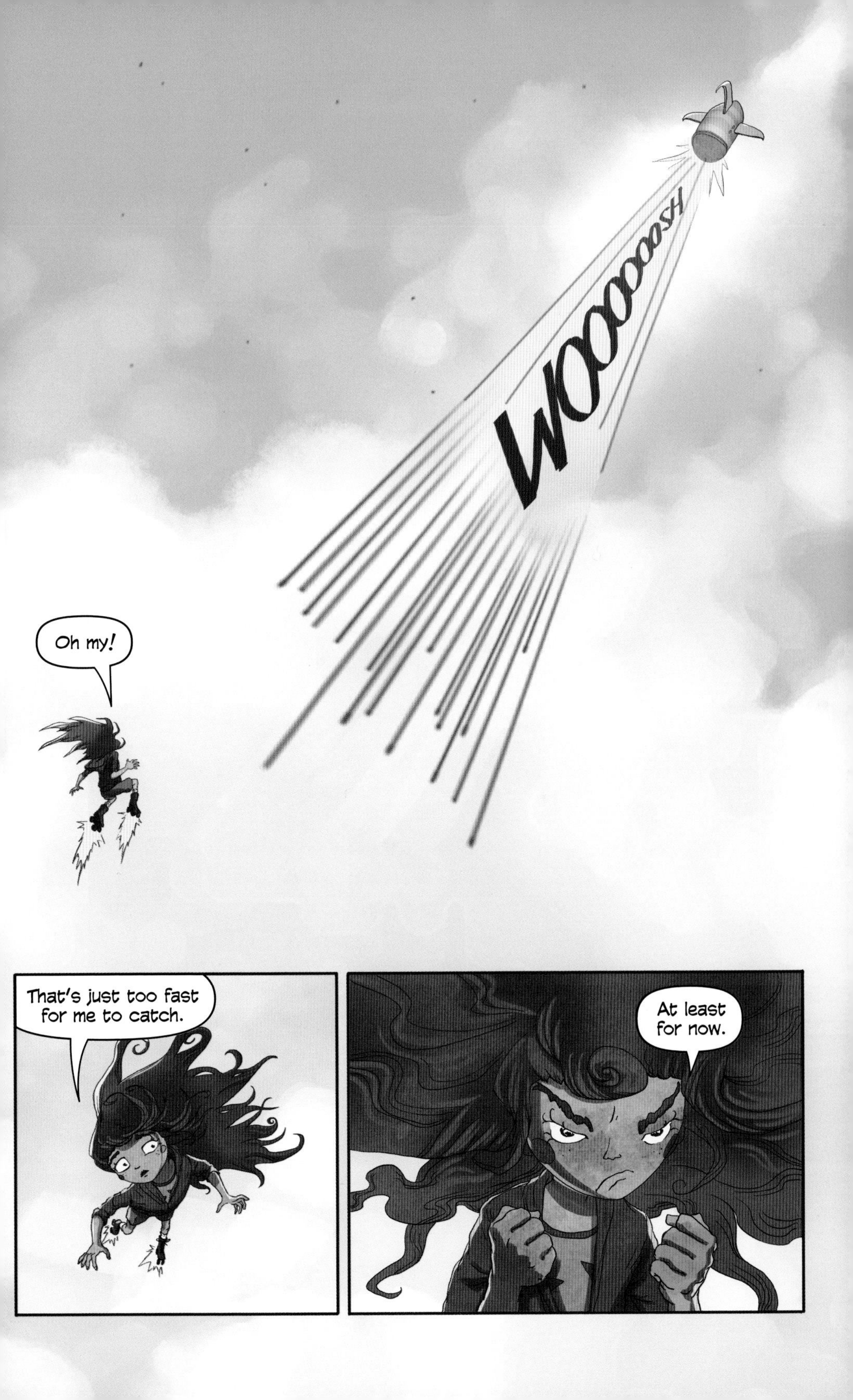
WOOOOOOOSH
Oh my!
That's just too fast for me to catch.
At least for now.

THE ROCKET SHIP

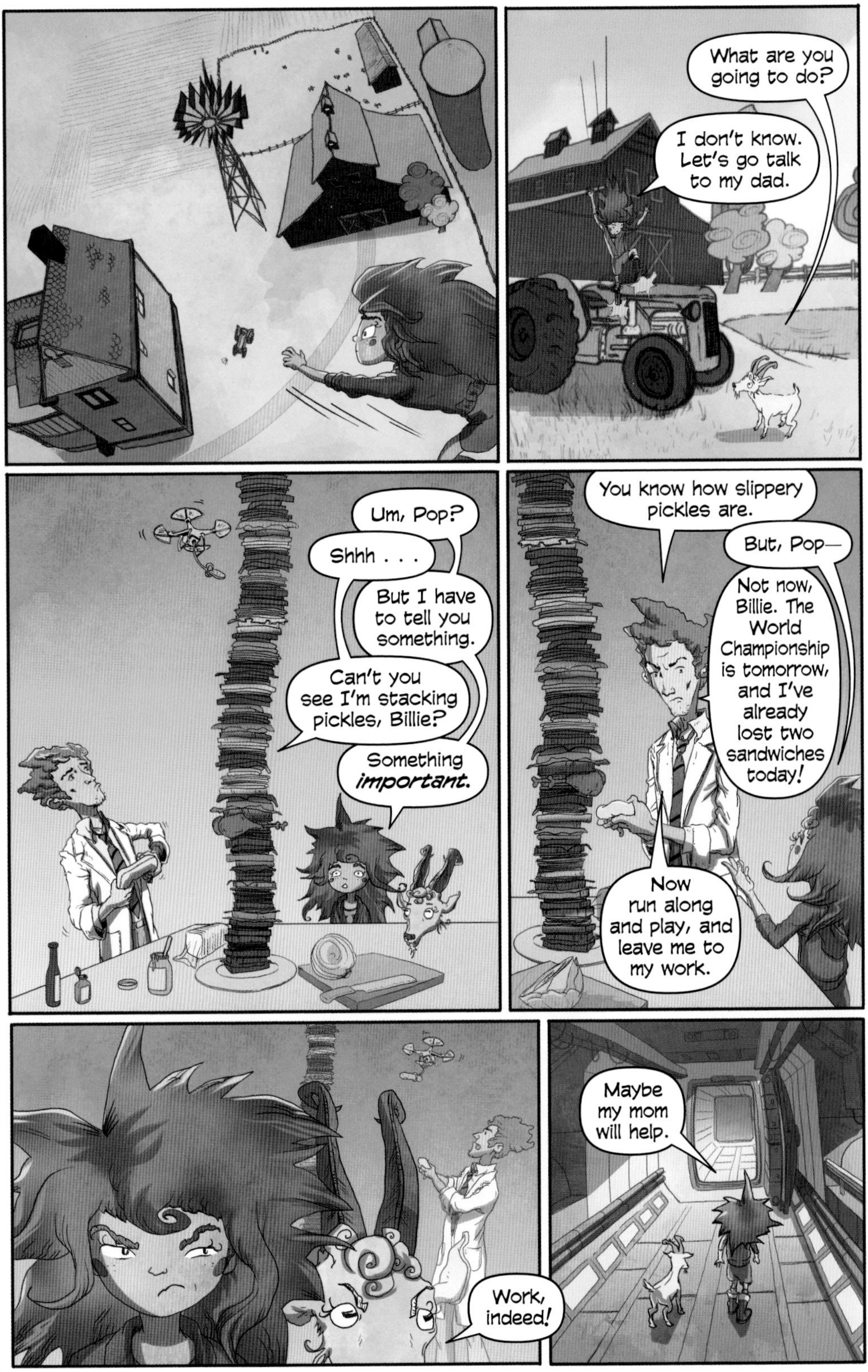
What are you going to do?
I don't know. Let's go talk to my dad.
Um, Pop?
Shhh . . .
But I have to tell you something.
Can't you see I'm stacking pickles, Billie?
Something *important*.
You know how slippery pickles are.
But, Pop—
Not now, Billie. The World Championship is tomorrow, and I've already lost two sandwiches today!
Now run along and play, and leave me to my work.
Work, indeed!
Maybe my mom will help.

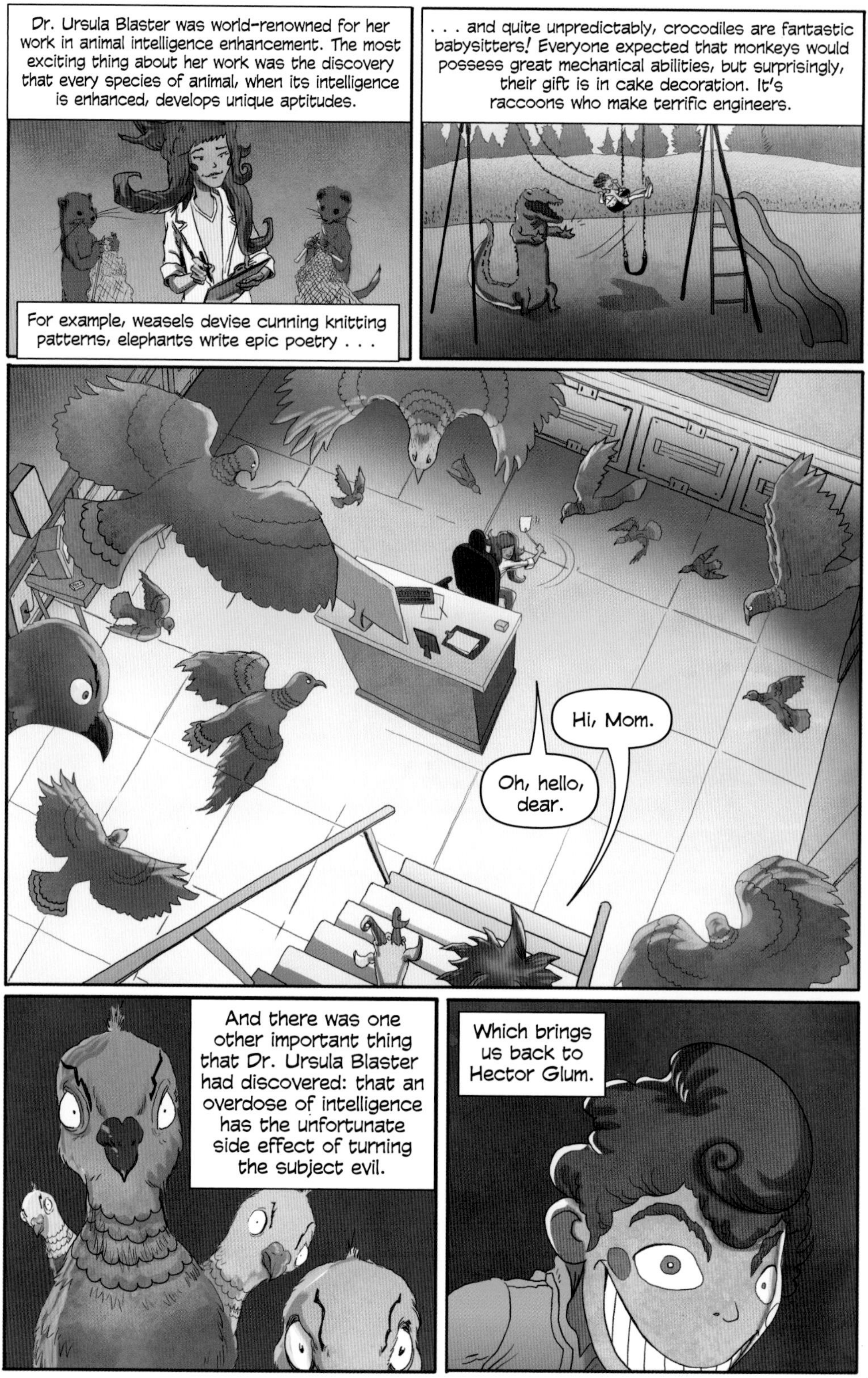
Dr. Ursula Blaster was world-renowned for her work in animal intelligence enhancement. The most exciting thing about her work was the discovery that every species of animal, when its intelligence is enhanced, develops unique aptitudes.
For example, weasels devise cunning knitting patterns, elephants write epic poetry . . .
. . . and quite unpredictably, crocodiles are fantastic babysitters! Everyone expected that monkeys would possess great mechanical abilities, but surprisingly, their gift is in cake decoration. It's raccoons who make terrific engineers.
Hi, Mom.
Oh, hello, dear.
And there was one other important thing that Dr. Ursula Blaster had discovered: that an overdose of intelligence has the unfortunate side effect of turning the subject evil.
Which brings us back to Hector Glum.

FLASHBACK INTERLUDE

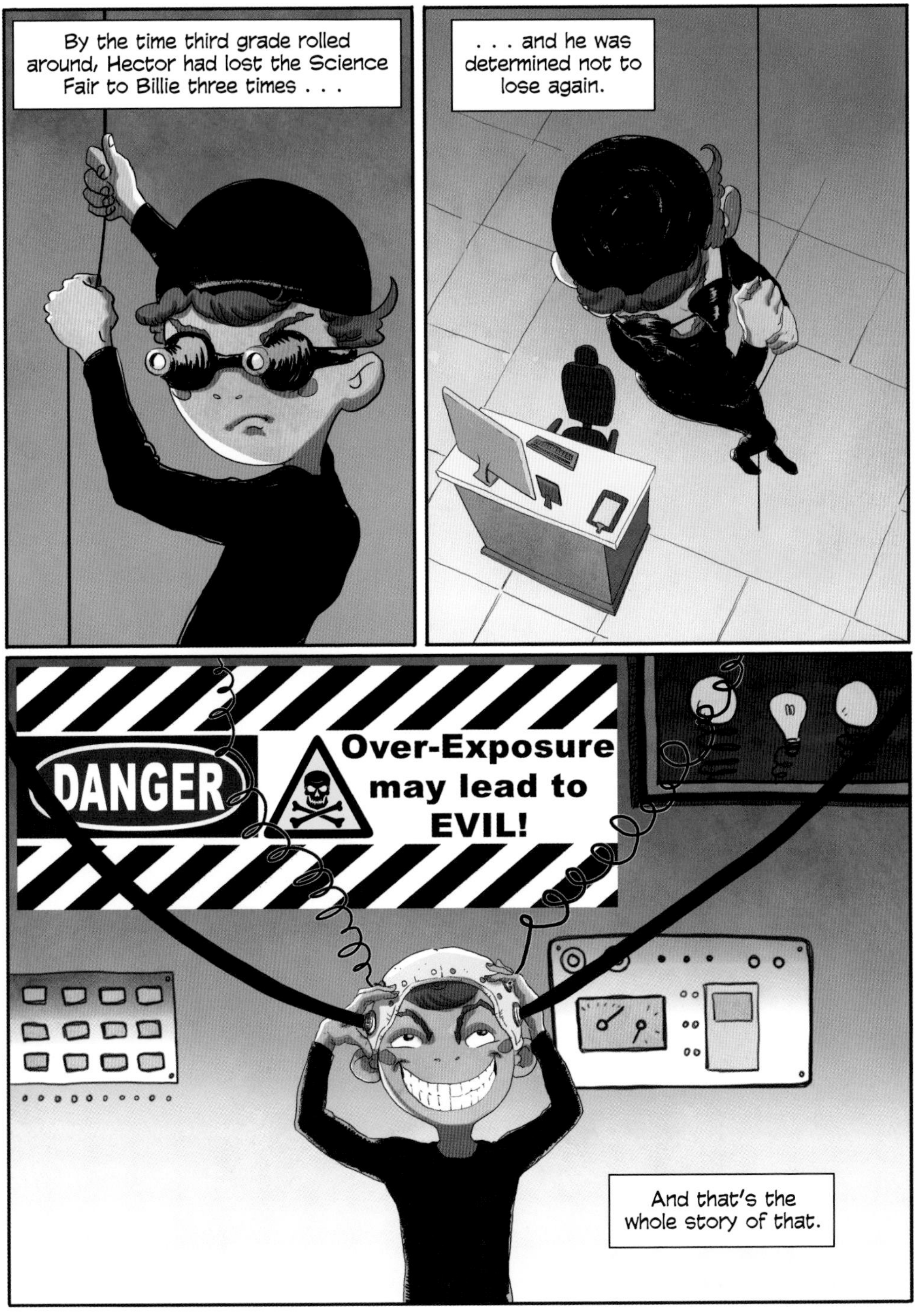

By the time third grade rolled around, Hector had lost the Science Fair to Billie three times . . .
. . . and he was determined not to lose again.
DANGER
Over-Exposure may lead to EVIL!
And that's the whole story of that.

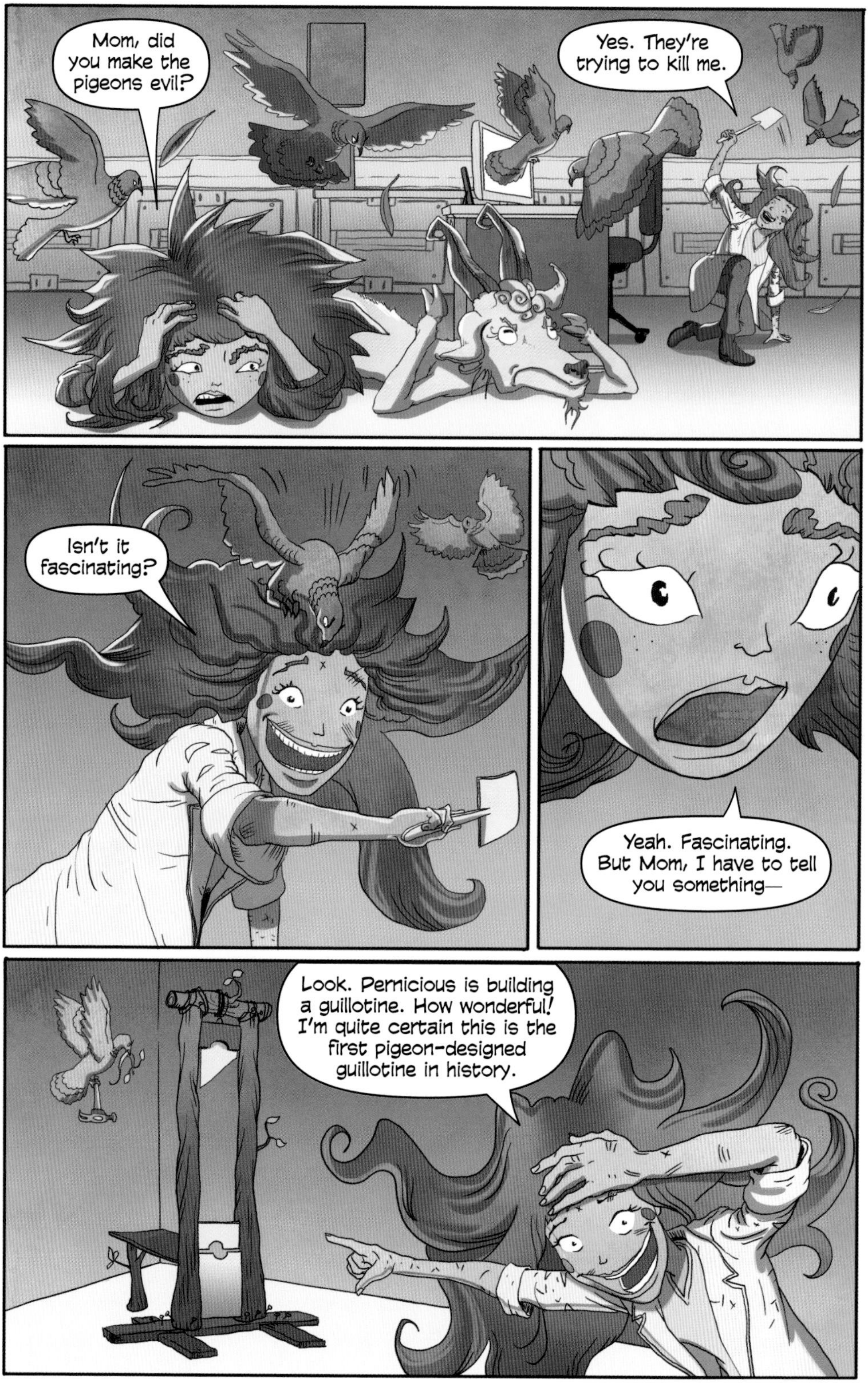
Mom, did you make the pigeons evil?
Yes. They're trying to kill me.
Isn't it fascinating?
Yeah. Fascinating. But Mom, I have to tell you something—
Look. Pernicious is building a guillotine. How wonderful! I'm quite certain this is the first pigeon-designed guillotine in history.

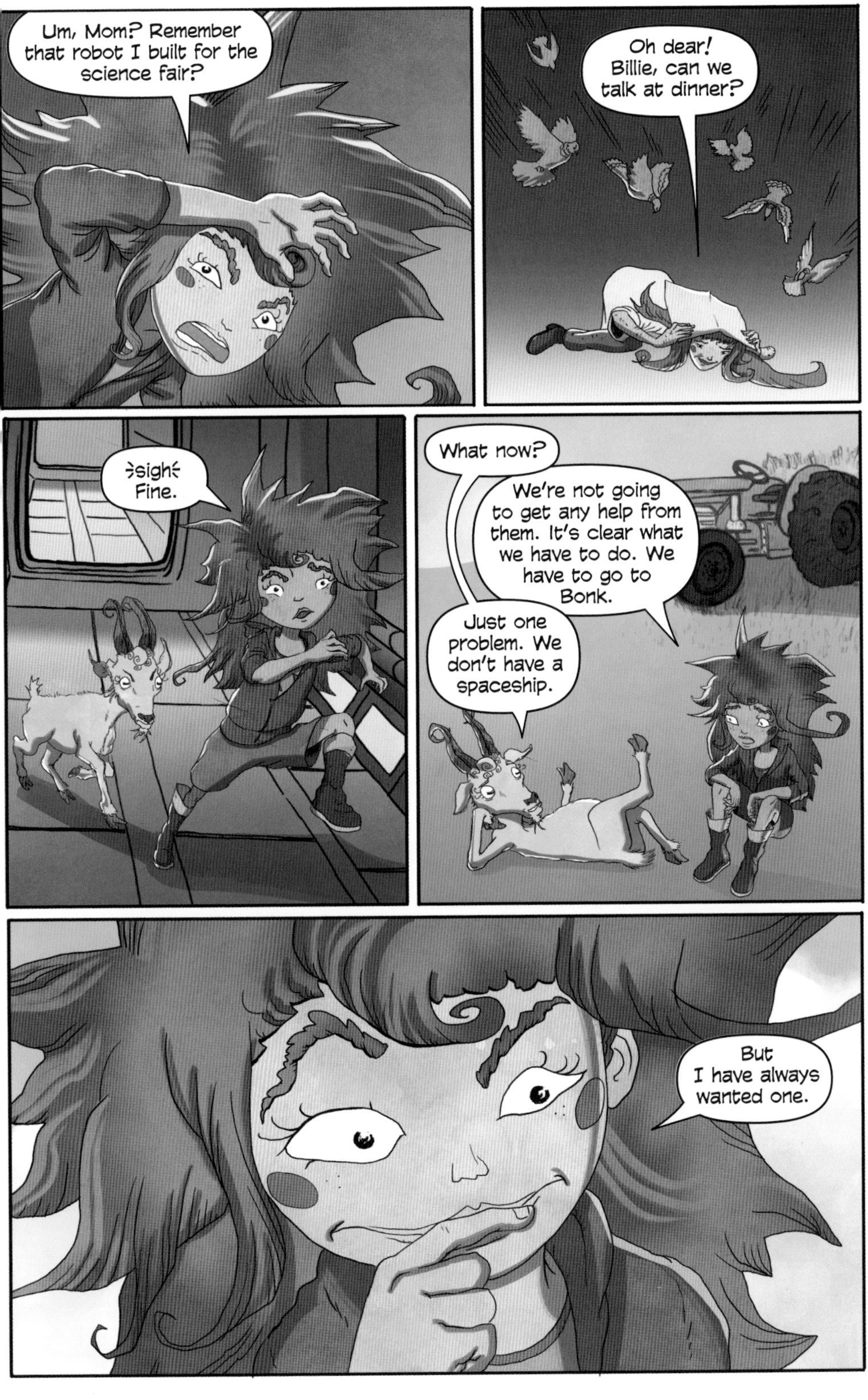
Um, Mom? Remember that robot I built for the science fair?
Oh dear! Billie, can we talk at dinner?
sigh Fine.
What now?
We're not going to get any help from them. It's clear what we have to do. We have to go to Bonk.
Just one problem. We don't have a spaceship.
But I have always wanted one.

BUILDING A ROCKET SHIP

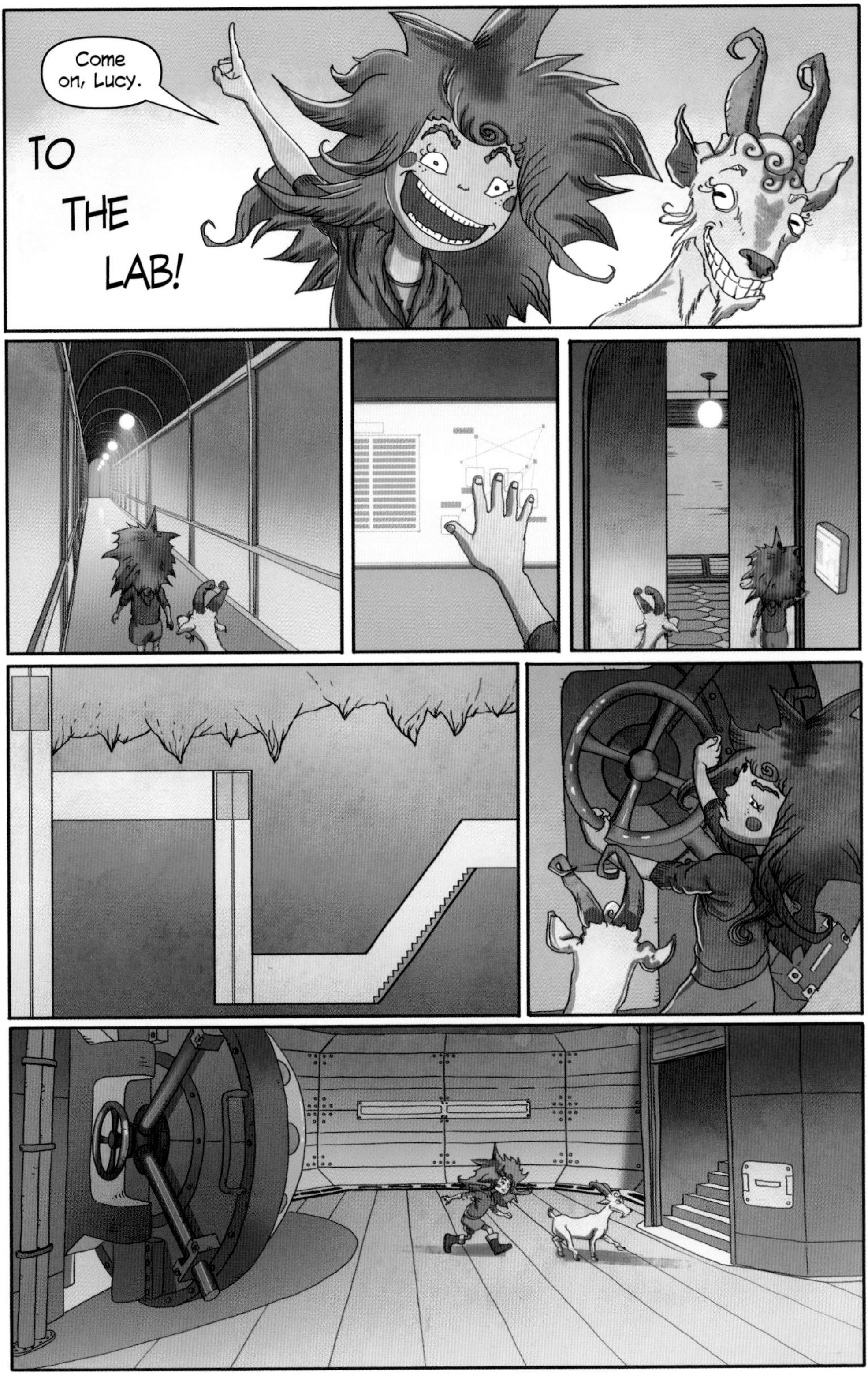
Come on, Lucy.
TO THE LAB!

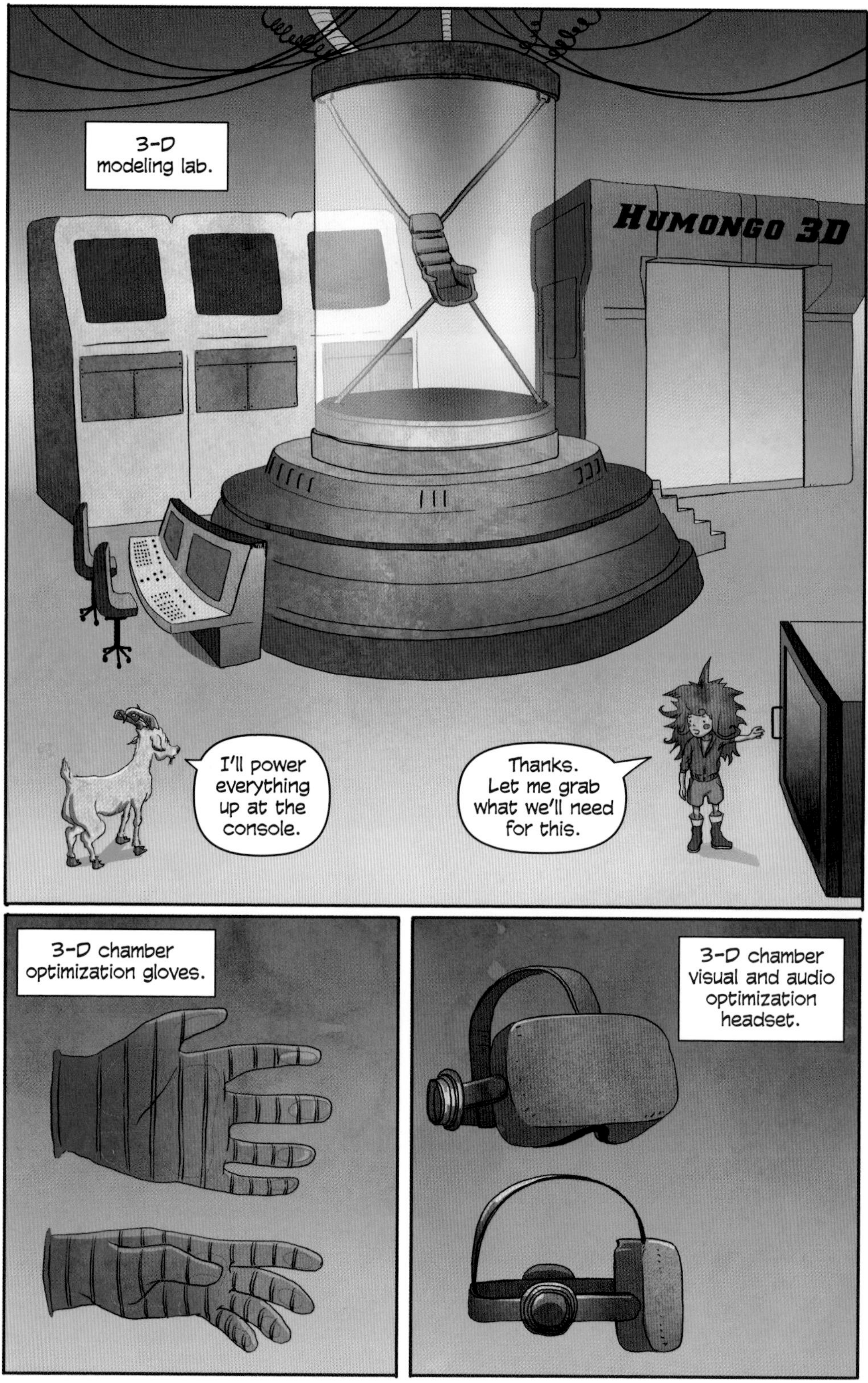
3-D modeling lab.
HUMONGO 3D
I'll power everything up at the console.
Thanks. Let me grab what we'll need for this.
3-D chamber optimization gloves.
3-D chamber visual and audio optimization headset.

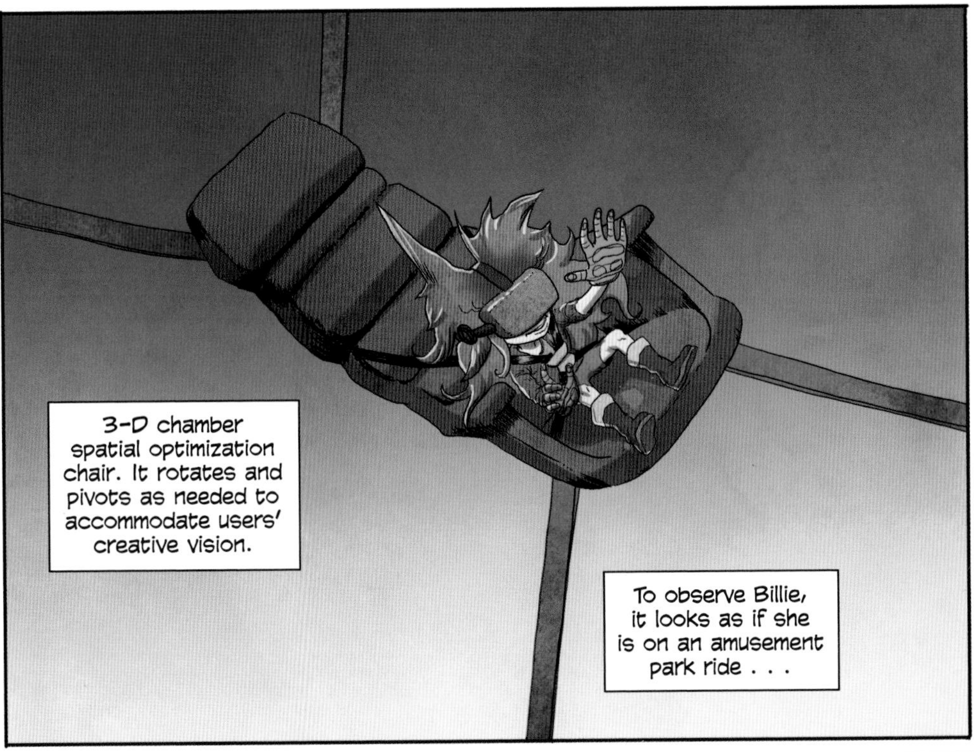
3-D chamber spatial optimization chair. It rotates and pivots as needed to accommodate users' creative vision.
To observe Billie, it looks as if she is on an amusement park ride . . .

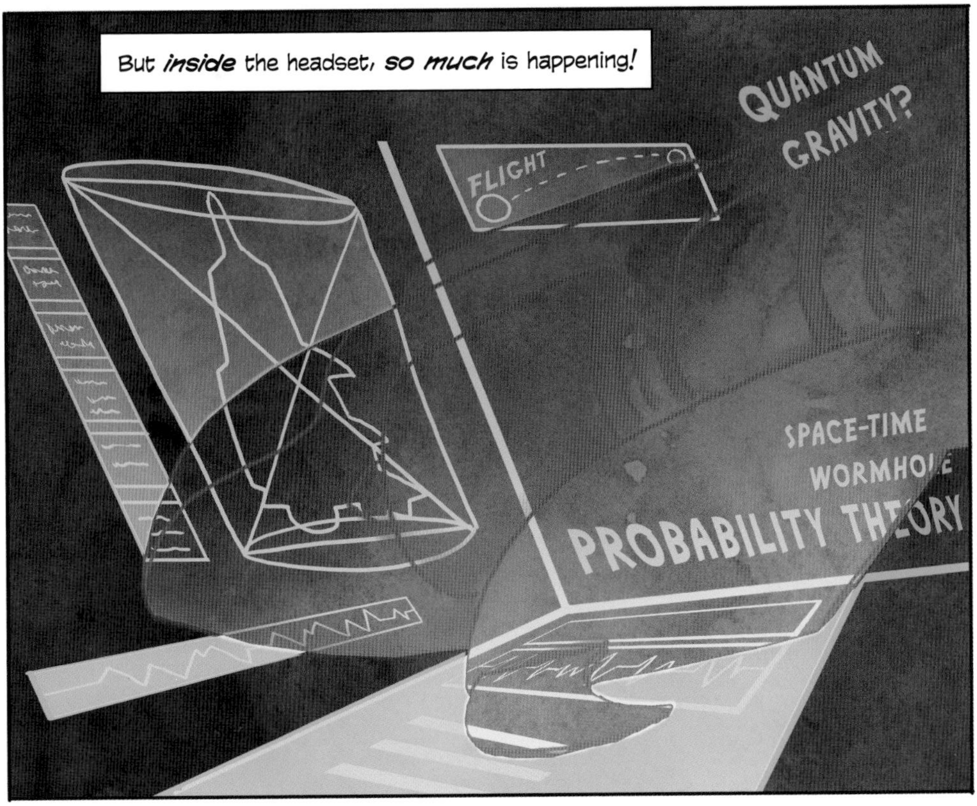
But *inside* the headset, *so much* is happening!
QUANTUM GRAVITY?
FLIGHT
SPACE-TIME
PROBABILITY THEORY

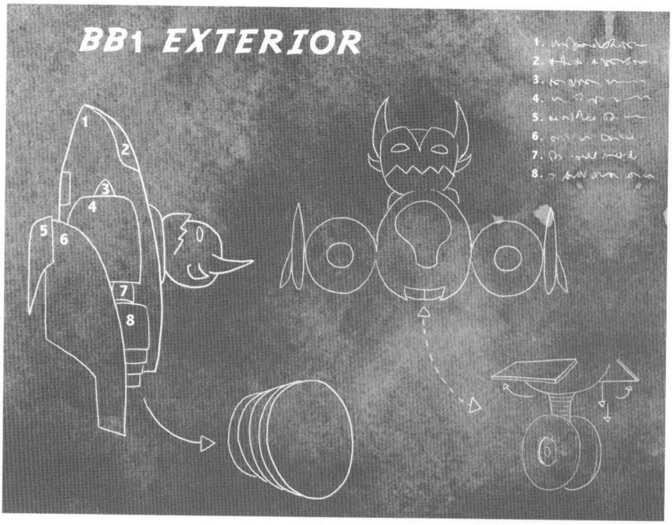
BB1 EXTERIOR
1
2
3
4
5
6
7
8

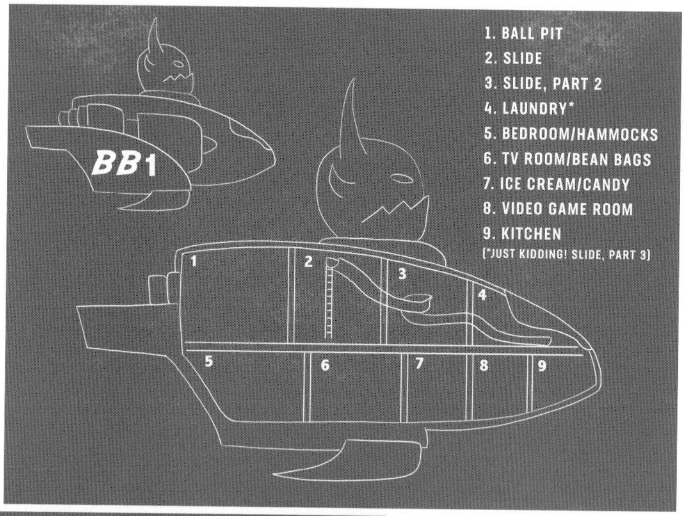
BB1
1. BALL PIT
2. SLIDE
3. SLIDE, PART 2
4. LAUNDRY*
5. BEDROOM/HAMMOCKS
6. TV ROOM/BEAN BAGS
7. ICE CREAM/CANDY
8. VIDEO GAME ROOM
9. KITCHEN
(*JUST KIDDING! SLIDE, PART 3)
1
2
3
4
5
6
7
8
9

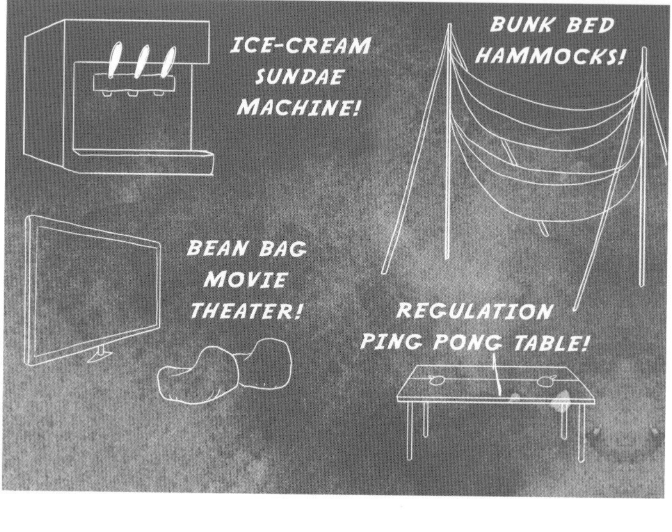
ICE-CREAM SUNDAE MACHINE!
BUNK BED HAMMOCKS!
BEAN BAG MOVIE THEATER!
REGULATION PING PONG TABLE!

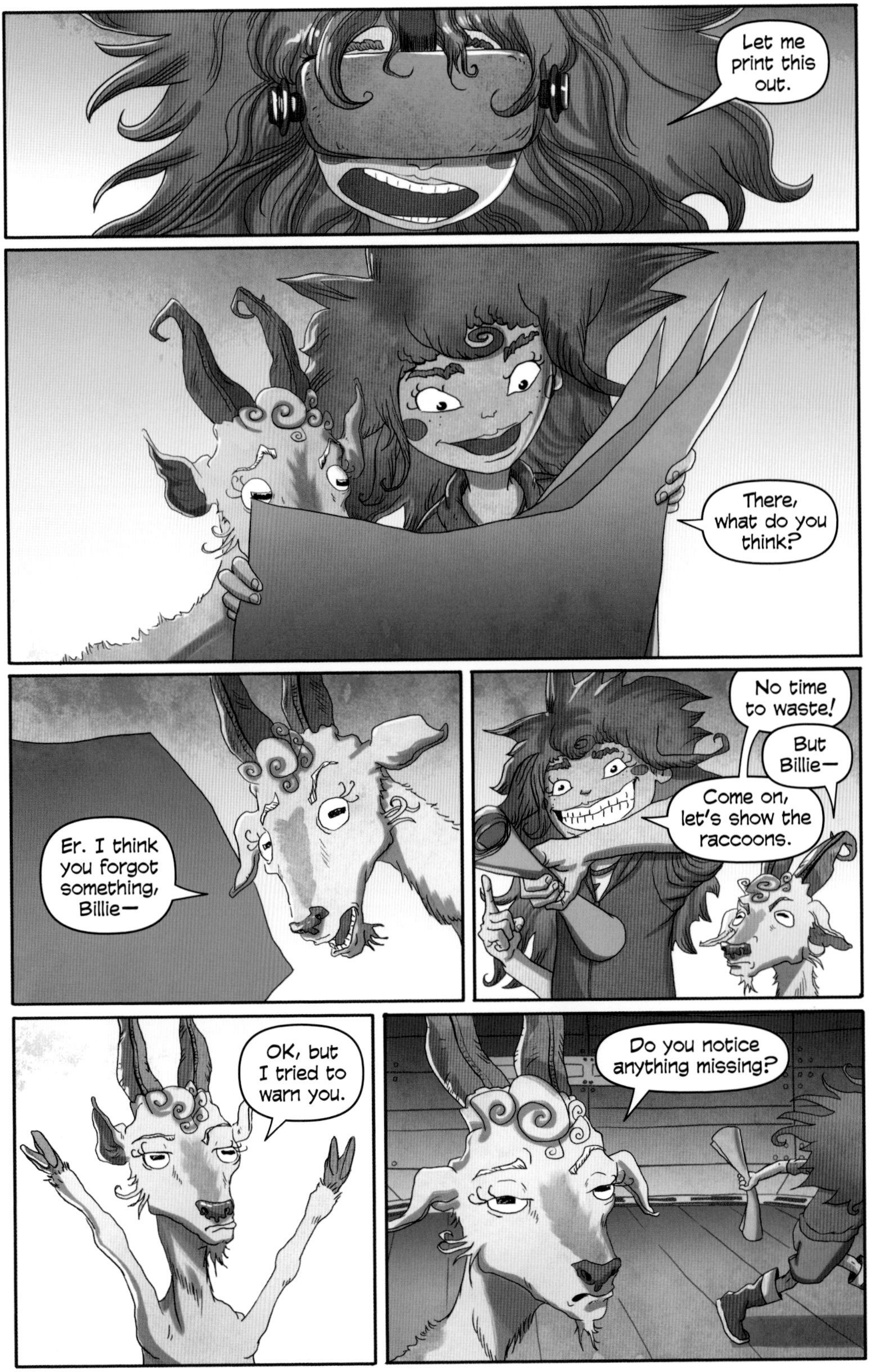
Let me print this out.
There, what do you think?
Er. I think you forgot something, Billie—
No time to waste!
But Billie—
Come on, let's show the raccoons.
OK, but I tried to warn you.
Do you notice anything missing?

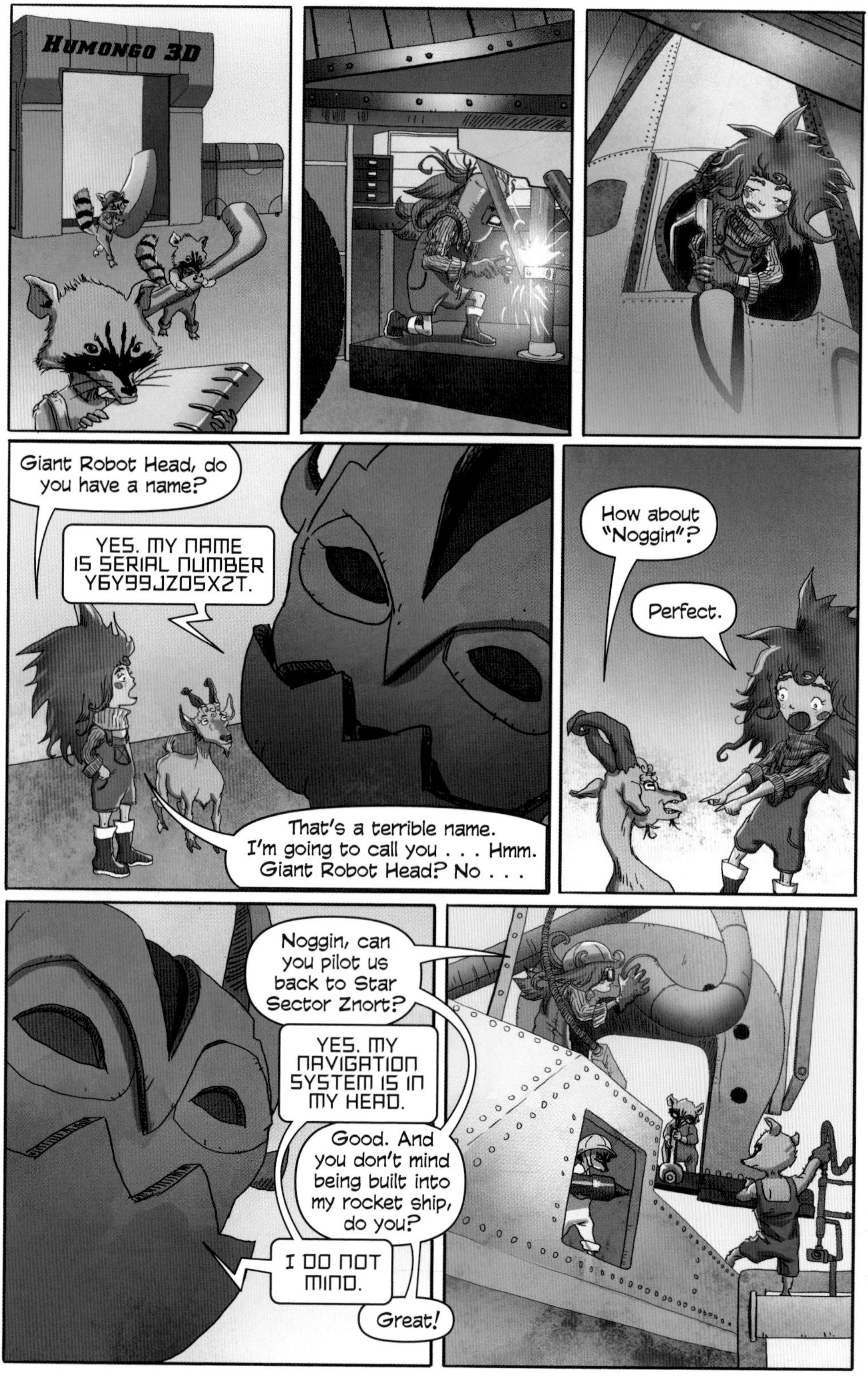
HUMONGO 3D
Giant Robot Head, do you have a name?
YES. MY NAME IS SERIAL NUMBER Y6Y99JZ05X2T.
That's a terrible name. I'm going to call you . . . Hmm. Giant Robot Head? No . . .
How about "Noggin"?
Perfect.
Noggin, can you pilot us back to Star Sector Znort?
YES. MY NAVIGATION SYSTEM IS IN MY HEAD.
Good. And you don't mind being built into my rocket ship, do you?
I DO NOT MIND.
Great!

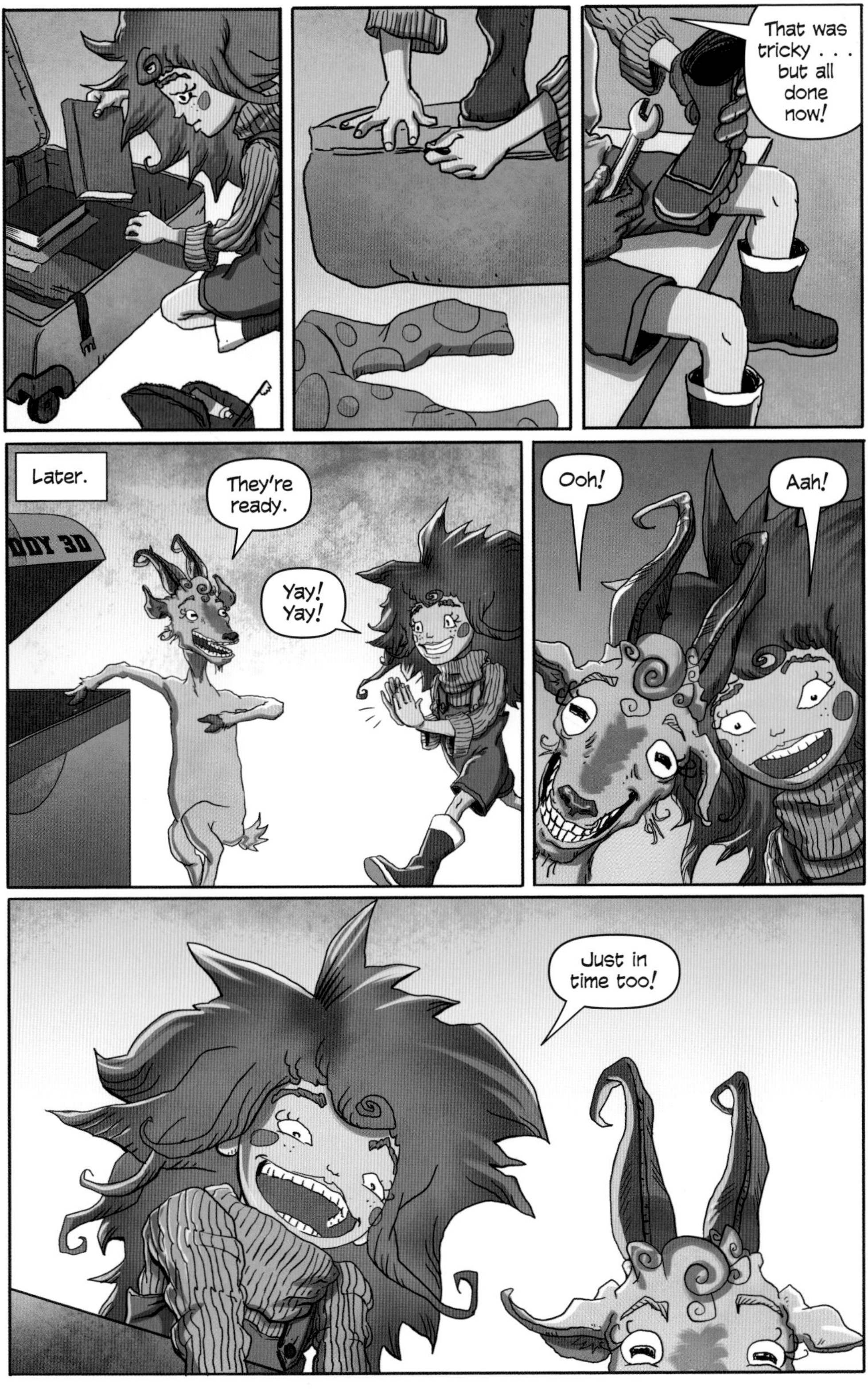
That was tricky . . . but all done now!
Later.
They're ready.
Yay! Yay!
Ooh!
Aah!
Just in time too!

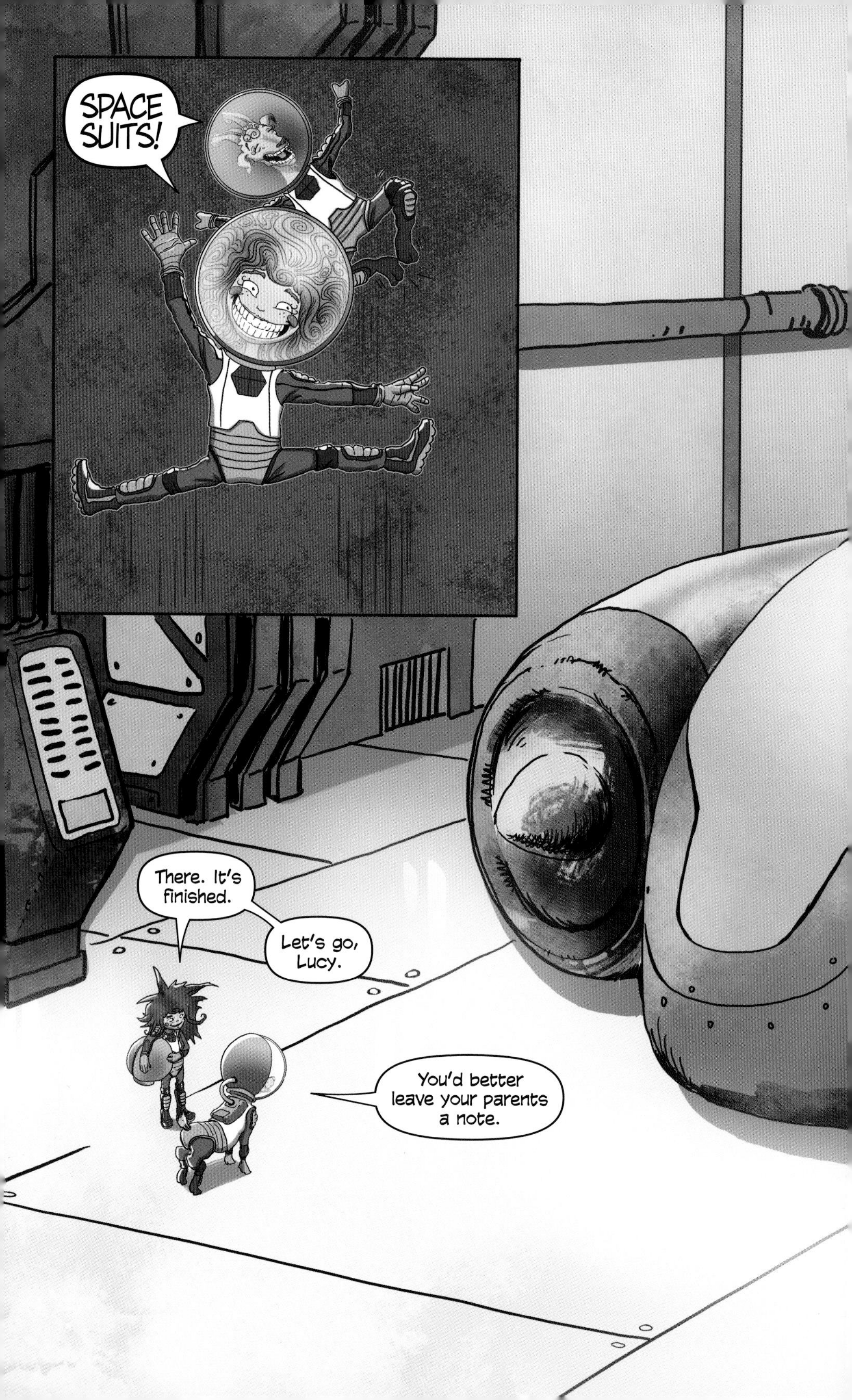
SPACE SUITS!
There. It's finished.
Let's go, Lucy.
You'd better leave your parents a note.

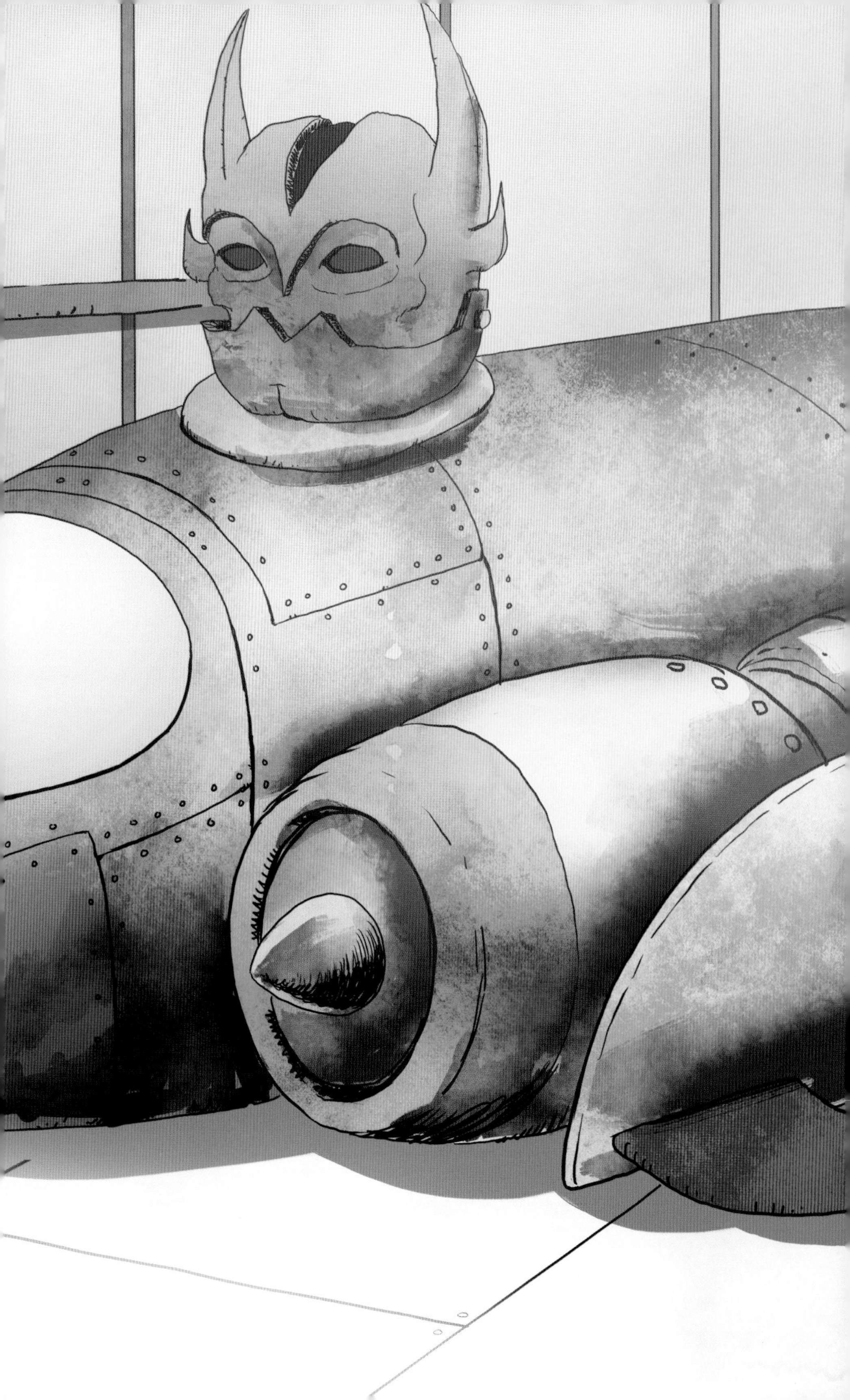

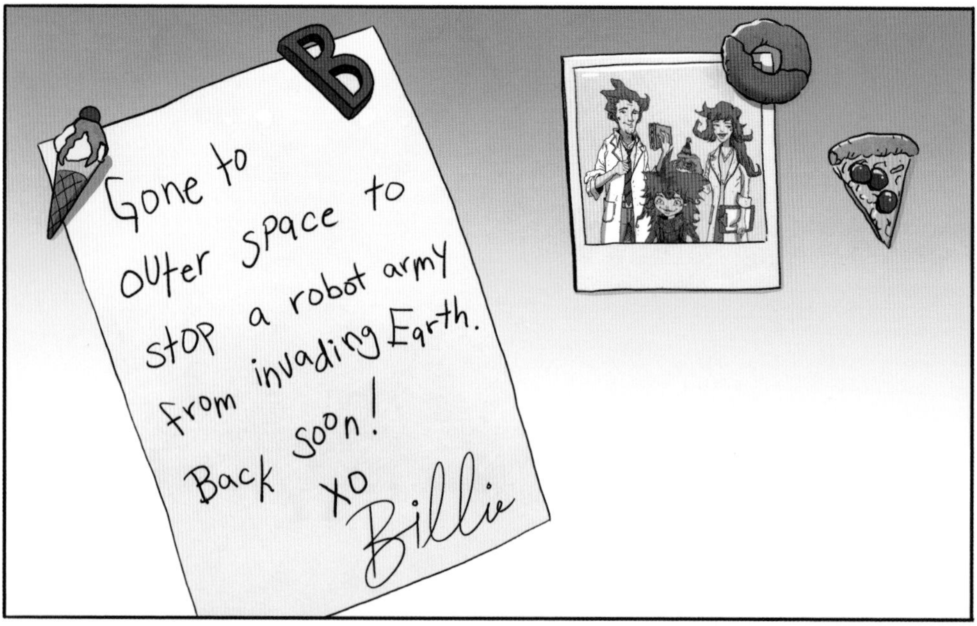
Gone to outer space to stop a robot army from invading Earth. Back soon!
XO Billie

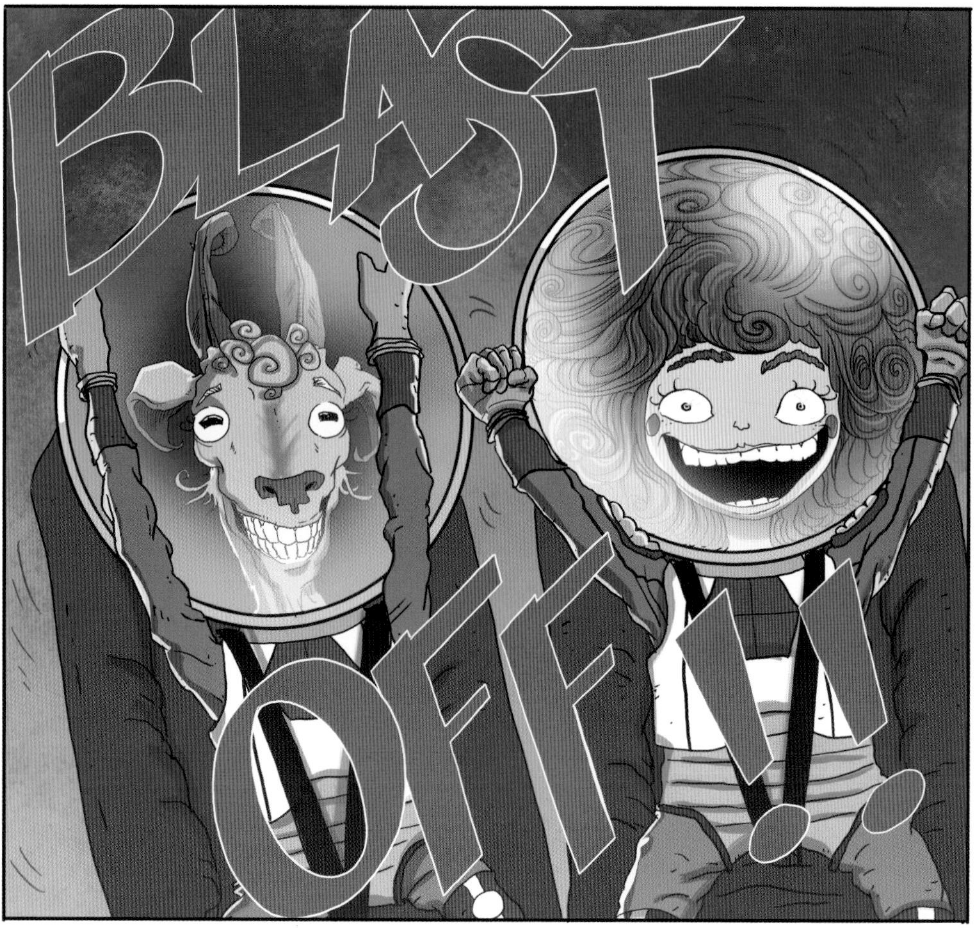
BLAST OFF!!

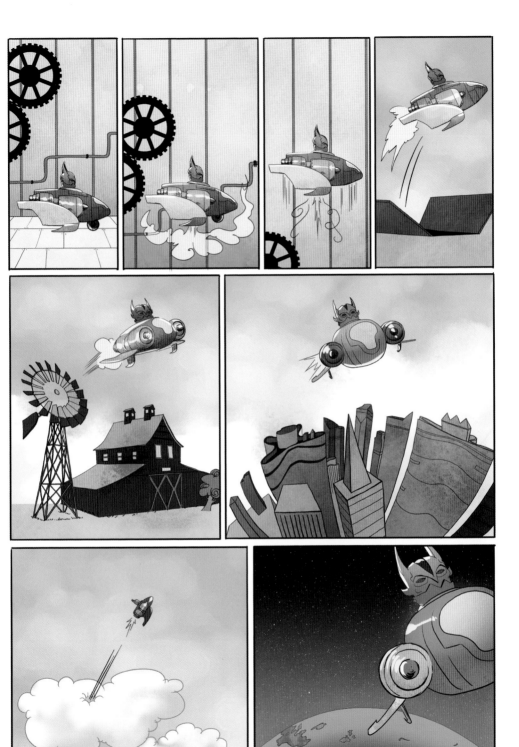

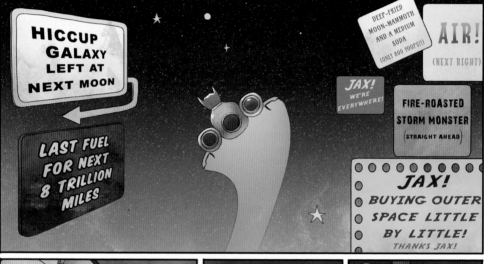

HICCUP GALAXY LEFT AT NEXT MOON

LAST FUEL FOR NEXT 8 TRILLION MILES

DEEP-FRIED MOON-MAMMOTH AND A MEDIUM SODA (ONLY 800 YOOPS!!)

AIR! (NEXT RIGHT)

JAX! WE'RE EVERYWHERE!

FIRE-ROASTED STORM MONSTER (STRAIGHT AHEAD)

JAX! BUYING OUTER SPACE LITTLE BY LITTLE! THANKS JAX!

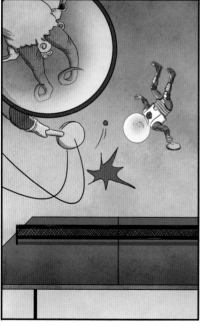

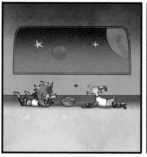

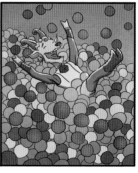

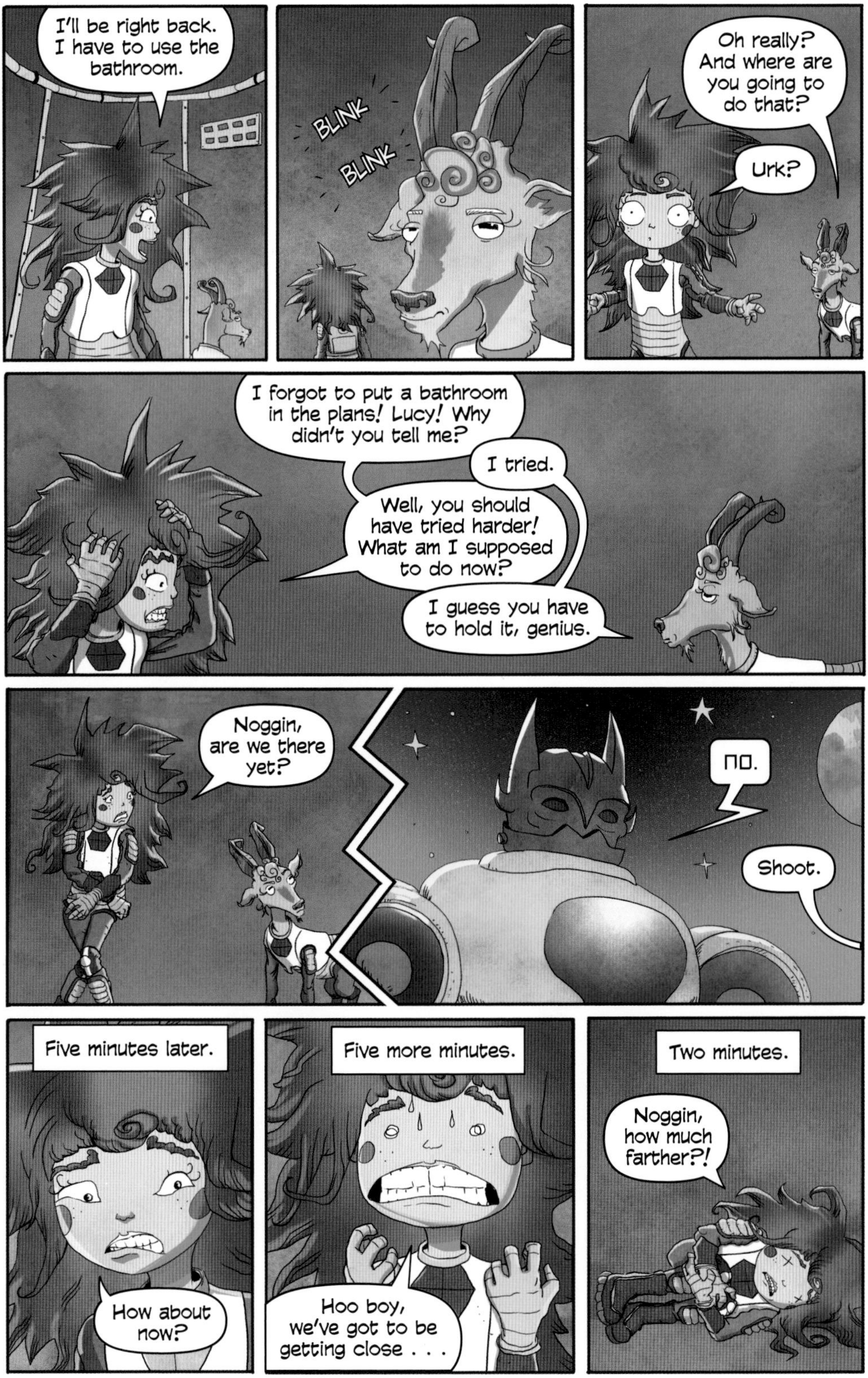
I'll be right back. I have to use the bathroom.
BLINK
BLINK
Oh really? And where are you going to do that?
Urk?
I forgot to put a bathroom in the plans! Lucy! Why didn't you tell me?
I tried.
Well, you should have tried harder! What am I supposed to do now?
I guess you have to hold it, genius.
Noggin, are we there yet?
no.
Shoot.
Five minutes later.
How about now?
Five more minutes.
Hoo boy, we've got to be getting close . . .
Two minutes.
Noggin, how much farther?!

BONK

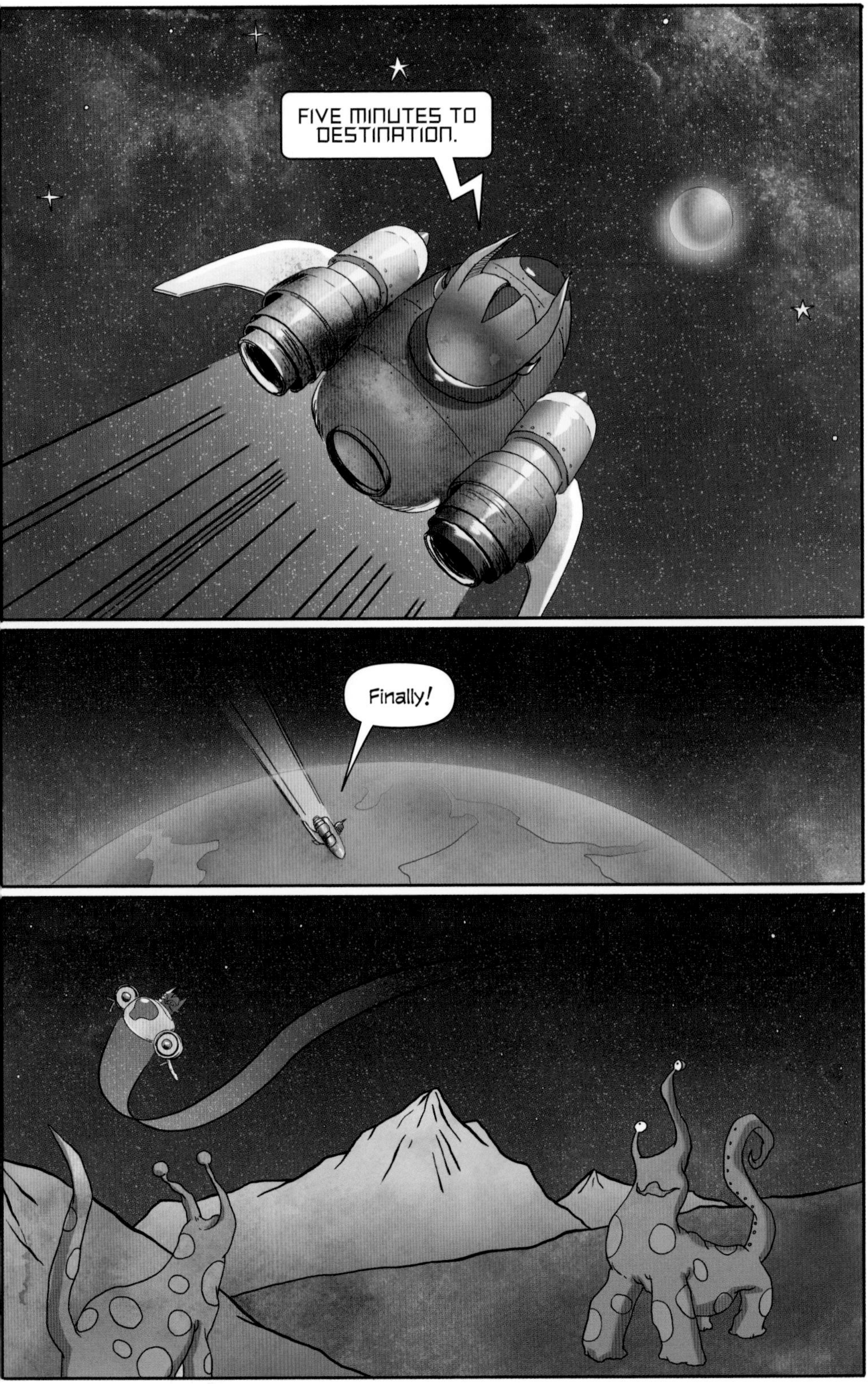
FIVE MINUTES TO DESTINATION.
Finally!

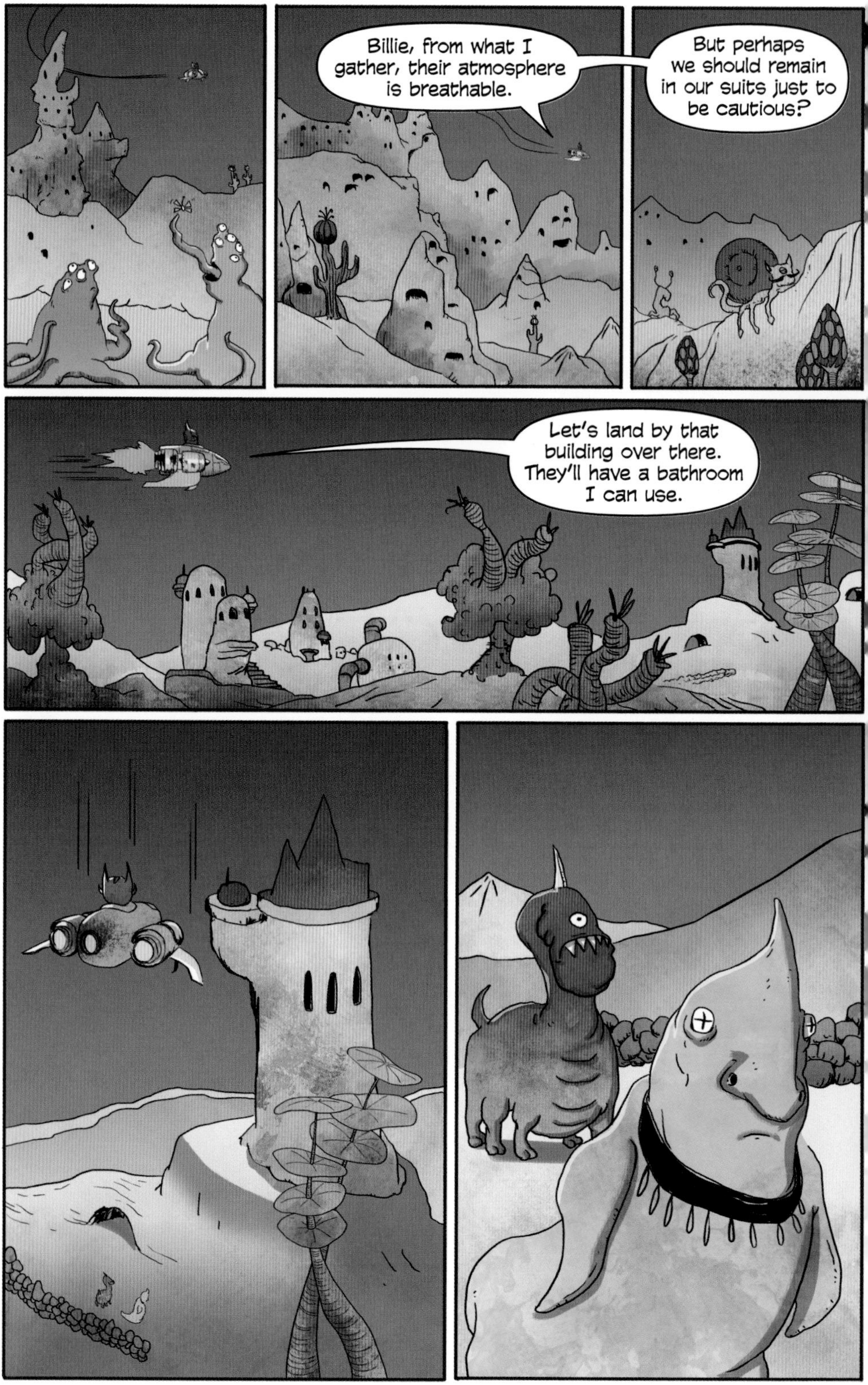
Billie, from what I gather, their atmosphere is breathable.
But perhaps we should remain in our suits just to be cautious?
Let's land by that building over there. They'll have a bathroom I can use.

Look, an alien!

Well, technically, it's us who are the aliens. If they came to Earth, they'd be aliens, but here on Bonk, they're Bonkers and we are aliens—

OK, OK, I get it.

Uh, greetings! I come in peace—

Well. Sort of.

Yeah, and anyway, I was wondering if I could use your bathroom?

ᚻᚾᚷᚻᚢᚾᛏᚷᛋᚷᚷᚷᛖᛖᛚᛋᛏ ᛏᛒᚢᛁᚠ ᛃᚫᛖᛏ ᚻᛁᛕ

What?

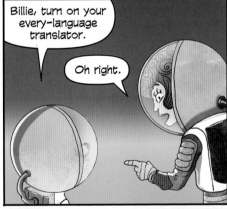

Billie, turn on your every-language translator.

Oh right.

"CLICK"

So, about that bathroom—?

Moo.

Moo?

Moo.

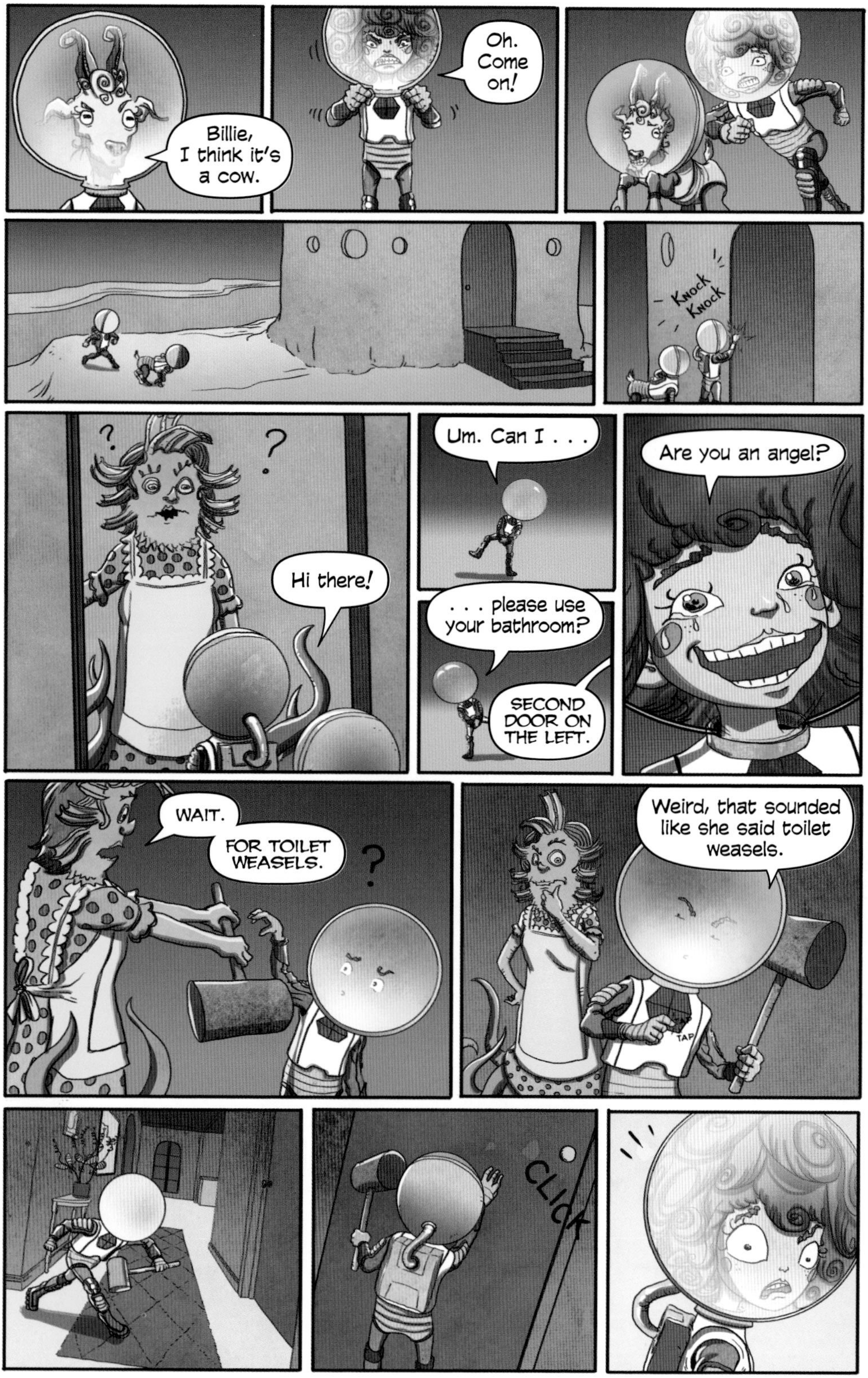
Billie, I think it's a cow.
Oh. Come on!
KNOCK KNOCK
?
?
Hi there!
Um. Can I . . .
. . . please use your bathroom?
SECOND DOOR ON THE LEFT.
Are you an angel?
WAIT.
FOR TOILET WEASELS.
?
Weird, that sounded like she said toilet weasels.
TAP TAP
CLICK

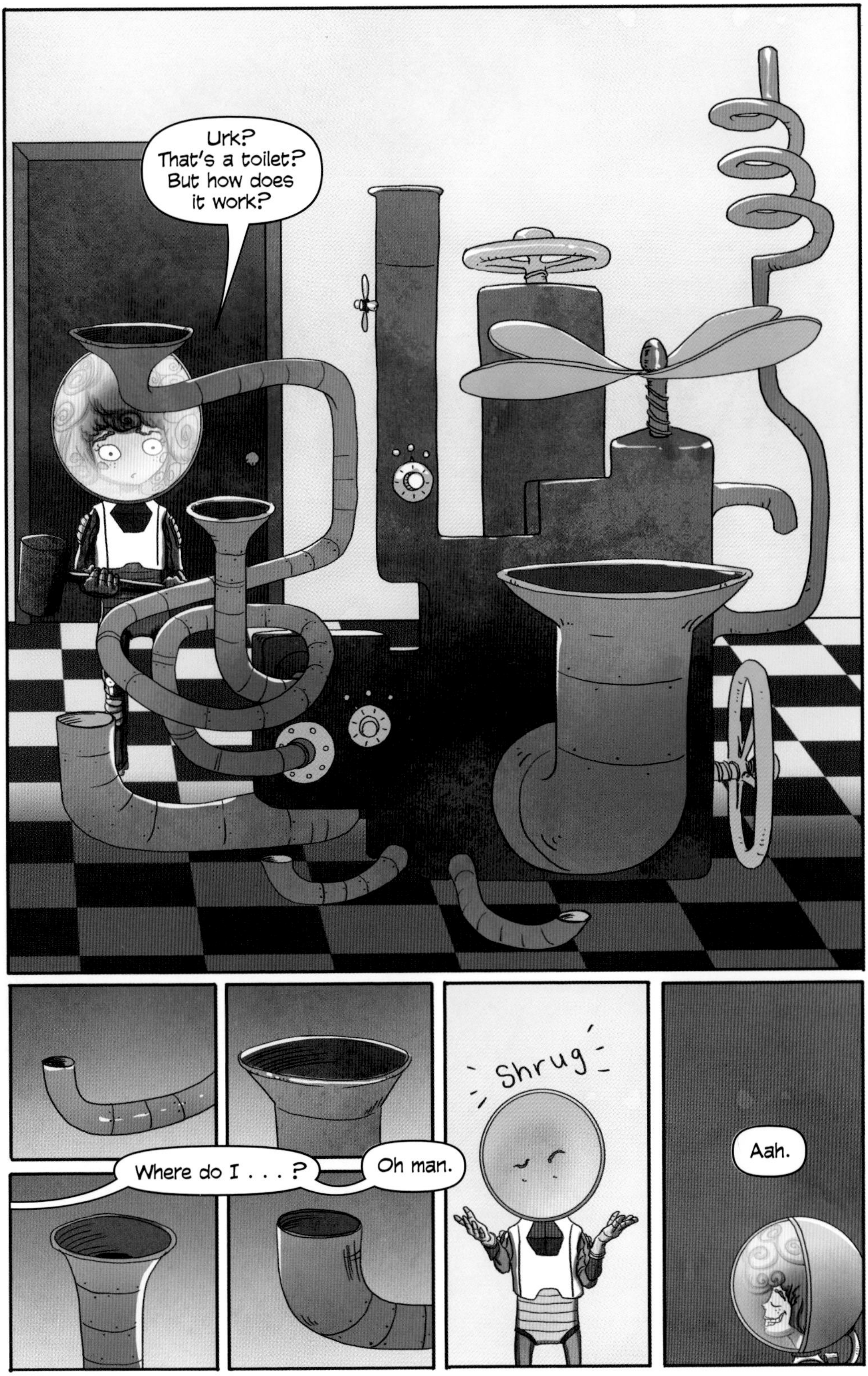
Urk?
That's a toilet?
But how does
it work?
Where do I . . . ?
Oh man.
Shrug
Aah.

Aaggghhh!

BLESS STARS! PLIMBO BE PEED ON BY ALIEN! THE GUYS, THEY WILL NOT BELIEVE!

WHAT IN WORLD . . . ?

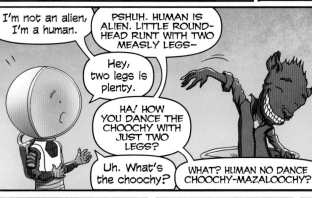

I'm not an alien, I'm a human.

PSHUH. HUMAN IS ALIEN. LITTLE ROUND-HEAD RUNT WITH TWO MEASLY LEGS—

Hey, two legs is plenty.

HA! HOW YOU DANCE THE CHOOCHY WITH JUST TWO LEGS?

Uh. What's the choochy?

WHAT? HUMAN NO DANCE CHOOCHY-MAZALOOCHY?

IS OFFICIAL DANCE OF BONK. LITTLE TWO-LEGS NO DANCING IT, IT PROVE SHE IS ALIEN!

BOOTY BOOTY BOOTY SHAKE!!!

FREEZE!!

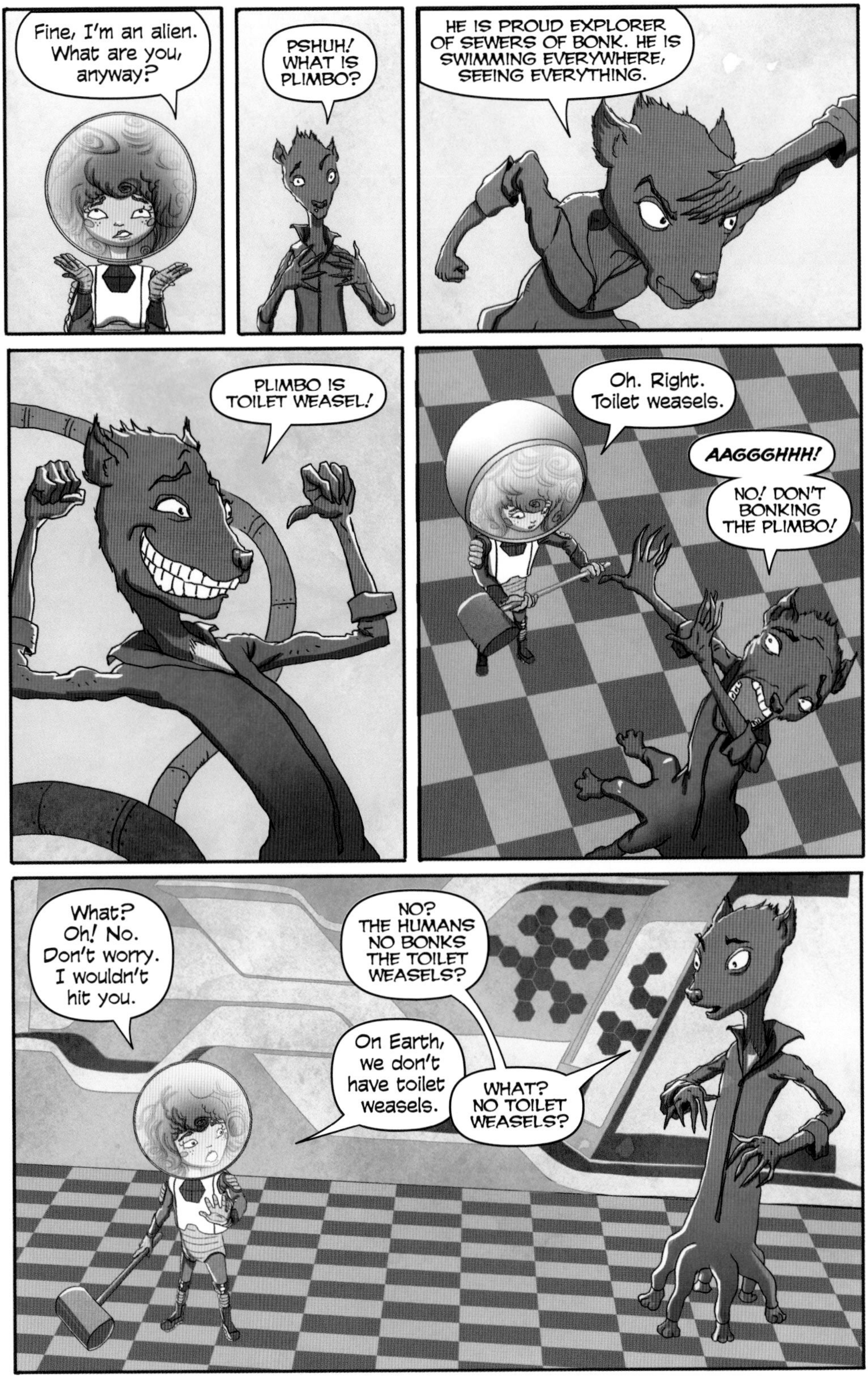
Fine, I'm an alien. What are you, anyway?
PSHUH! WHAT IS PLIMBO?
HE IS PROUD EXPLORER OF SEWERS OF BONK. HE IS SWIMMING EVERYWHERE, SEEING EVERYTHING.
PLIMBO IS TOILET WEASEL!
Oh. Right. Toilet weasels.
AAGGGHHH!
NO! DON'T BONKING THE PLIMBO!
What? Oh! No. Don't worry. I wouldn't hit you.
NO? THE HUMANS NO BONKS THE TOILET WEASELS?
On Earth, we don't have toilet weasels.
WHAT? NO TOILET WEASELS?

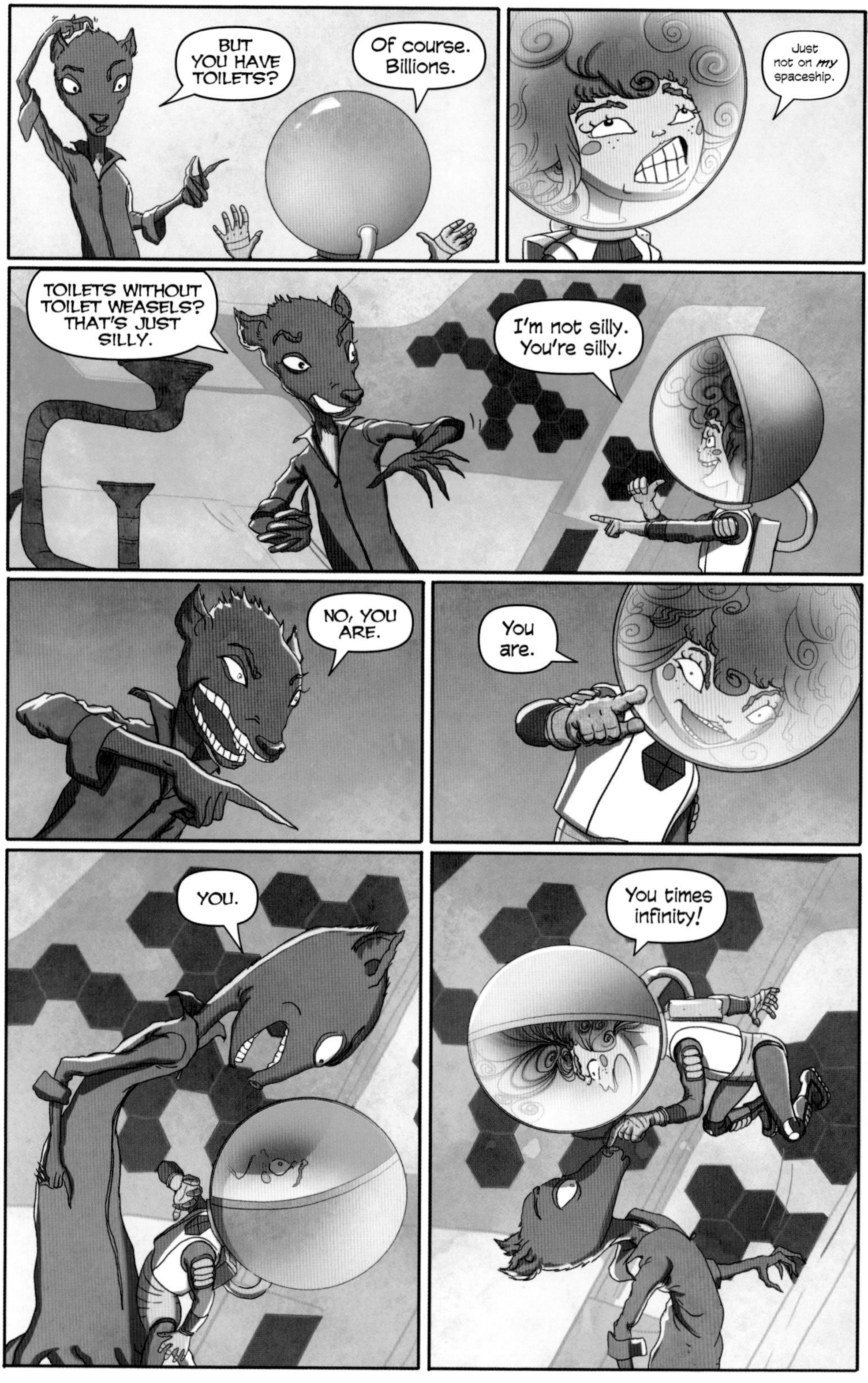
BUT YOU HAVE TOILETS?
Of course. Billions.
Just not on *my* spaceship.
TOILETS WITHOUT TOILET WEASELS? THAT'S JUST SILLY.
I'm not silly. You're silly.
NO, YOU ARE.
You are.
YOU.
You times infinity!

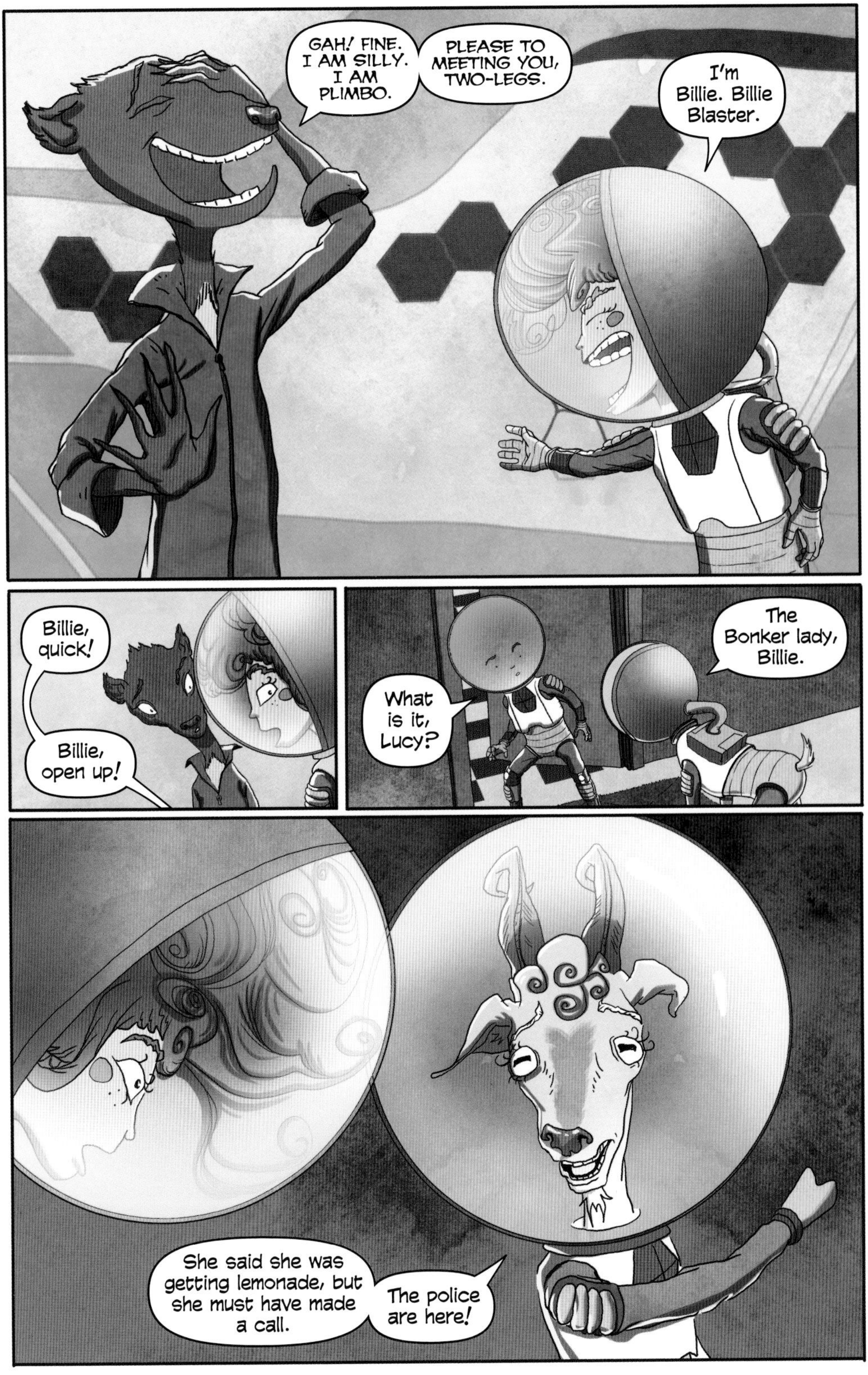
GAH! FINE. I AM SILLY. I AM PLIMBO.
PLEASE TO MEETING YOU, TWO-LEGS.
I'm Billie. Billie Blaster.
Billie, quick!
Billie, open up!
What is it, Lucy?
The Bonker lady, Billie.
She said she was getting lemonade, but she must have made a call.
The police are here!

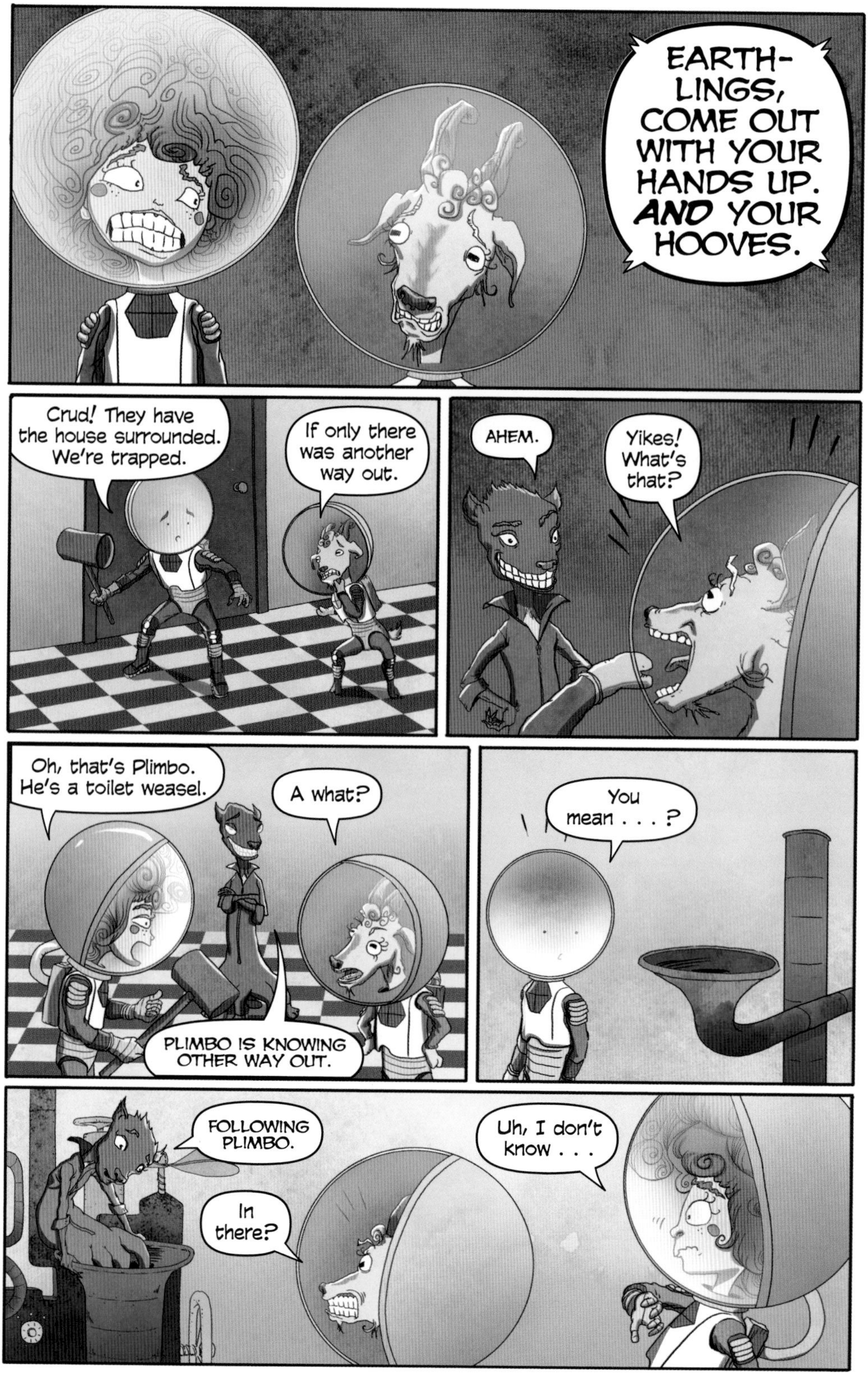
EARTH-LINGS, COME OUT WITH YOUR HANDS UP. **AND** YOUR HOOVES.
Crud! They have the house surrounded. We're trapped.
If only there was another way out.
AHEM.
Yikes! What's that?
Oh, that's Plimbo. He's a toilet weasel.
A what?
PLIMBO IS KNOWING OTHER WAY OUT.
You mean . . . ?
FOLLOWING PLIMBO.
In there?
Uh, I don't know . . .

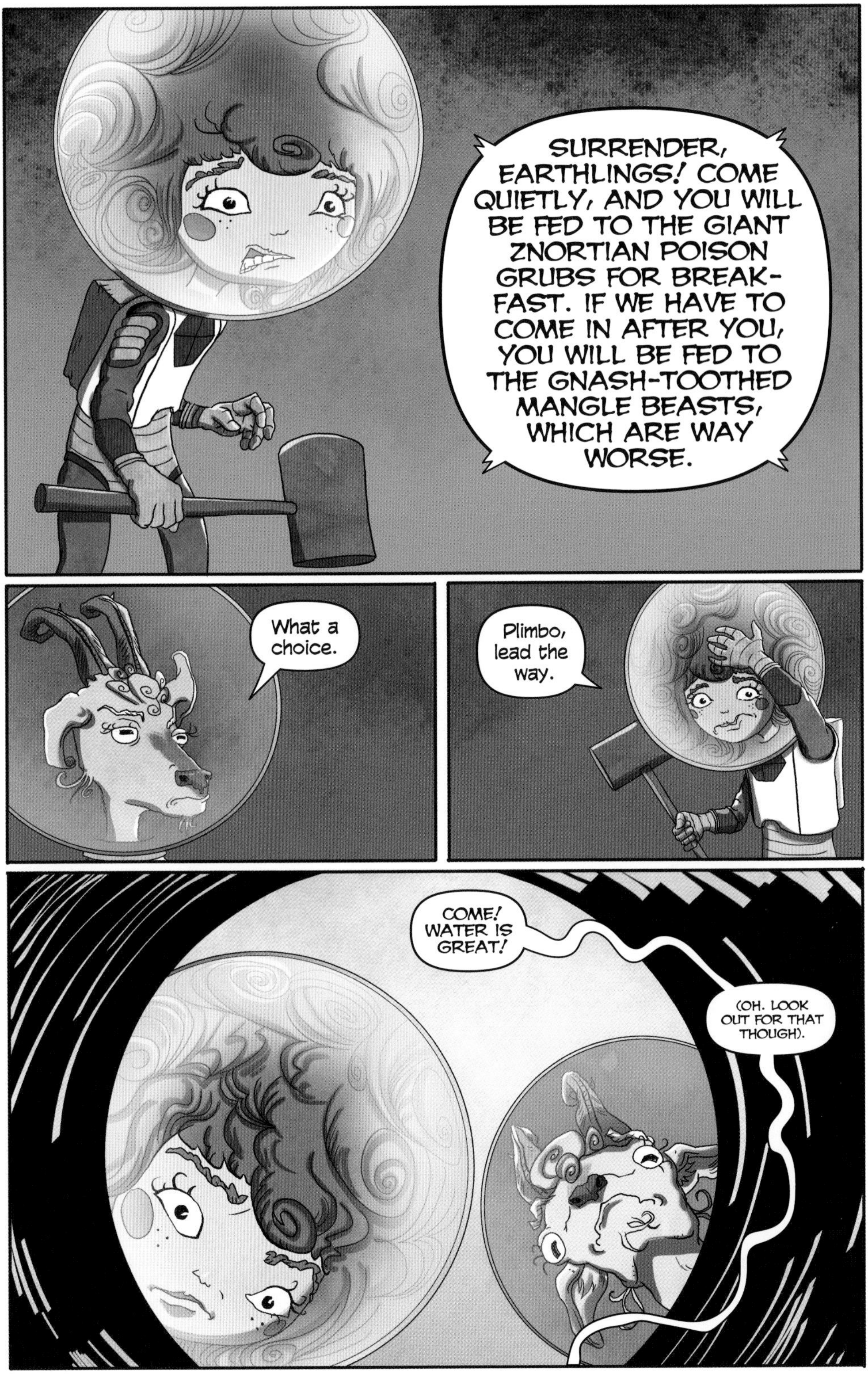
SURRENDER, EARTHLINGS! COME QUIETLY, AND YOU WILL BE FED TO THE GIANT ZNORTIAN POISON GRUBS FOR BREAK-FAST. IF WE HAVE TO COME IN AFTER YOU, YOU WILL BE FED TO THE GNASH-TOOTHED MANGLE BEASTS, WHICH ARE WAY WORSE.
What a choice.
Plimbo, lead the way.
COME! WATER IS GREAT!
(OH. LOOK OUT FOR THAT THOUGH).

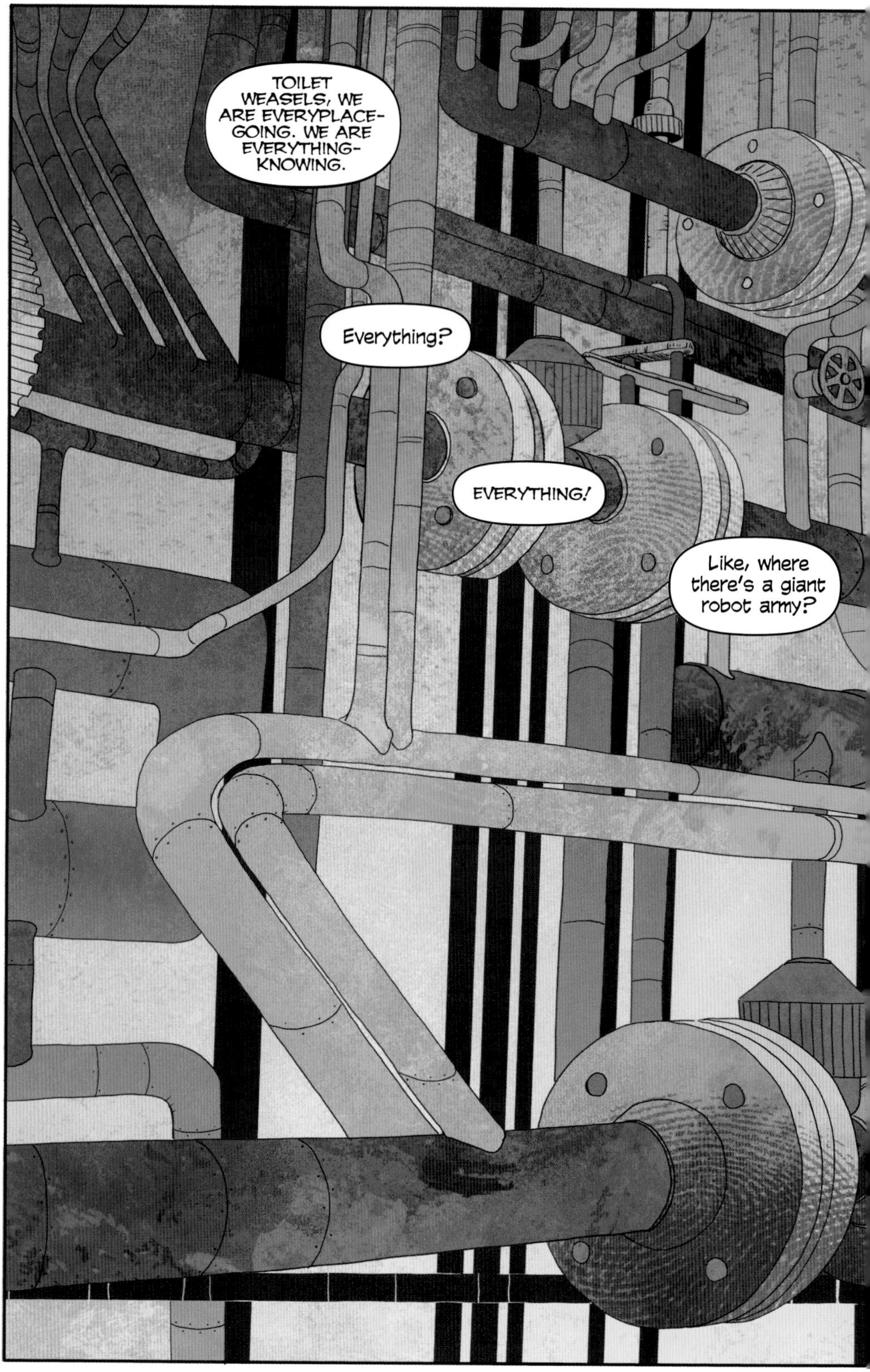
TOILET WEASELS, WE ARE EVERYPLACE-GOING. WE ARE EVERYTHING-KNOWING.
Everything?
EVERYTHING!
Like, where there's a giant robot army?

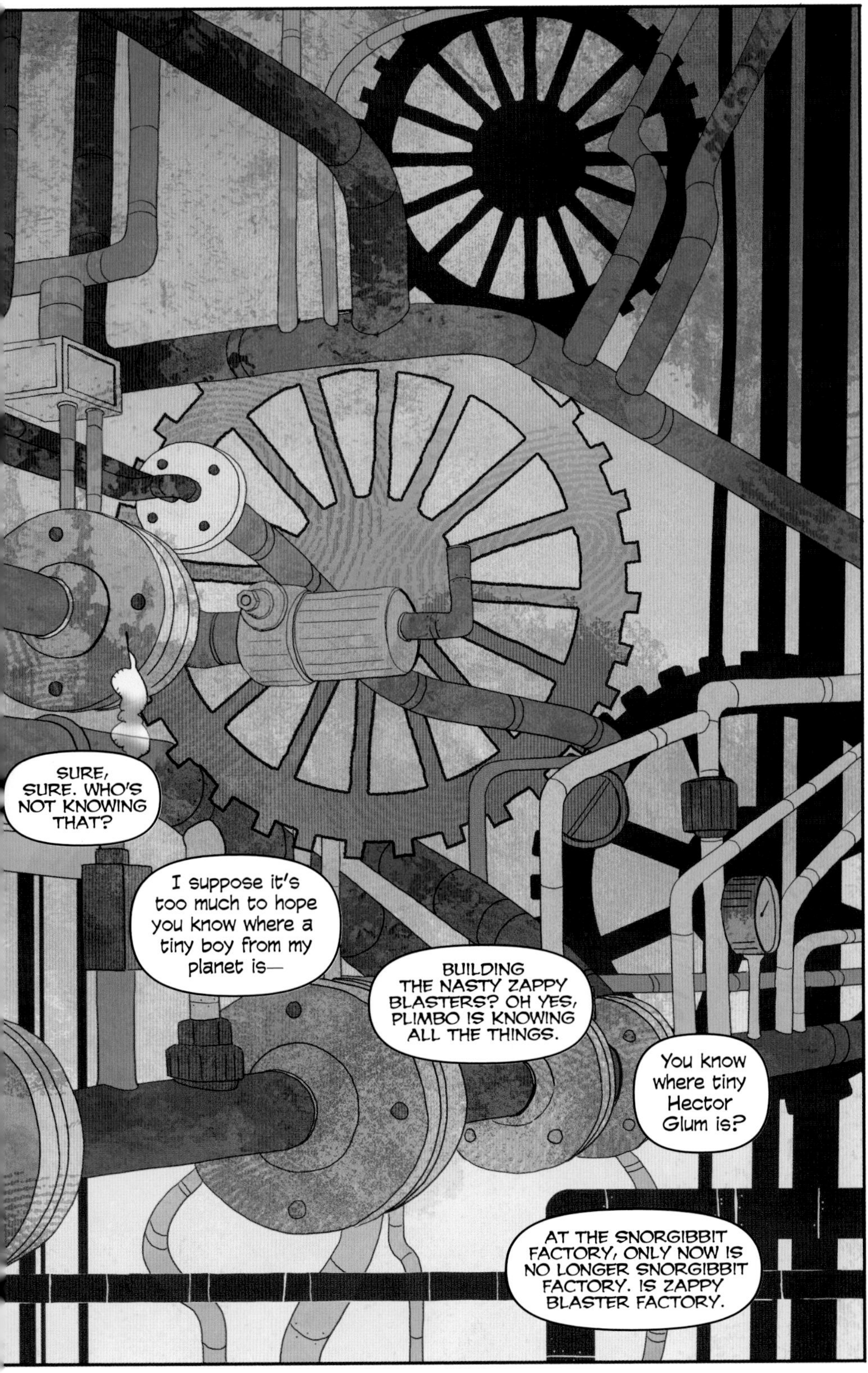
SURE, SURE. WHO'S NOT KNOWING THAT?
I suppose it's too much to hope you know where a tiny boy from my planet is—
BUILDING THE NASTY ZAPPY BLASTERS? OH YES, PLIMBO IS KNOWING ALL THE THINGS.
You know where tiny Hector Glum is?
AT THE SNORGIBBIT FACTORY, ONLY NOW IS NO LONGER SNORGIBBIT FACTORY. IS ZAPPY BLASTER FACTORY.

THE BLASTER FACTORY

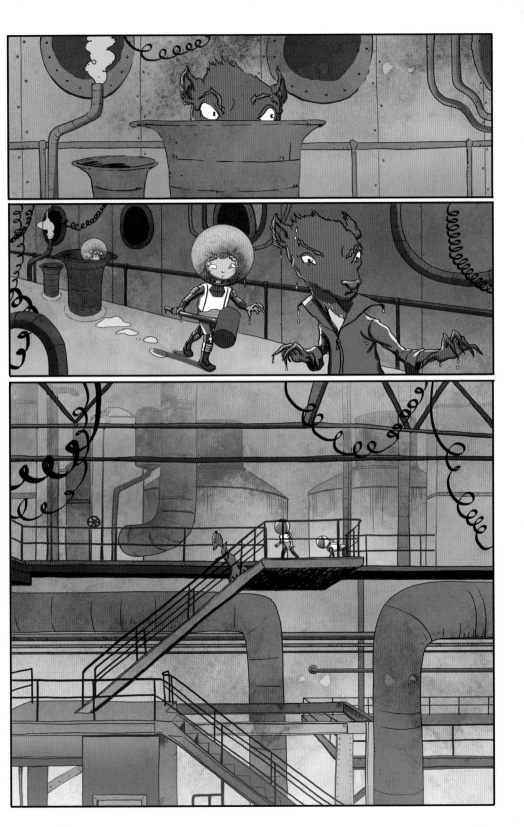

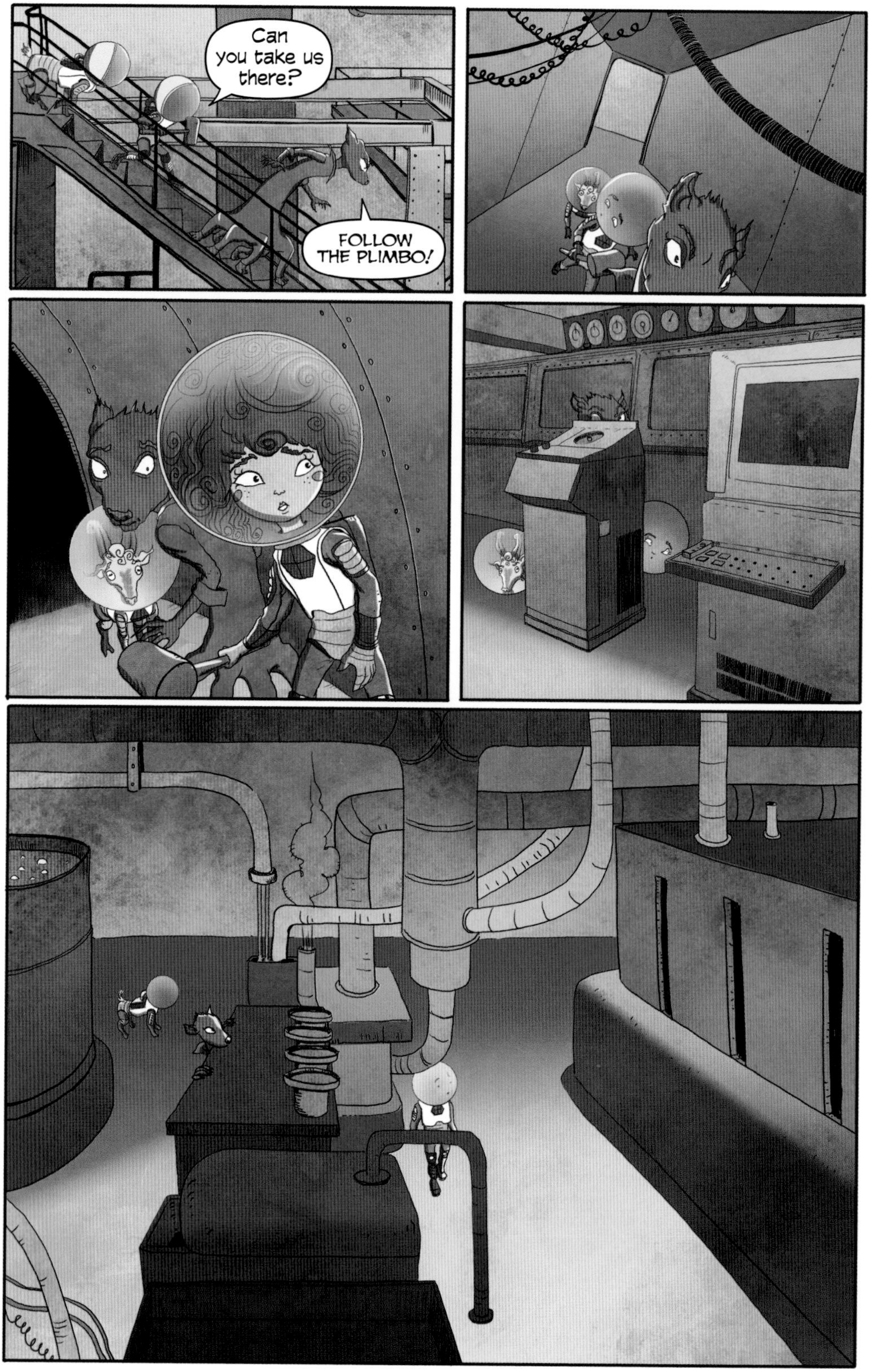
Can you take us there?
FOLLOW THE PLIMBO!

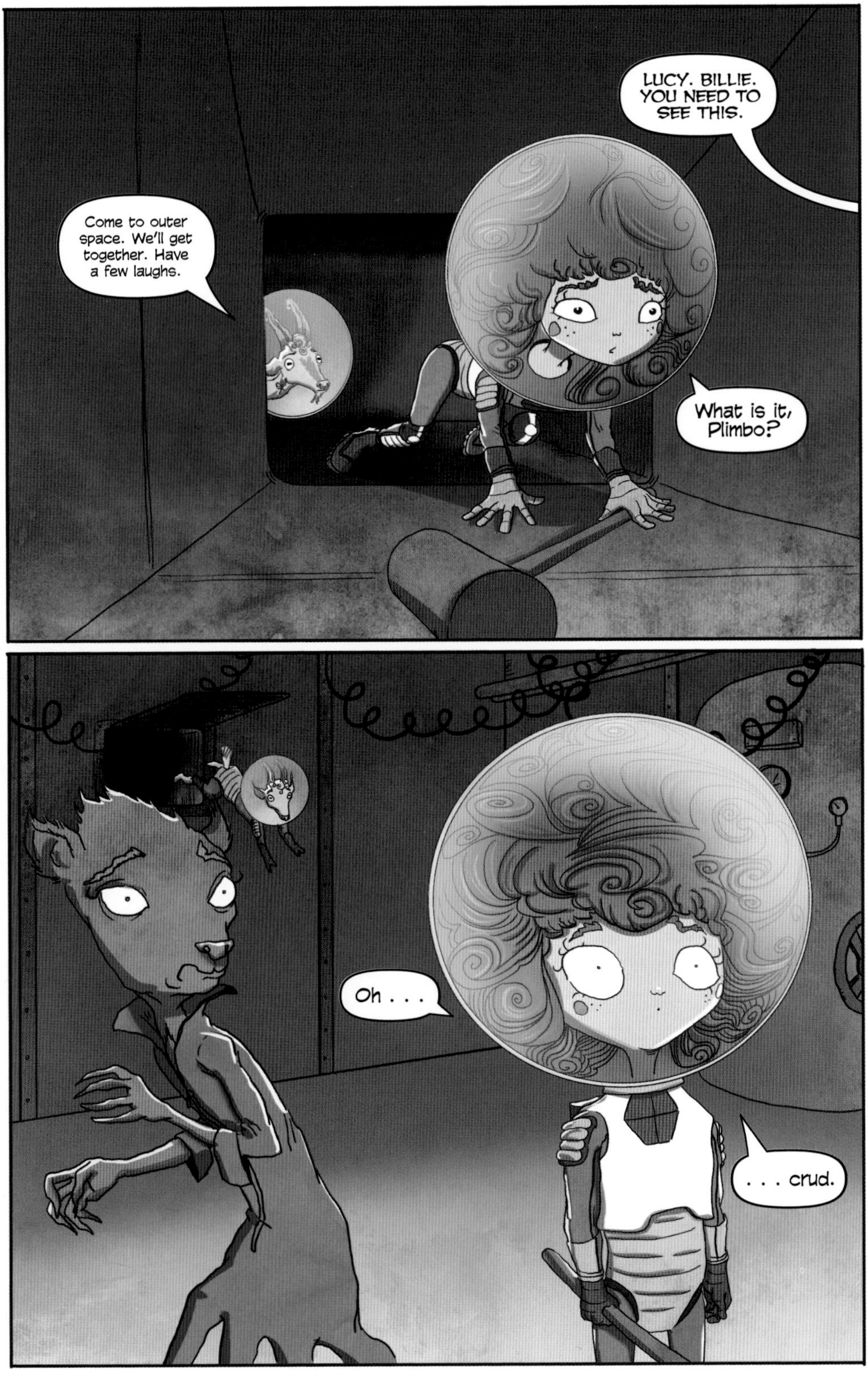
LUCY. BILLIE. YOU NEED TO SEE THIS.
Come to outer space. We'll get together. Have a few laughs.
What is it, Plimbo?
Oh . . .
. . . crud.

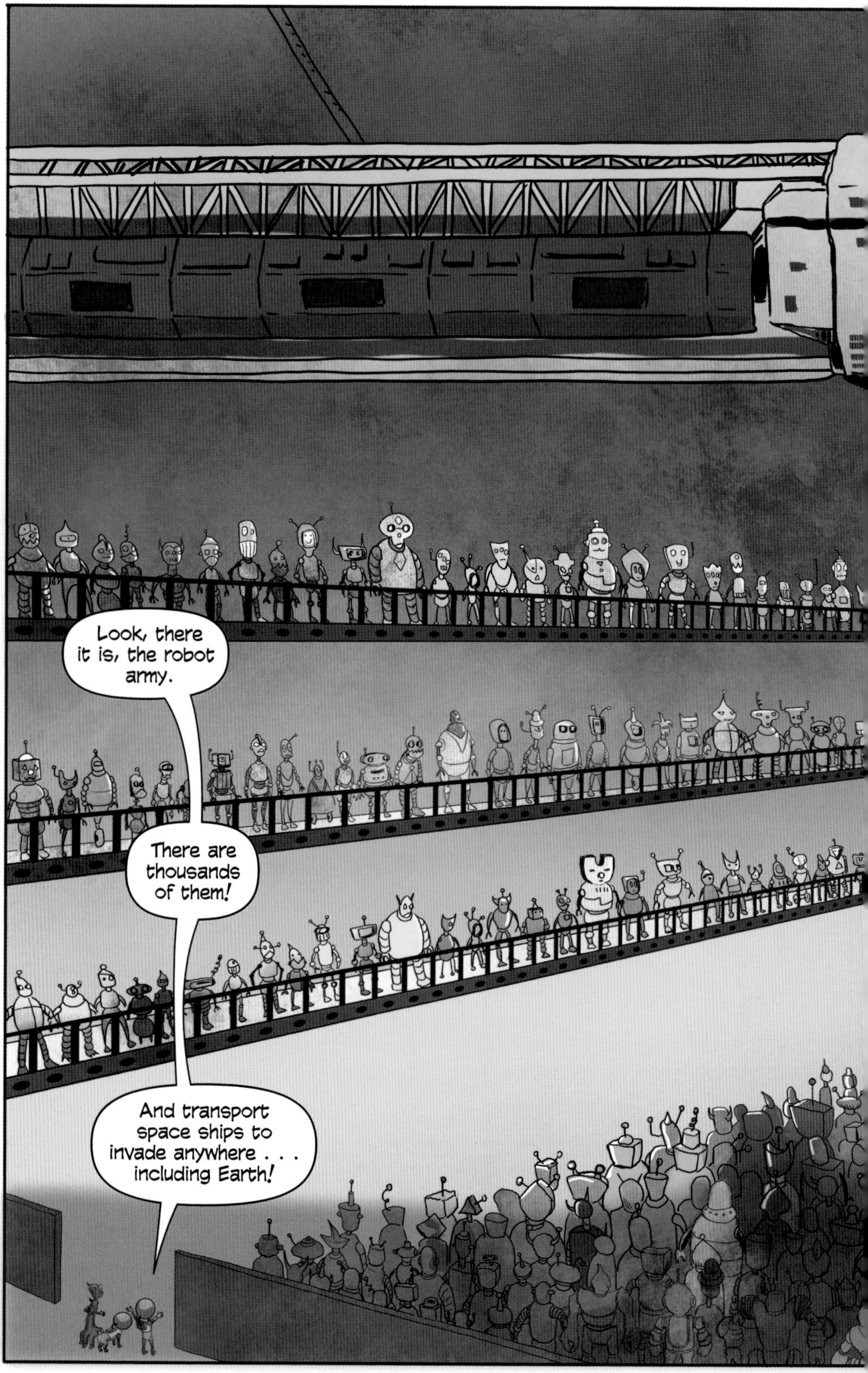
Look, there it is, the robot army.
There are thousands of them!
And transport space ships to invade anywhere . . . including Earth!

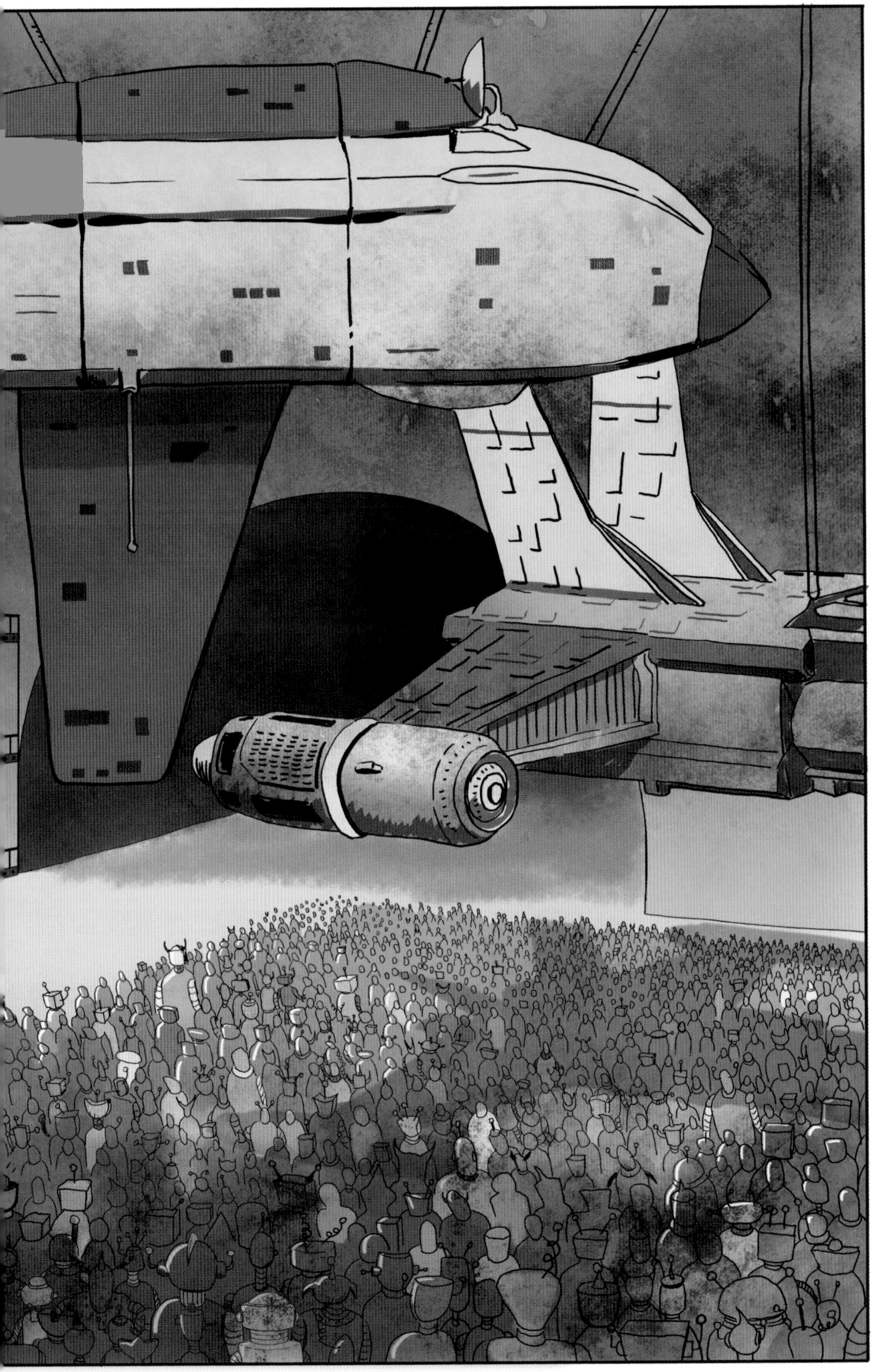

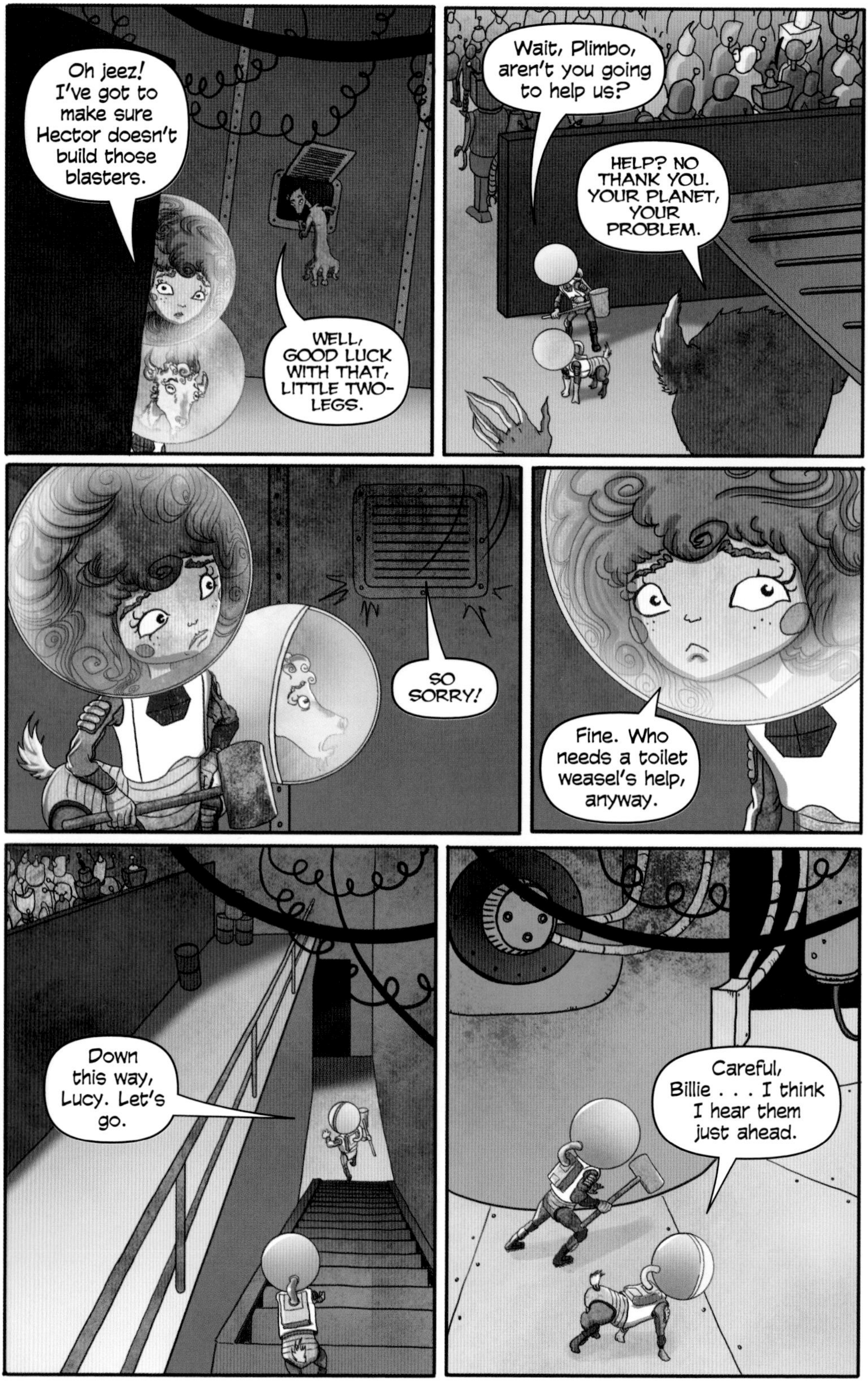
Oh jeez! I've got to make sure Hector doesn't build those blasters.
WELL, GOOD LUCK WITH THAT, LITTLE TWO-LEGS.
Wait, Plimbo, aren't you going to help us?
HELP? NO THANK YOU. YOUR PLANET, YOUR PROBLEM.
SO SORRY!
Fine. Who needs a toilet weasel's help, anyway.
Down this way, Lucy. Let's go.
Careful, Billie . . . I think I hear them just ahead.

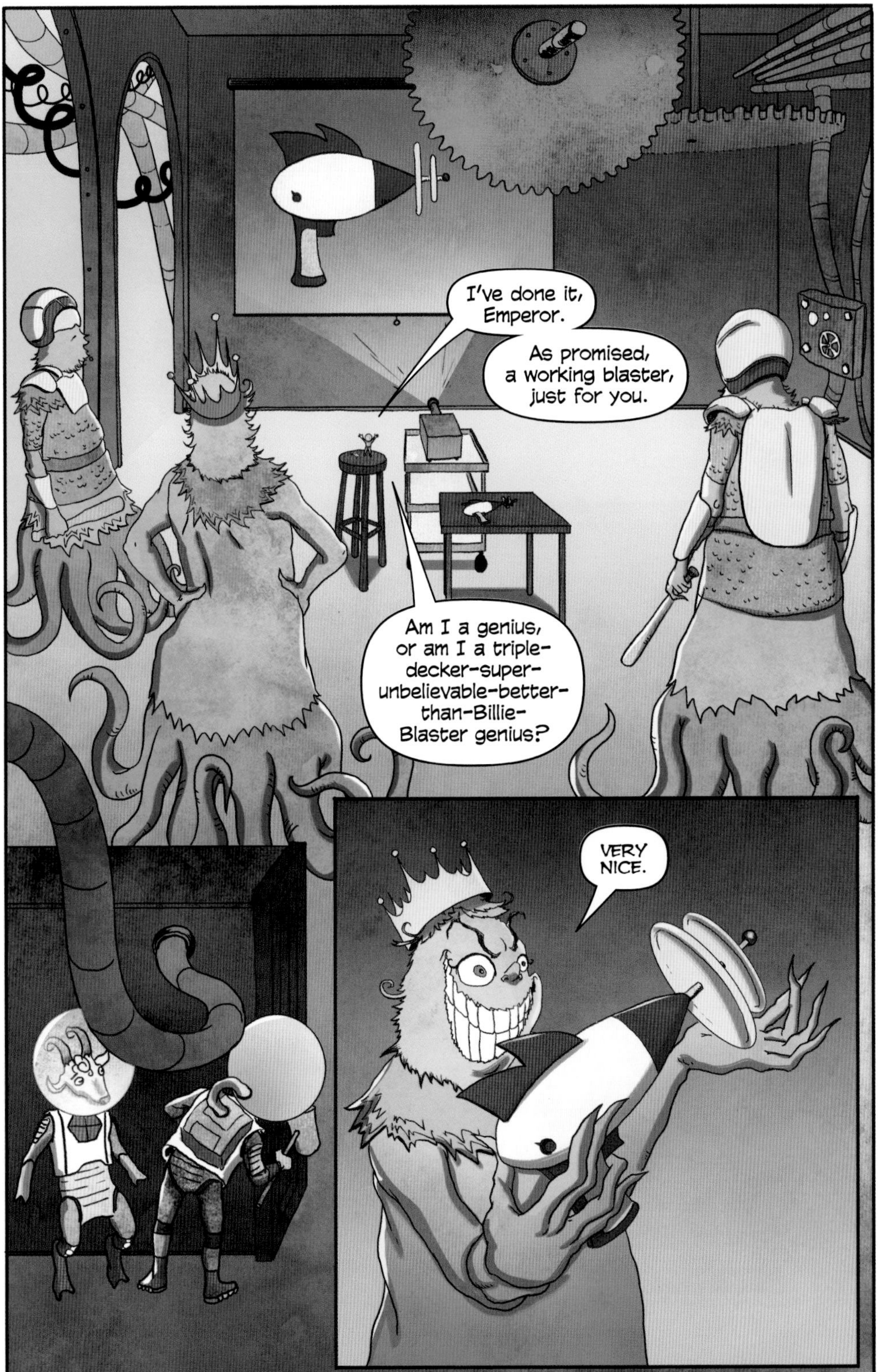
I've done it, Emperor.
As promised, a working blaster, just for you.
Am I a genius, or am I a triple-decker-super-unbelievable-better-than-Billie-Blaster genius?
VERY NICE.

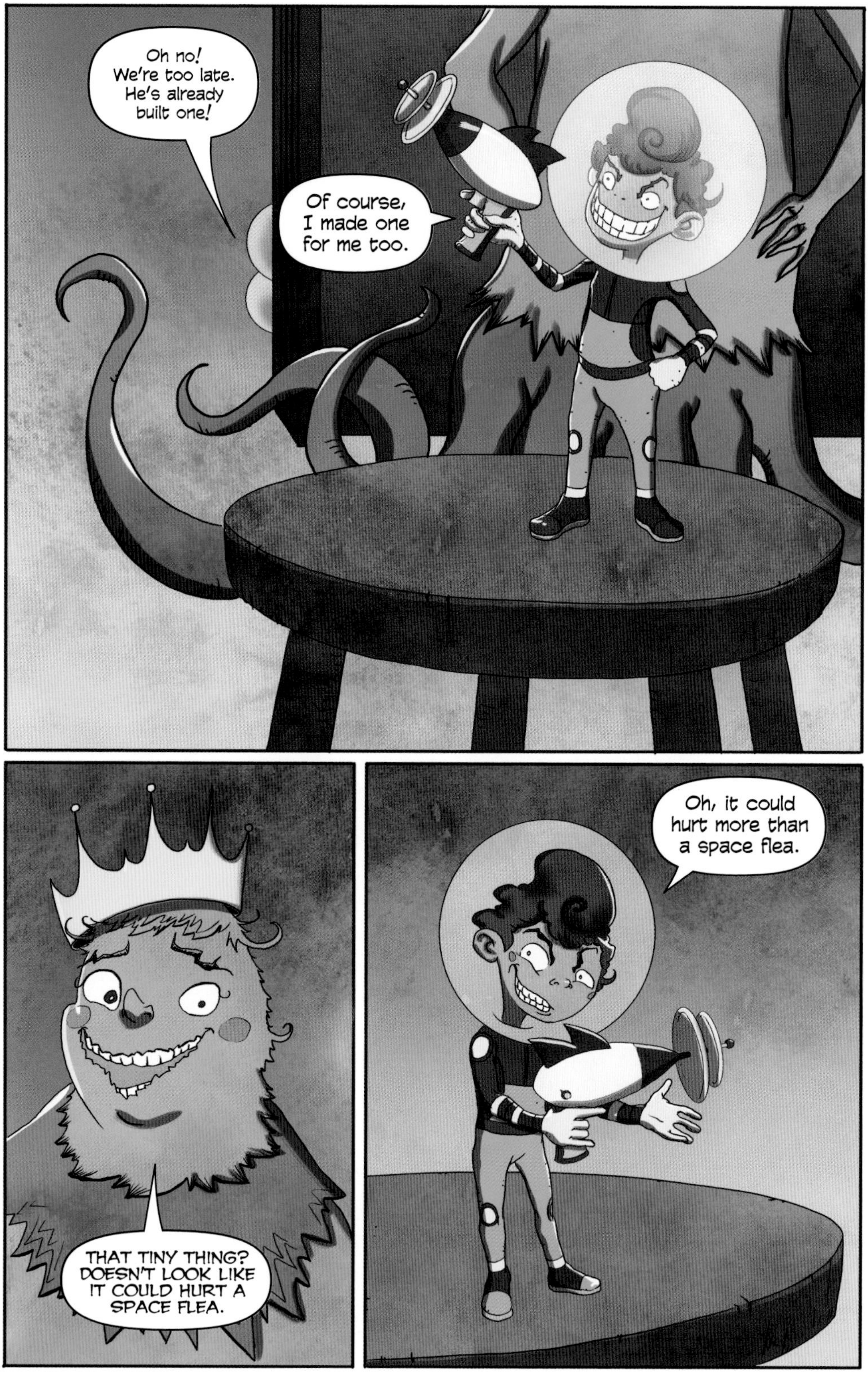
Oh no! We're too late. He's already built one!
Of course, I made one for me too.
THAT TINY THING? DOESN'T LOOK LIKE IT COULD HURT A SPACE FLEA.
Oh, it could hurt more than a space flea.

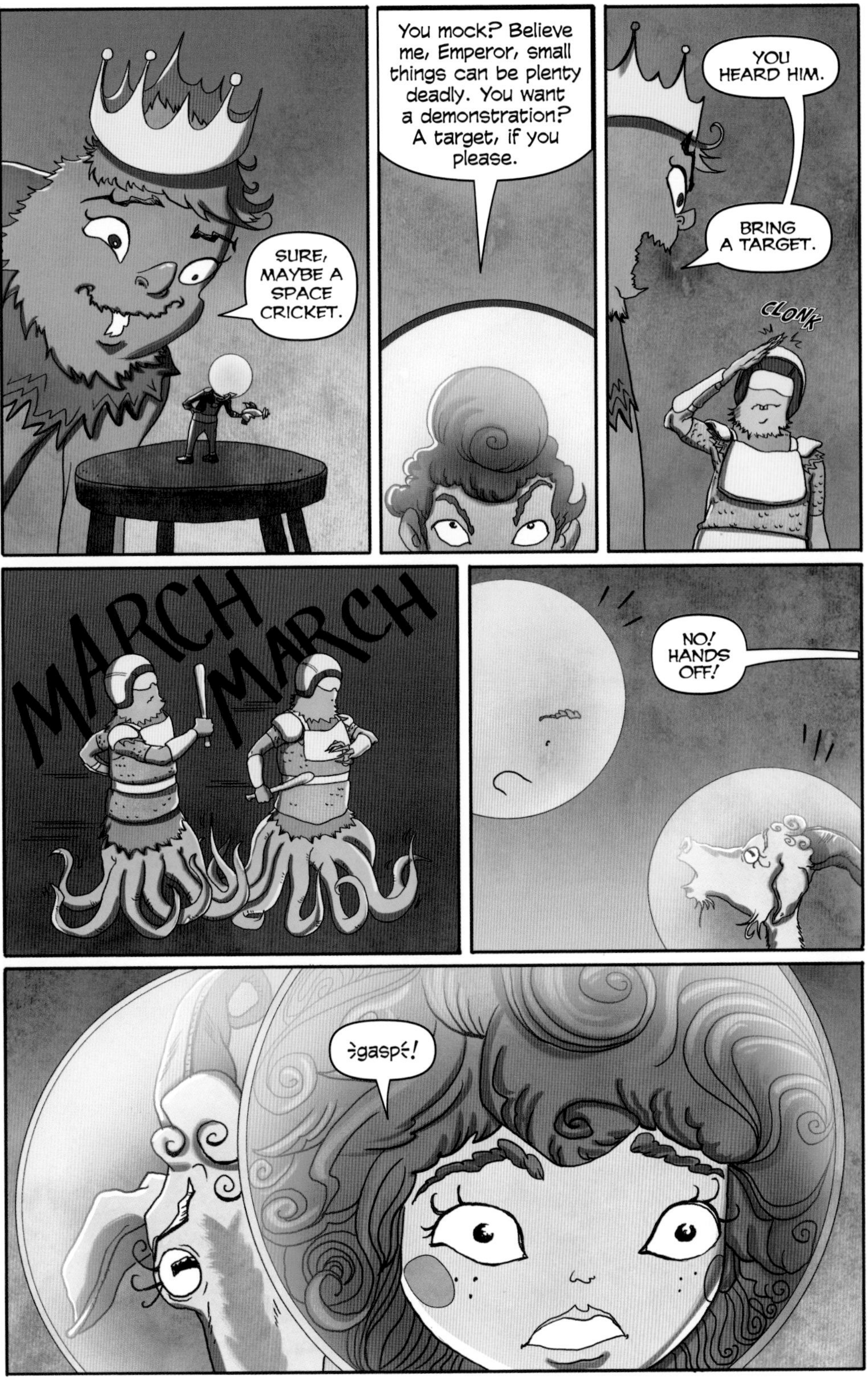
SURE, MAYBE A SPACE CRICKET.
You mock? Believe me, Emperor, small things can be plenty deadly. You want a demonstration? A target, if you please.
YOU HEARD HIM.
BRING A TARGET.
CLONK
MARCH MARCH
NO! HANDS OFF!
≑gasp≑!

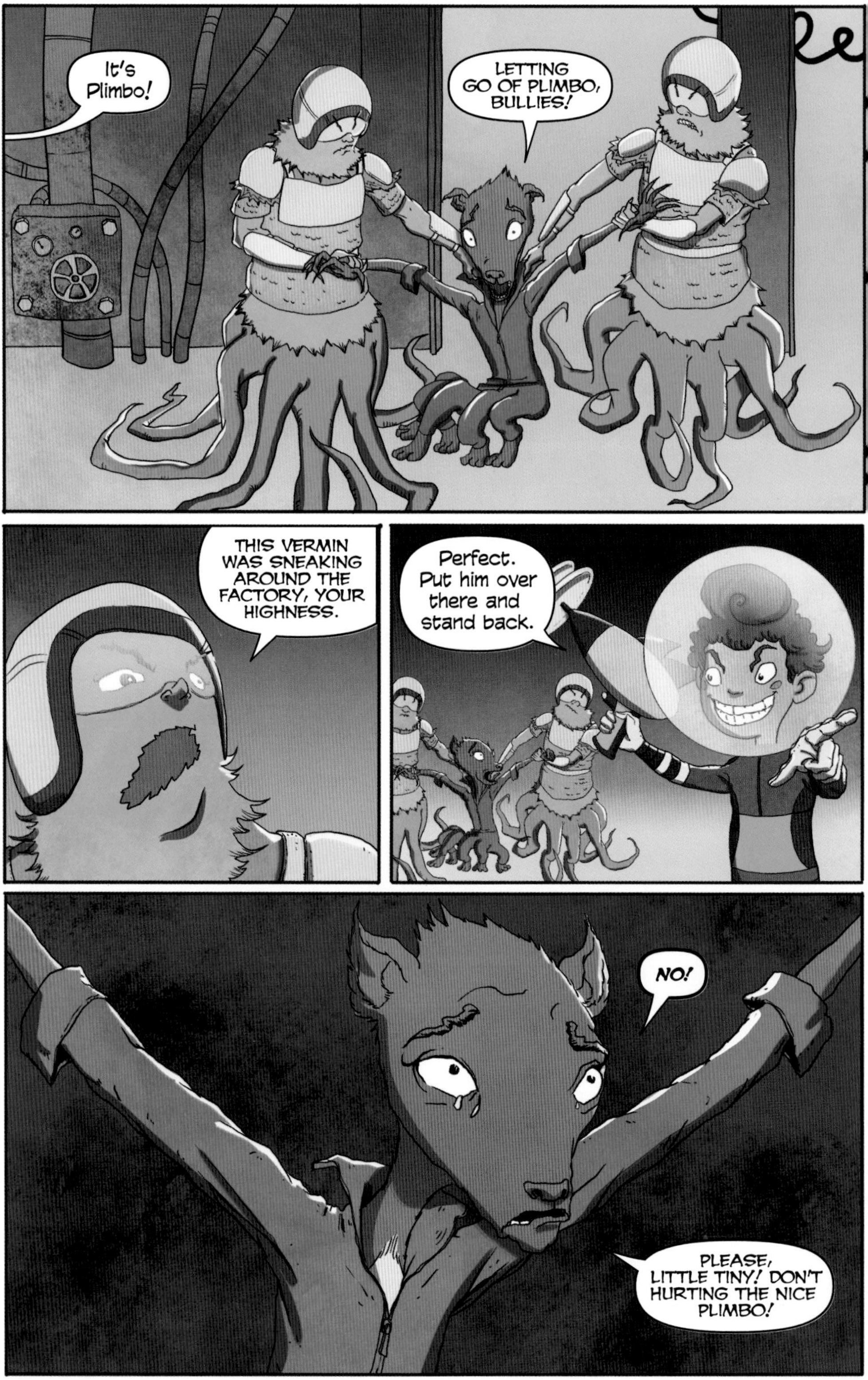
It's Plimbo!
LETTING GO OF PLIMBO, BULLIES!
THIS VERMIN WAS SNEAKING AROUND THE FACTORY, YOUR HIGHNESS.
Perfect. Put him over there and stand back.
NO!
PLEASE, LITTLE TINY! DON'T HURTING THE NICE PLIMBO!

Billie, we have to stop him.

He won't do it. Not even tiny Hector Glum could be so vicious.

You will note, the blaster has two settings: MELT and STUN.

STUN MELT

Melt?!

He'll just stun him—

And since stunning is for weenies, I will demonstrate MELT.

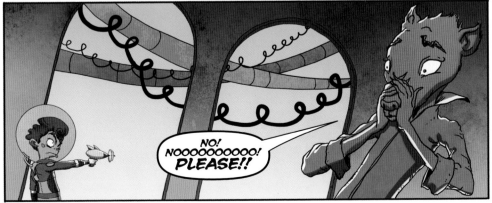

NO! NOOOOOOOOOO! PLEASE!!

115

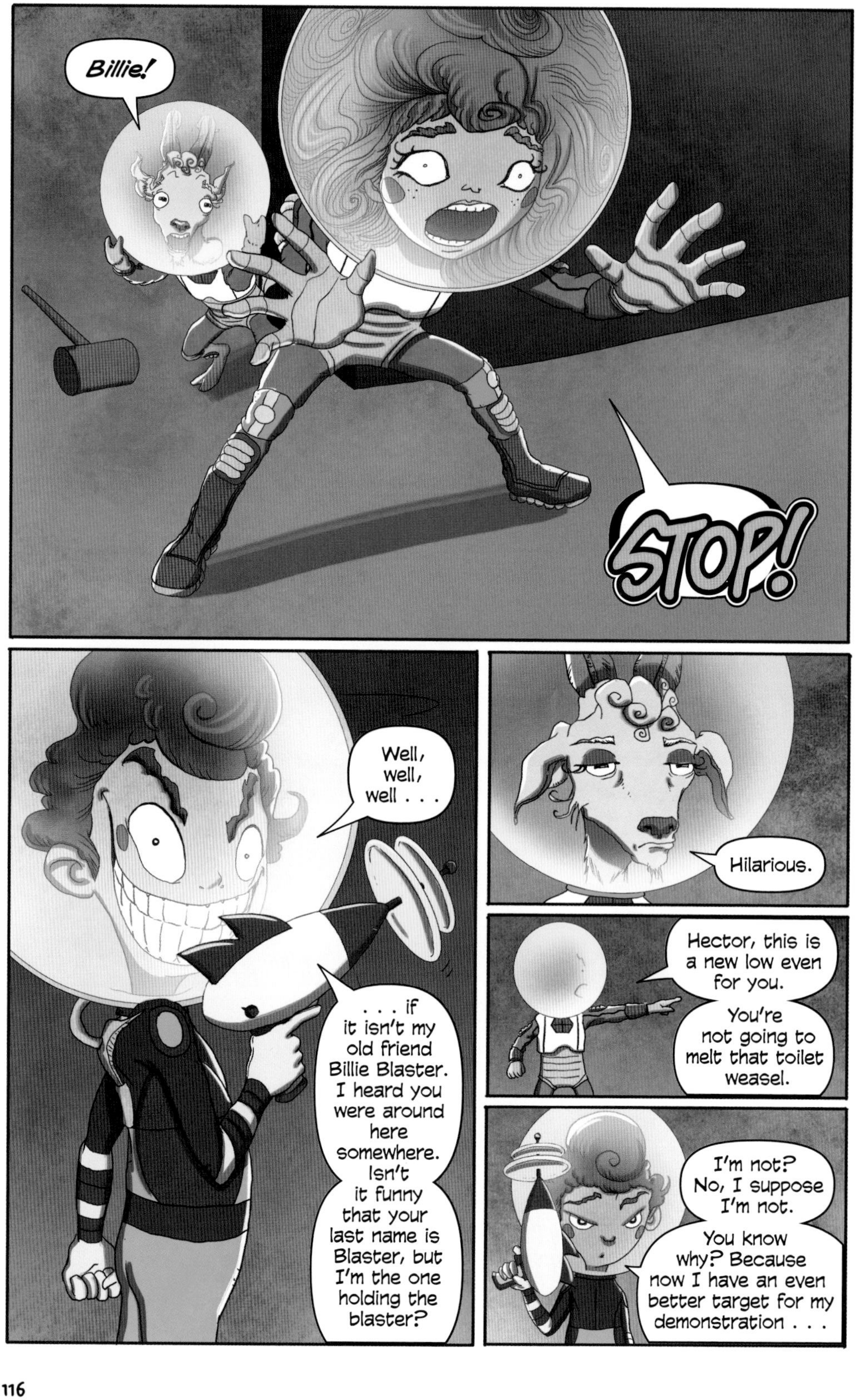

Billie!
STOP!
Well, well, well . . .
. . . if it isn't my old friend Billie Blaster. I heard you were around here somewhere. Isn't it funny that your last name is Blaster, but I'm the one holding the blaster?
Hilarious.
Hector, this is a new low even for you.
You're not going to melt that toilet weasel.
I'm not? No, I suppose I'm not.
You know why? Because now I have an even better target for my demonstration . . .

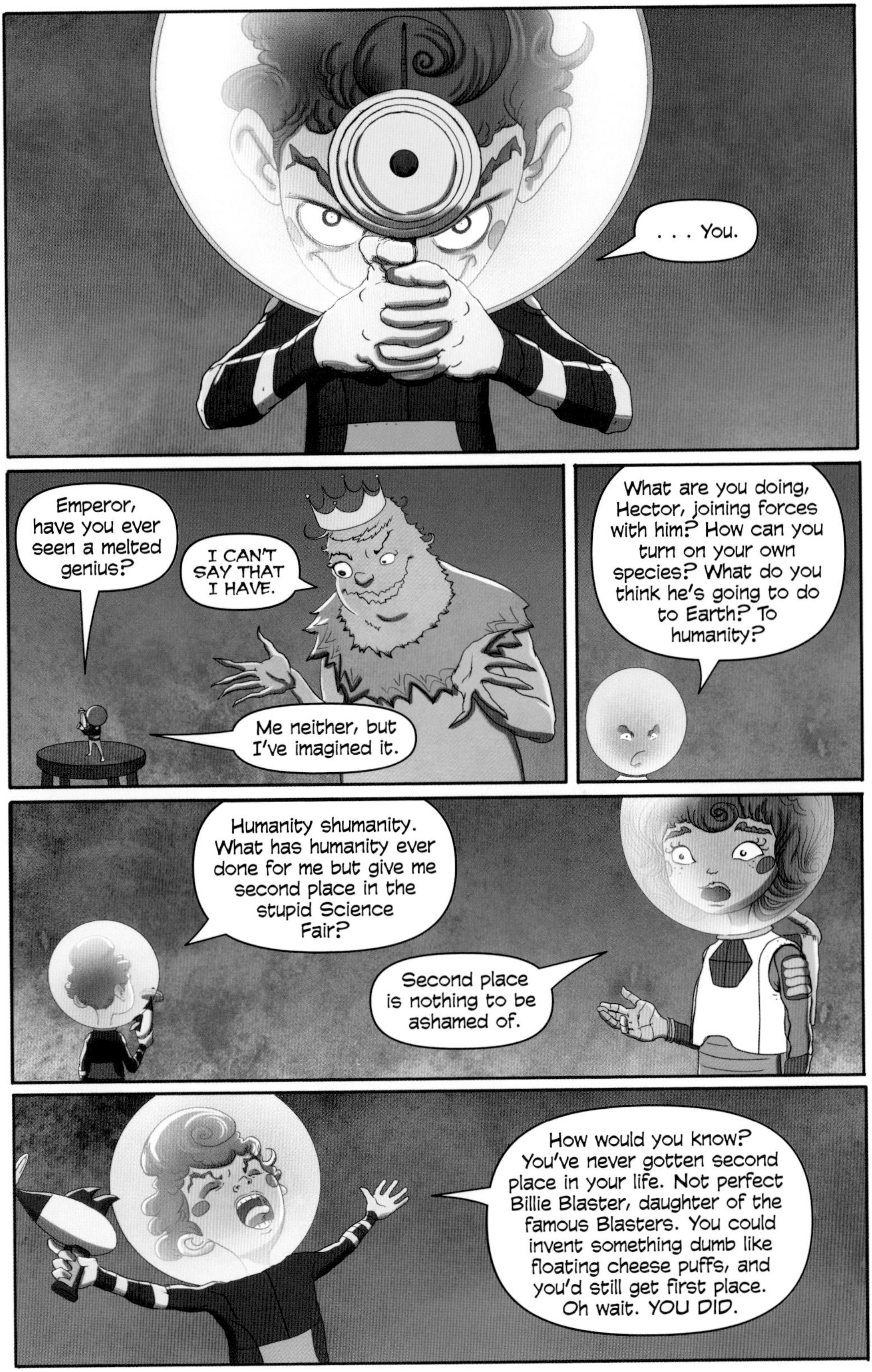
. . . You.
Emperor, have you ever seen a melted genius?
I CAN'T SAY THAT I HAVE.
Me neither, but I've imagined it.
What are you doing, Hector, joining forces with him? How can you turn on your own species? What do you think he's going to do to Earth? To humanity?
Humanity shumanity. What has humanity ever done for me but give me second place in the stupid Science Fair?
Second place is nothing to be ashamed of.
How would you know? You've never gotten second place in your life. Not perfect Billie Blaster, daughter of the famous Blasters. You could invent something dumb like floating cheese puffs, and you'd still get first place. Oh wait. YOU DID.

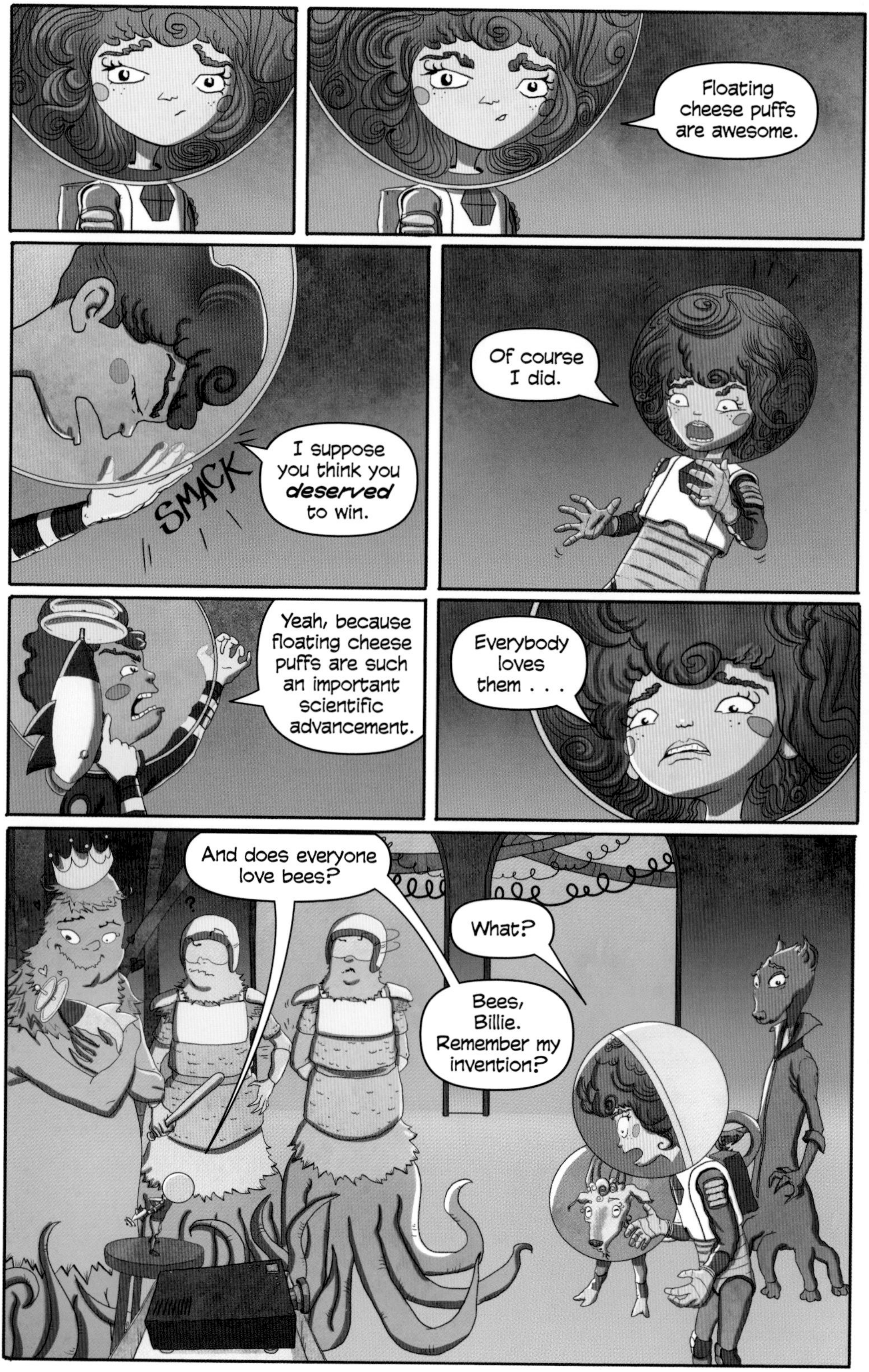
Floating cheese puffs are awesome.
SMACK
I suppose you think you *deserved* to win.
Of course I did.
Yeah, because floating cheese puffs are such an important scientific advancement.
Everybody loves them . . .
And does everyone love bees?
What?
Bees, Billie. Remember my invention?

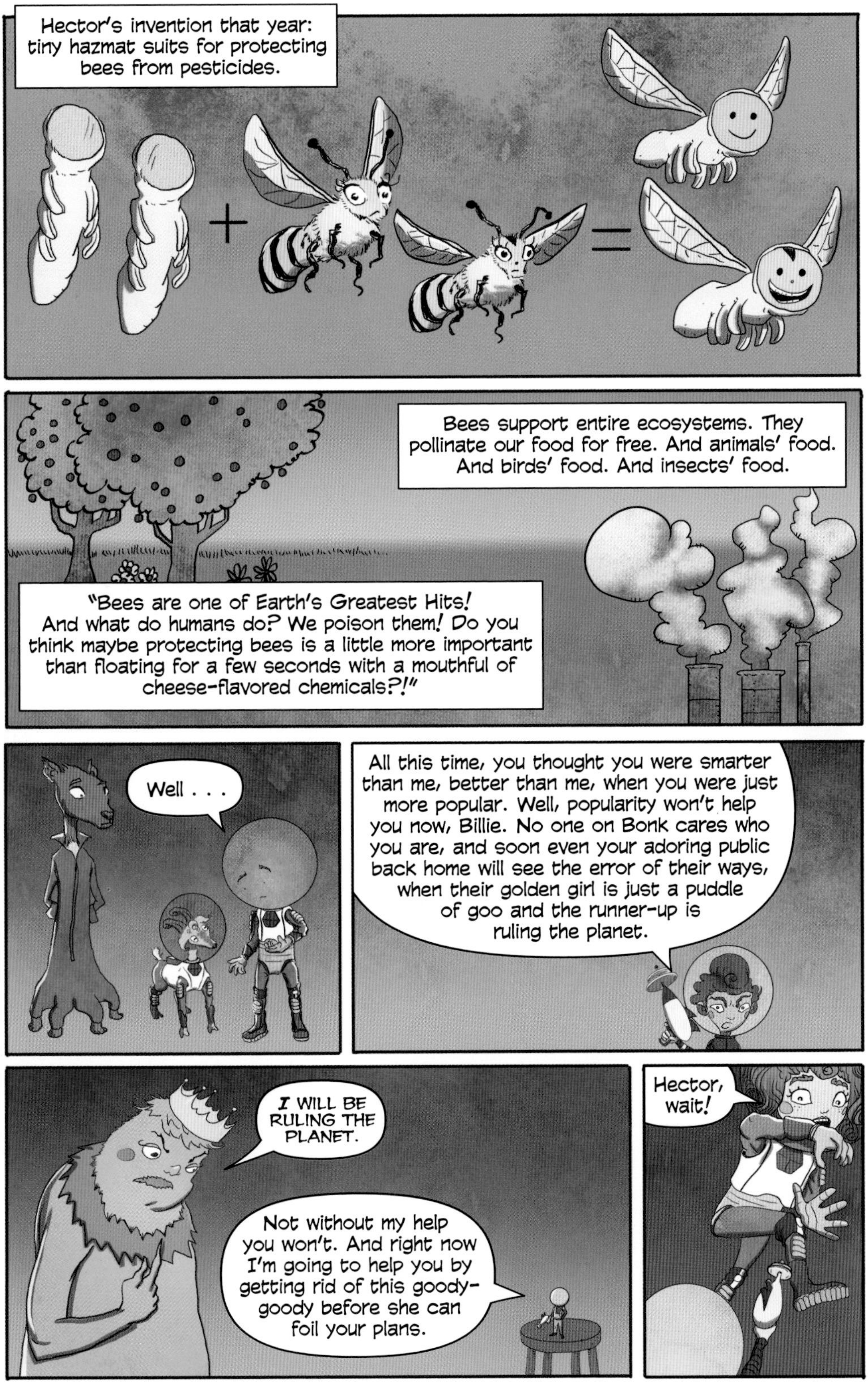
Hector's invention that year: tiny hazmat suits for protecting bees from pesticides.
+
=
Bees support entire ecosystems. They pollinate our food for free. And animals' food. And birds' food. And insects' food.
"Bees are one of Earth's Greatest Hits! And what do humans do? We poison them! Do you think maybe protecting bees is a little more important than floating for a few seconds with a mouthful of cheese-flavored chemicals?!"
Well . . .
All this time, you thought you were smarter than me, better than me, when you were just more popular. Well, popularity won't help you now, Billie. No one on Bonk cares who you are, and soon even your adoring public back home will see the error of their ways, when their golden girl is just a puddle of goo and the runner-up is ruling the planet.
I WILL BE RULING THE PLANET.
Not without my help you won't. And right now I'm going to help you by getting rid of this goody-goody before she can foil your plans.
Hector, wait!

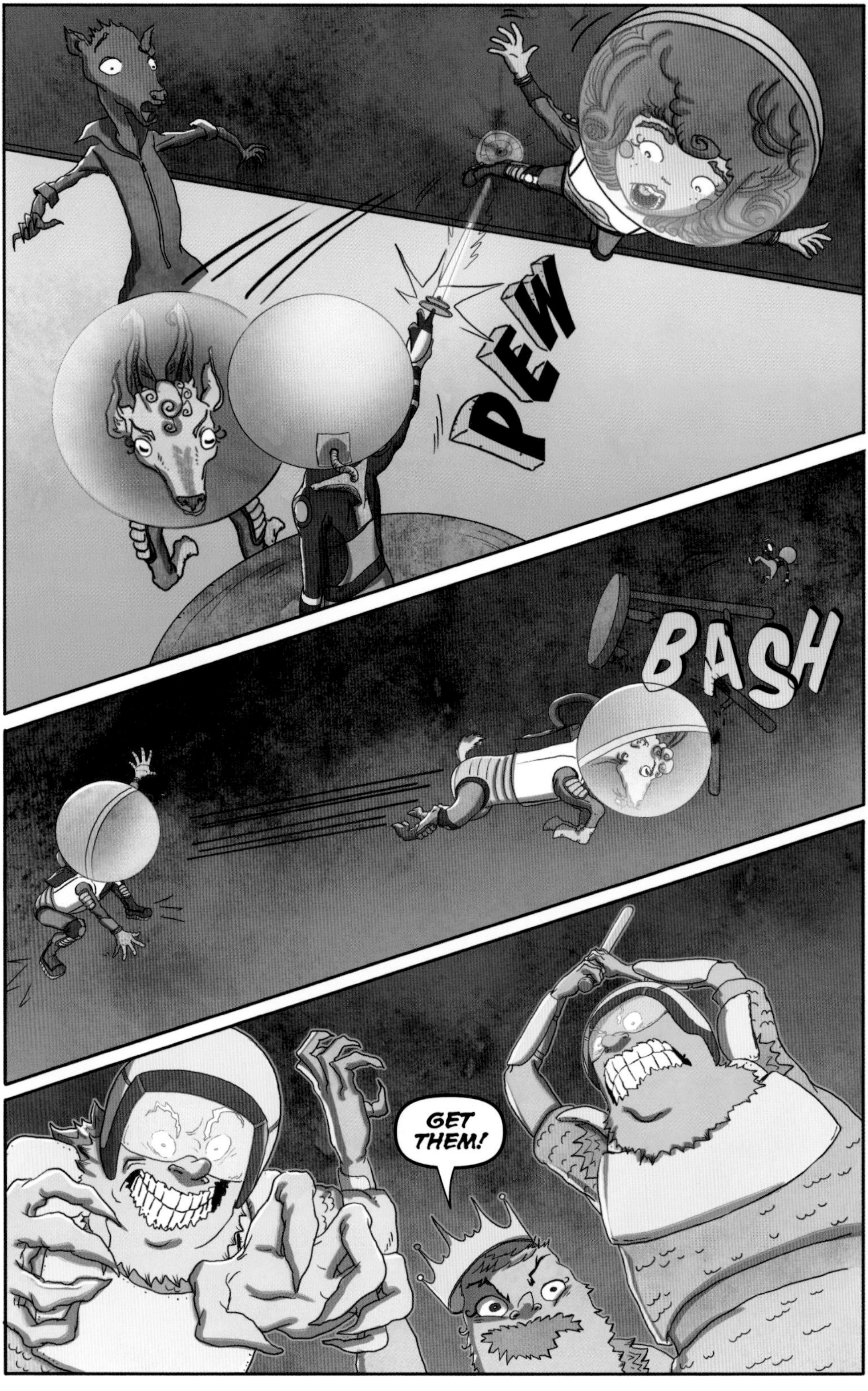
PEW
BASH
GET THEM!

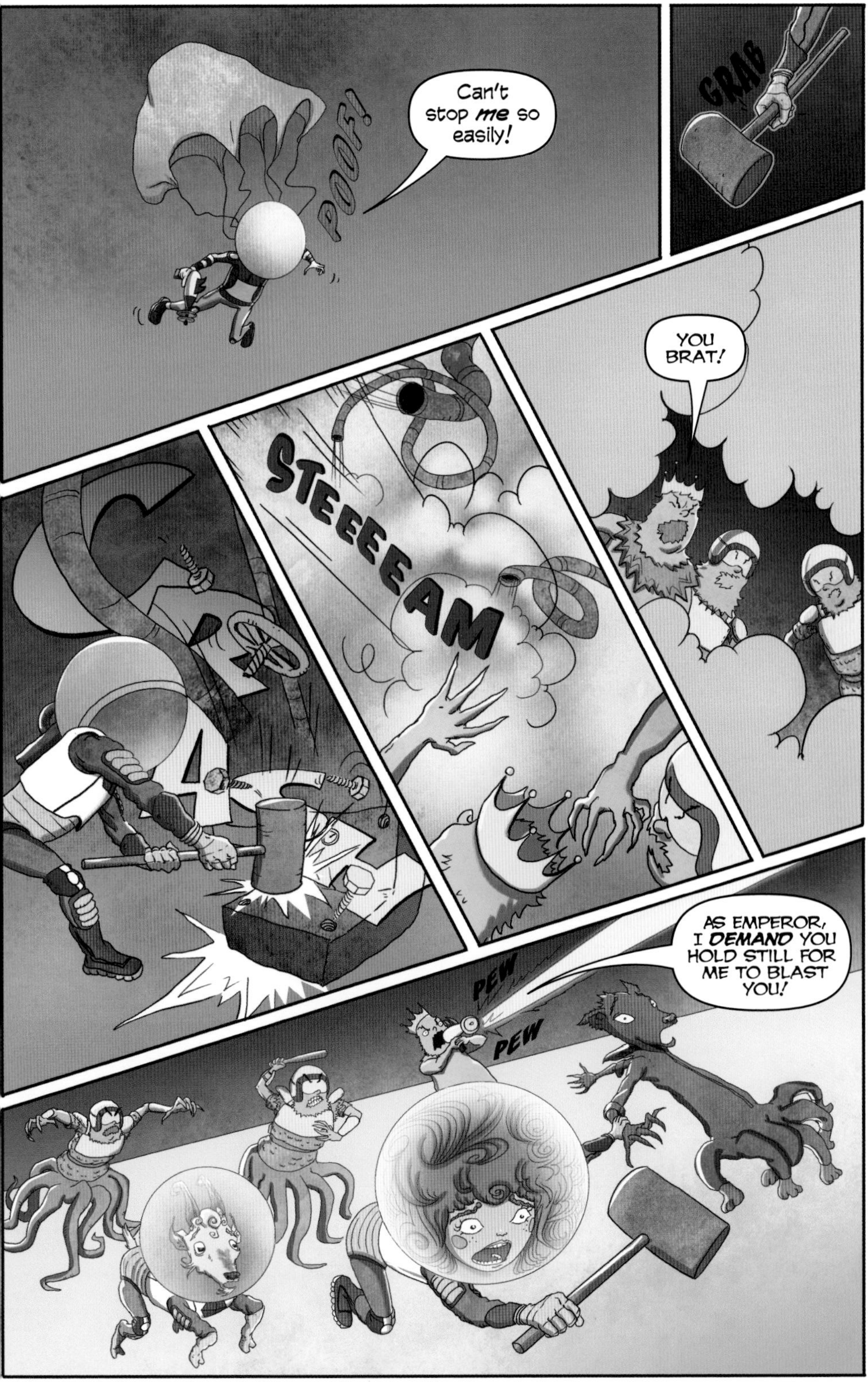

POOF!
Can't stop *me* so easily!
GRAB
STEEEEAM
YOU BRAT!
AS EMPEROR, I *DEMAND* YOU HOLD STILL FOR ME TO BLAST YOU!
PEW
PEW

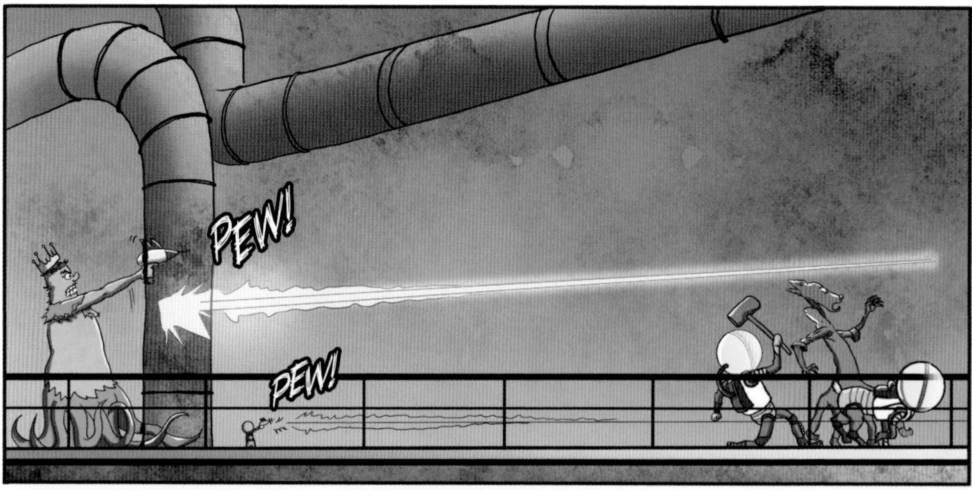
PEW!
PEW!

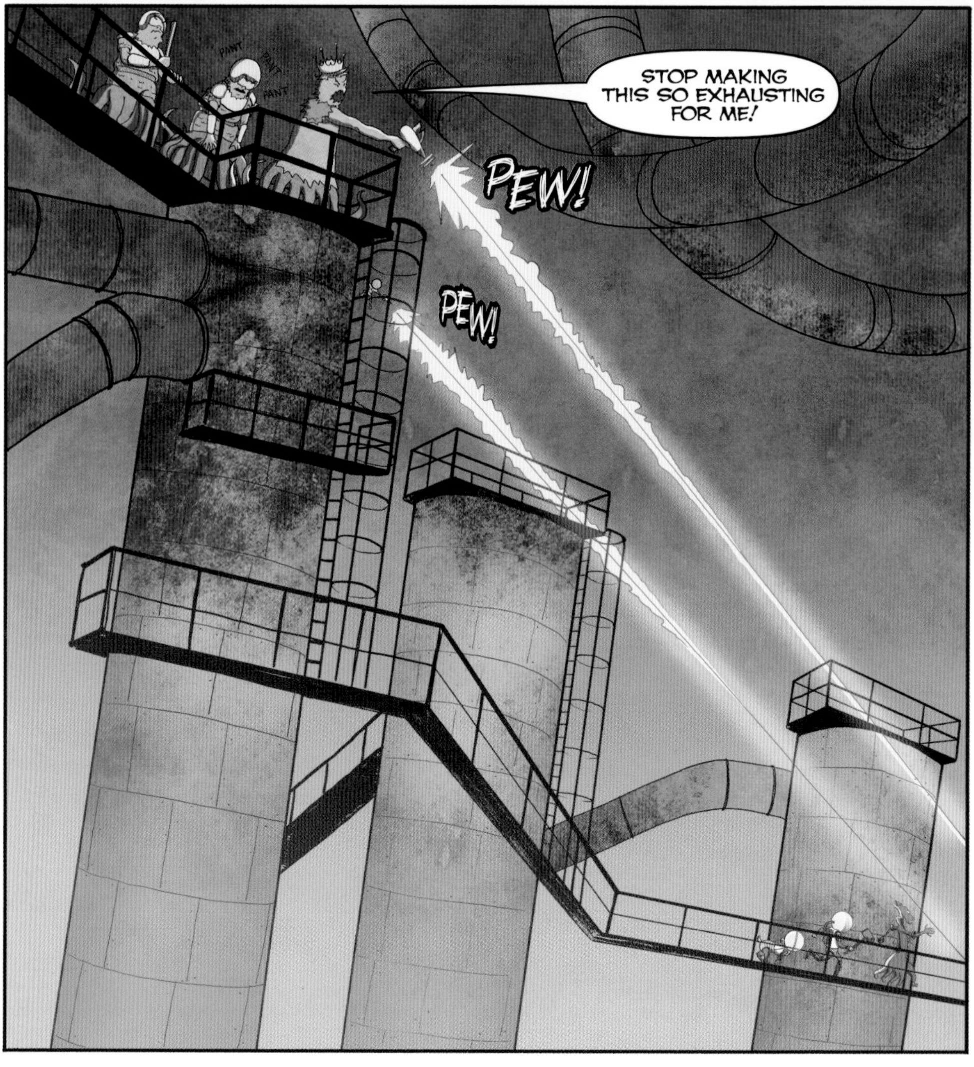
PANT
PANT
PANT
STOP MAKING THIS SO EXHAUSTING FOR ME!
PEW!
PEW!

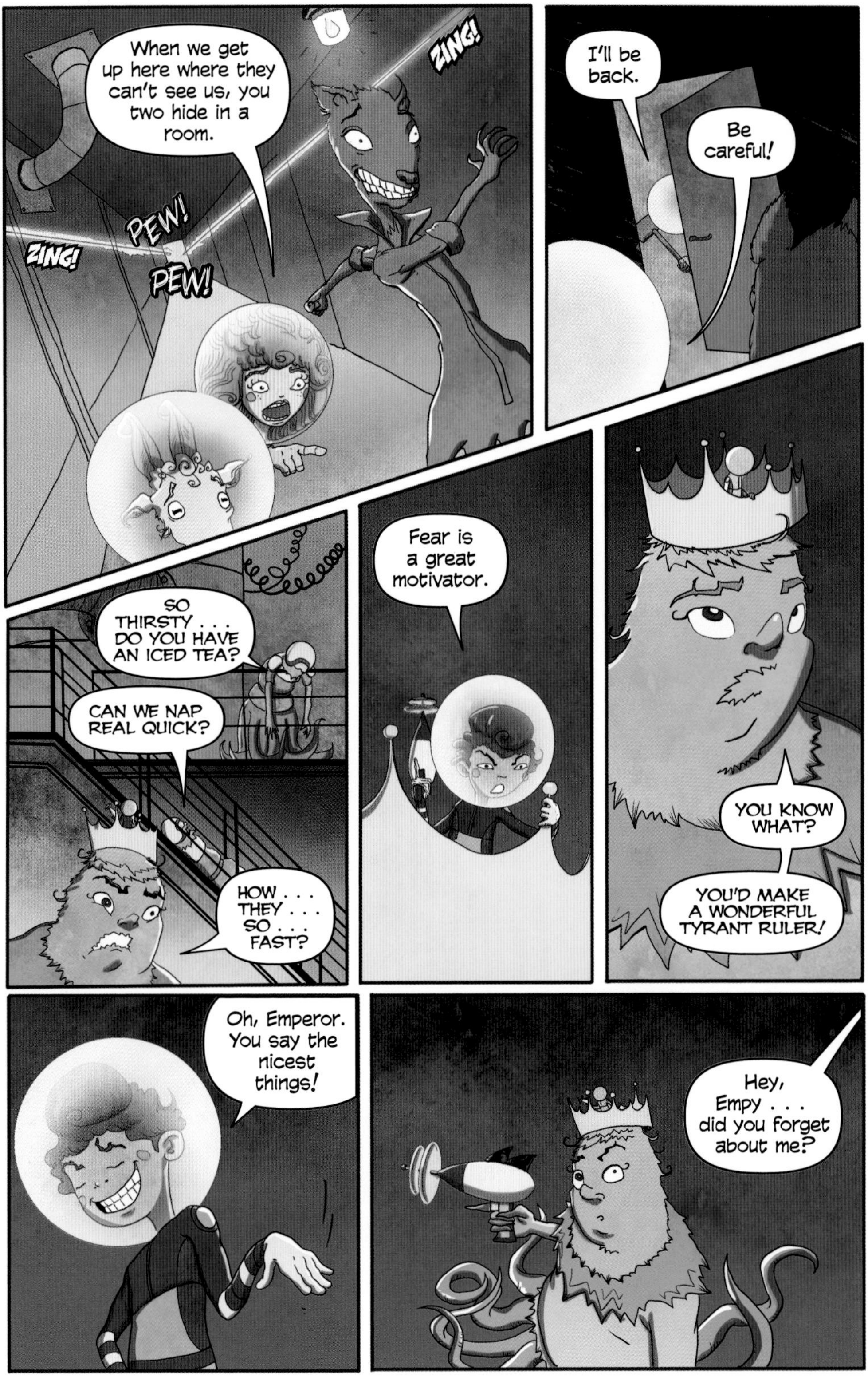
When we get up here where they can't see us, you two hide in a room.
ZING!
PEW!
ZING!
PEW!
I'll be back.
Be careful!
SO THIRSTY . . . DO YOU HAVE AN ICED TEA?
CAN WE NAP REAL QUICK?
HOW . . . THEY . . . SO . . . FAST?
Fear is a great motivator.
YOU KNOW WHAT?
YOU'D MAKE A WONDERFUL TYRANT RULER!
Oh, Emperor. You say the nicest things!
Hey, Empy . . . did you forget about me?

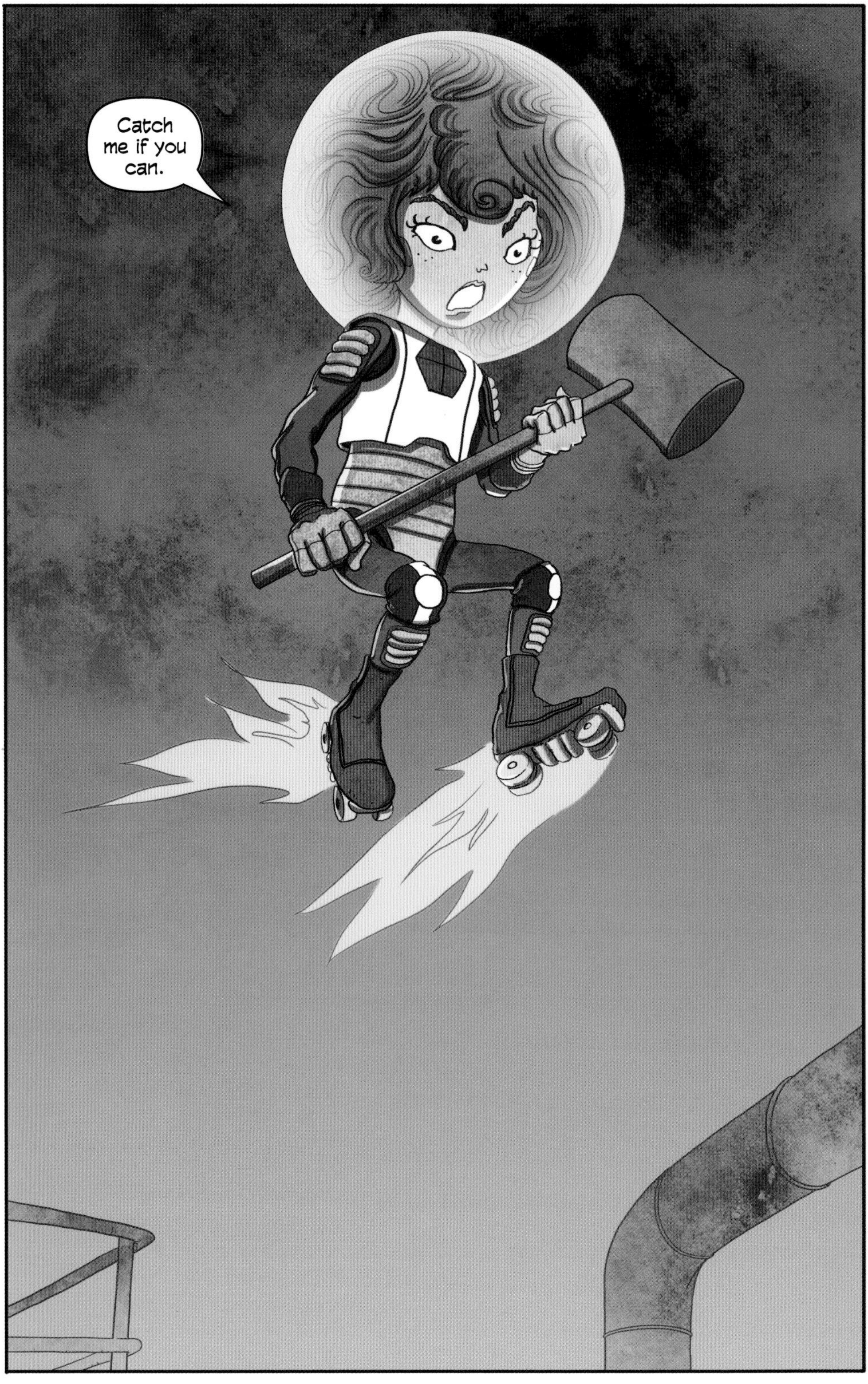
Catch me if you can.

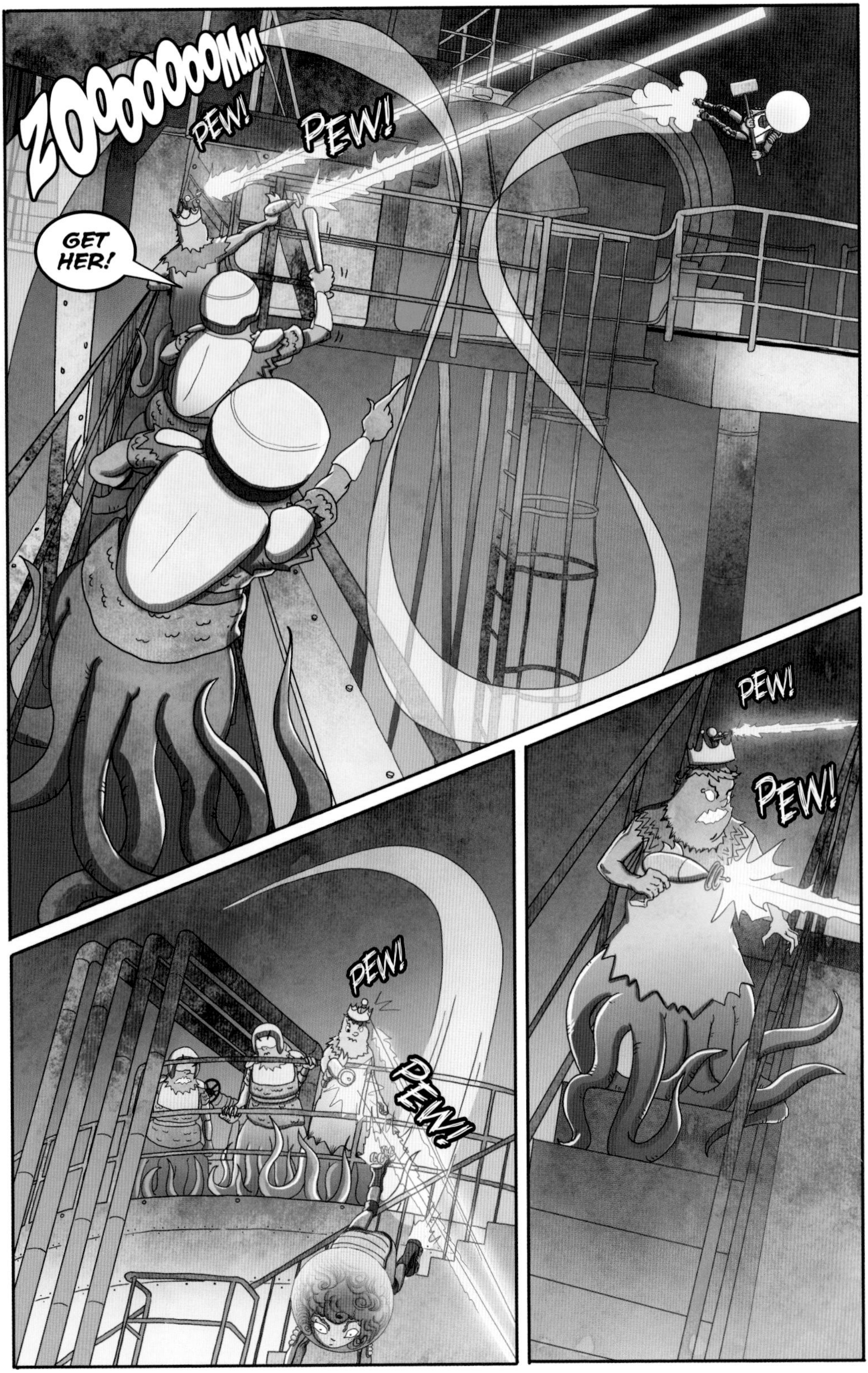
ZOOOOOOOMM
PEW!
PEW!
GET HER!
PEW!
PEW!
PEW!
PEW!

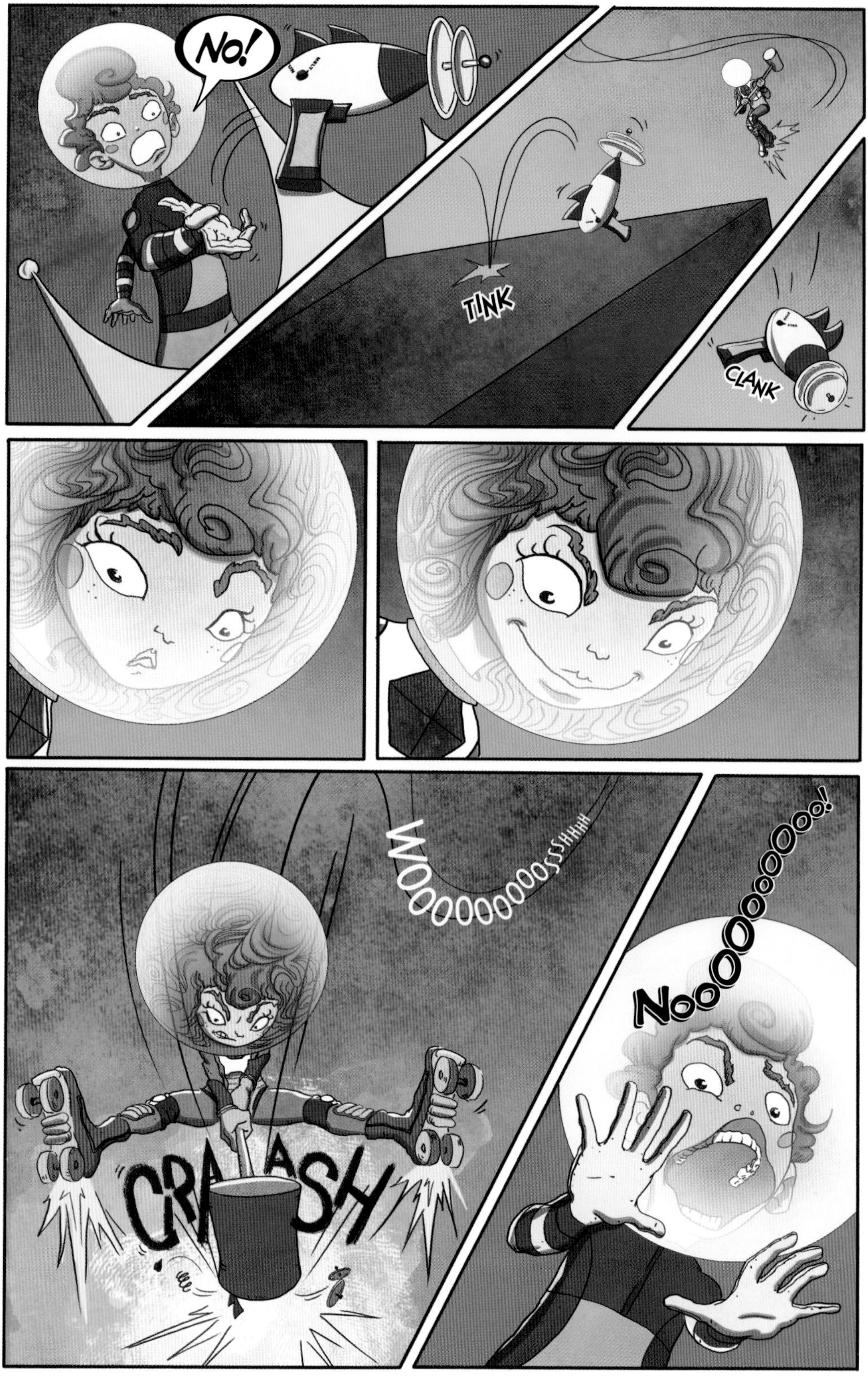
No!
TINK
CLANK
WOOOOOOOOOSSHHHH
CRASH
NooOOOOOOOOoo!

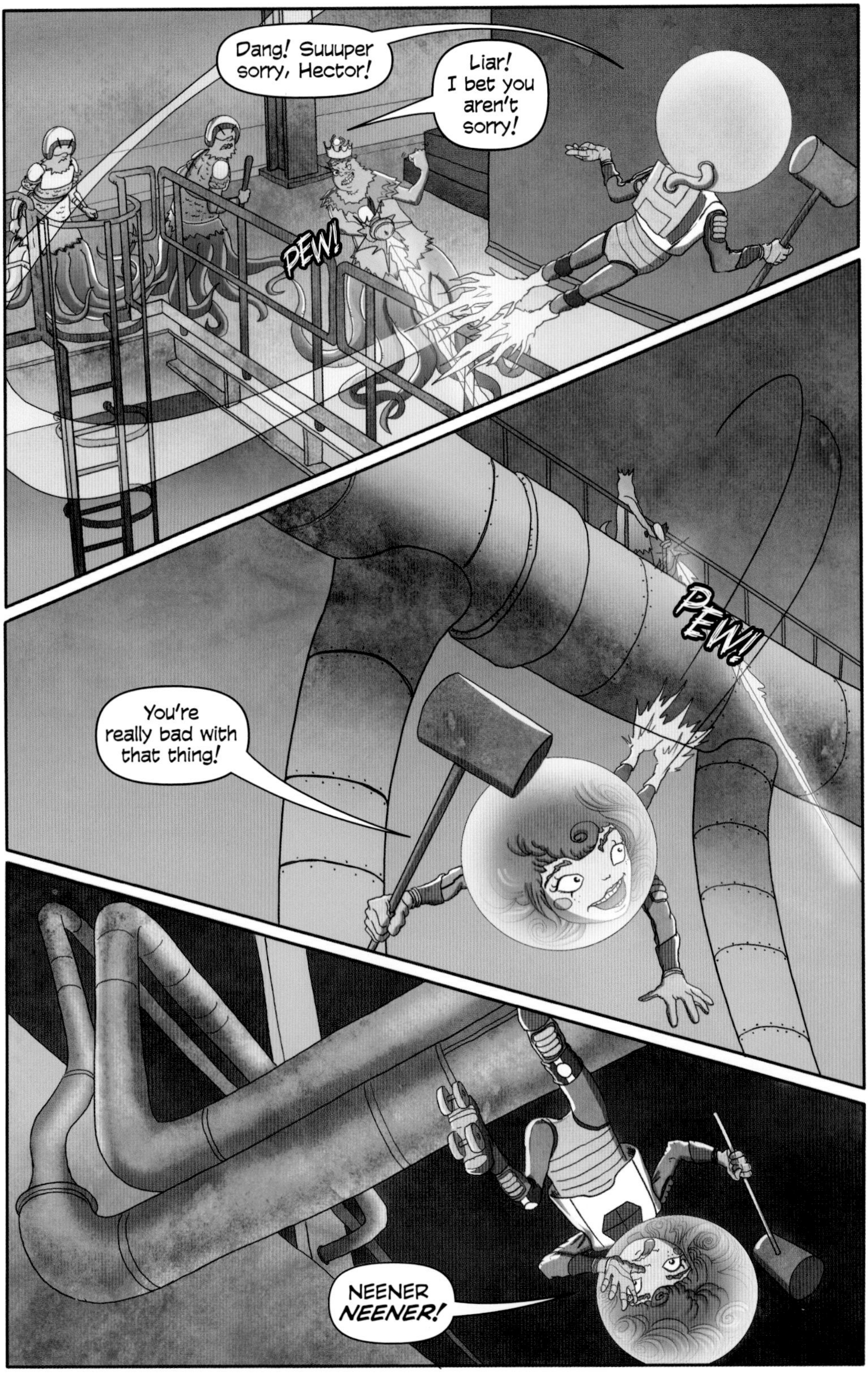
Dang! Suuuper sorry, Hector!
Liar! I bet you aren't sorry!
PEW!
PEW!
You're really bad with that thing!
NEENER NEENER!

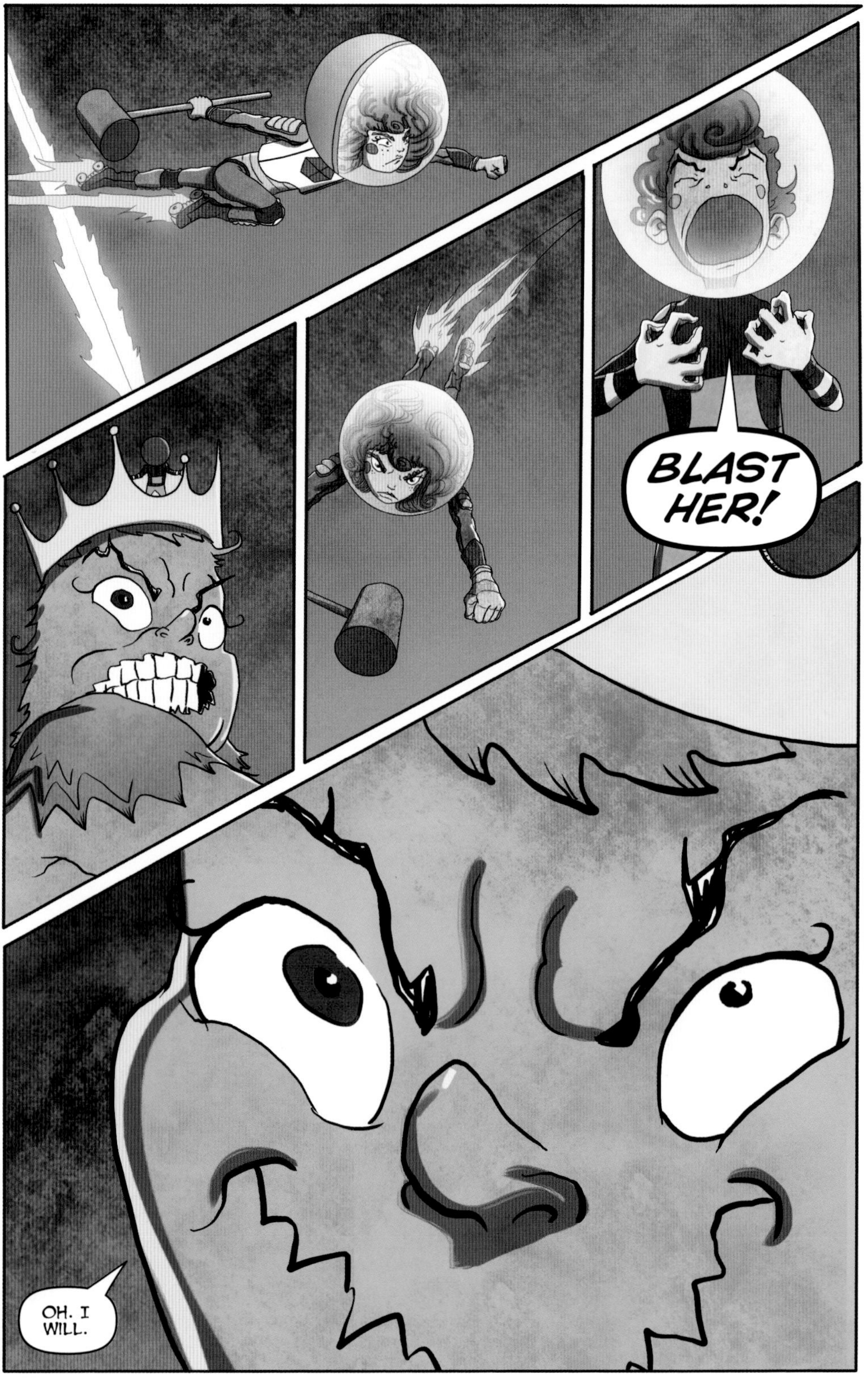
BLAST HER!
OH. I WILL.

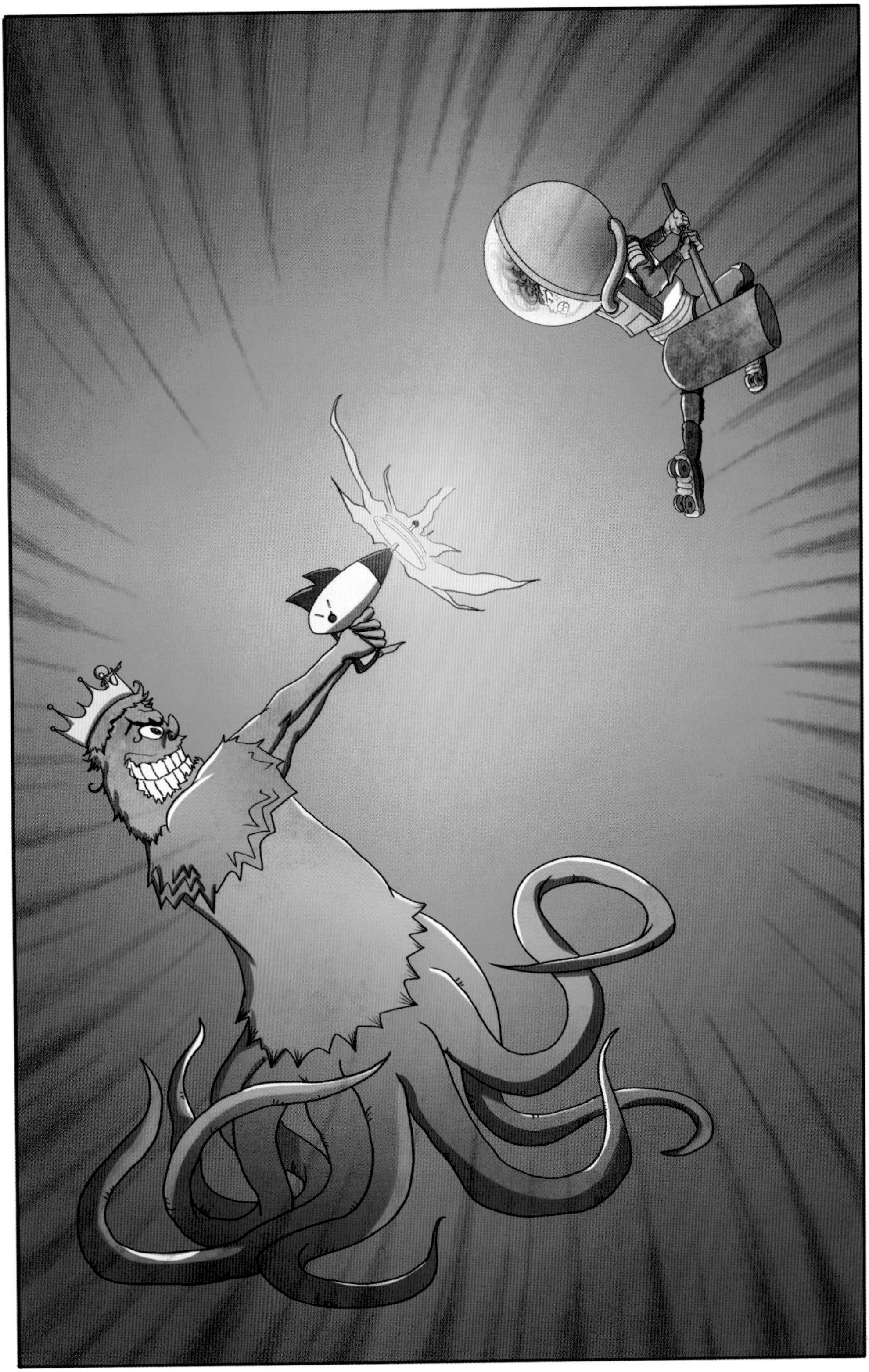

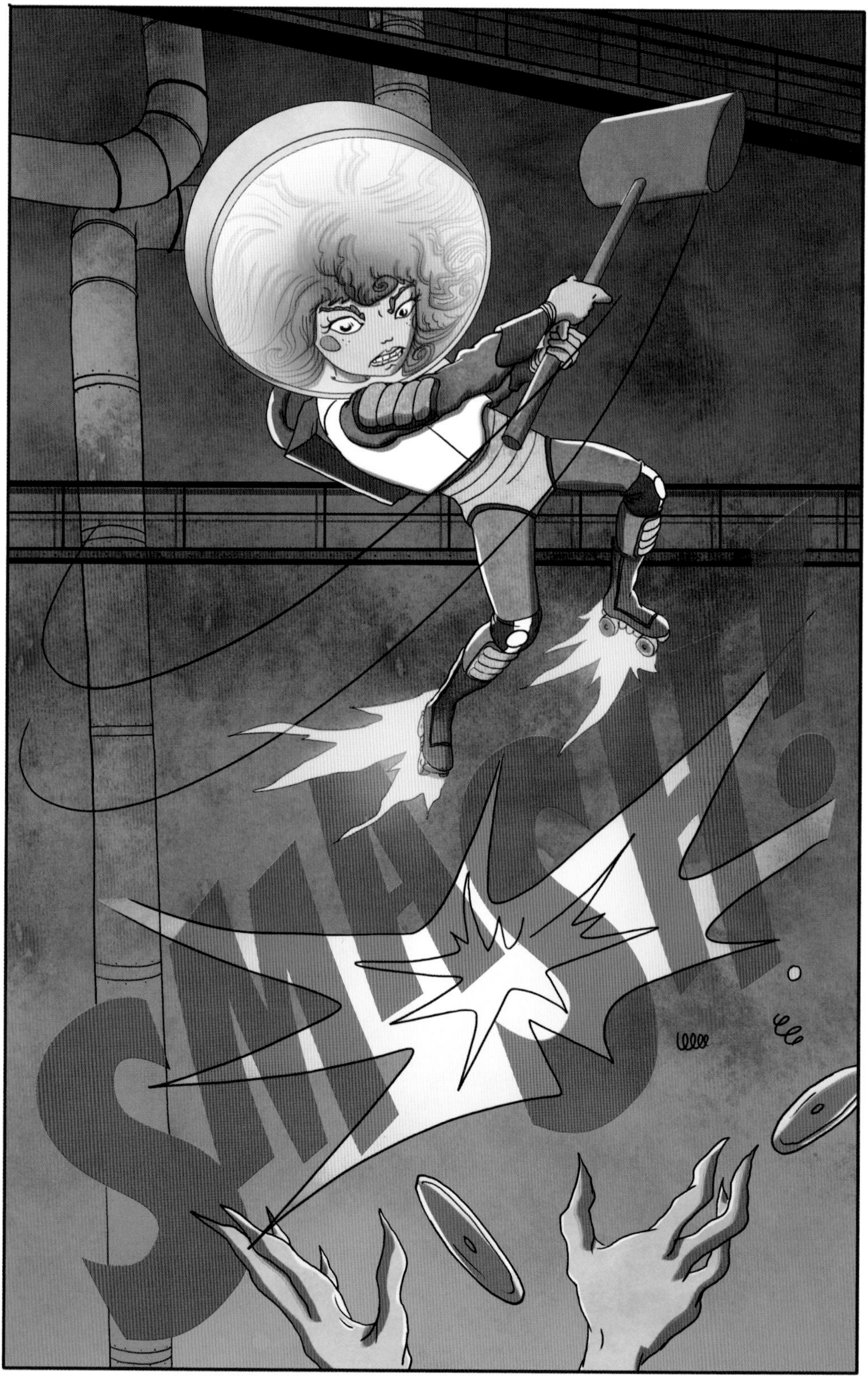
SMASH!

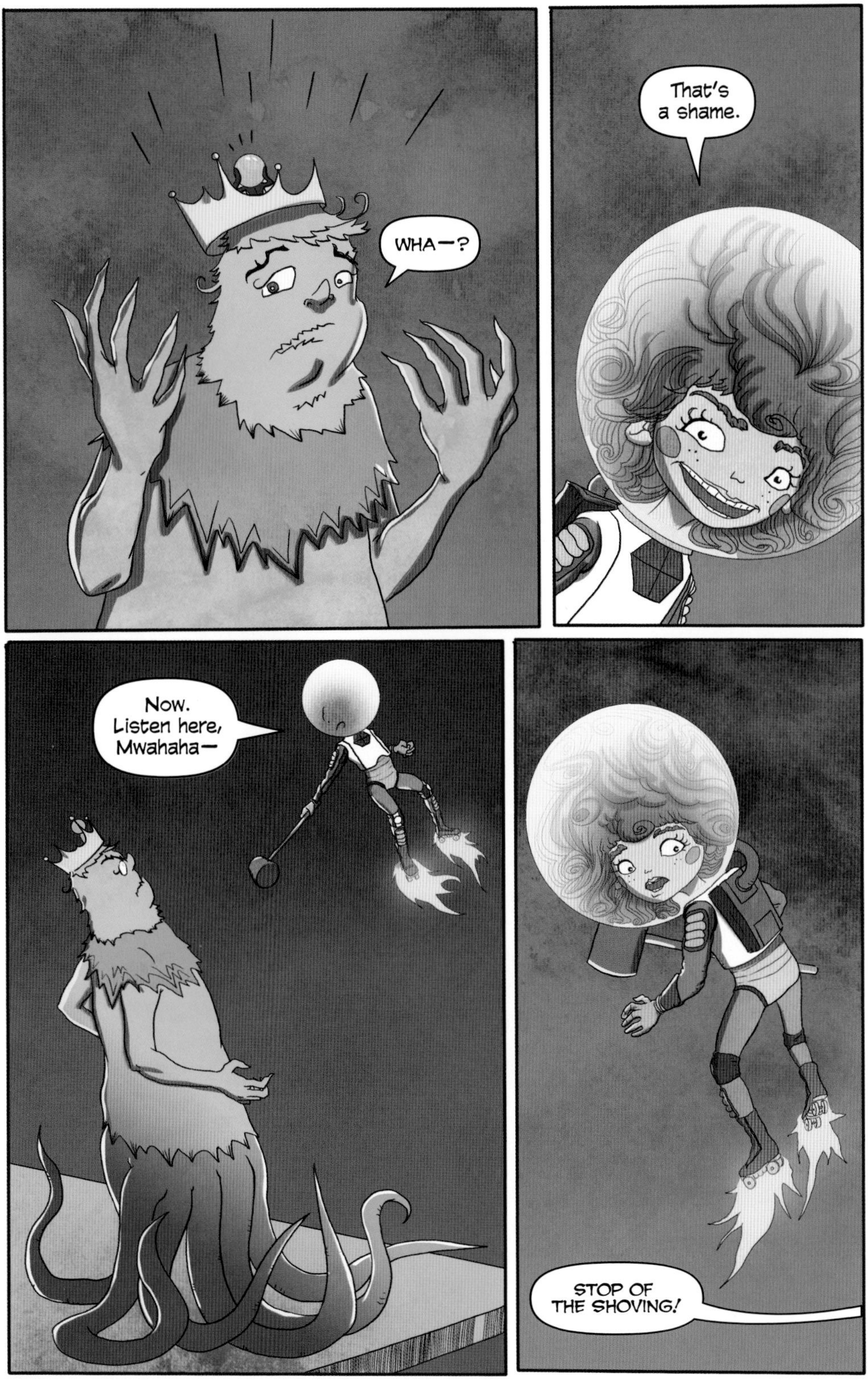
WHA—?
That's a shame.
Now. Listen here, Mwahaha—
STOP OF THE SHOVING!

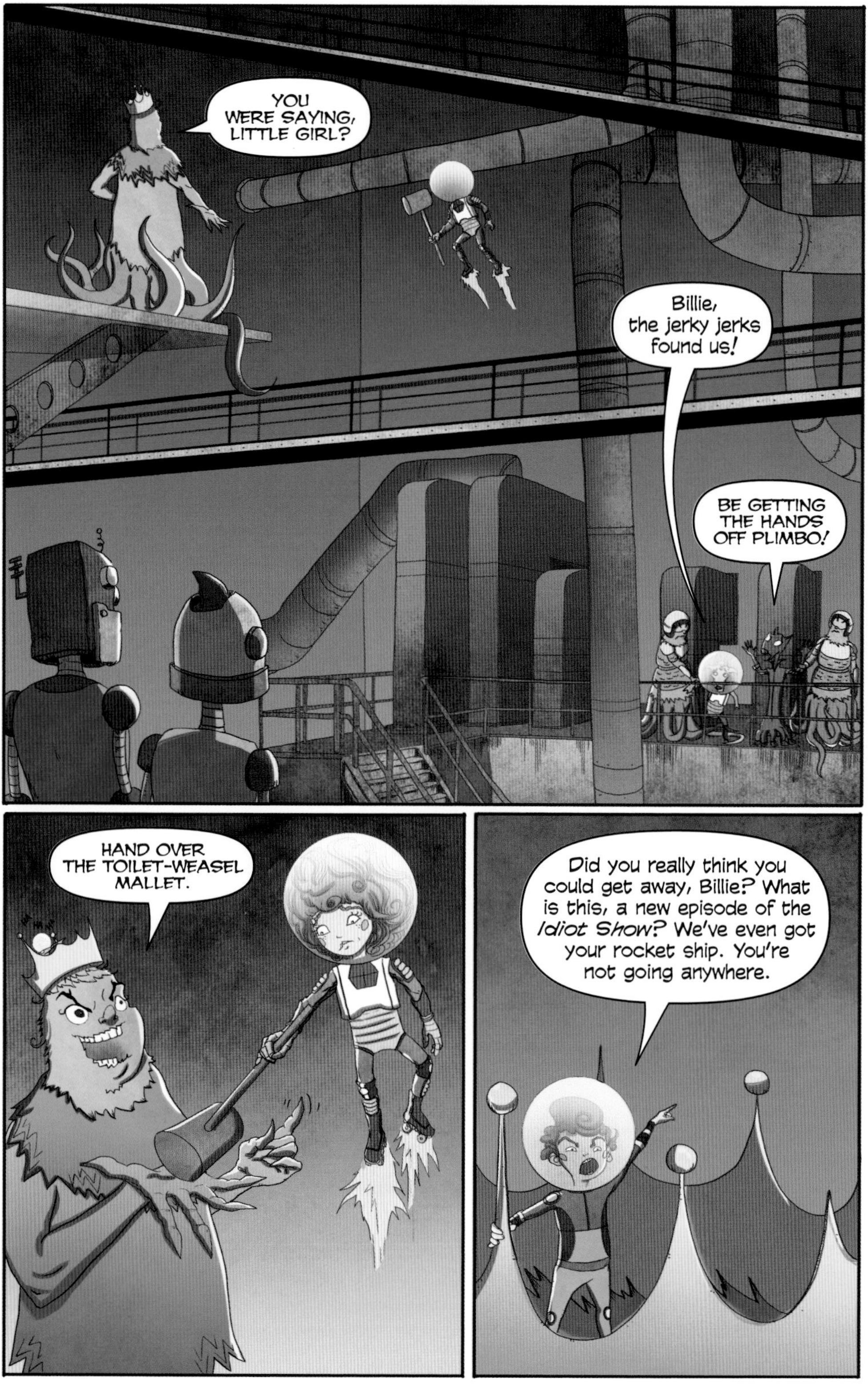
YOU WERE SAYING, LITTLE GIRL?
Billie, the jerky jerks found us!
BE GETTING THE HANDS OFF PLIMBO!
HAND OVER THE TOILET-WEASEL MALLET.
Did you really think you could get away, Billie? What is this, a new episode of the *Idiot Show*? We've even got your rocket ship. You're not going anywhere.

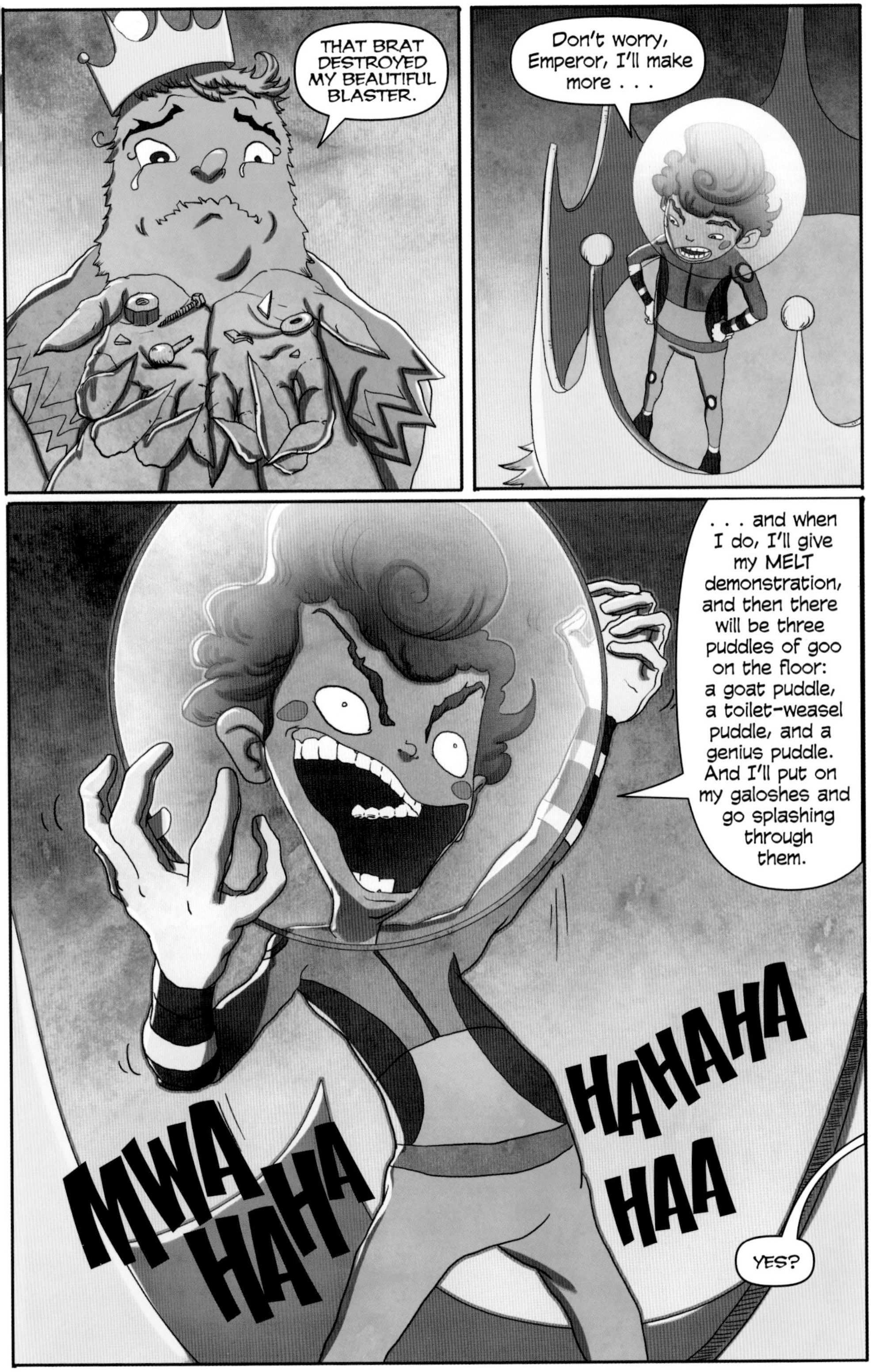
THAT BRAT DESTROYED MY BEAUTIFUL BLASTER.
Don't worry, Emperor, I'll make more . . .
. . . and when I do, I'll give my MELT demonstration, and then there will be three puddles of goo on the floor: a goat puddle, a toilet-weasel puddle, and a genius puddle. And I'll put on my galoshes and go splashing through them.
MWA HAHA HAHA
HAHAHA HAA
YES?

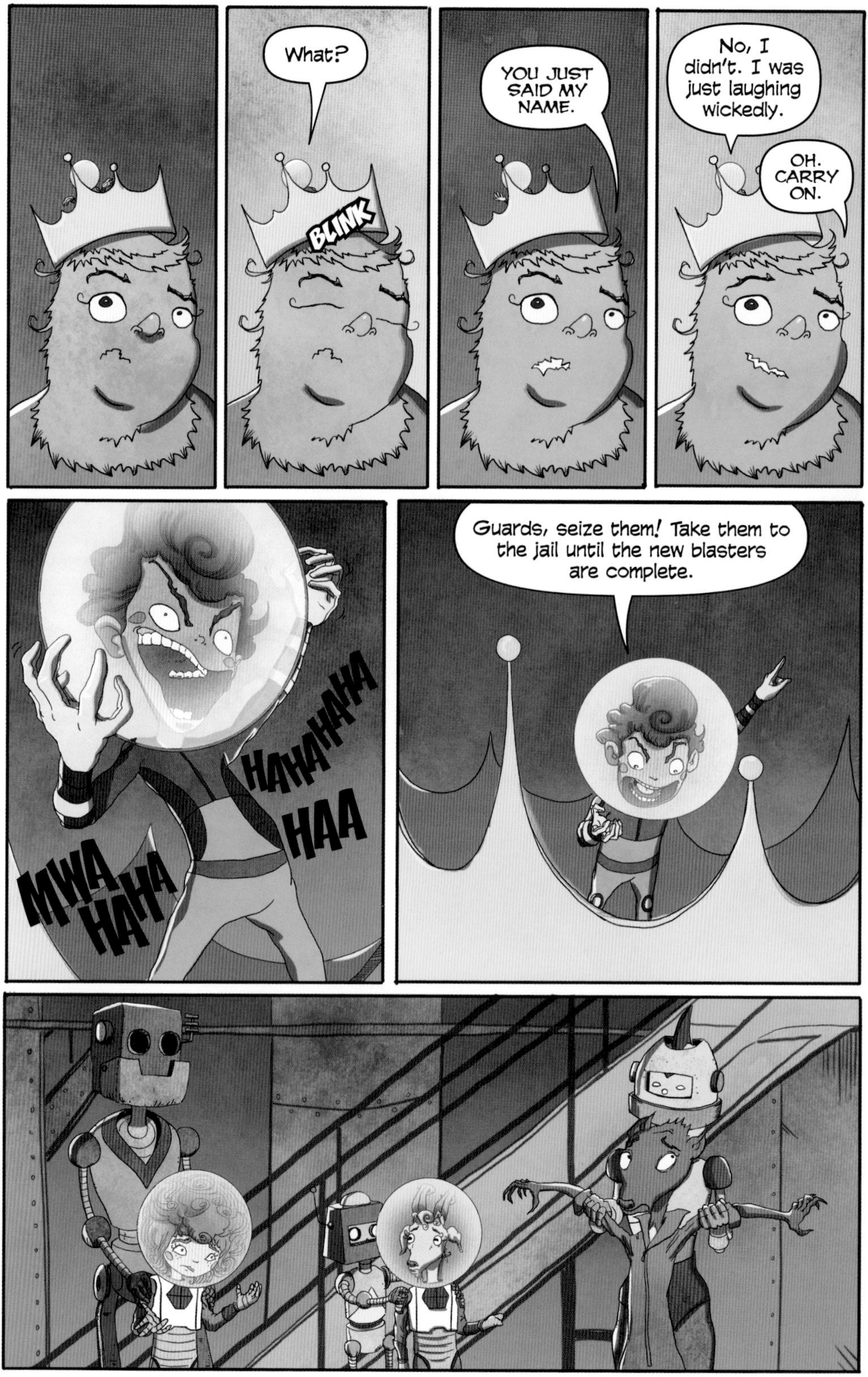
What?
BLINK
YOU JUST SAID MY NAME.
No, I didn't. I was just laughing wickedly.
OH. CARRY ON.
MWA HAHAHA
HAHAHAHA HAA
Guards, seize them! Take them to the jail until the new blasters are complete.

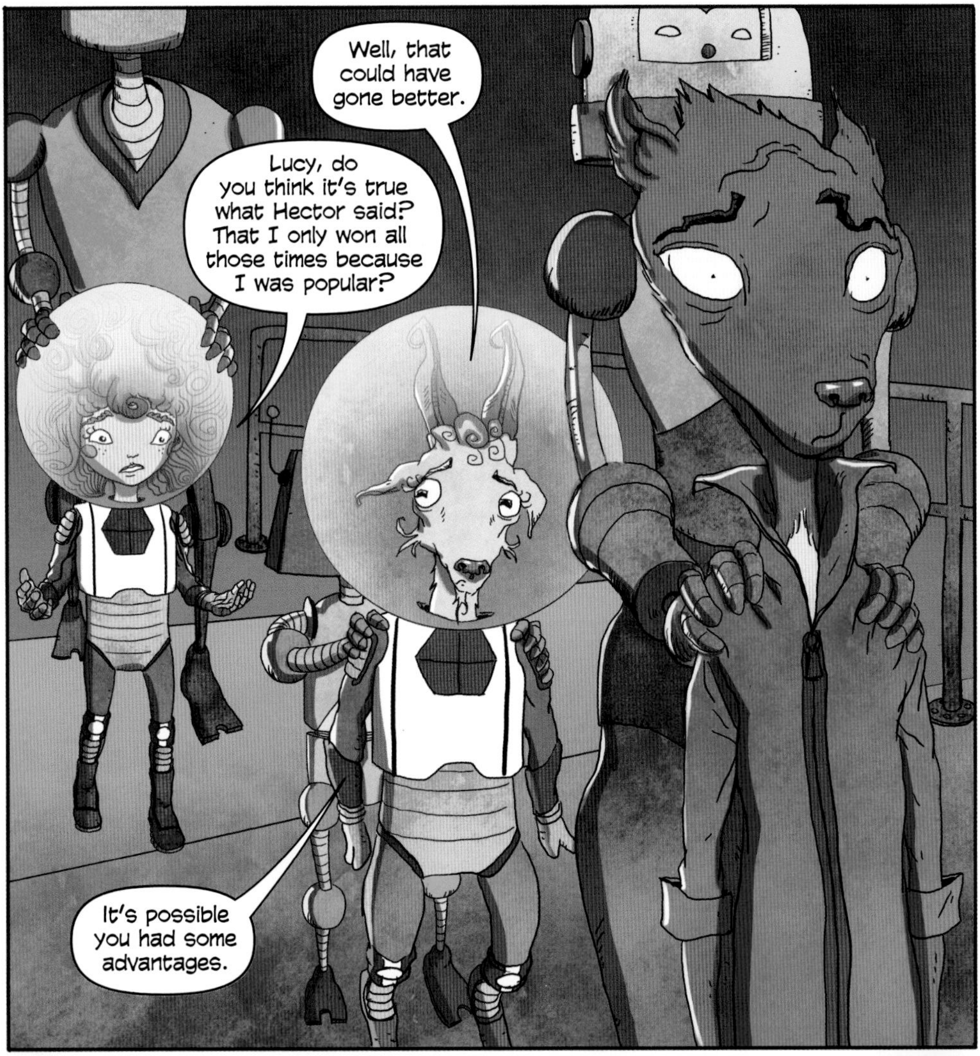
Well, that could have gone better.
Lucy, do you think it's true what Hector said? That I only won all those times because I was popular?
It's possible you had some advantages.

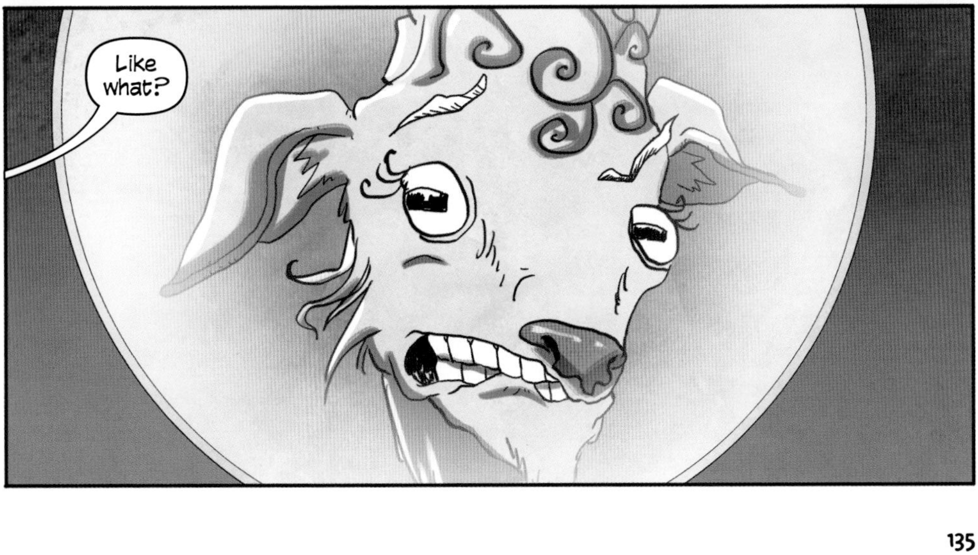
Like what?

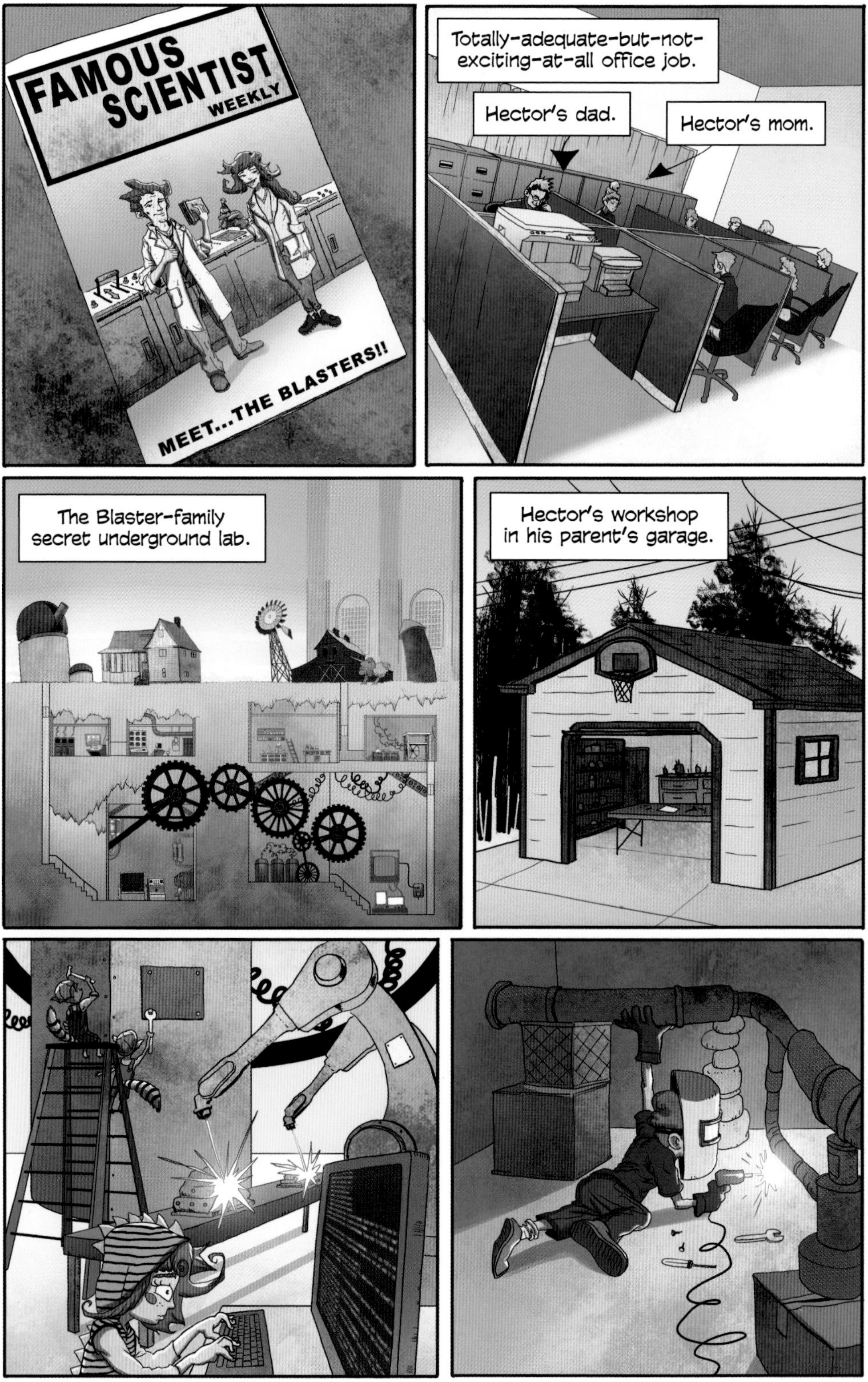
FAMOUS SCIENTIST WEEKLY
MEET...THE BLASTERS!!
Totally-adequate-but-not-exciting-at-all office job.
Hector's dad.
Hector's mom.
The Blaster-family secret underground lab.
Hector's workshop in his parent's garage.

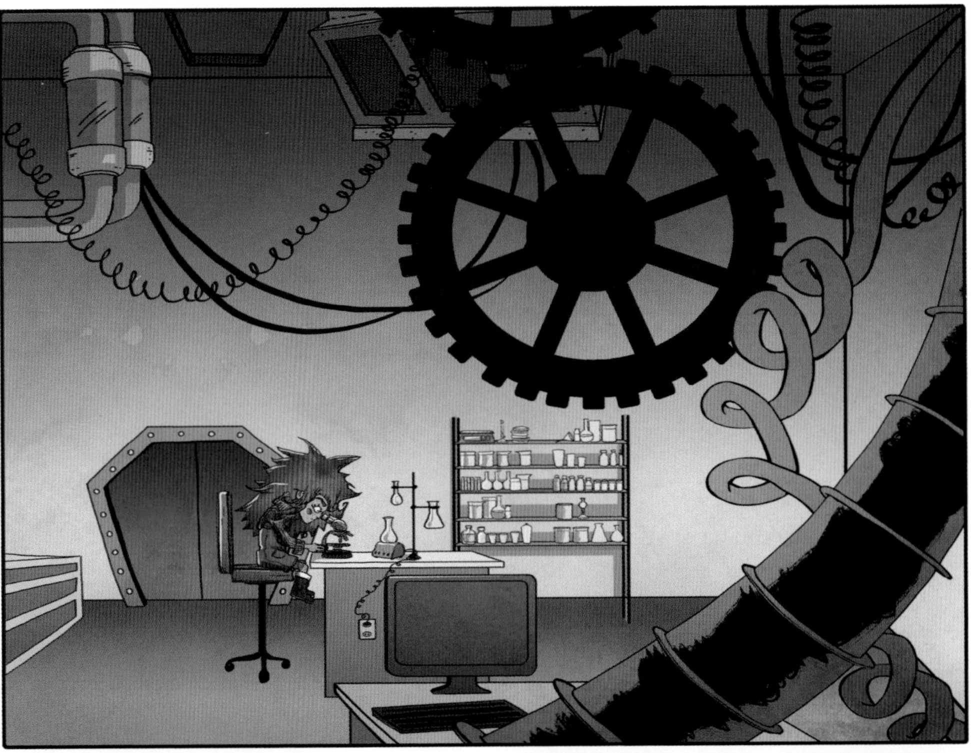

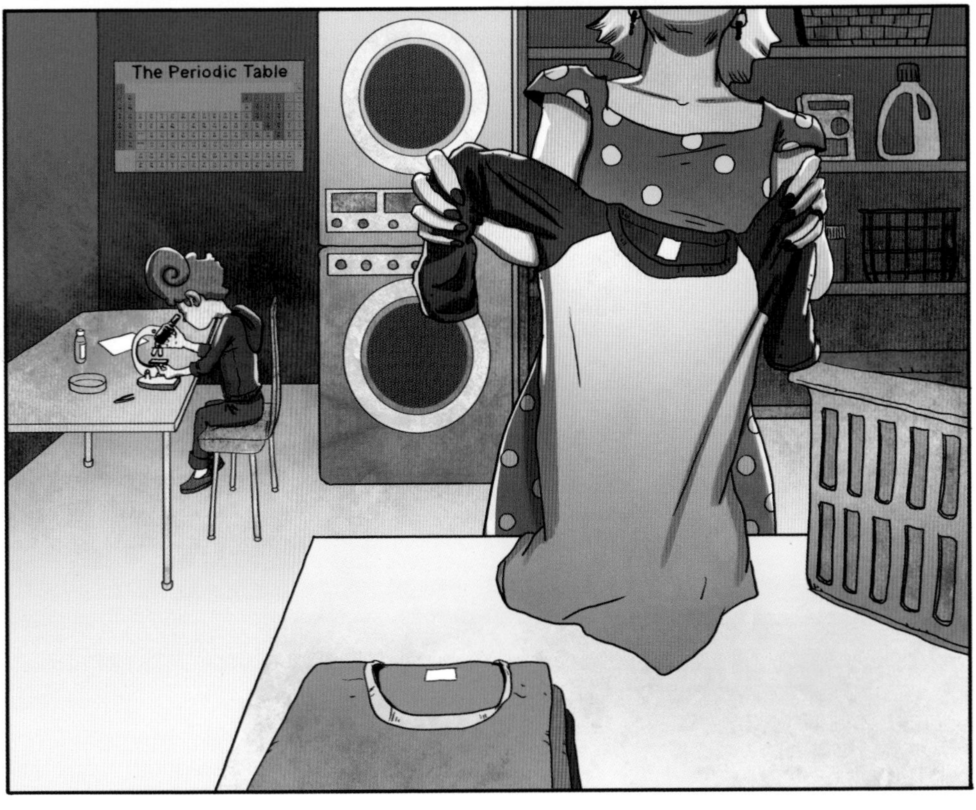
The Periodic Table

I'm a fraud. Lucy, what if Hector actually is smarter than me?
What if he is? Smart people can be pretty dumb. Look at your parents.
I mean, look at me. I may not be as smart as you, but I'm much wiser. Maybe it's how you use your intelligence that counts.
You mean like *not* on floating cheese puffs?
Floating cheese puffs are awesome. Don't let anyone tell you different. Endlessly replicating robots? Not so much.

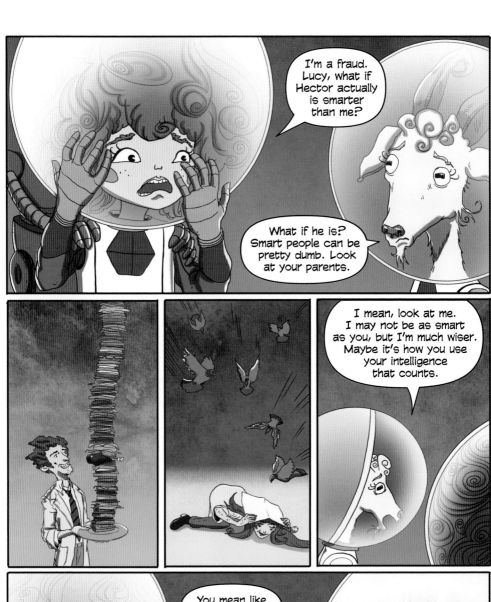

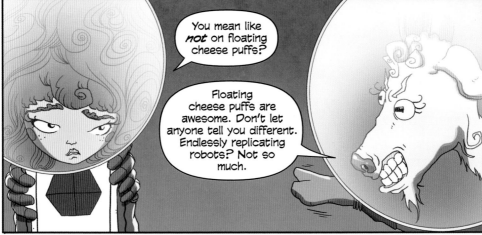

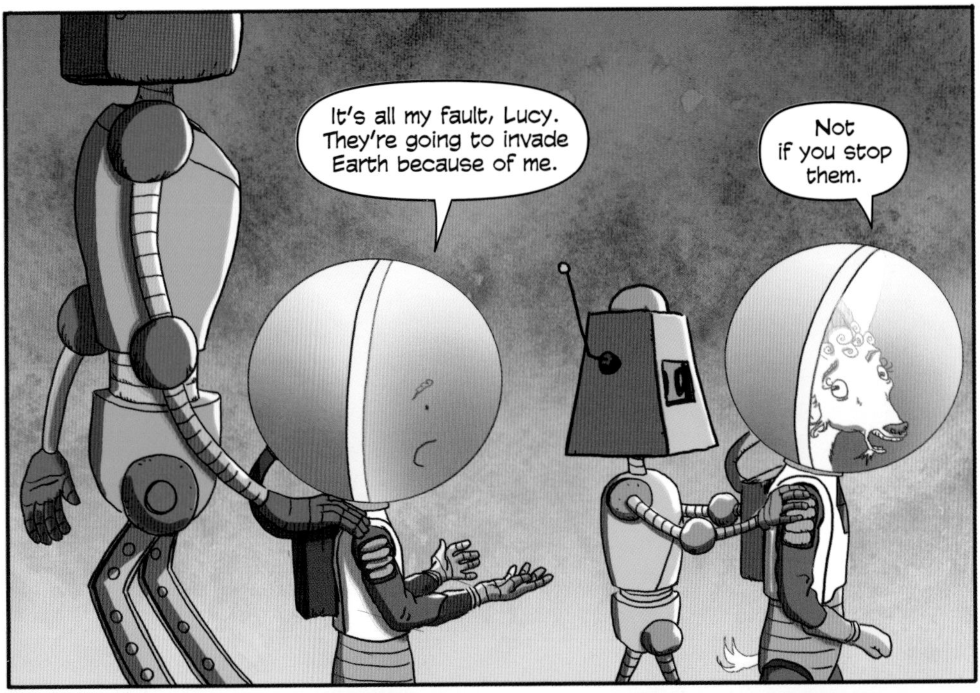
It's all my fault, Lucy. They're going to invade Earth because of me.
Not if you stop them.

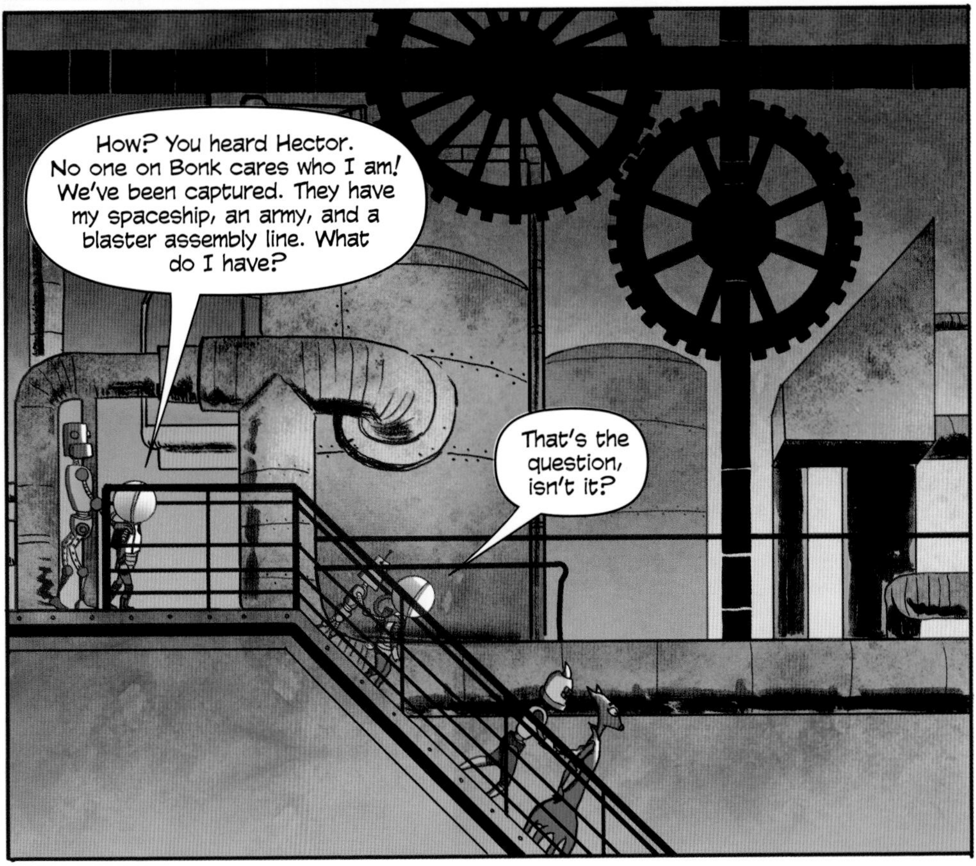
How? You heard Hector. No one on Bonk cares who I am! We've been captured. They have my spaceship, an army, and a blaster assembly line. What do I have?
That's the question, isn't it?

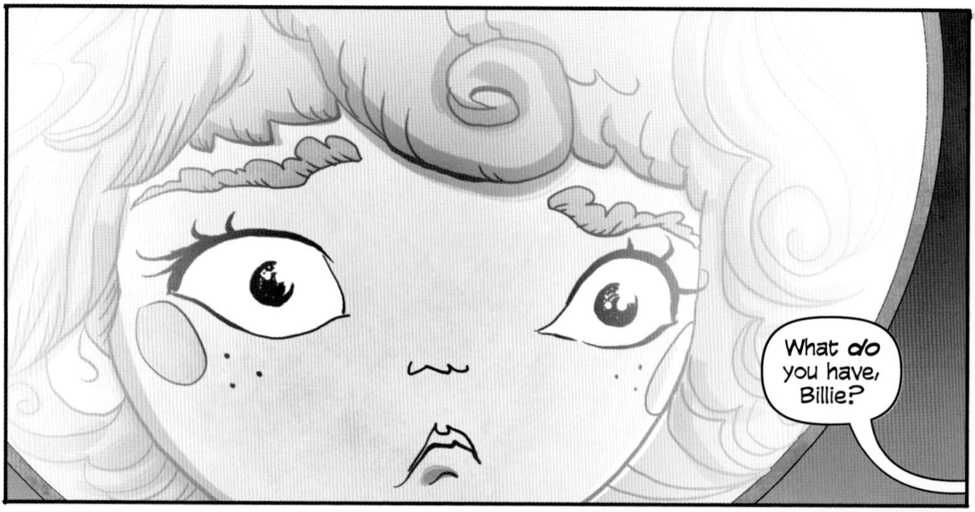
What do you have, Billie?

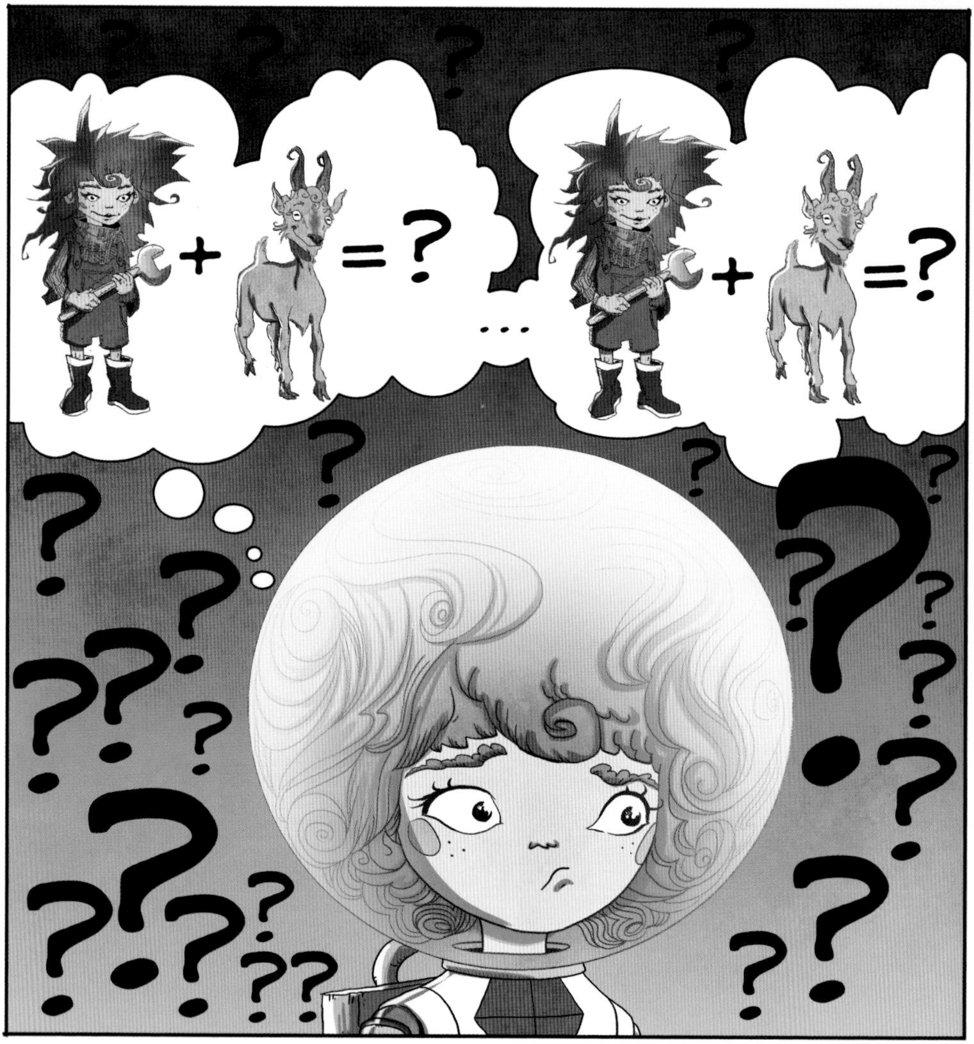
+ =?
...
+ =?

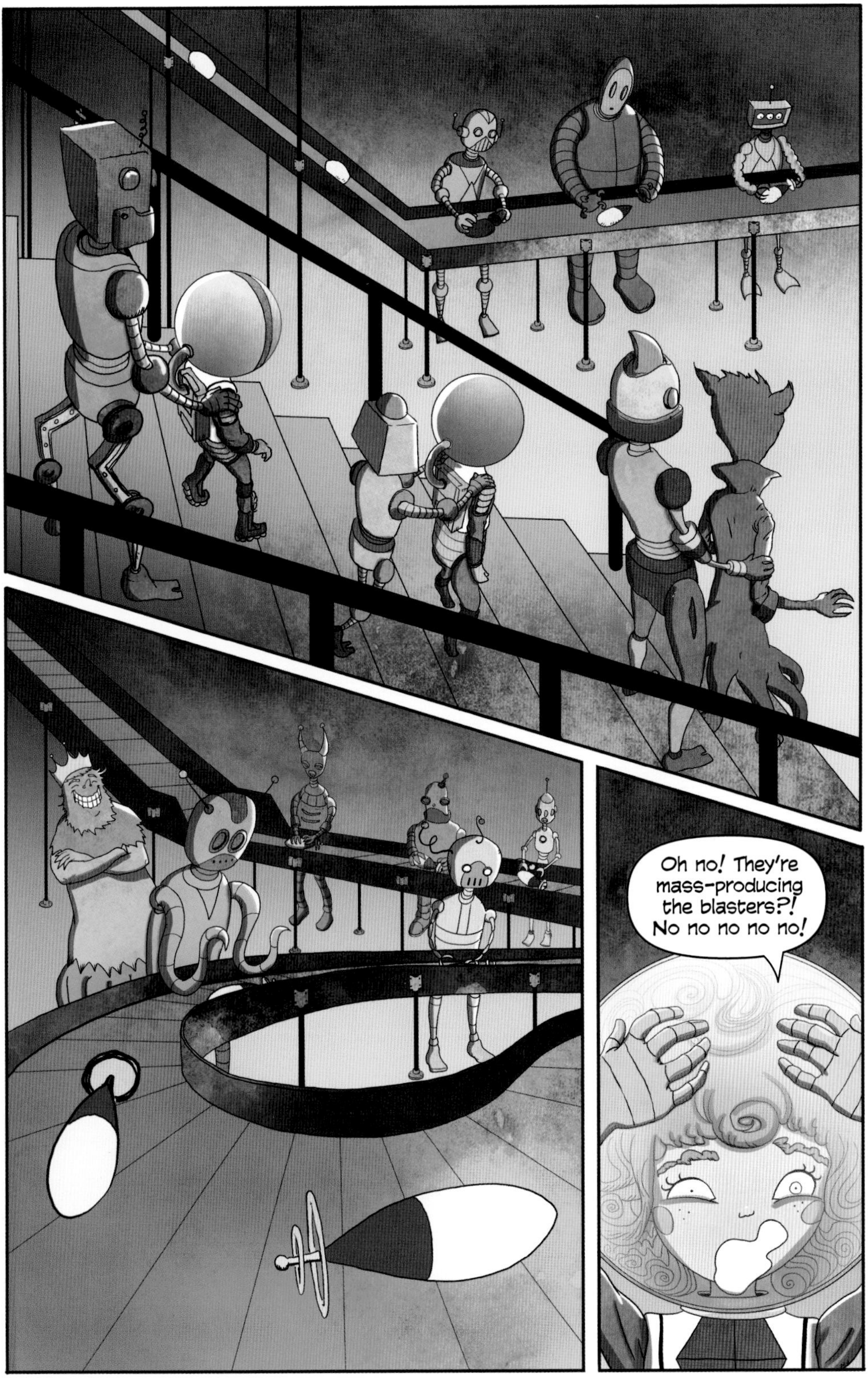
Oh no! They're mass-producing the blasters?! No no no no no!

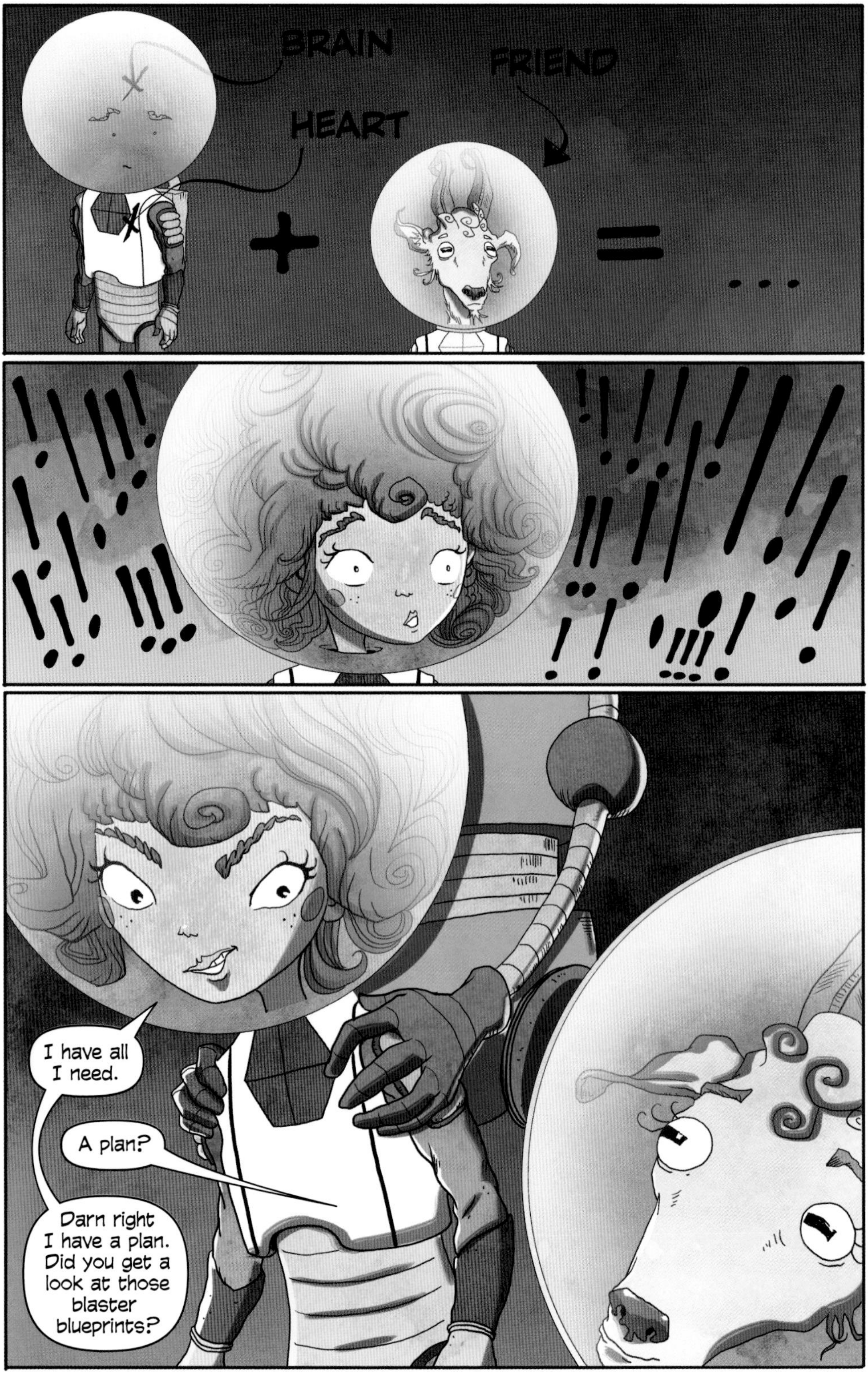
BRAIN
HEART
FRIEND
+
=
...
I have all I need.
A plan?
Darn right I have a plan. Did you get a look at those blaster blueprints?

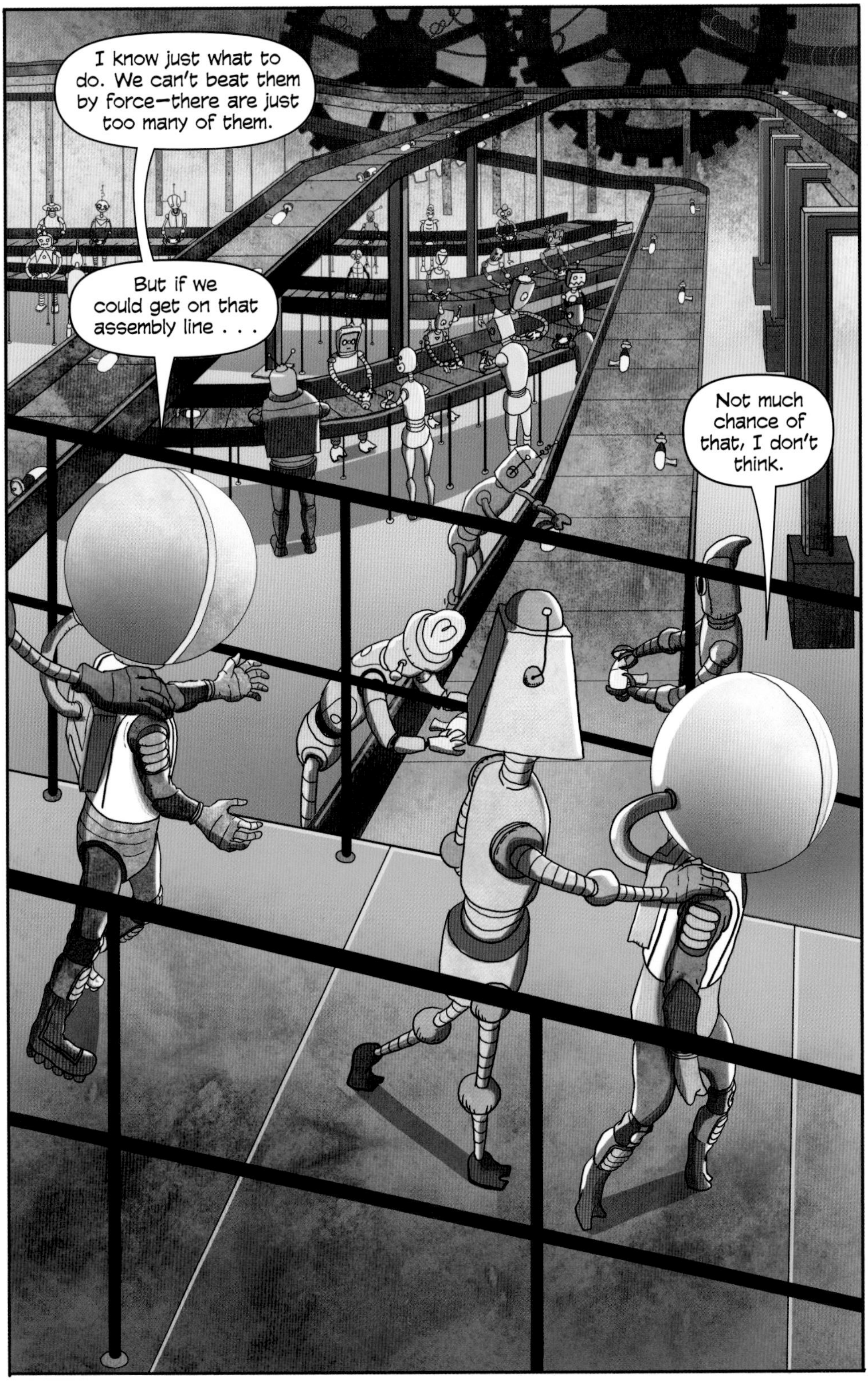
I know just what to do. We can't beat them by force—there are just too many of them.
But if we could get on that assembly line . . .
Not much chance of that, I don't think.

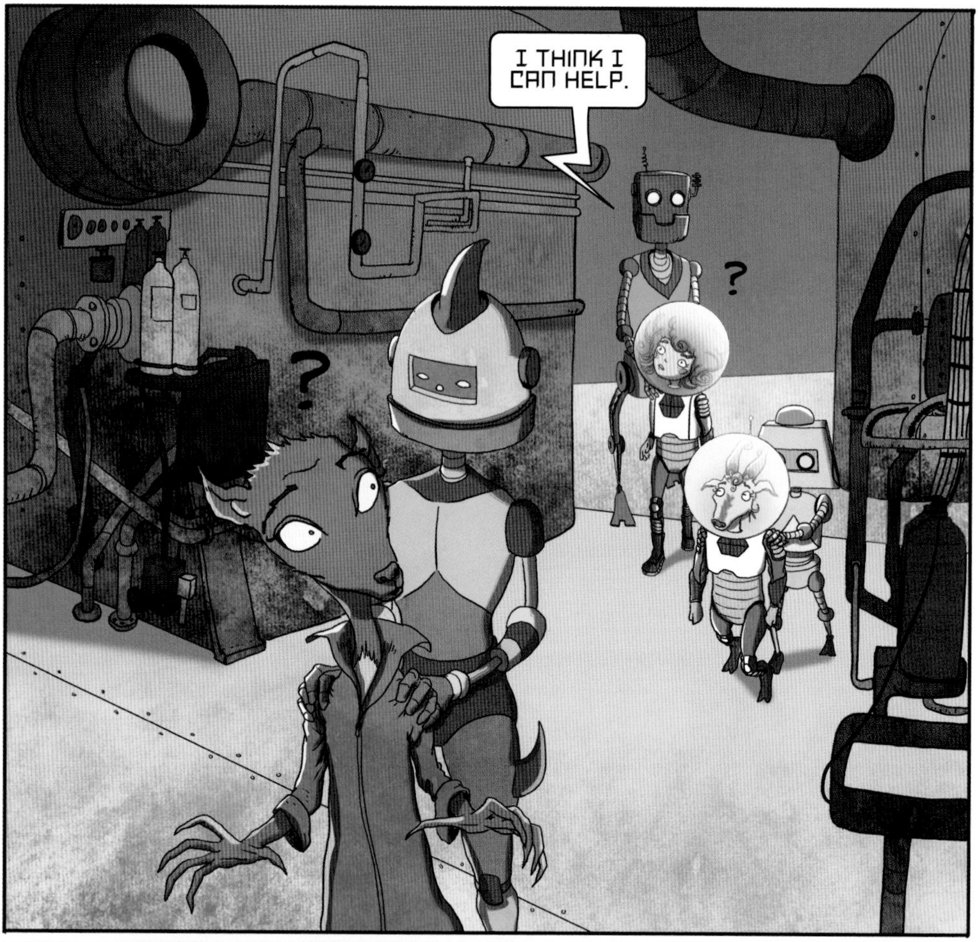
I THINK I CAN HELP.
?
?

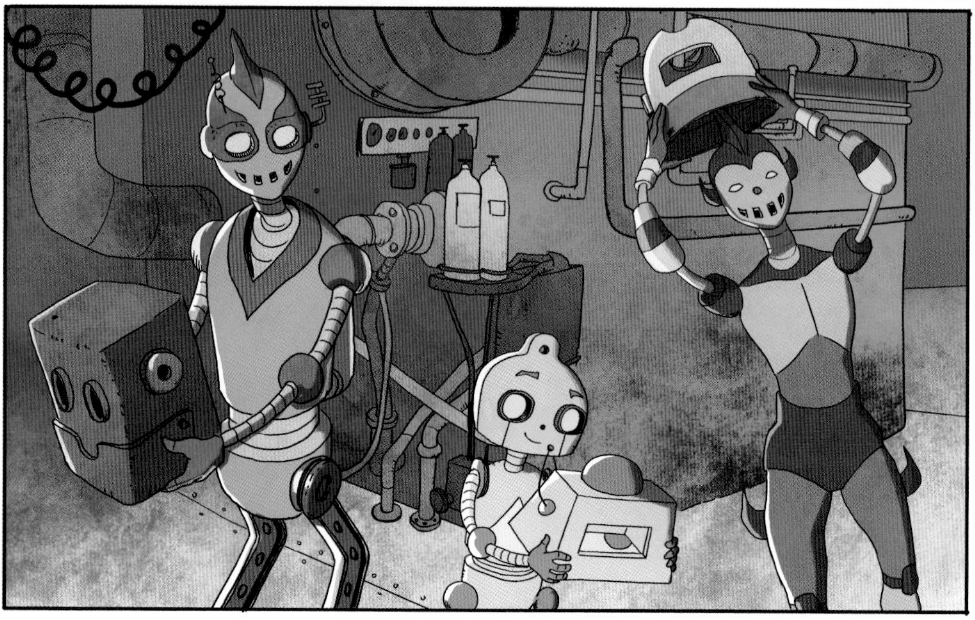

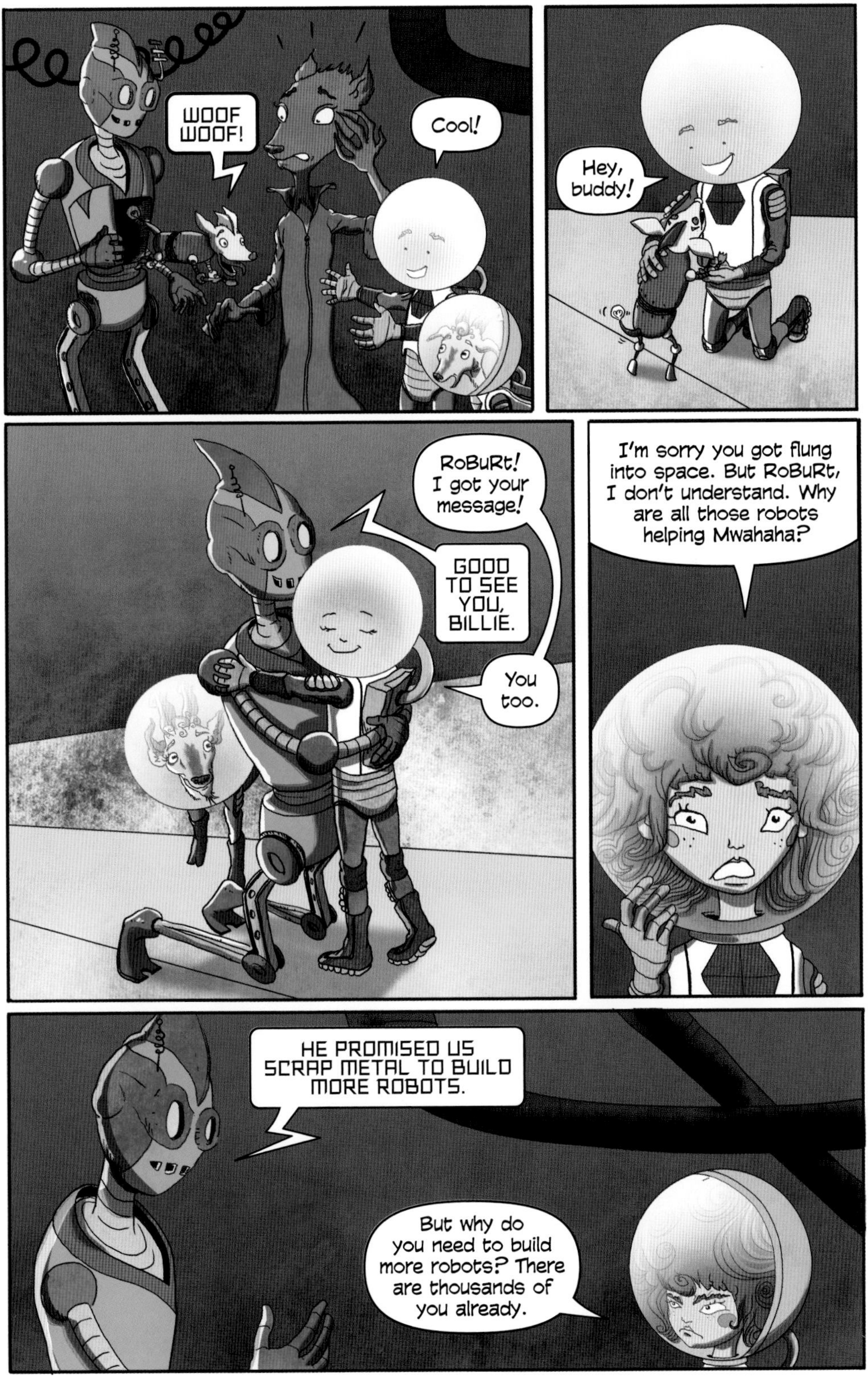
WOOF WOOF!
Cool!
Hey, buddy!
RoBuRt! I got your message!
GOOD TO SEE YOU, BILLIE.
You too.
I'm sorry you got flung into space. But RoBuRt, I don't understand. Why are all those robots helping Mwahaha?
HE PROMISED US SCRAP METAL TO BUILD MORE ROBOTS.
But why do you need to build more robots? There are thousands of you already.

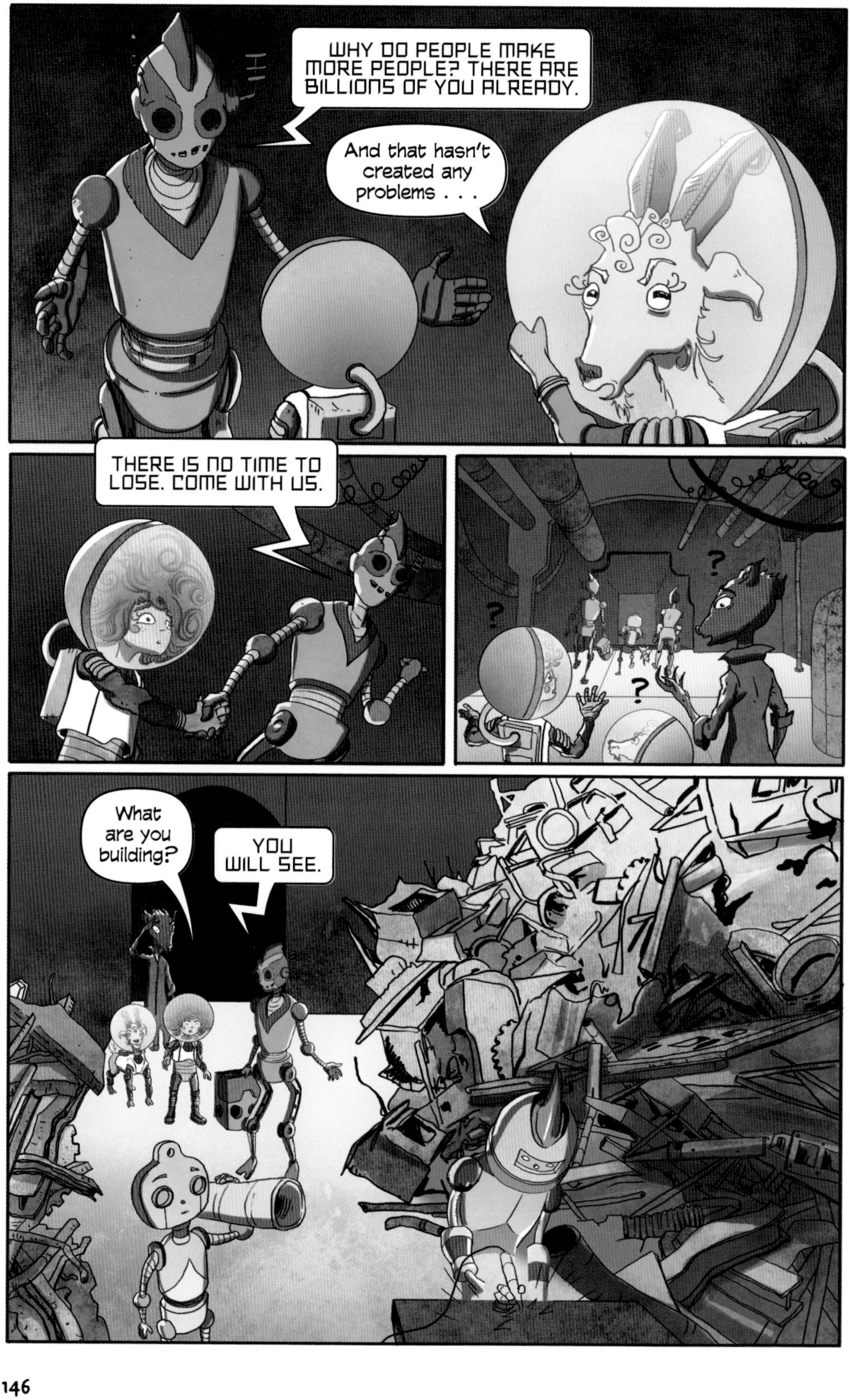
WHY DO PEOPLE MAKE MORE PEOPLE? THERE ARE BILLIONS OF YOU ALREADY.
And that hasn't created any problems . . .
THERE IS NO TIME TO LOSE. COME WITH US.
?
?
?
What are you building?
YOU WILL SEE.

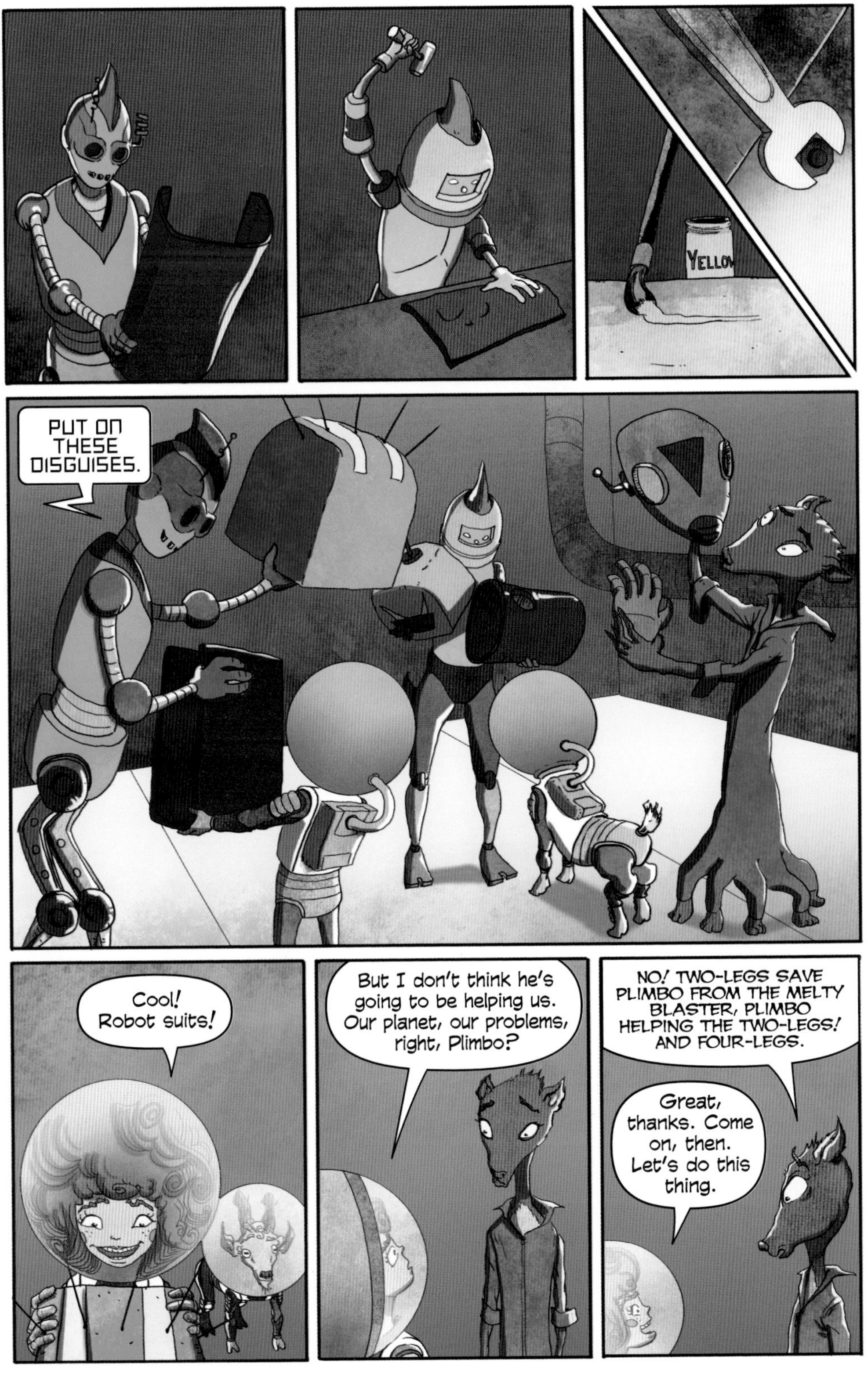
YELLOW
PUT ON THESE DISGUISES.
Cool! Robot suits!
But I don't think he's going to be helping us. Our planet, our problems, right, Plimbo?
NO! TWO-LEGS SAVE PLIMBO FROM THE MELTY BLASTER, PLIMBO HELPING THE TWO-LEGS! AND FOUR-LEGS.
Great, thanks. Come on, then. Let's do this thing.

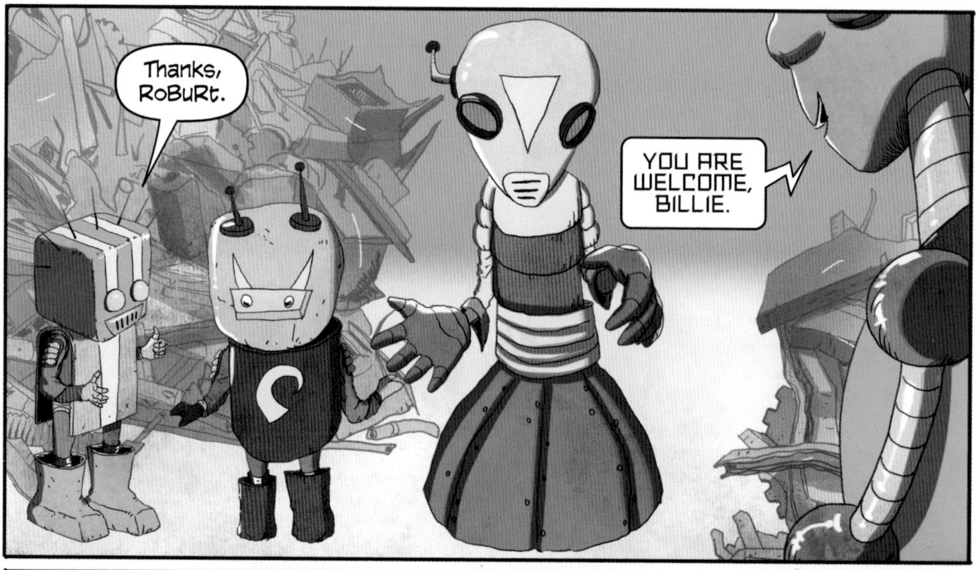
Thanks, RoBuRt.
YOU ARE WELCOME, BILLIE.

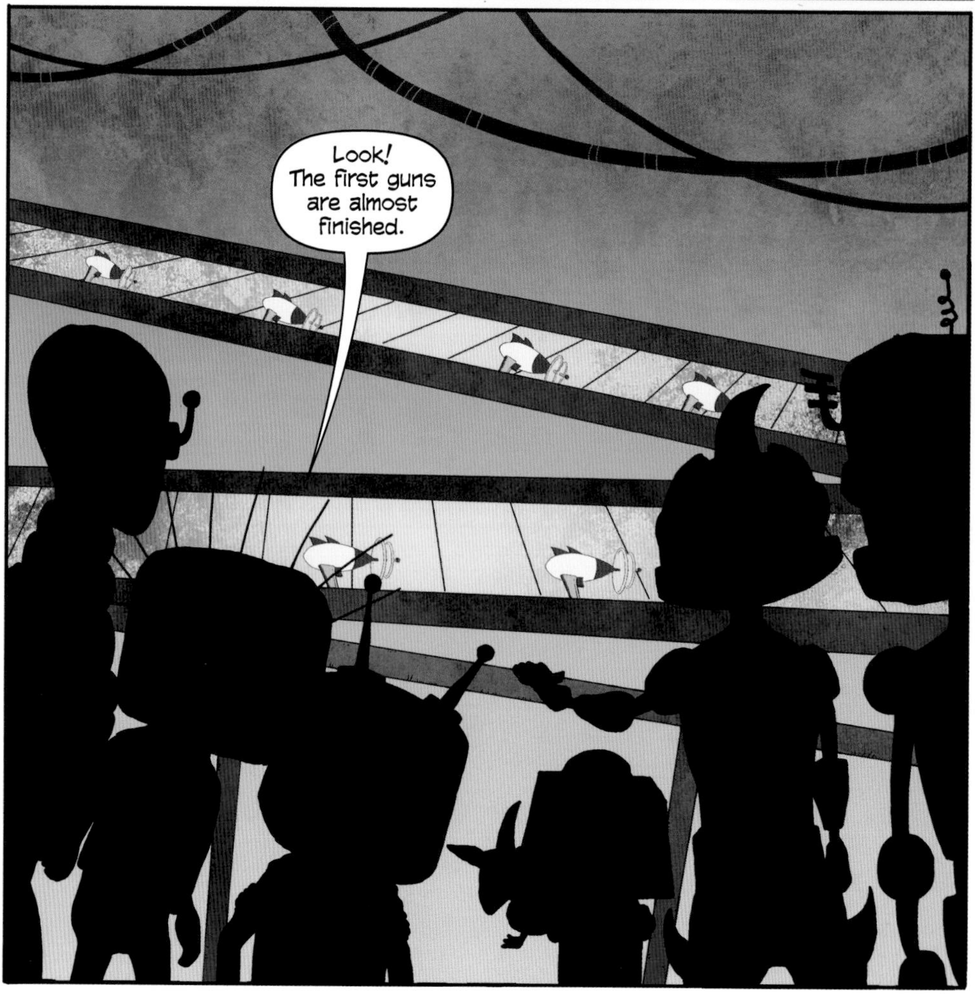
Look! The first guns are almost finished.

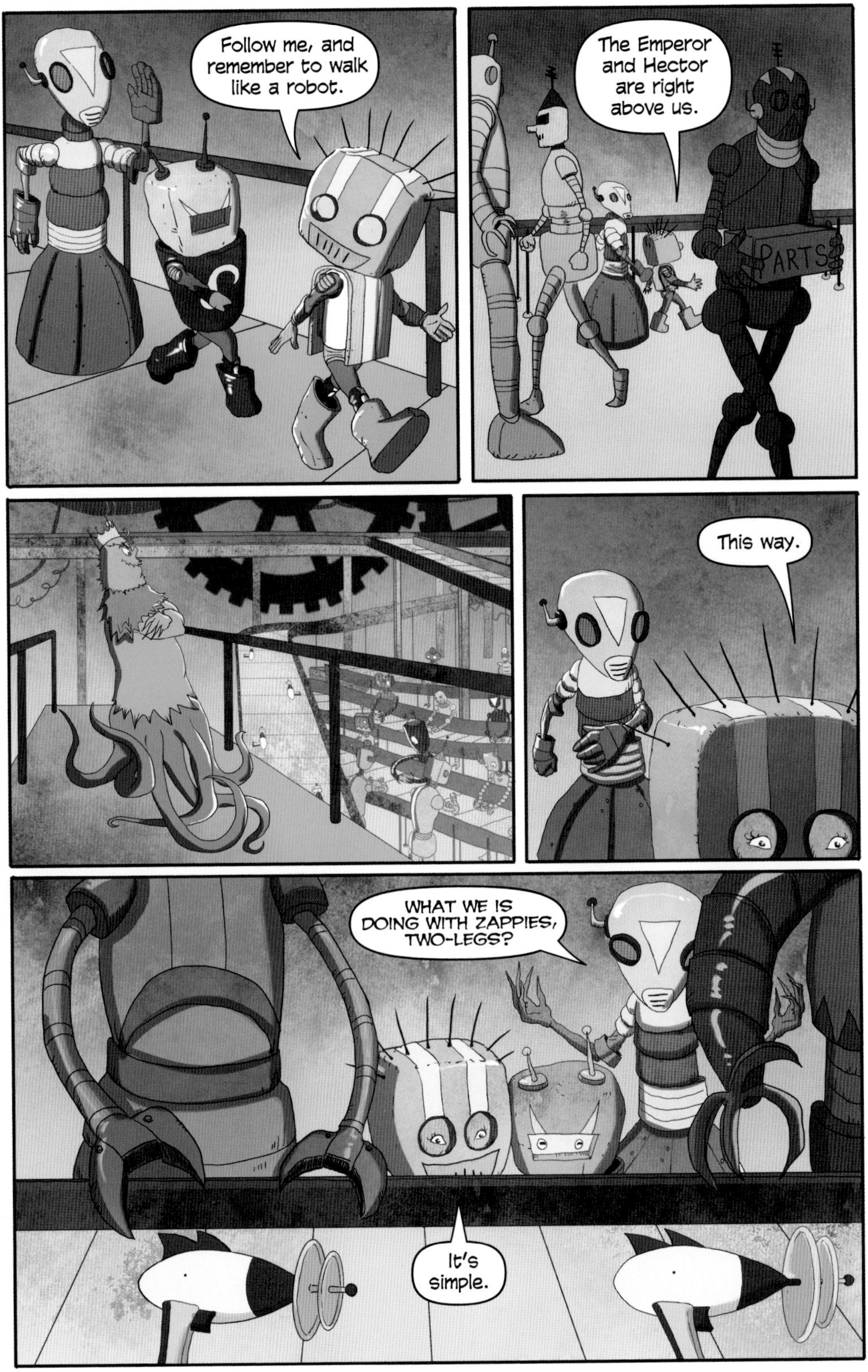

Follow me, and remember to walk like a robot.
The Emperor and Hector are right above us.
PARTS
This way.
WHAT WE IS DOING WITH ZAPPIES, TWO-LEGS?
It's simple.

We need to reverse the radioactive toggle-widgets and disable the incremental zap accelerators, then twist the gyro wires together and invert the spastic modular kerfuffle.

PSHUH. **SIMPLE,** SHE SAY!

Liiiike . . .

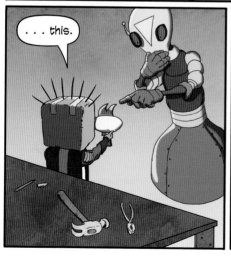

. . . this.

YES. ME LOVE IT. YOU CAN'T SEE THE PLIMBO, BUT HE IS TRYING NOT TO LAUGH.

LET'S SNEAK ONTO THE VERY END OF THE ASSEMBLY LINE AND GET TO WORK.

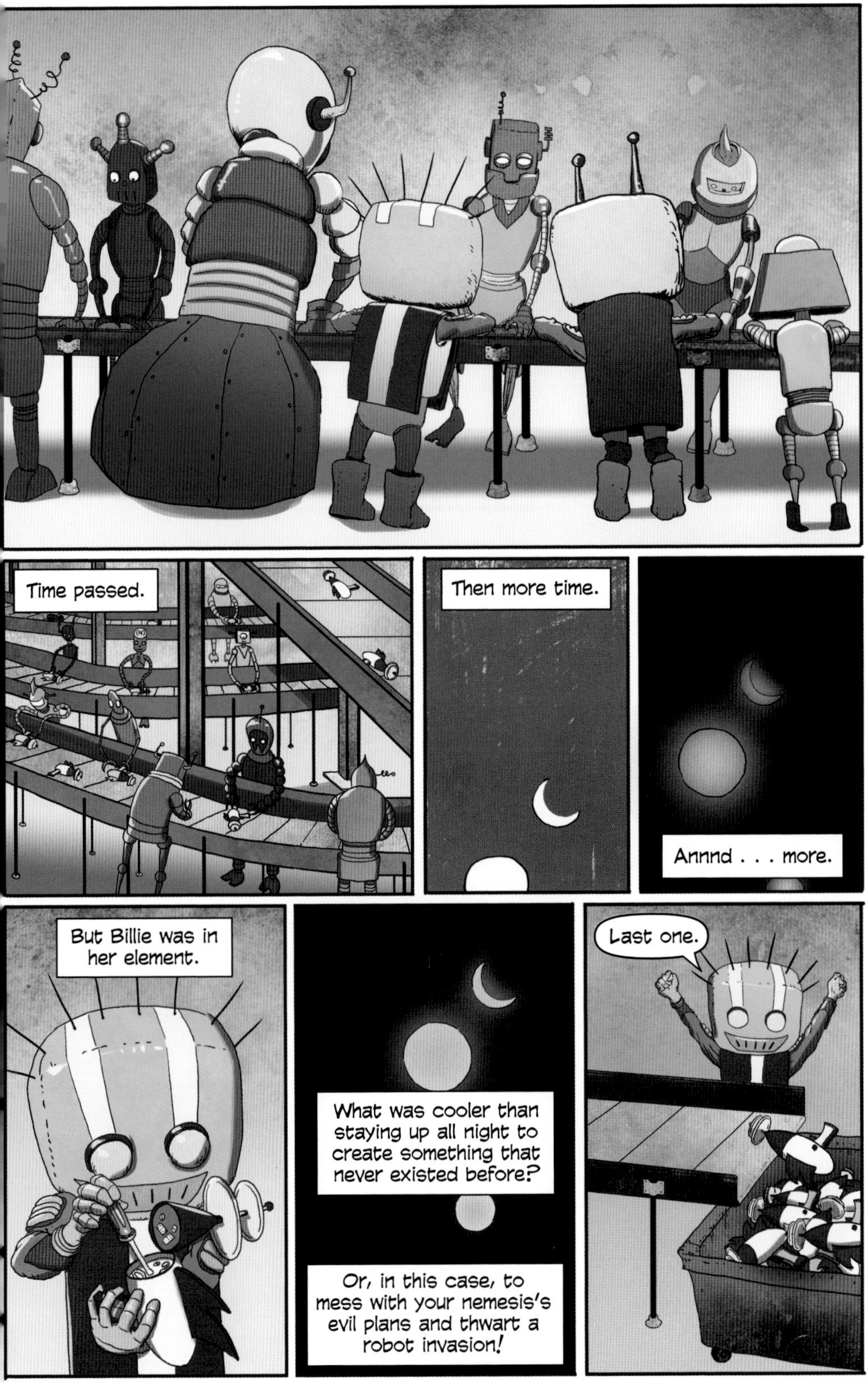
Time passed.
Then more time.
Annnd . . . more.
But Billie was in her element.
What was cooler than staying up all night to create something that never existed before?
Or, in this case, to mess with your nemesis's evil plans and thwart a robot invasion!
Last one.

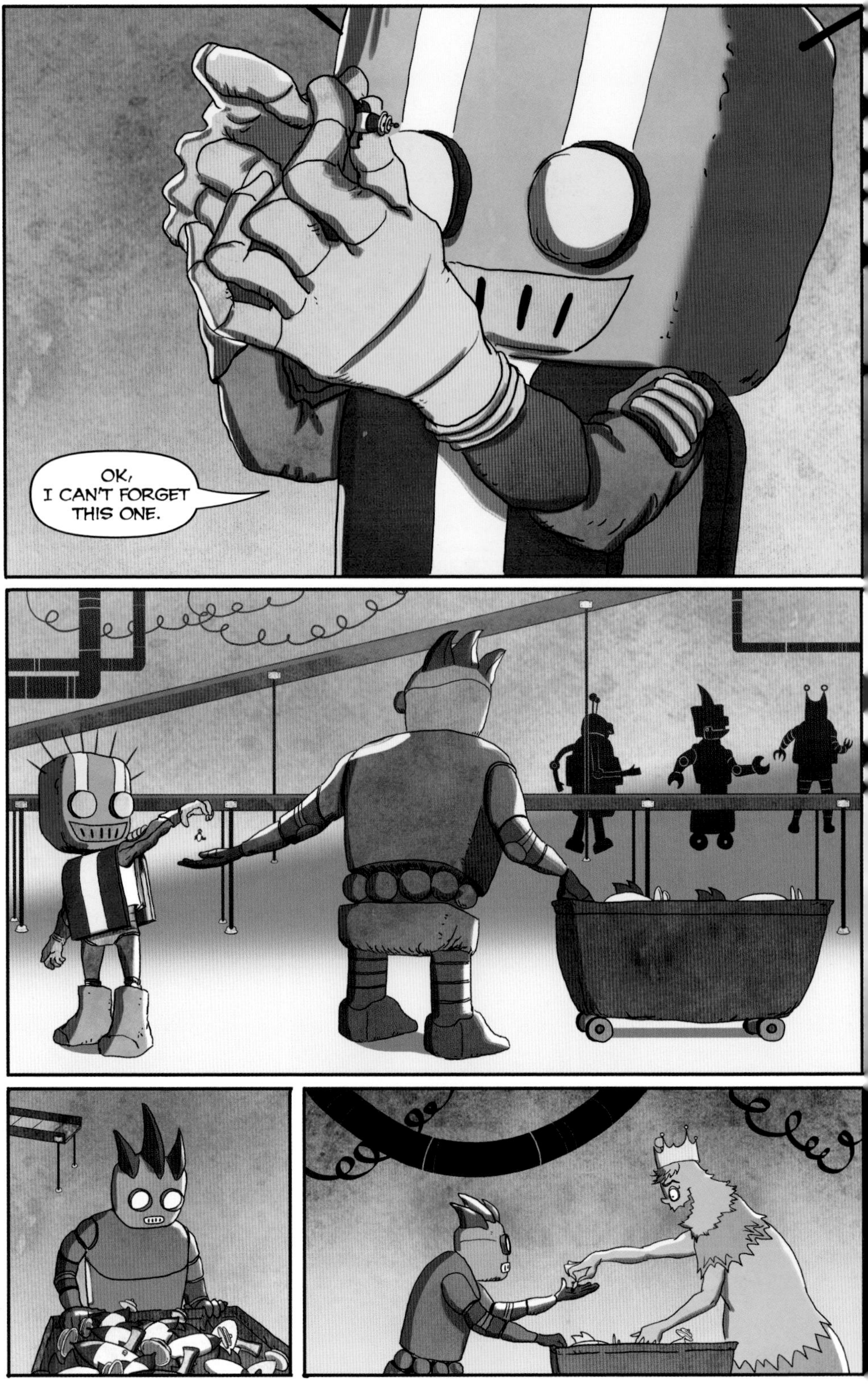
OK,
I CAN'T FORGET
THIS ONE.

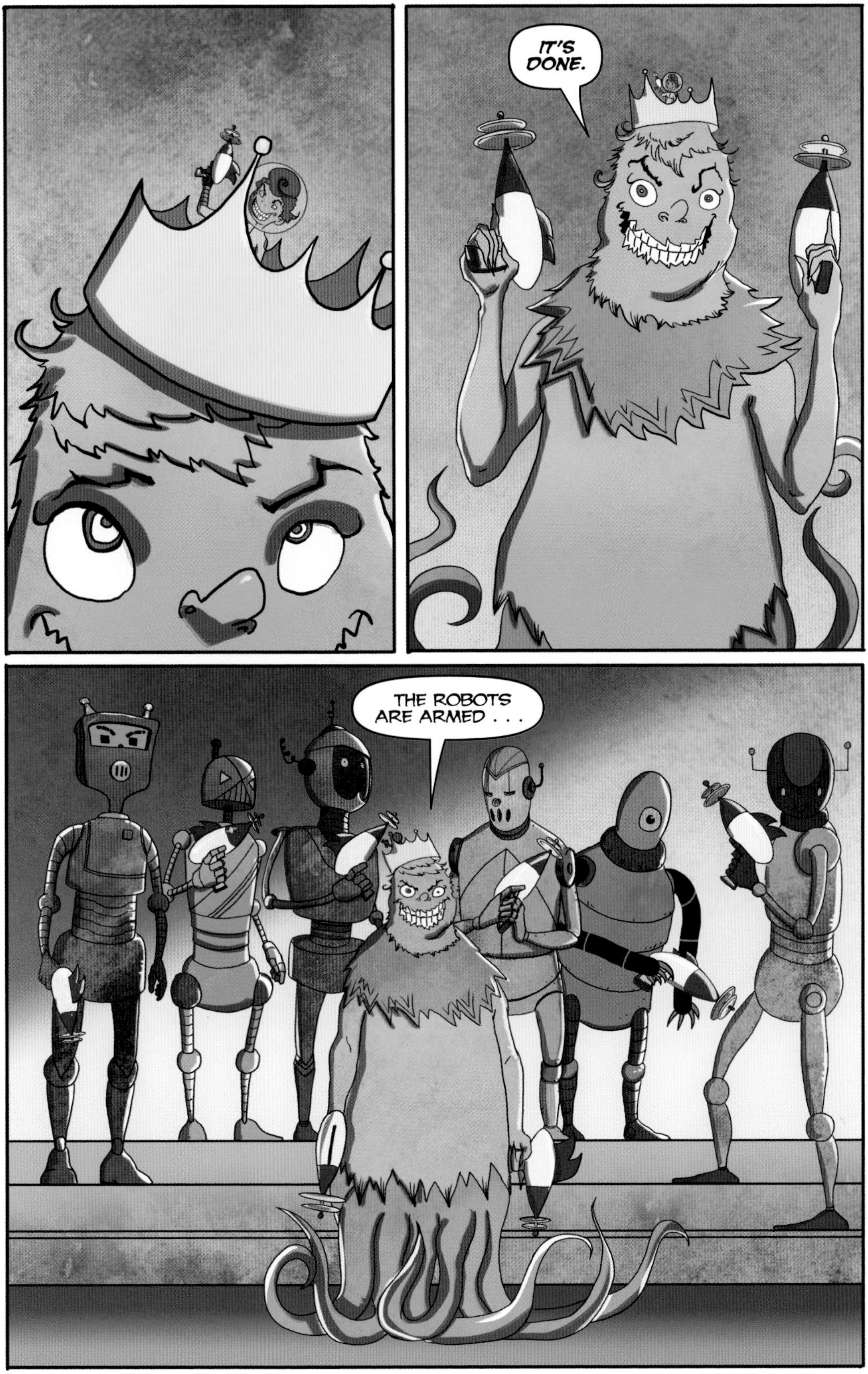
IT'S DONE.
THE ROBOTS ARE ARMED . . .

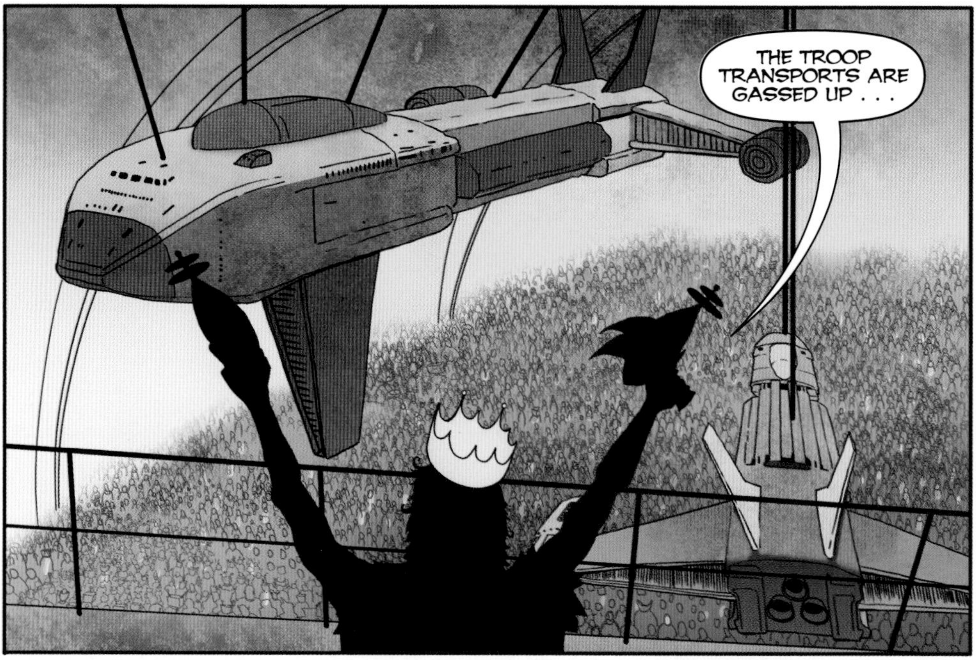
THE TROOP TRANSPORTS ARE GASSED UP . . .

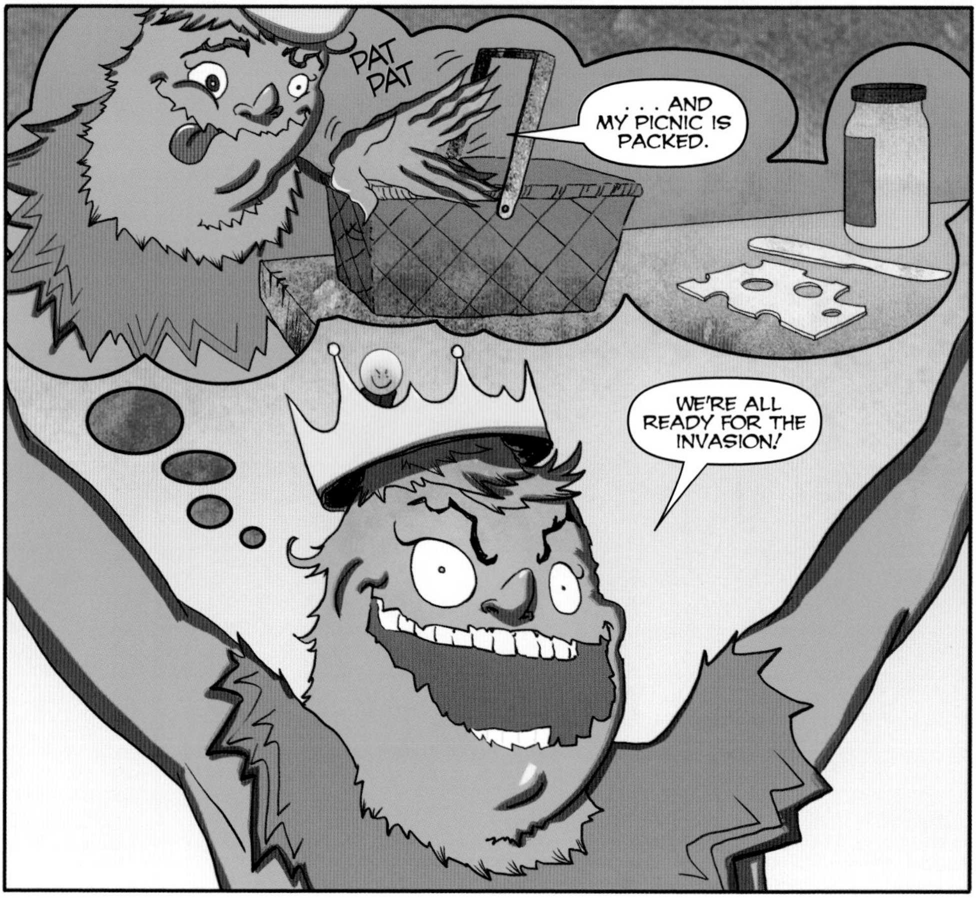
PAT PAT
. . . AND MY PICNIC IS PACKED.
WE'RE ALL READY FOR THE INVASION!

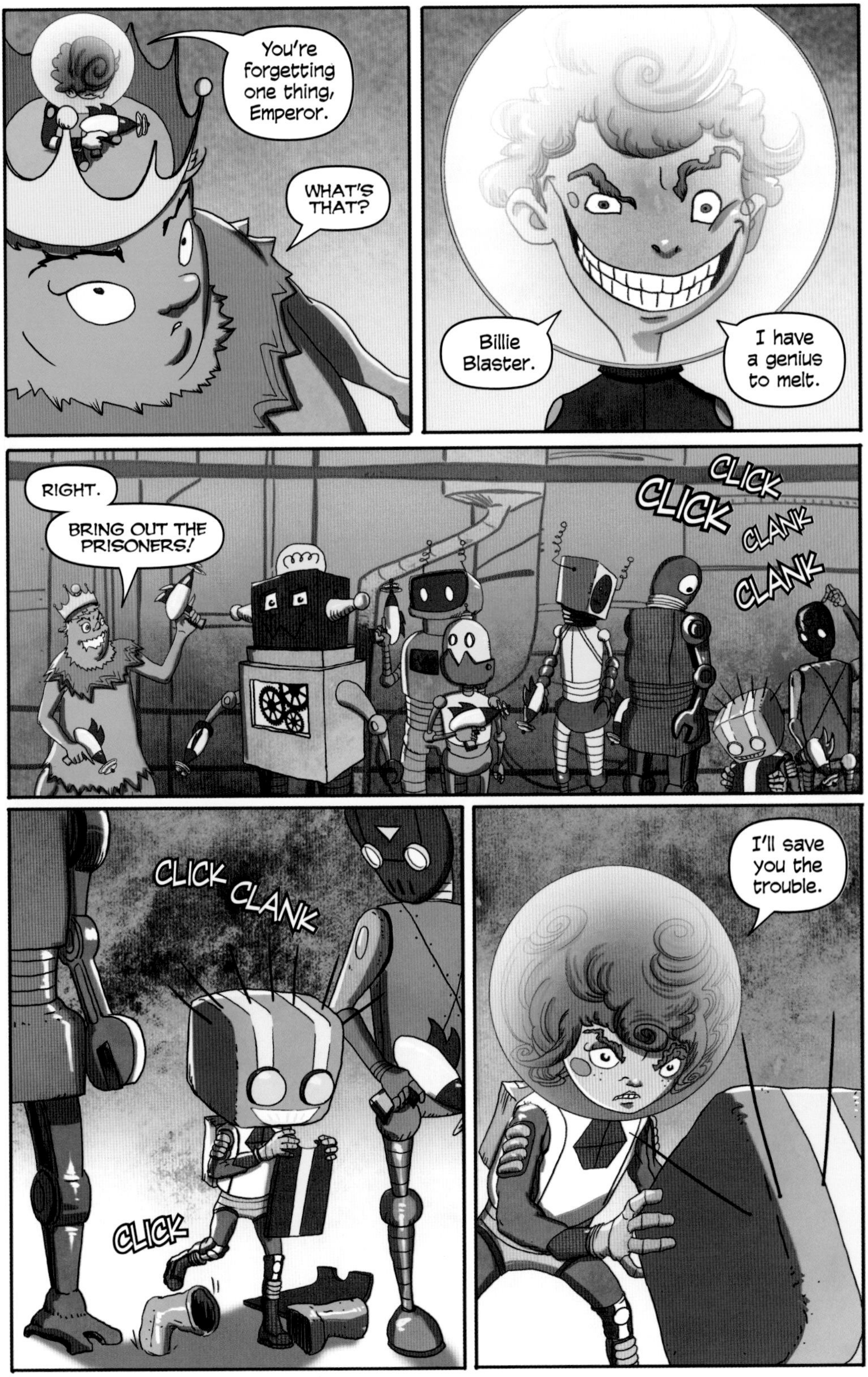
You're forgetting one thing, Emperor.
WHAT'S THAT?
Billie Blaster.
I have a genius to melt.
RIGHT.
BRING OUT THE PRISONERS!
CLICK
CLICK
CLANK
CLANK
CLICK
CLANK
CLICK
I'll save you the trouble.

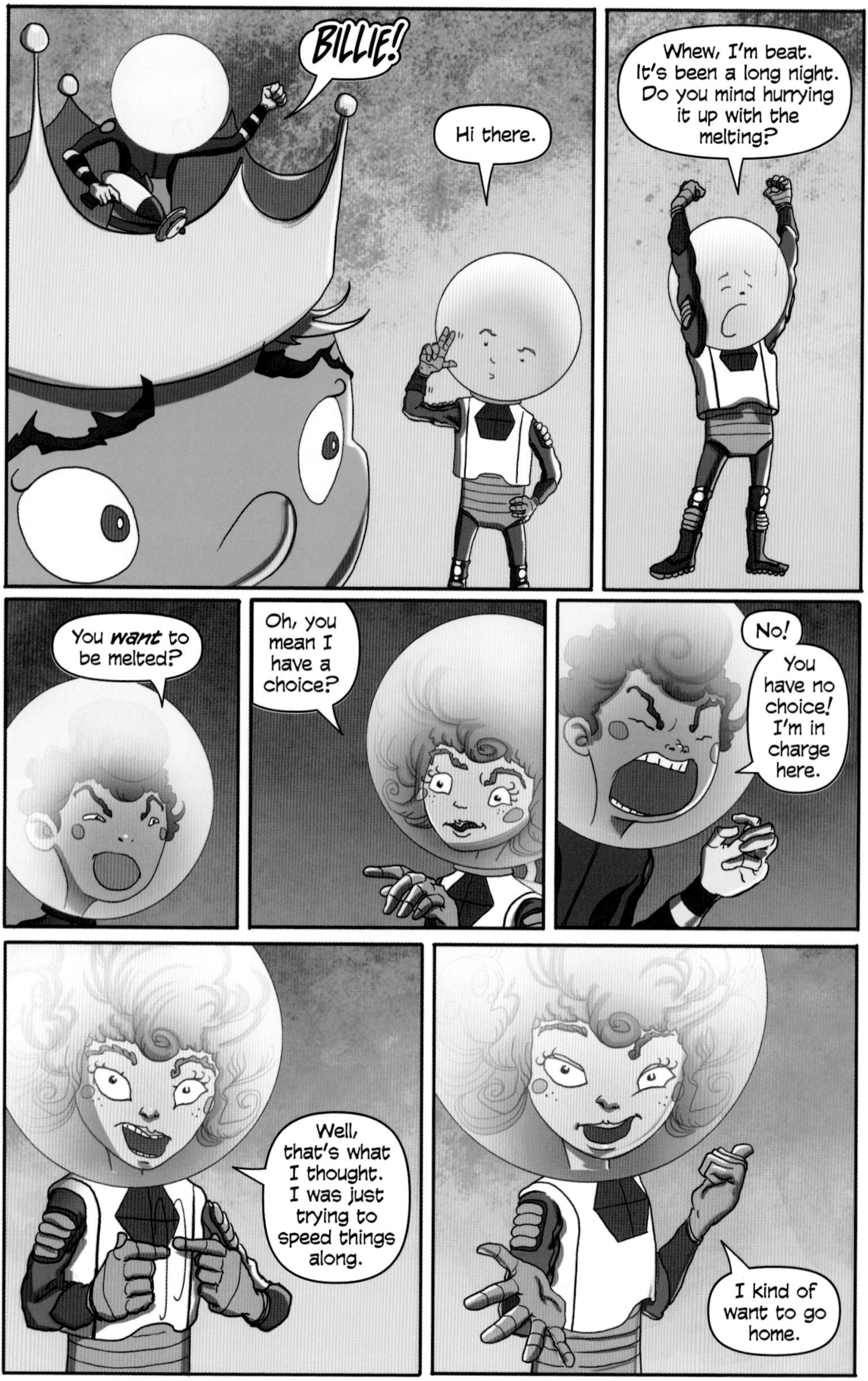
BILLIE!
Hi there.
Whew, I'm beat. It's been a long night. Do you mind hurrying it up with the melting?
You *want* to be melted?
Oh, you mean I have a choice?
No!
You have no choice! I'm in charge here.
Well, that's what I thought. I was just trying to speed things along.
I kind of want to go home.

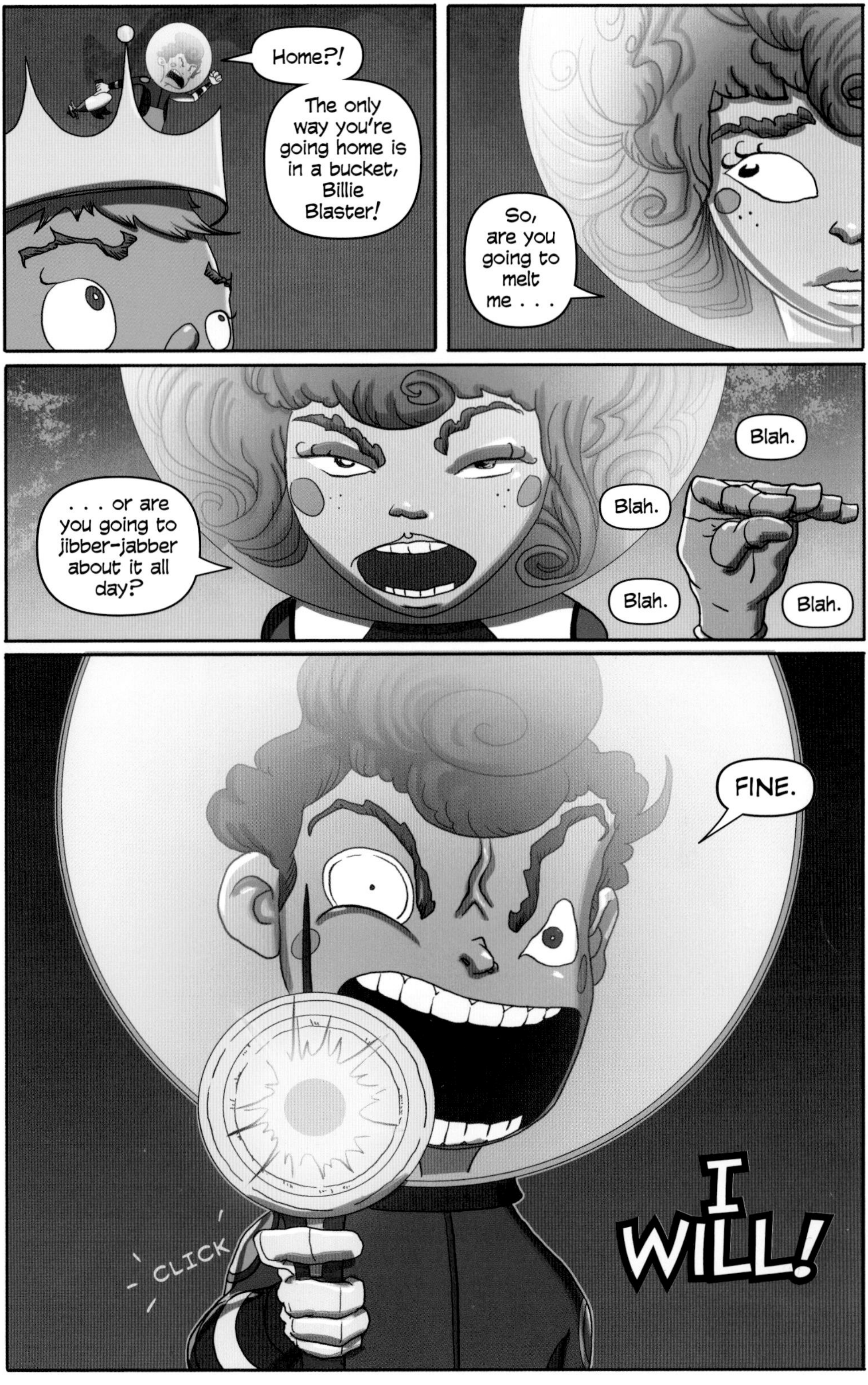
Home?!
The only way you're going home is in a bucket, Billie Blaster!
So, are you going to melt me . . .
. . . or are you going to jibber-jabber about it all day?
Blah.
Blah.
Blah.
Blah.
FINE.
I WILL!
CLICK

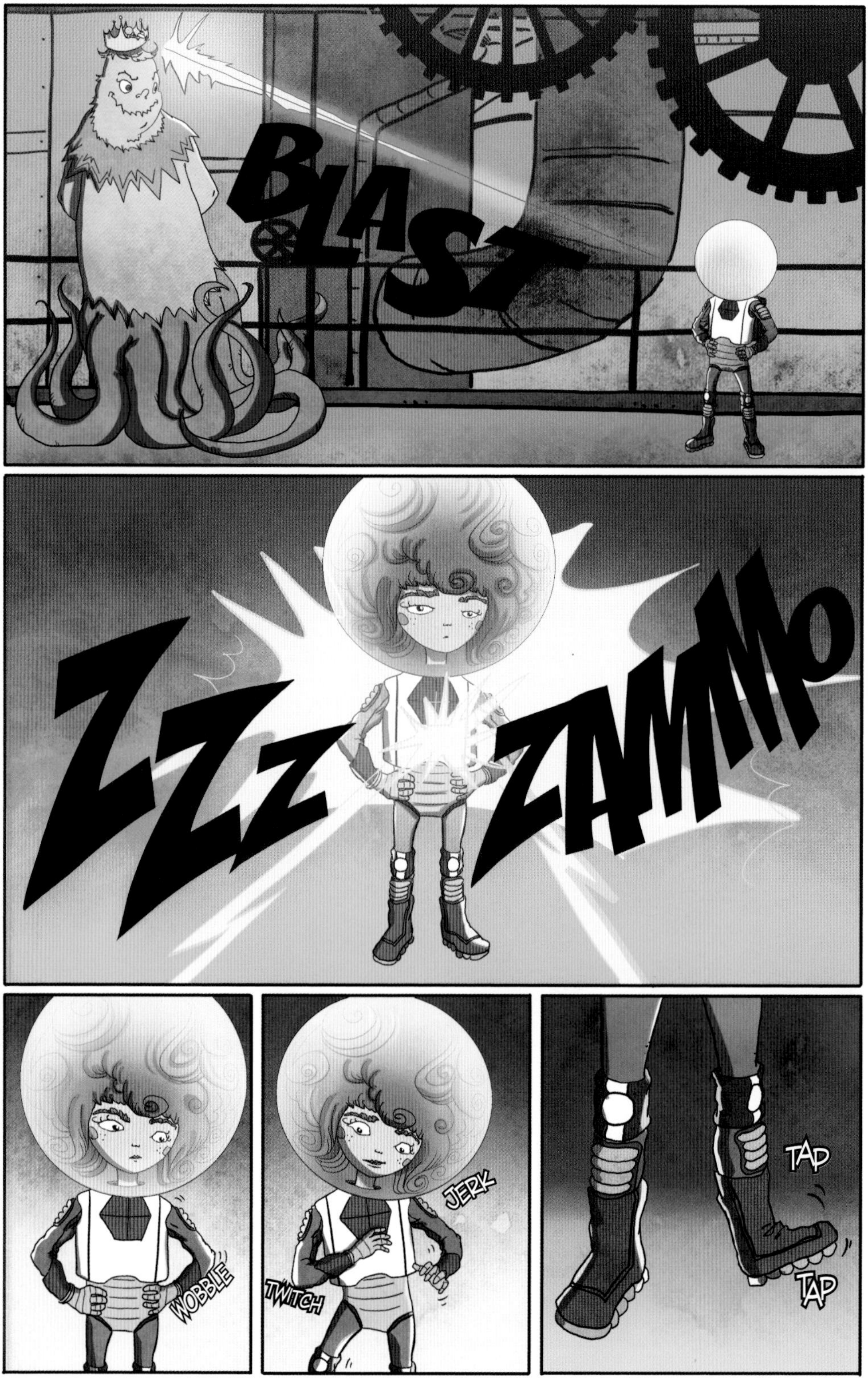
BLAST
ZZZ ZAMMO
WOBBLE
JERK
TWITCH
TAP
TAP

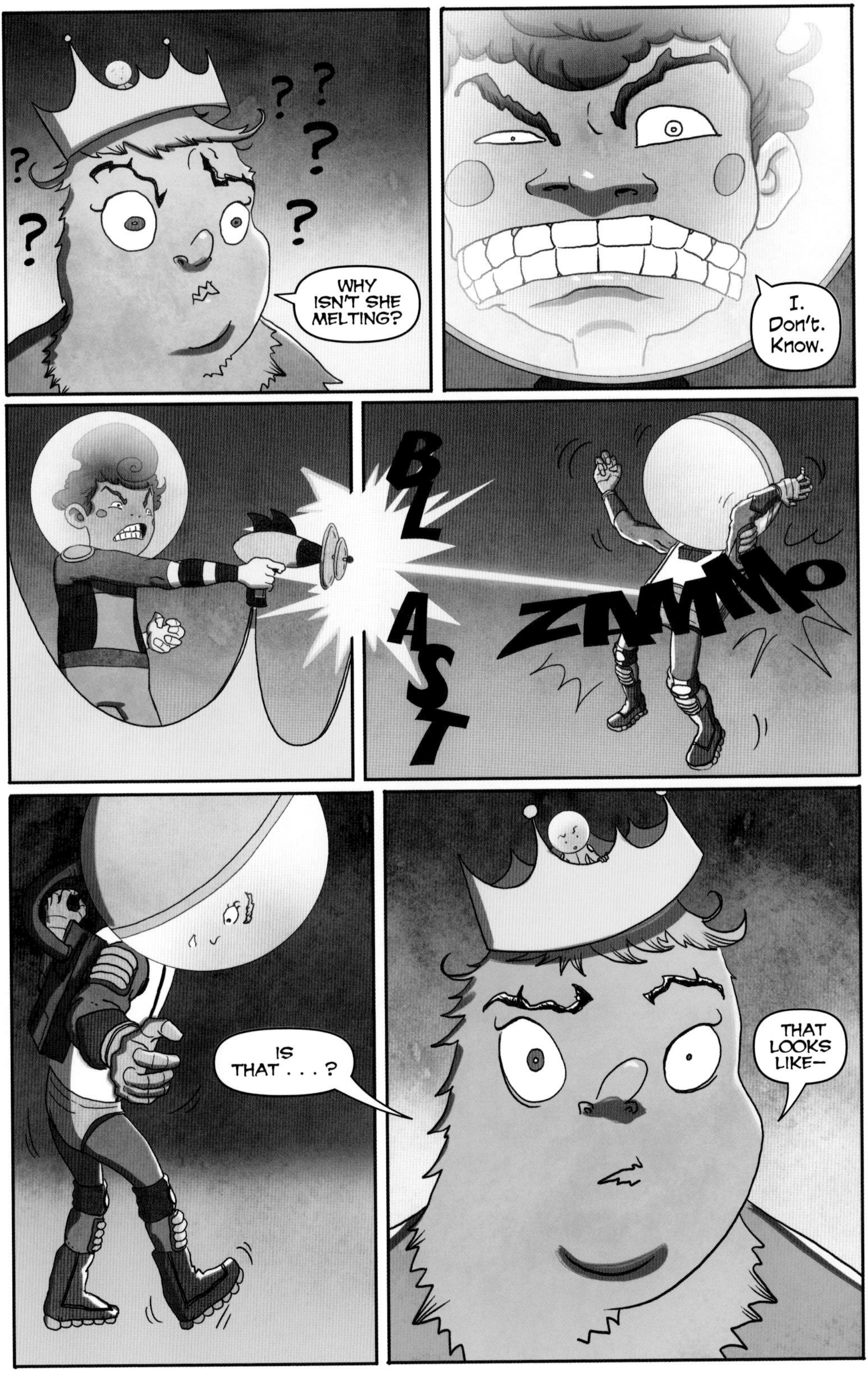

? ? ? ? ? ?
WHY ISN'T SHE MELTING?
I. Don't. Know.
BLAST
ZAMMO
IS THAT . . . ?
THAT LOOKS LIKE—

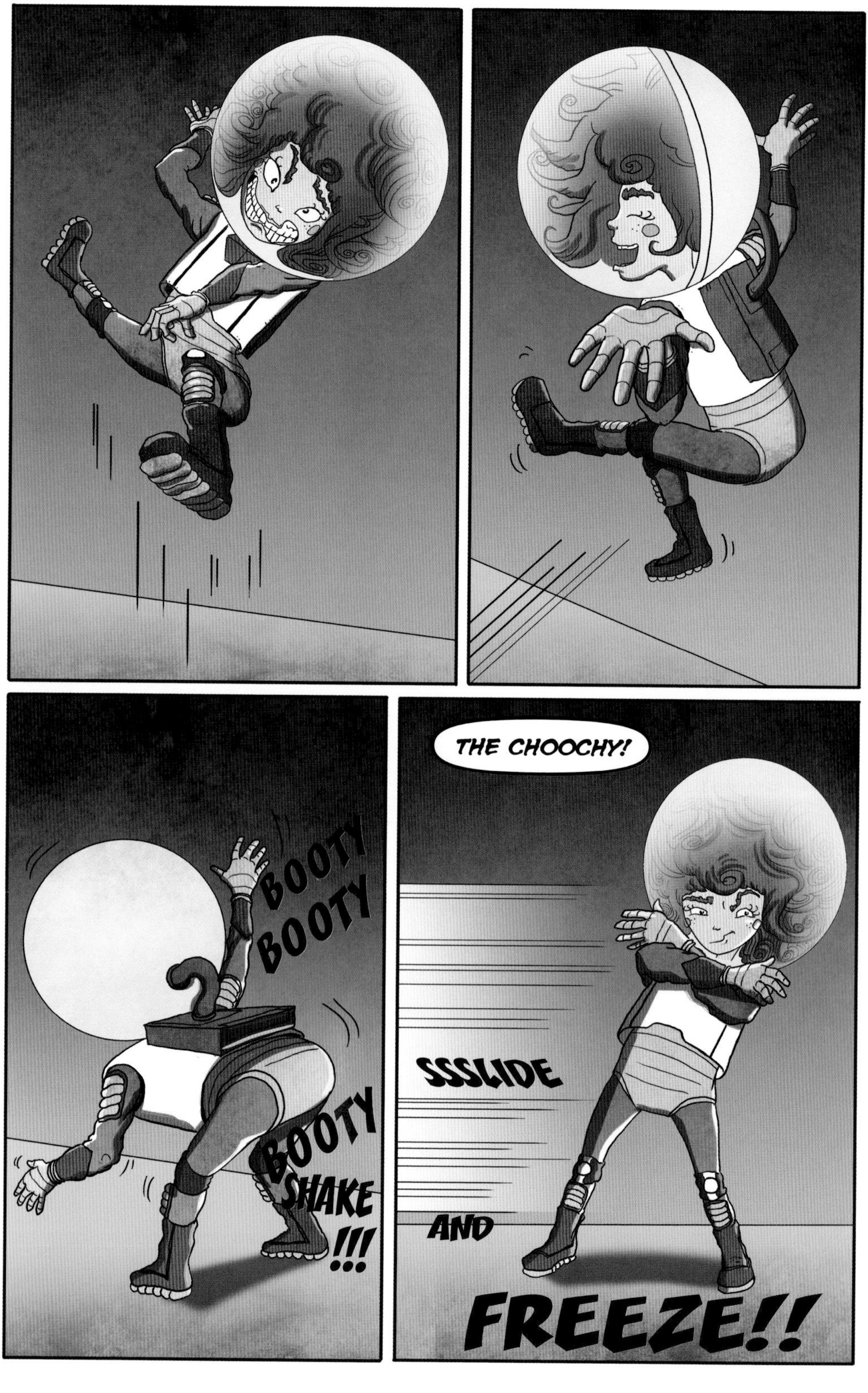
BOOTY
BOOTY
BOOTY
SHAKE
!!!
THE CHOOCHY!
SSSLIDE
AND
FREEZE!!

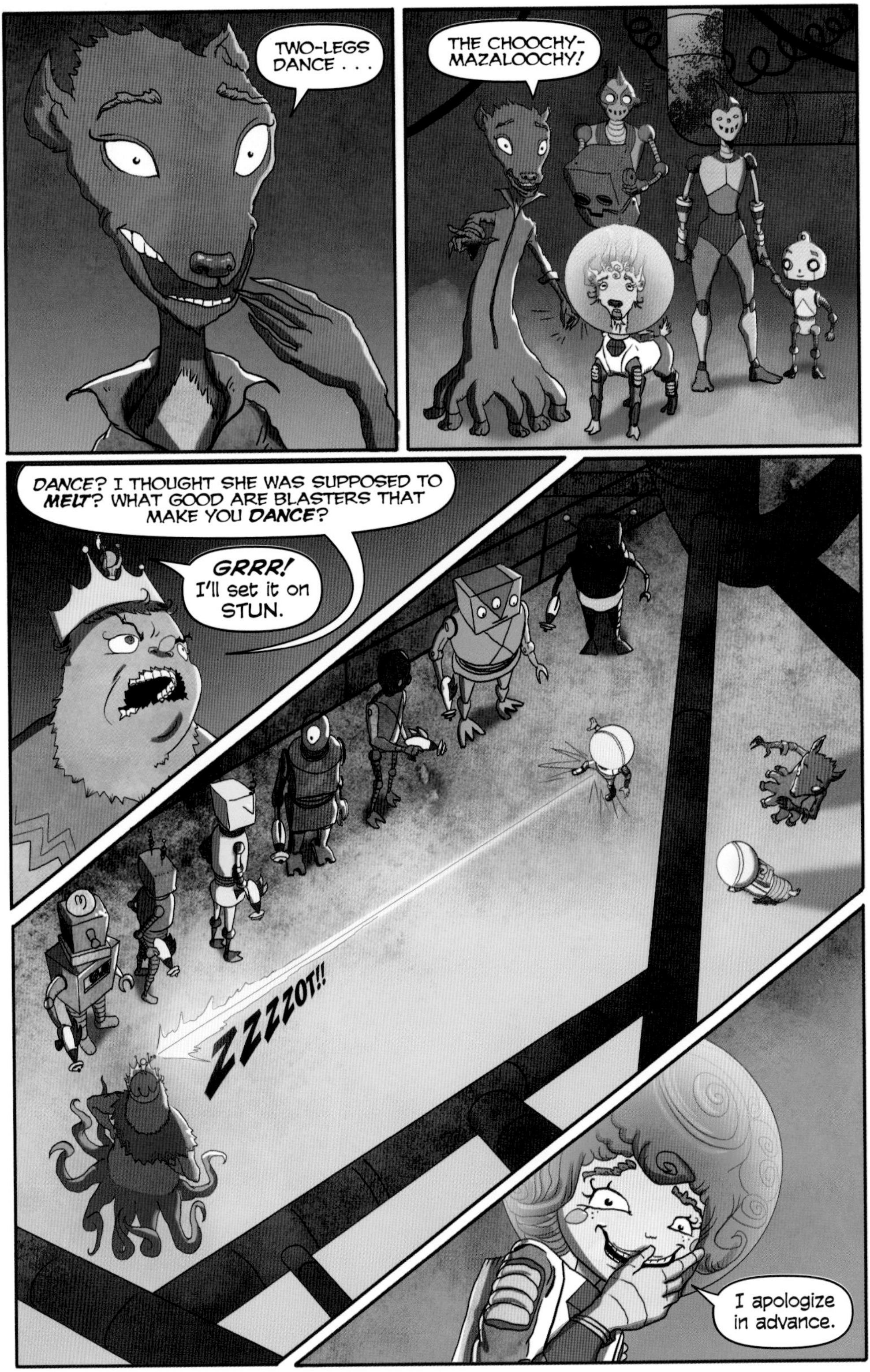
TWO-LEGS DANCE . . .
THE CHOOCHY-MAZALOOCHY!
DANCE? I THOUGHT SHE WAS SUPPOSED TO MELT? WHAT GOOD ARE BLASTERS THAT MAKE YOU DANCE?
GRRR! I'll set it on STUN.
ZZZZOT!!
I apologize in advance.

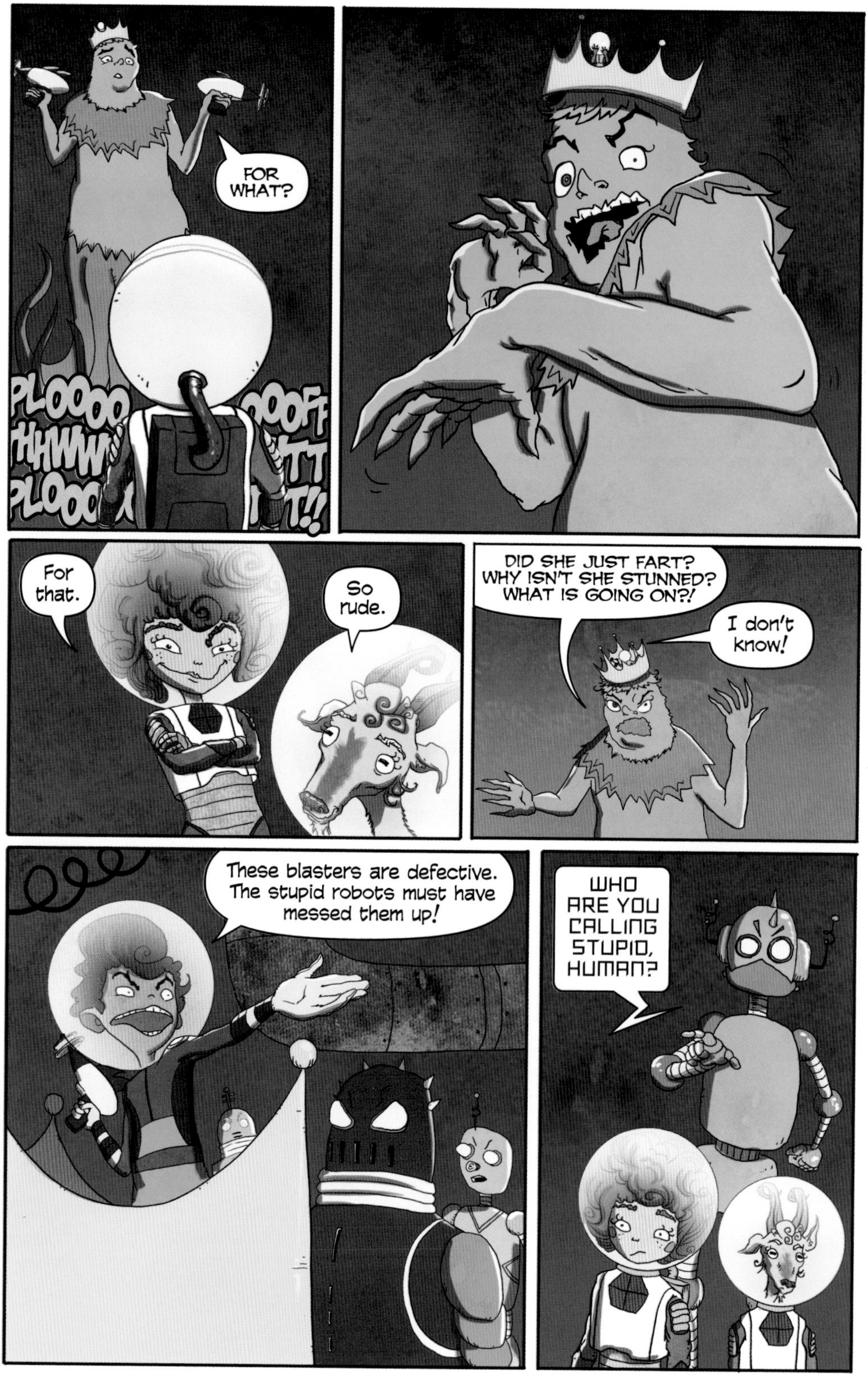
FOR WHAT?
PLOOOOO THHWWW PLOOO
OOOFF TTT T!!
For that.
So rude.
DID SHE JUST FART? WHY ISN'T SHE STUNNED? WHAT IS GOING ON?!
I don't know!
These blasters are defective. The stupid robots must have messed them up!
WHO ARE YOU CALLING STUPID, HUMAN?

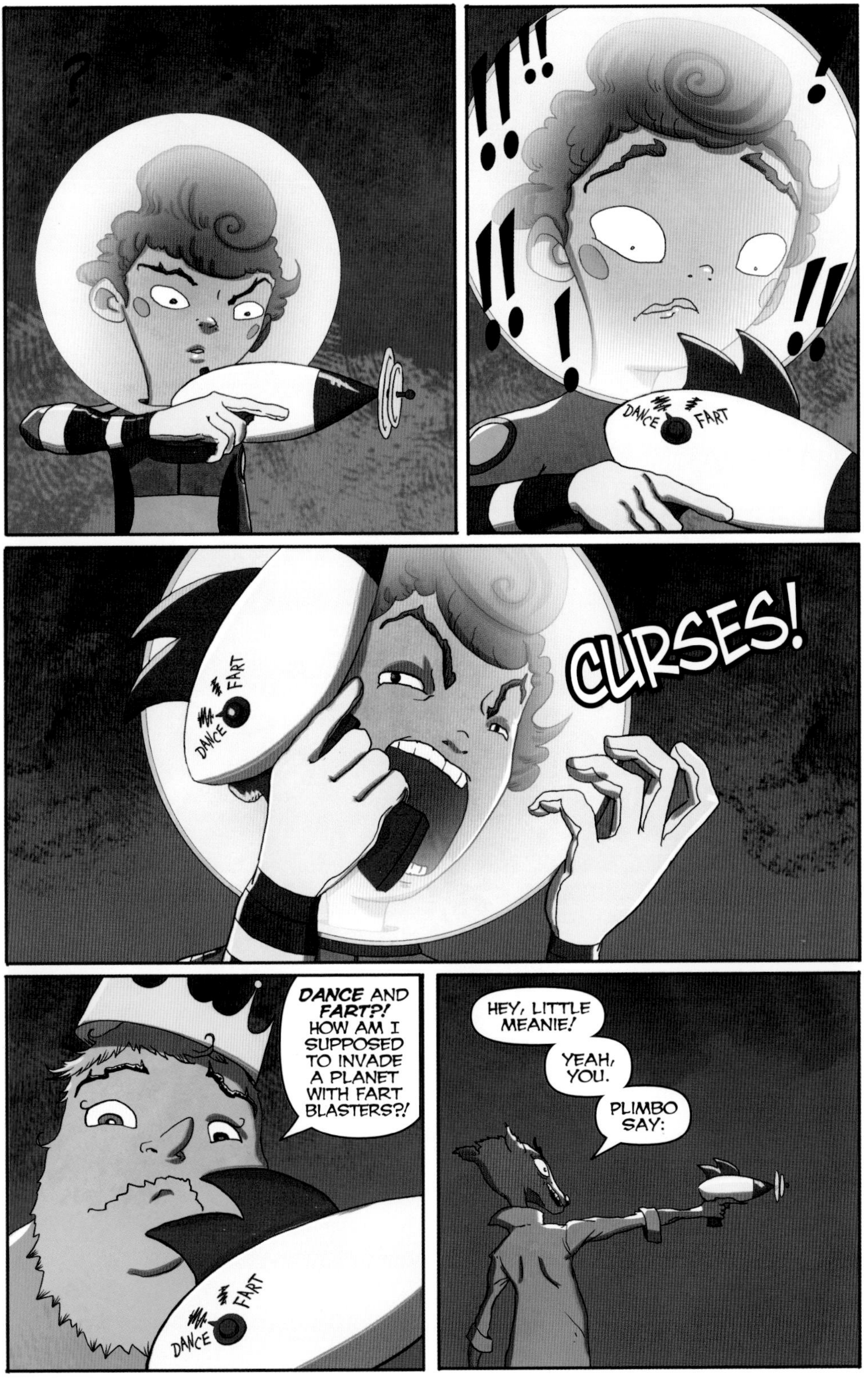

?
?
DANCE
FART
CURSES!
DANCE
FART
DANCE
FART
DANCE AND FART?! HOW AM I SUPPOSED TO INVADE A PLANET WITH FART BLASTERS?!
HEY, LITTLE MEANIE!
YEAH, YOU.
PLIMBO SAY:

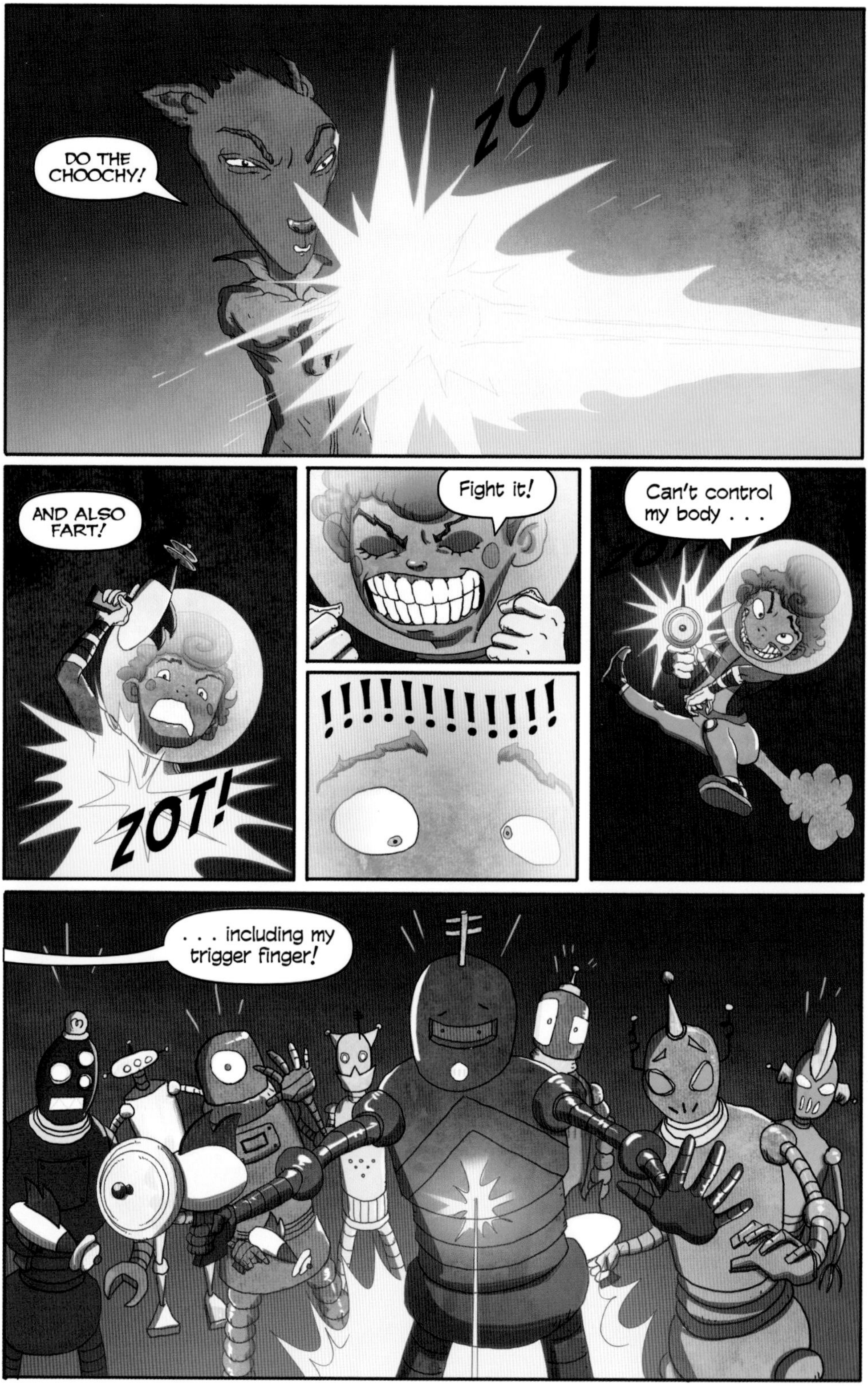
DO THE CHOOCHY!
ZOT!
AND ALSO FART!
ZOT!
Fight it!
!!!!!!!!!!!!
Can't control my body . . .
. . . including my trigger finger!

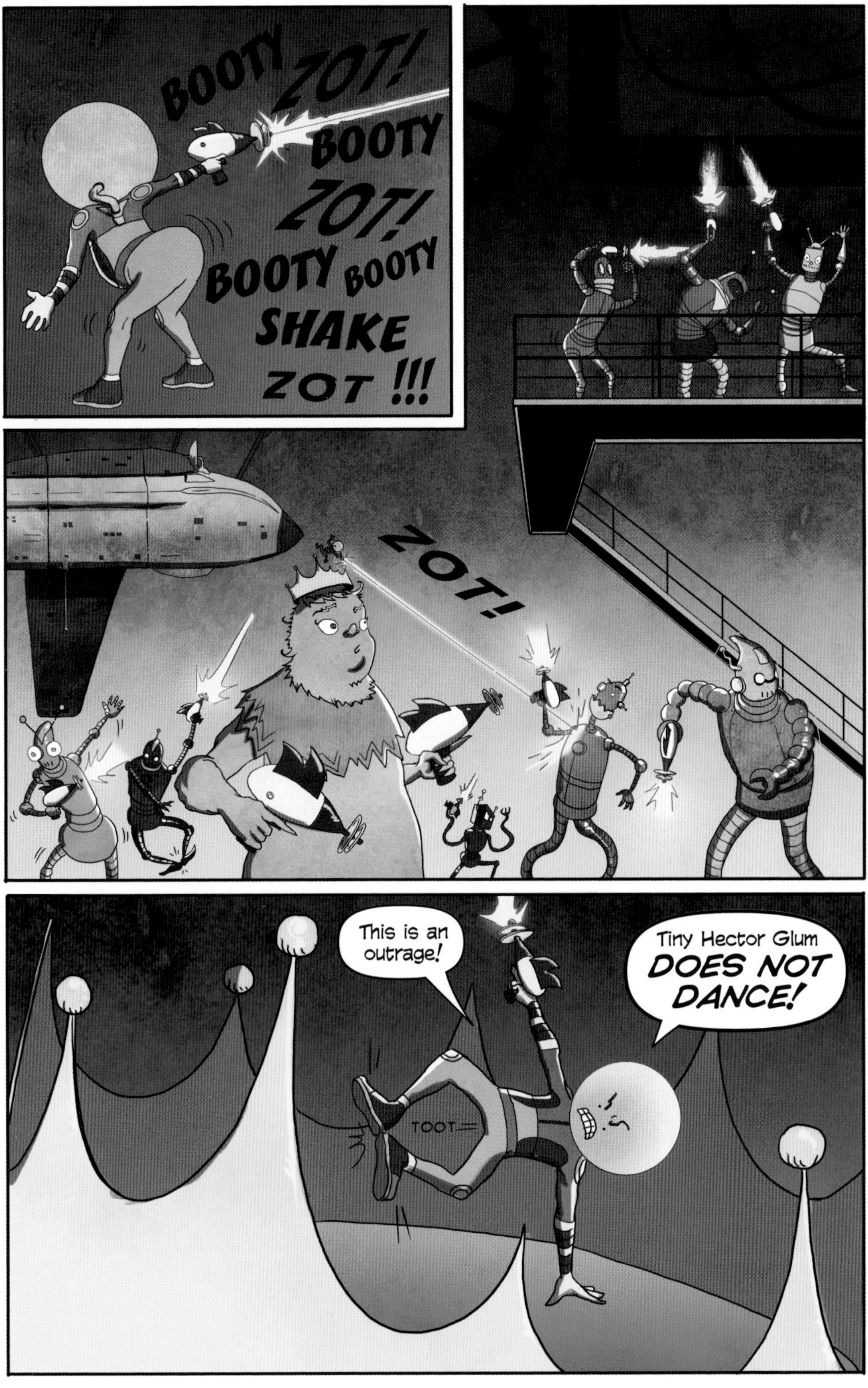
BOOTY ZOT! BOOTY ZOT! BOOTY BOOTY SHAKE ZOT !!!
ZOT!
This is an outrage!
Tiny Hector Glum DOES NOT DANCE!
TOOT

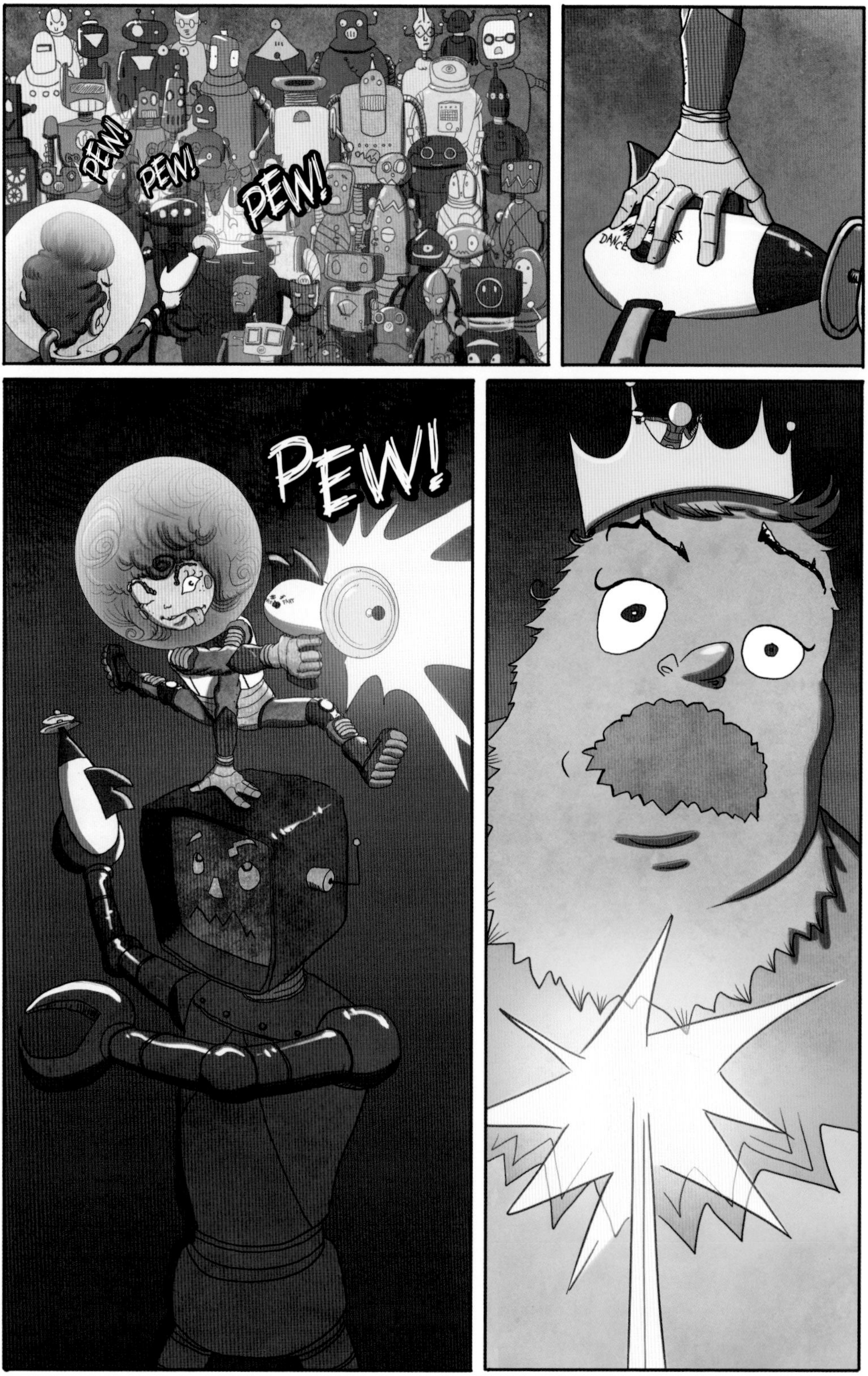
PEW!
PEW!
PEW!
DANCE
PEW!

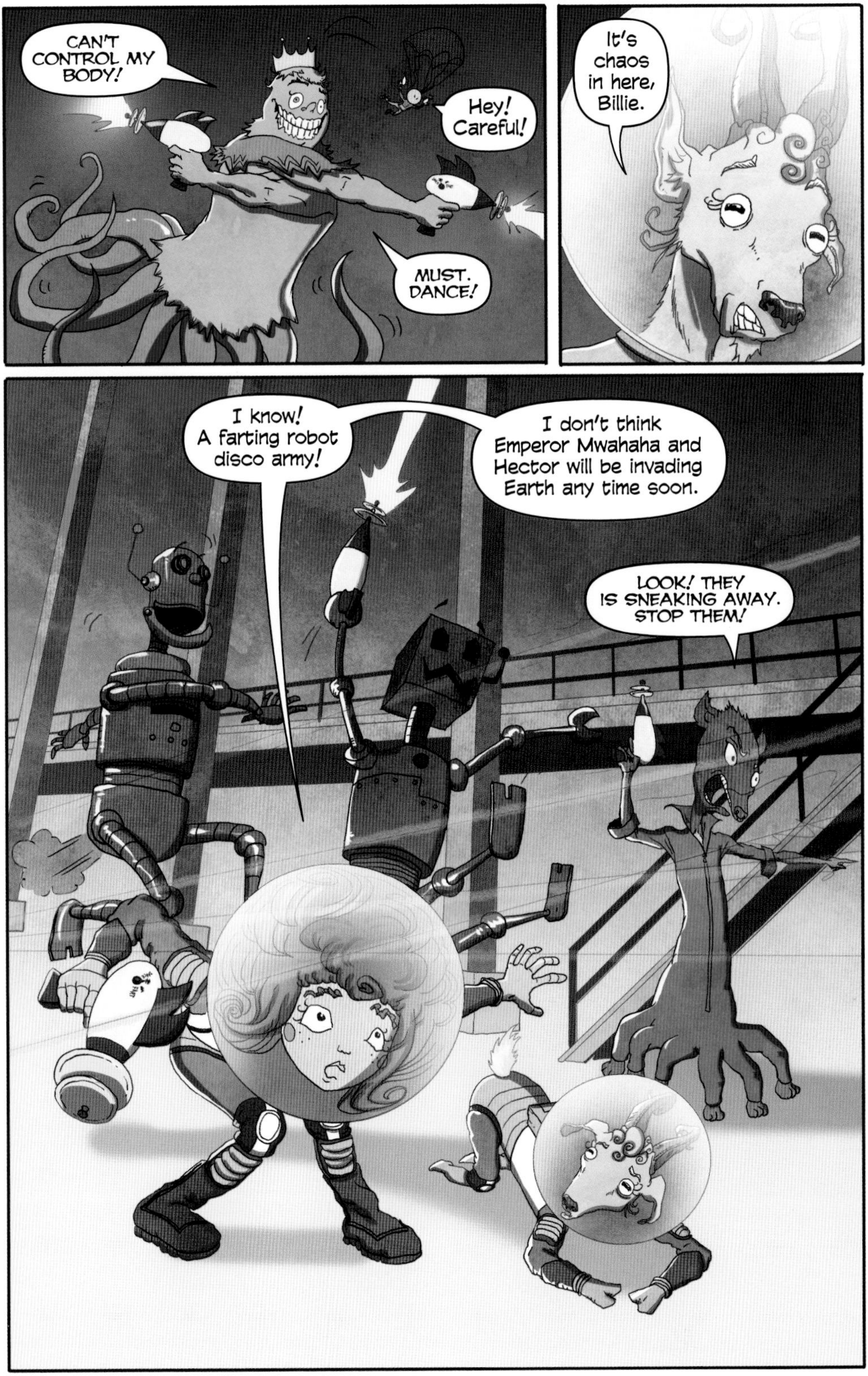
CAN'T CONTROL MY BODY!
Hey! Careful!
MUST. DANCE!
It's chaos in here, Billie.
I know! A farting robot disco army!
I don't think Emperor Mwahaha and Hector will be invading Earth any time soon.
LOOK! THEY IS SNEAKING AWAY. STOP THEM!

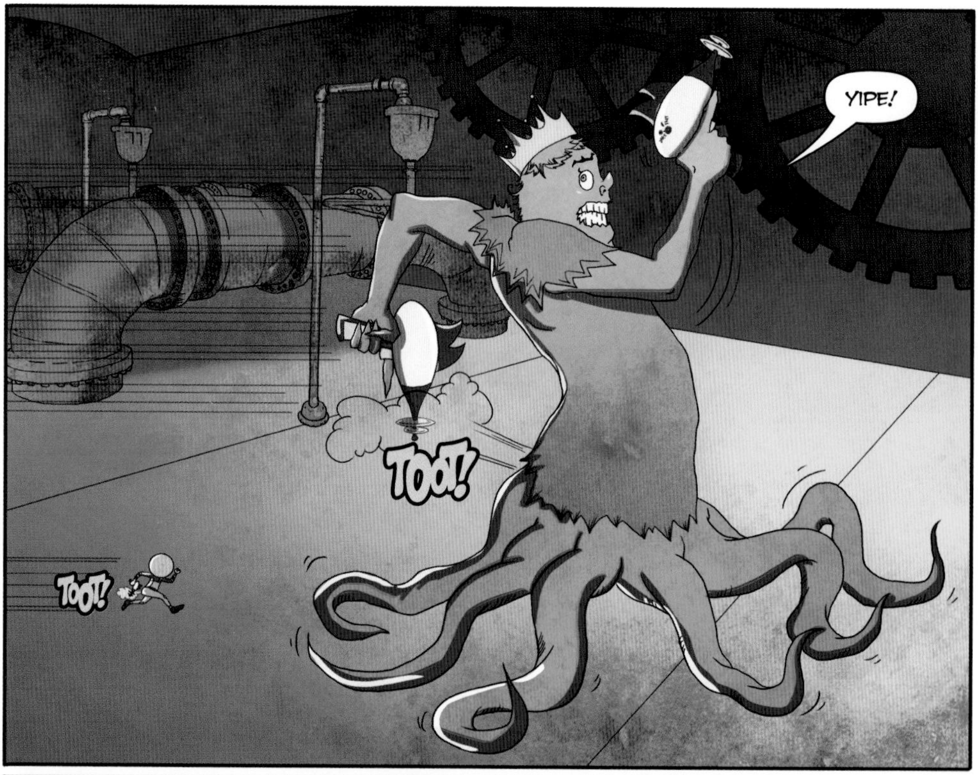
YIPE!
TOOT!
TOOT!

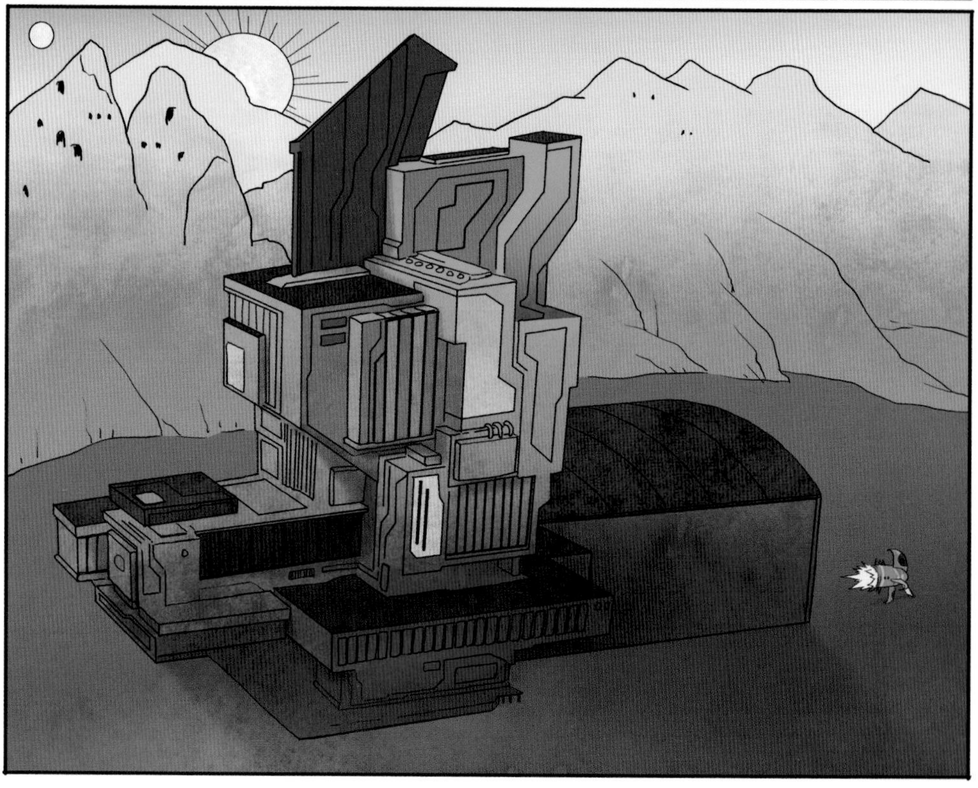

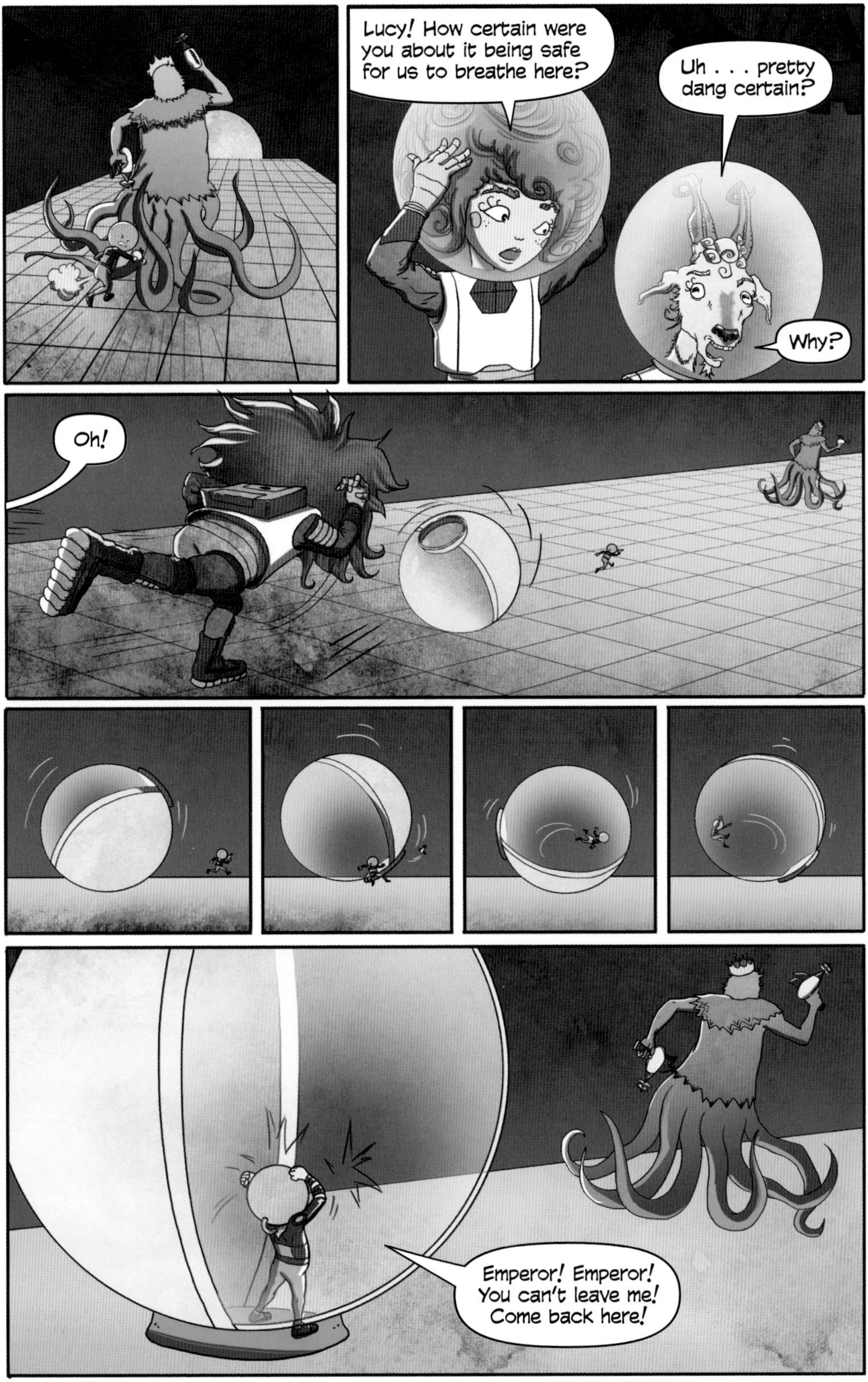
Lucy! How certain were you about it being safe for us to breathe here?
Uh . . . pretty dang certain?
Why?
Oh!
Emperor! Emperor! You can't leave me! Come back here!

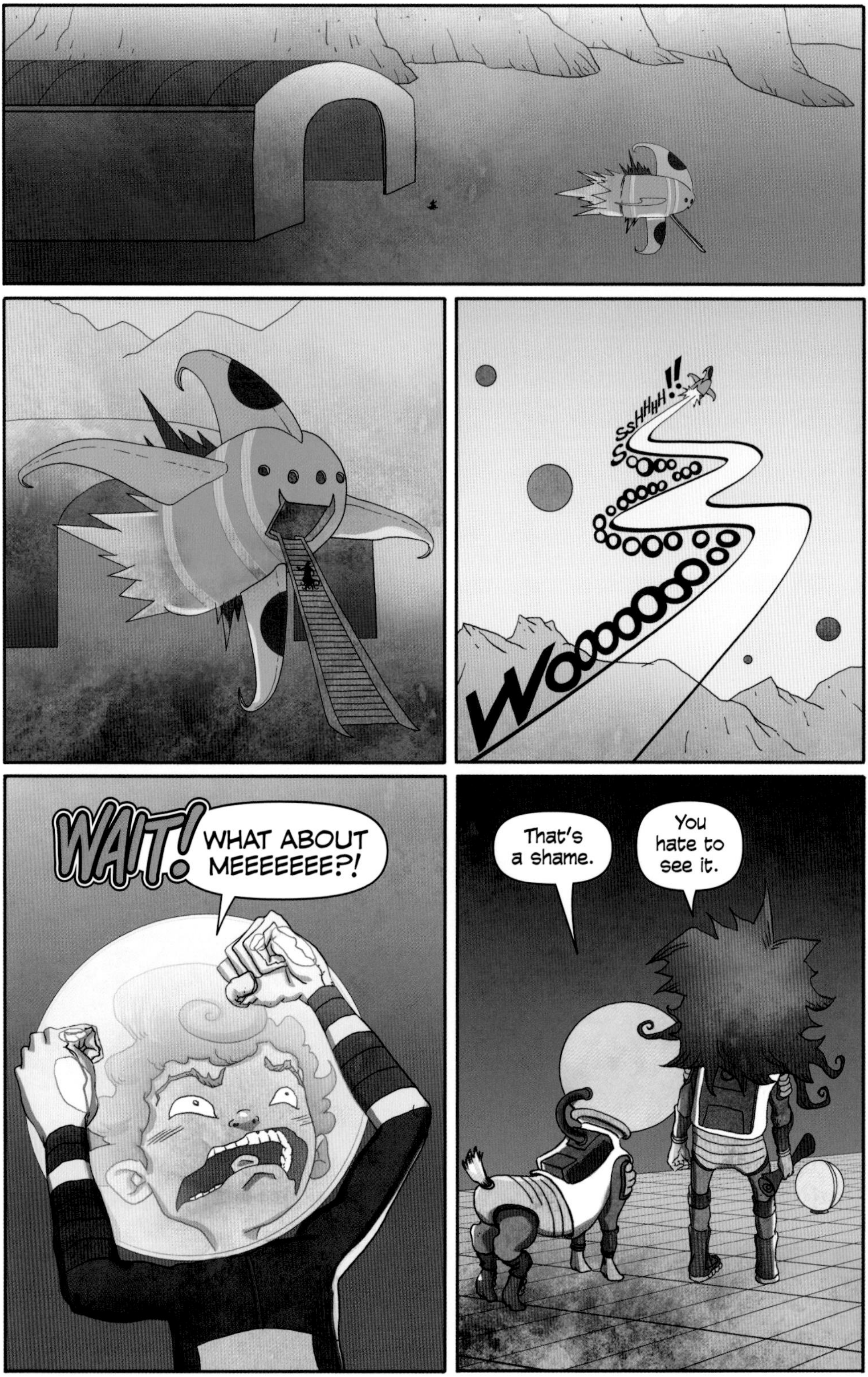
SSHHHH!!
SOOOOOOOOOOOOOOOOOOO
WOOOOOO
WAIT!
WHAT ABOUT MEEEEEEE?!
That's a shame.
You hate to see it.

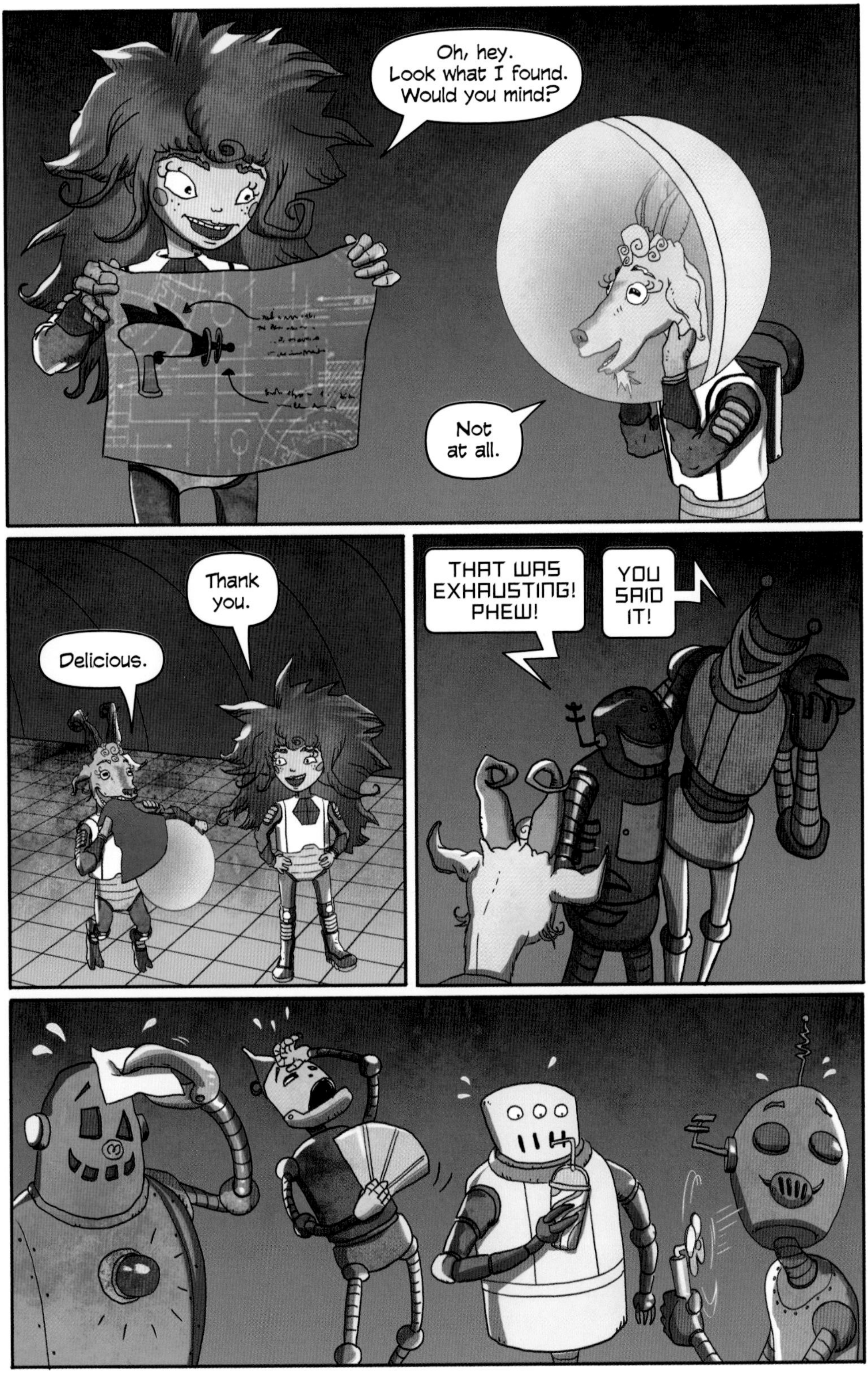
Oh, hey.
Look what I found.
Would you mind?
Not at all.
Thank you.
Delicious.
THAT WAS EXHAUSTING! PHEW!
YOU SAID IT!

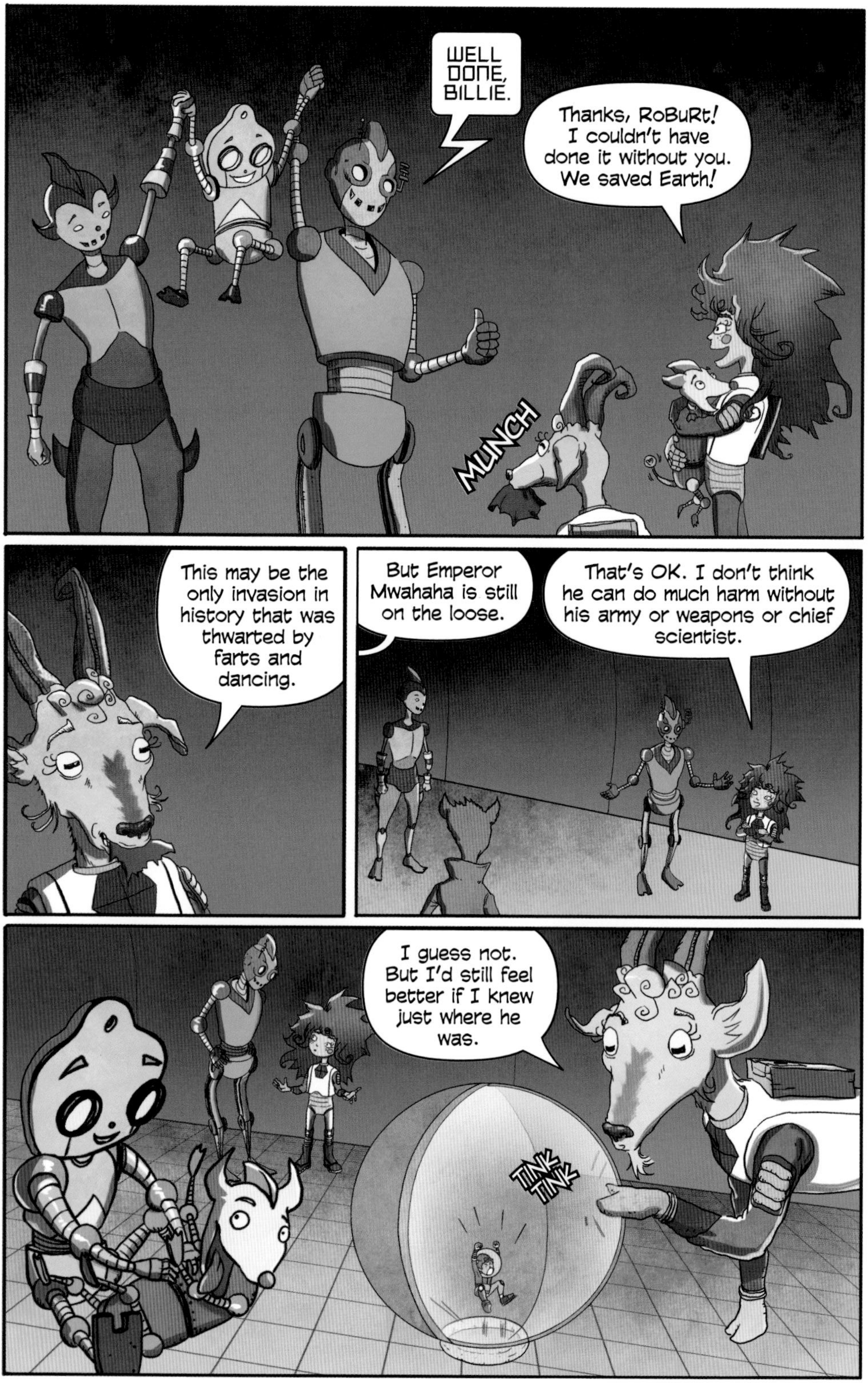
WELL DONE, BILLIE.
Thanks, RoBuRt! I couldn't have done it without you. We saved Earth!
MUNCH
This may be the only invasion in history that was thwarted by farts and dancing.
But Emperor Mwahaha is still on the loose.
That's OK. I don't think he can do much harm without his army or weapons or chief scientist.
I guess not. But I'd still feel better if I knew just where he was.
TINK TINK

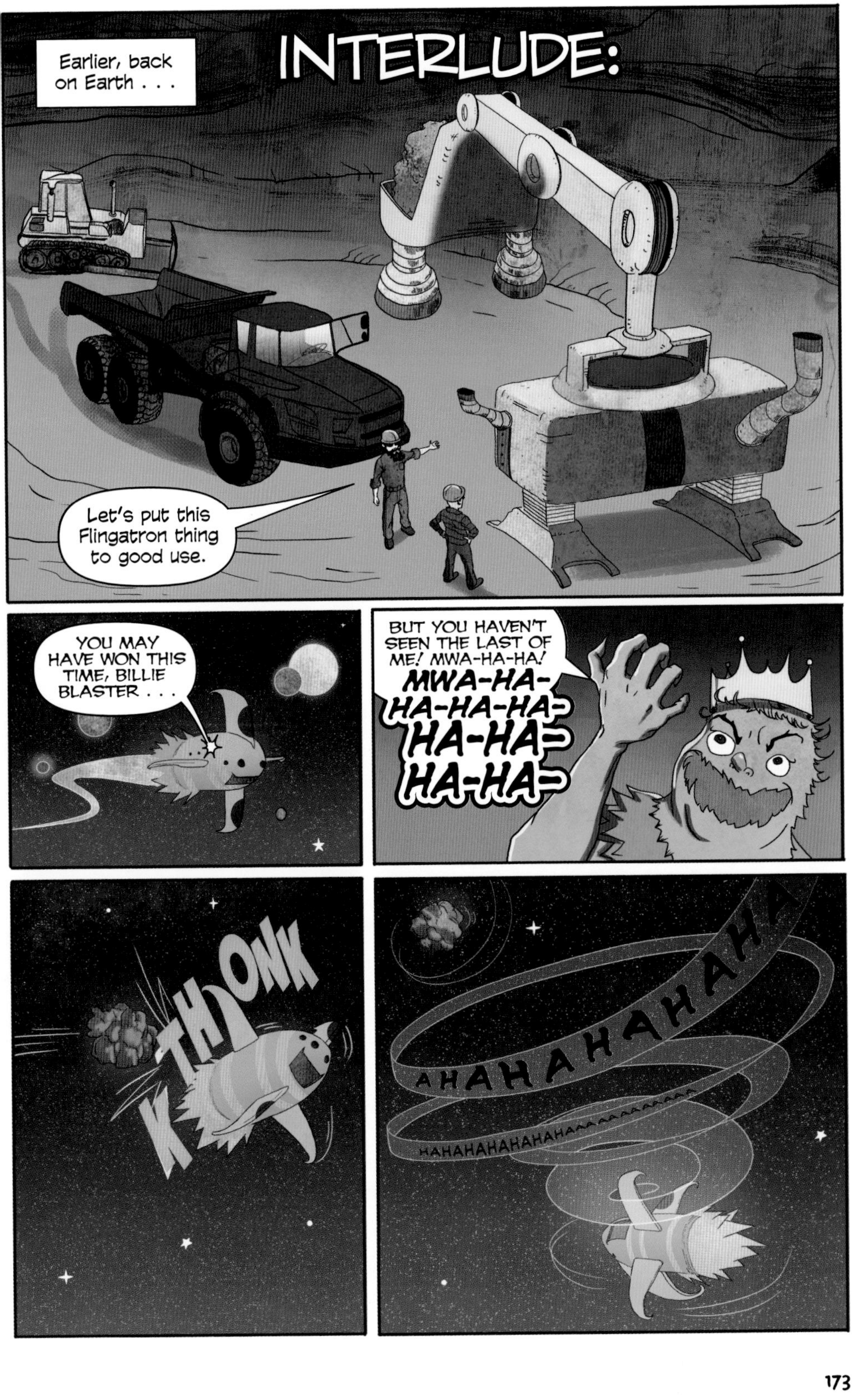
INTERLUDE:
Earlier, back on Earth . . .
Let's put this Flingatron thing to good use.
YOU MAY HAVE WON THIS TIME, BILLIE BLASTER . . .
BUT YOU HAVEN'T SEEN THE LAST OF ME! MWA-HA-HA!
MWA-HA-HA-HA-HA-HA-HA-HA-HA-
KTHONK
AHAHAHAHAHAHA
HAHAHAHAHAHAHAaaaaaaaaaaa

THE AFTERMATH

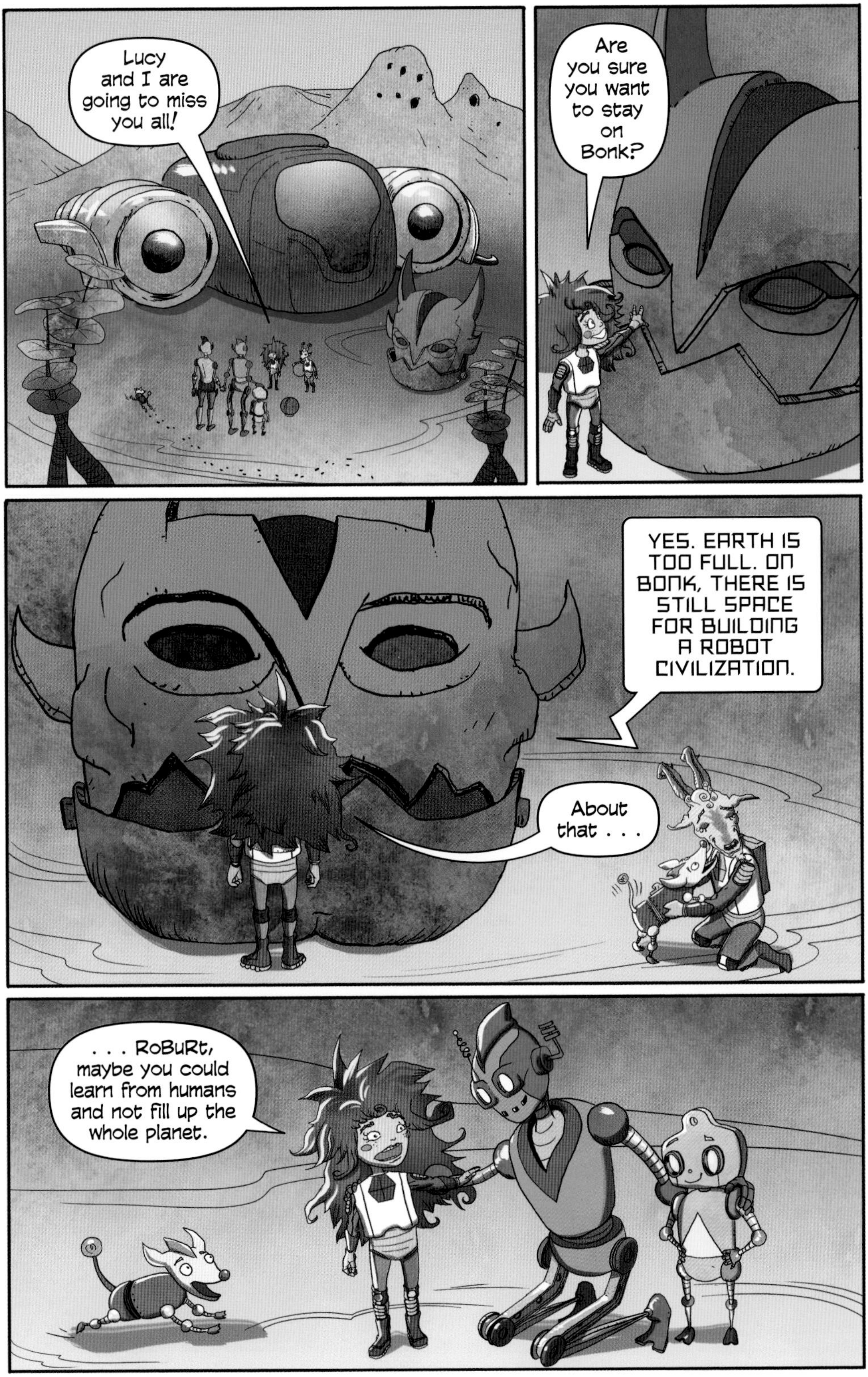
Lucy and I are going to miss you all!
Are you sure you want to stay on Bonk?
YES. EARTH IS TOO FULL. ON BONK, THERE IS STILL SPACE FOR BUILDING A ROBOT CIVILIZATION.
About that . . .
. . . RoBuRt, maybe you could learn from humans and not fill up the whole planet.

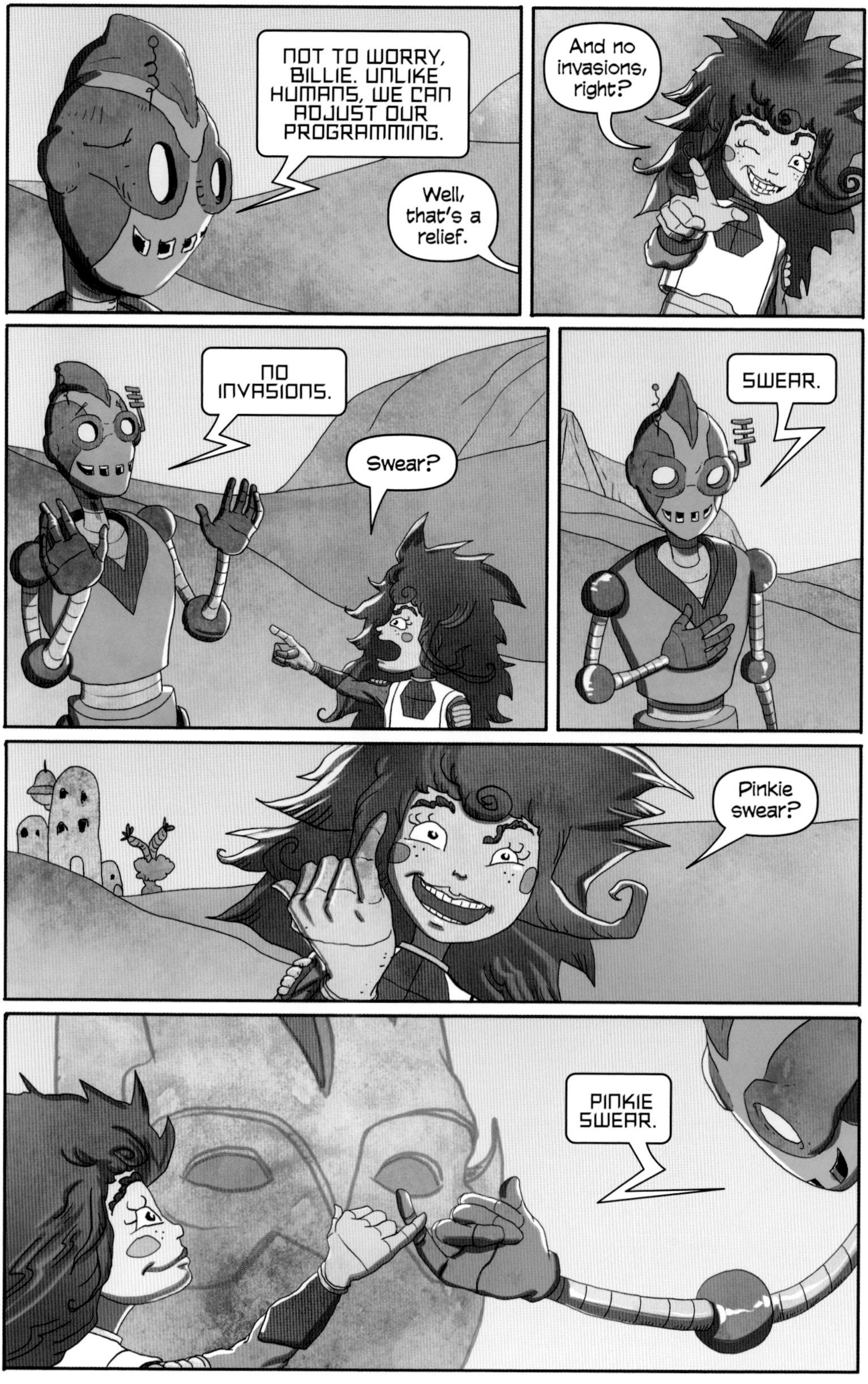
NOT TO WORRY, BILLIE. UNLIKE HUMANS, WE CAN ADJUST OUR PROGRAMMING.
Well, that's a relief.
And no invasions, right?
NO INVASIONS.
Swear?
SWEAR.
Pinkie swear?
PINKIE SWEAR.

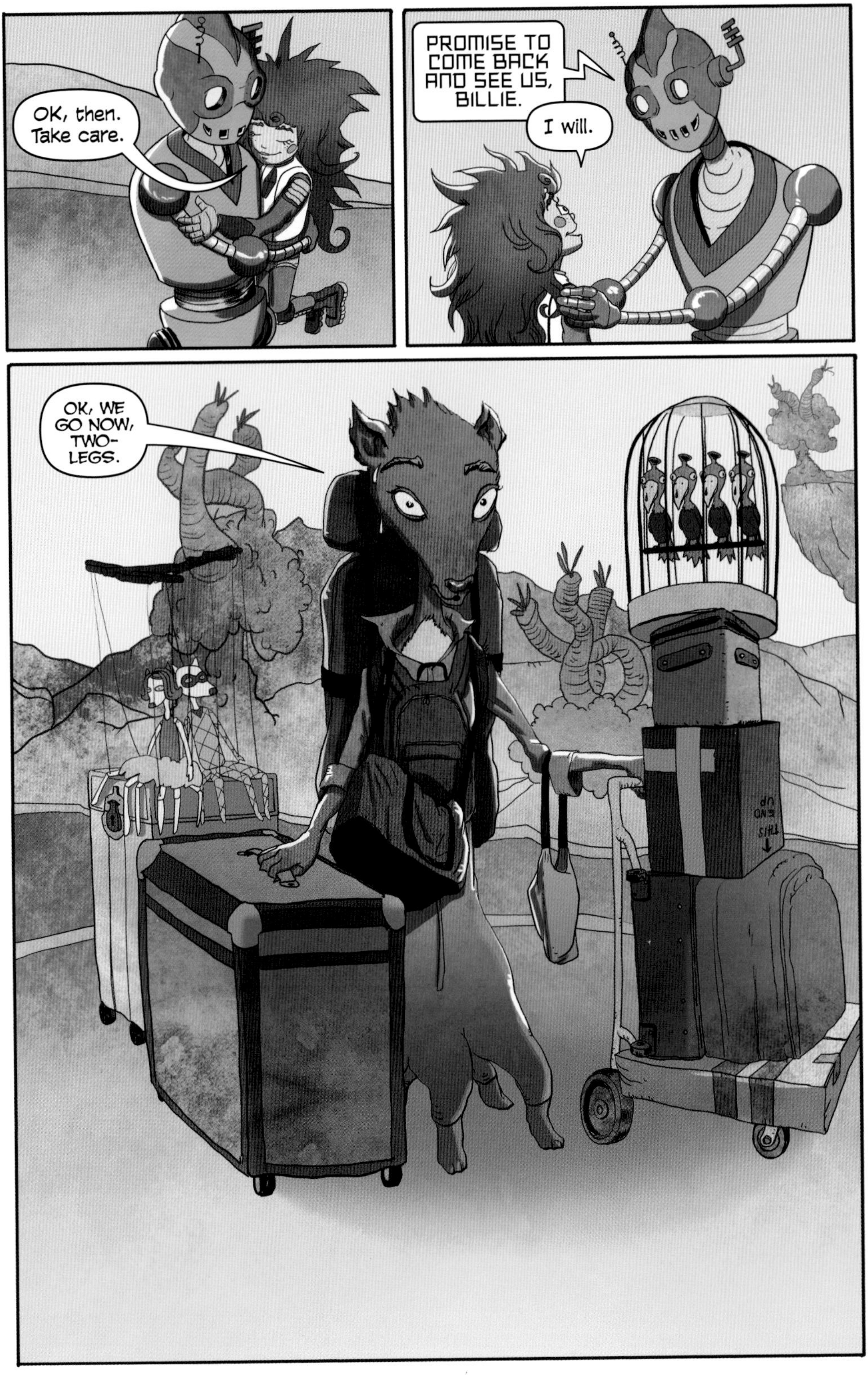
OK, then. Take care.
PROMISE TO COME BACK AND SEE US, BILLIE.
I will.
OK, WE GO NOW, TWO-LEGS.

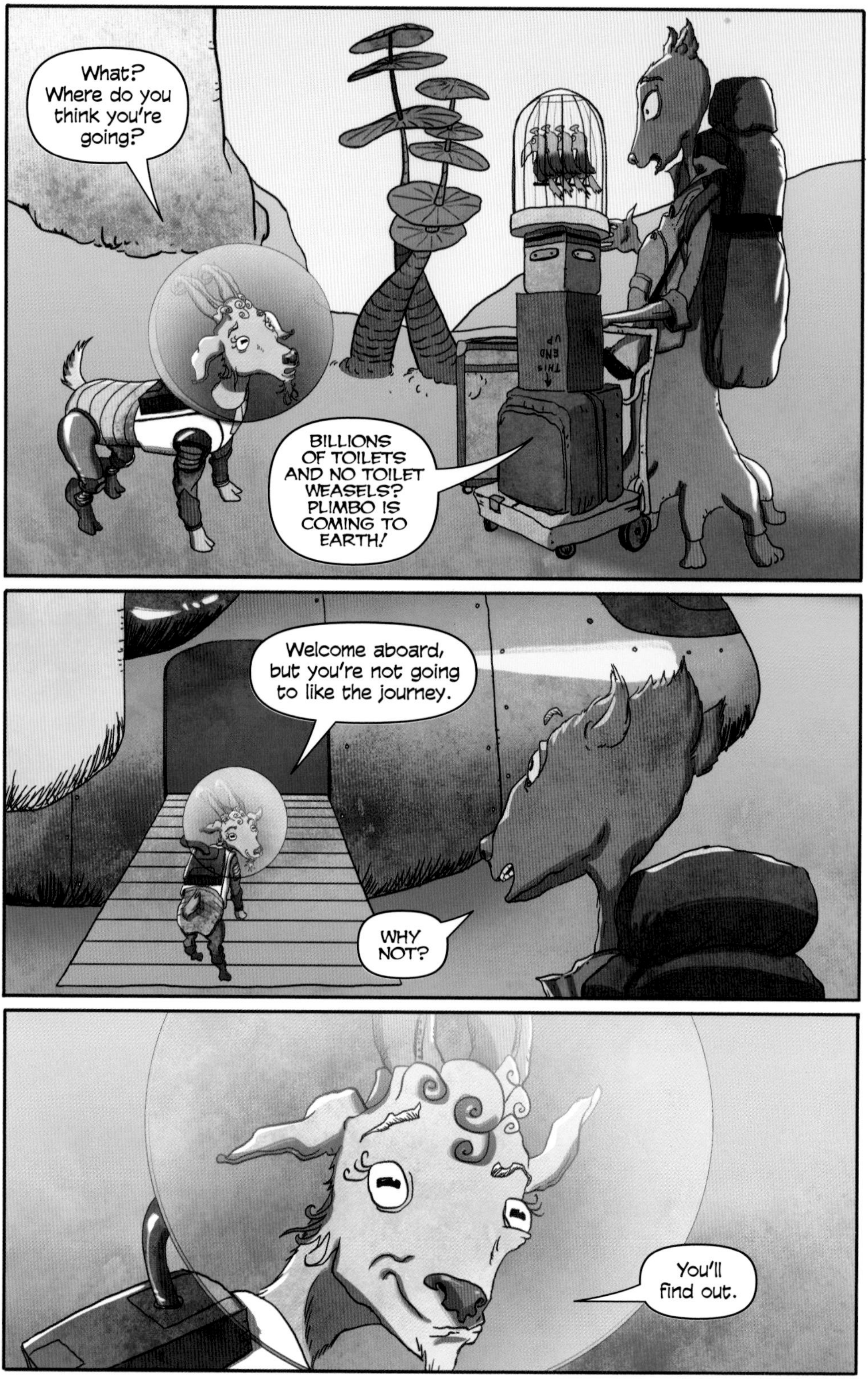
What? Where do you think you're going?
THIS END UP
BILLIONS OF TOILETS AND NO TOILET WEASELS? PLIMBO IS COMING TO EARTH!
Welcome aboard, but you're not going to like the journey.
WHY NOT?
You'll find out.

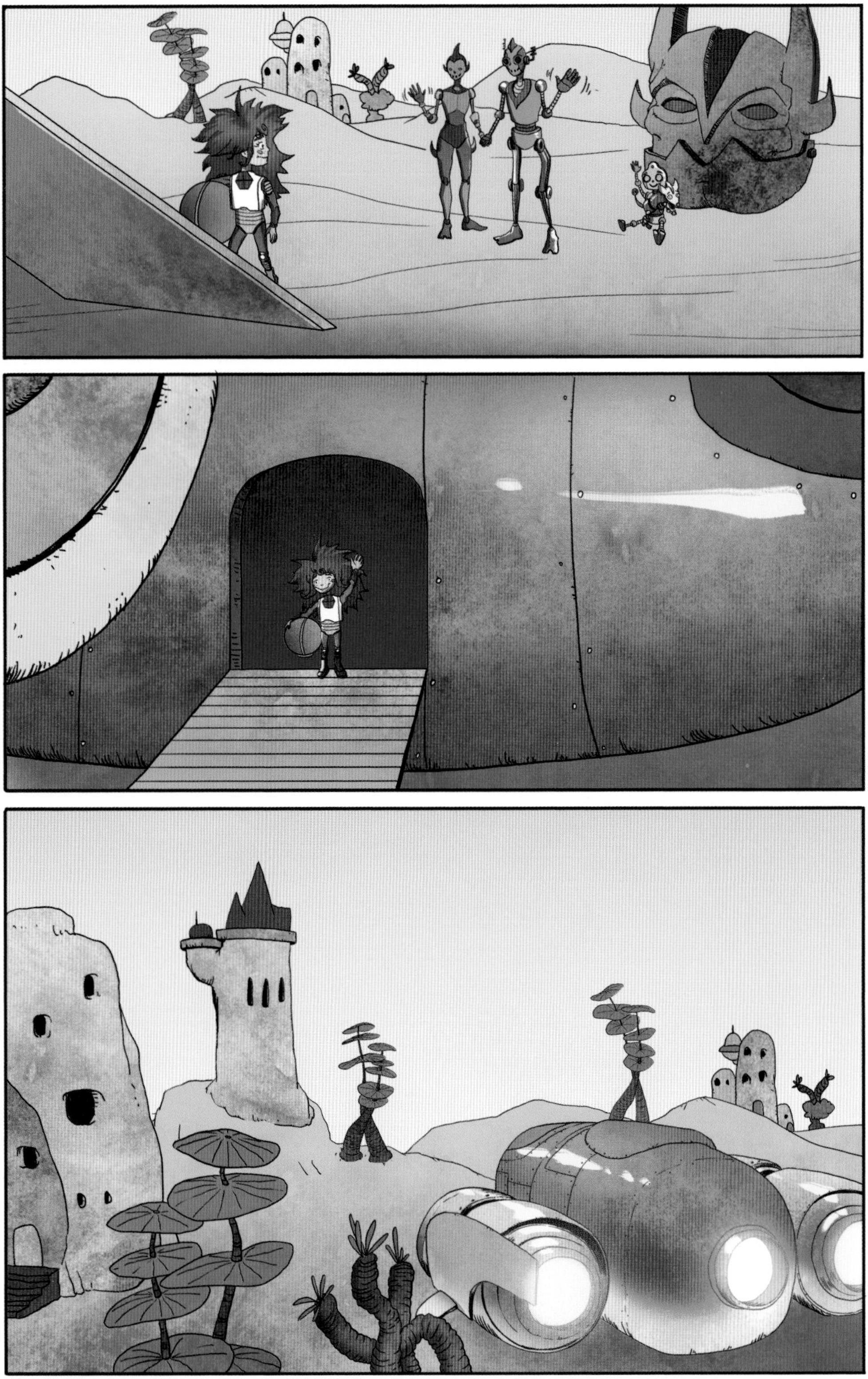

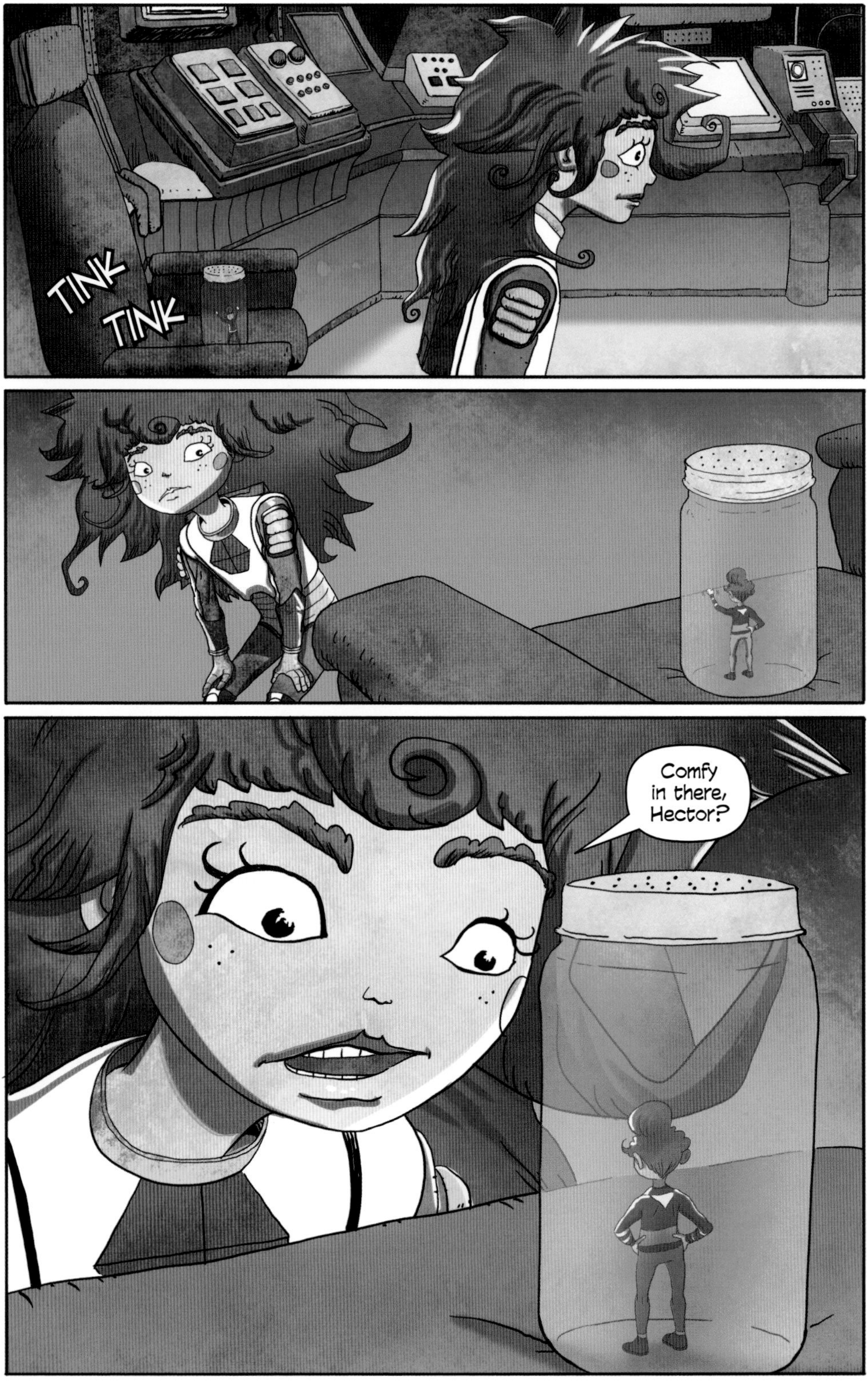
TINK
TINK
Comfy in there, Hector?

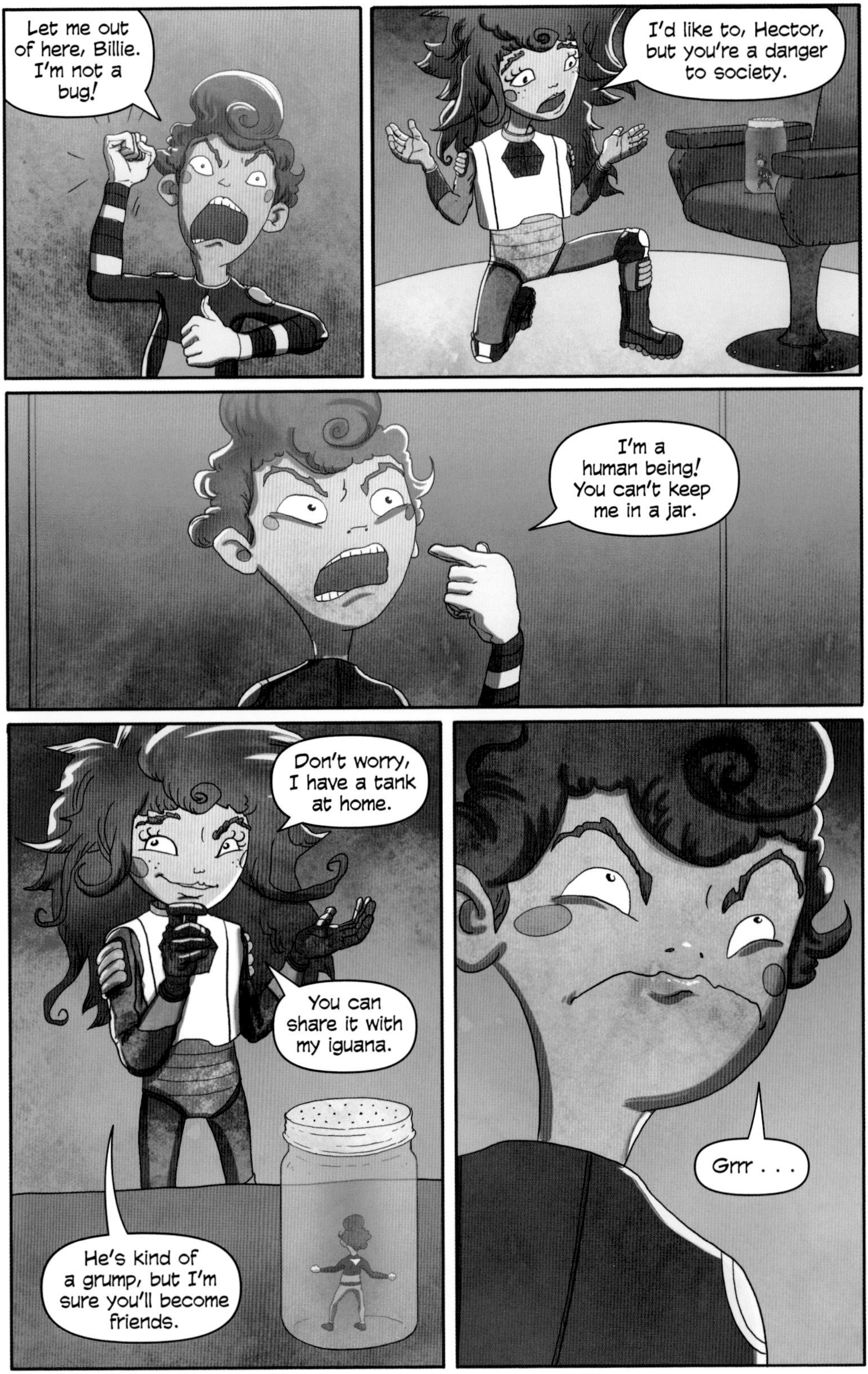
Let me out of here, Billie. I'm not a bug!
I'd like to, Hector, but you're a danger to society.
I'm a human being! You can't keep me in a jar.
Don't worry, I have a tank at home.
You can share it with my iguana.
He's kind of a grump, but I'm sure you'll become friends.
Grrr . . .

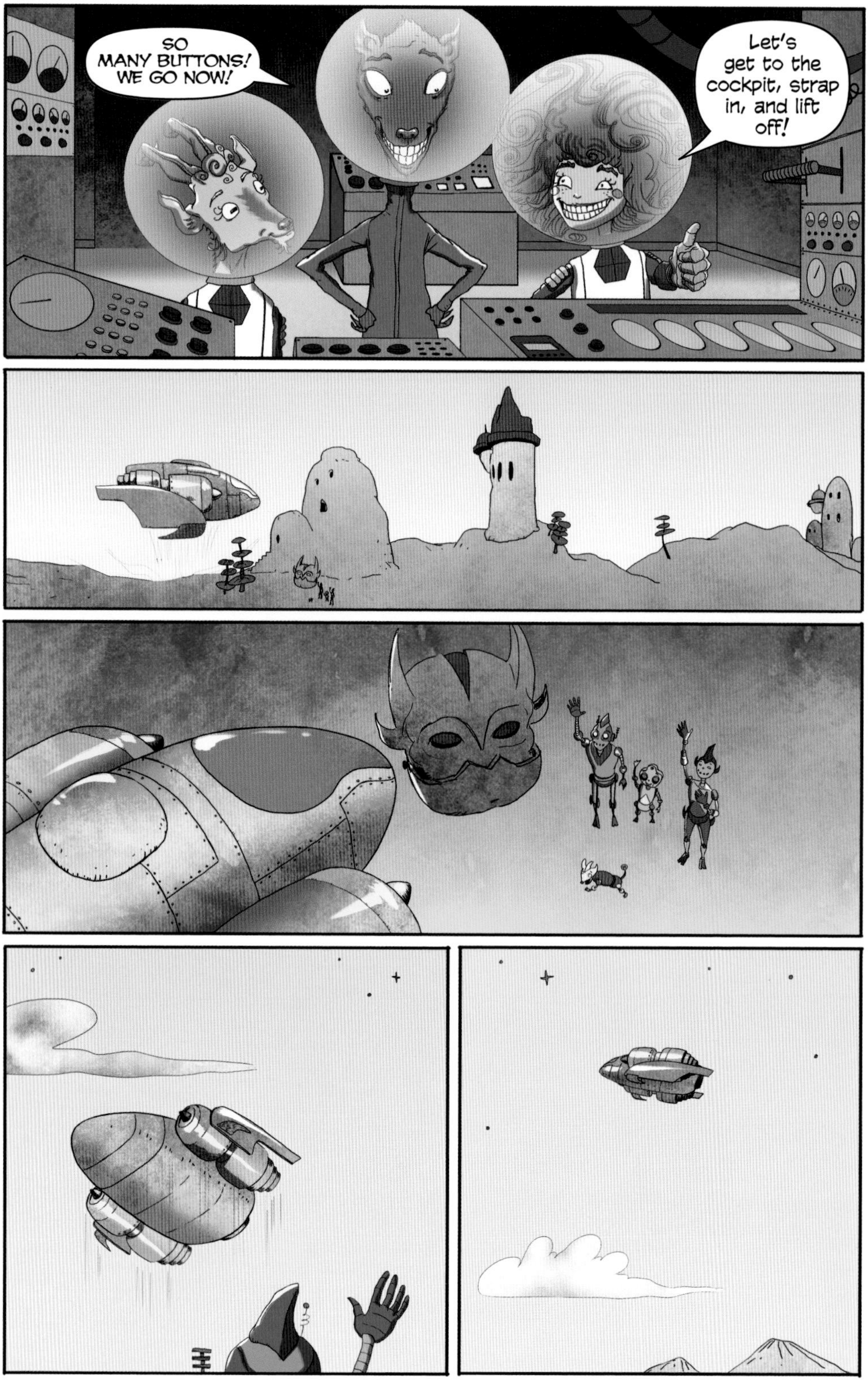
SO MANY BUTTONS! WE GO NOW!
Let's get to the cockpit, strap in, and lift off!

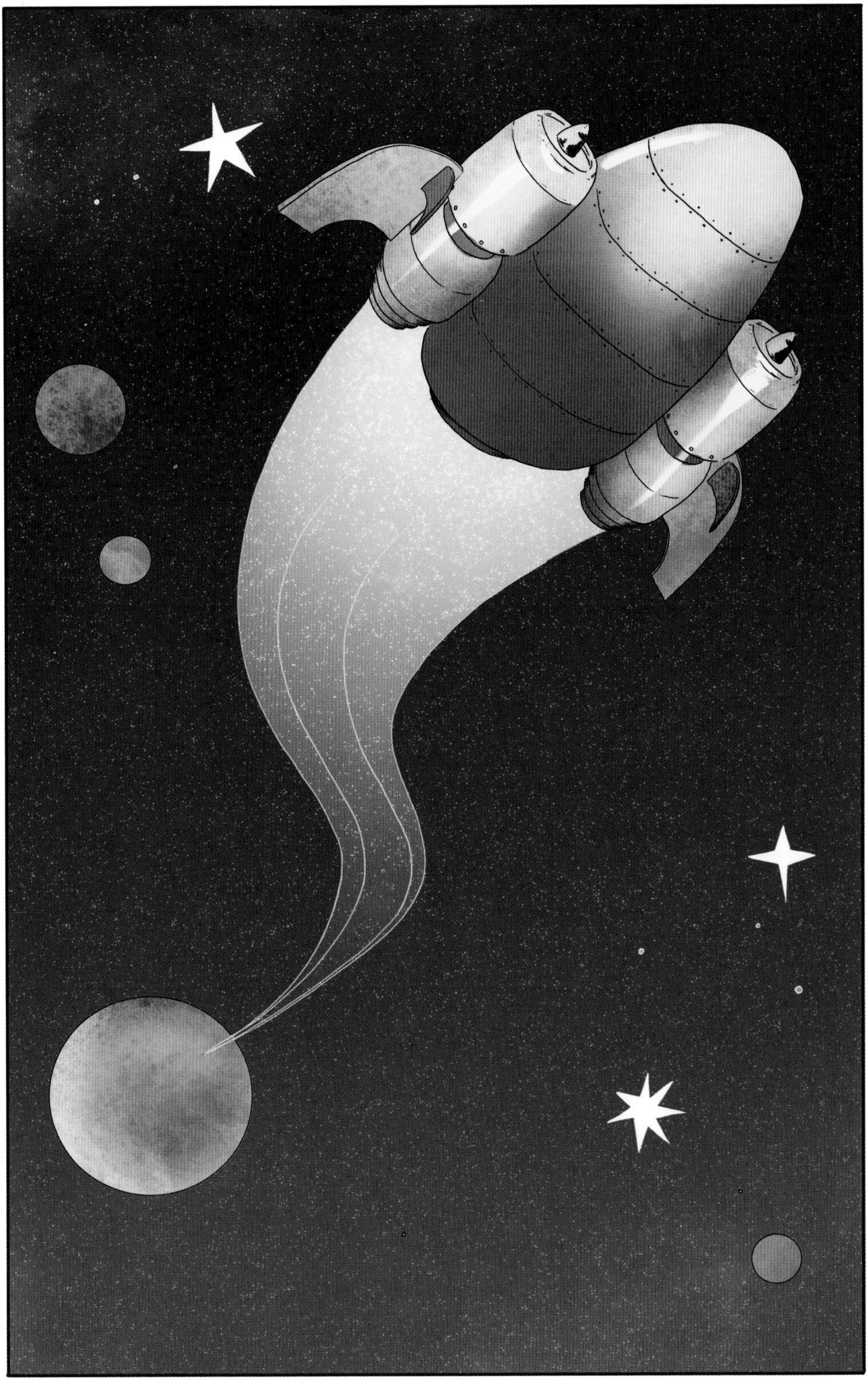

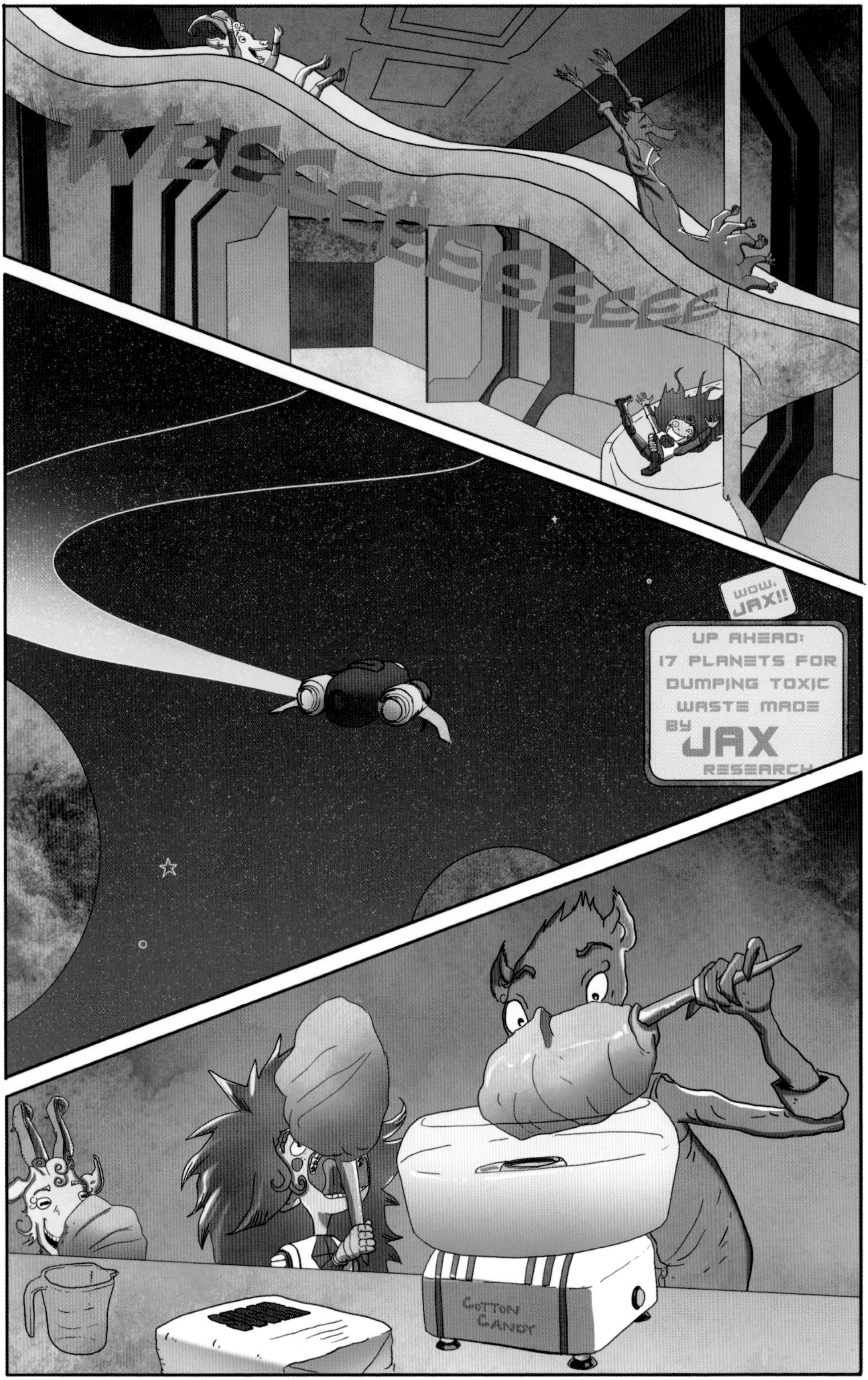
WOW, JAX!!
UP AHEAD: 17 PLANETS FOR DUMPING TOXIC WASTE MADE BY JAX RESEARCH
COTTON CANDY

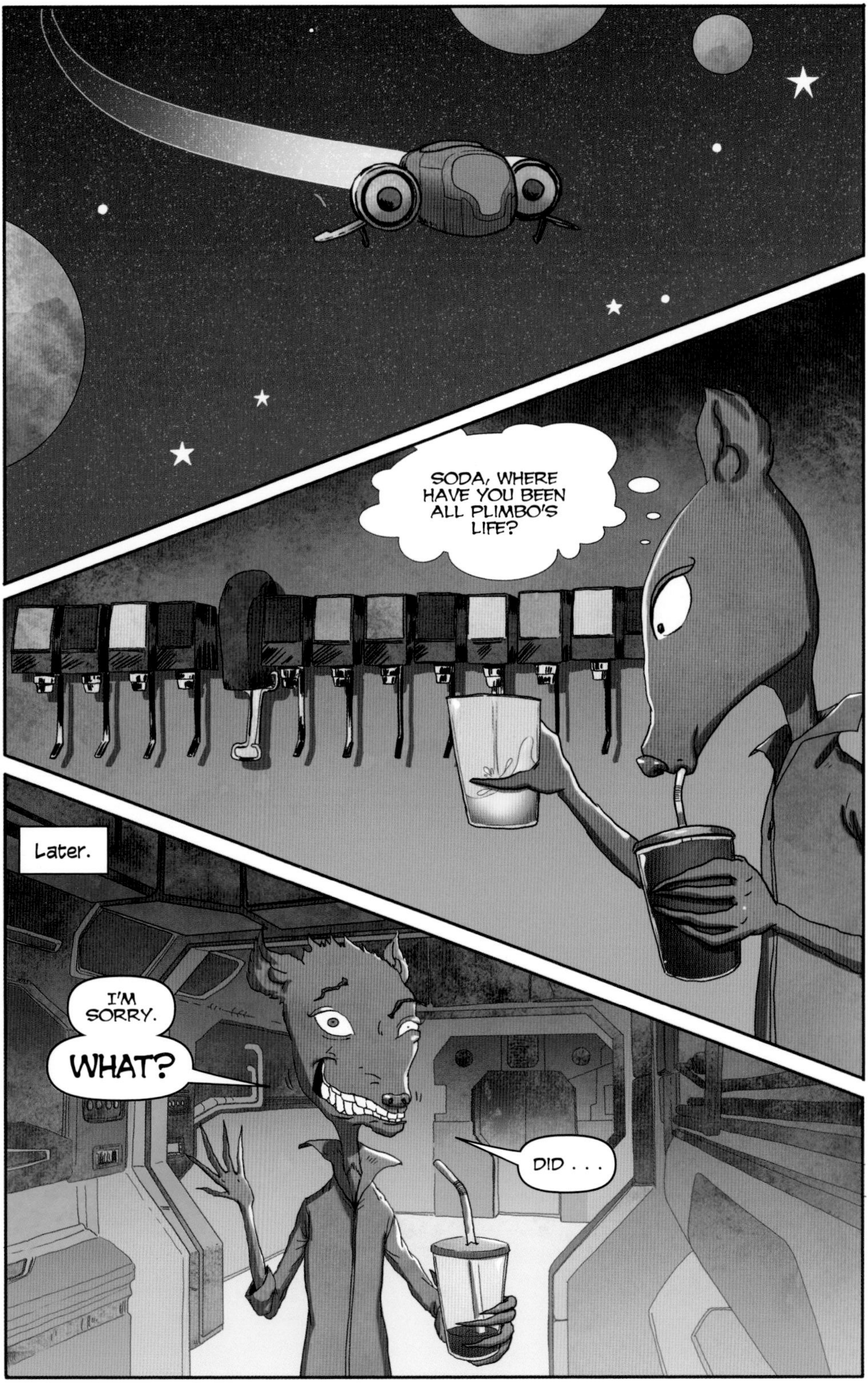
SODA, WHERE HAVE YOU BEEN ALL PLIMBO'S LIFE?
Later.
I'M SORRY.
WHAT?
DID . . .

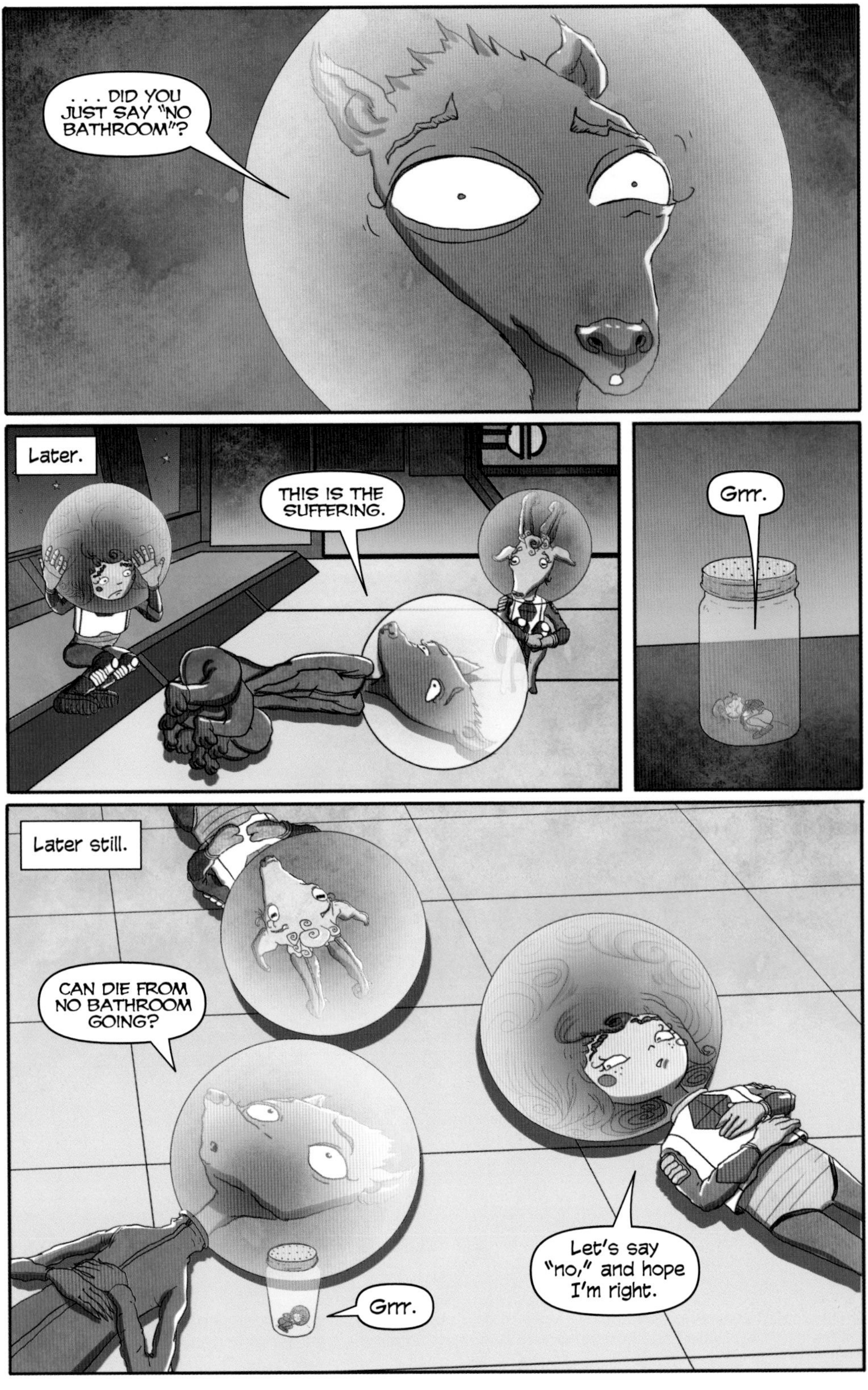
. . . DID YOU JUST SAY "NO BATHROOM"?
Later.
THIS IS THE SUFFERING.
Grrr.
Later still.
CAN DIE FROM NO BATHROOM GOING?
Grrr.
Let's say "no," and hope I'm right.

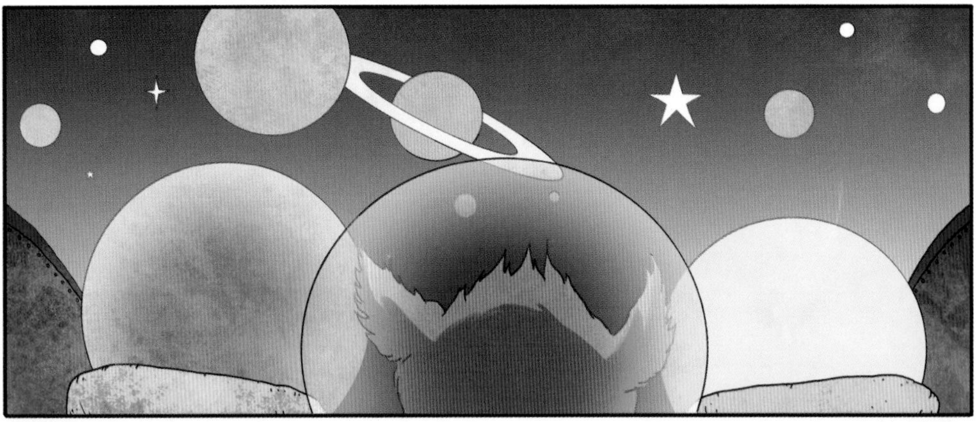

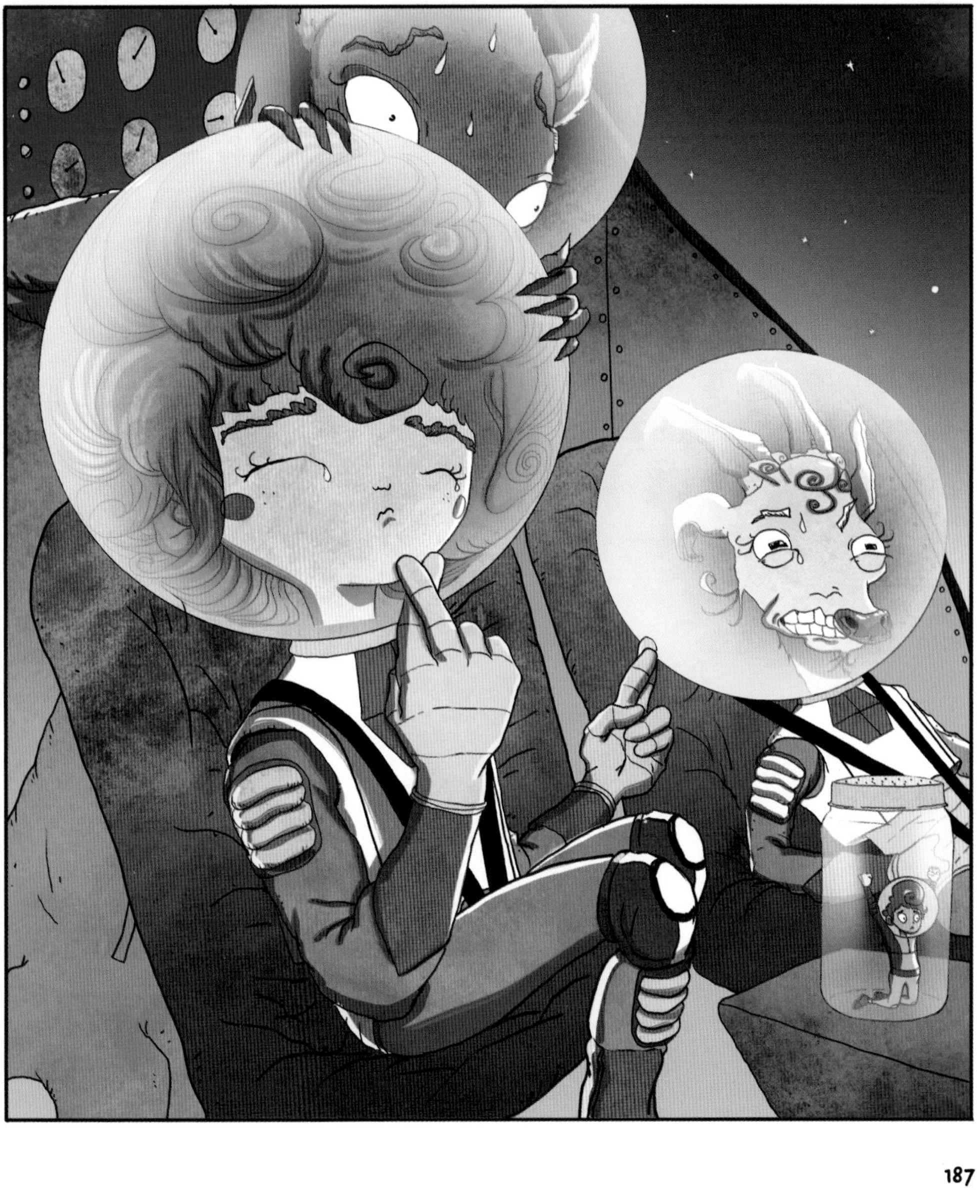

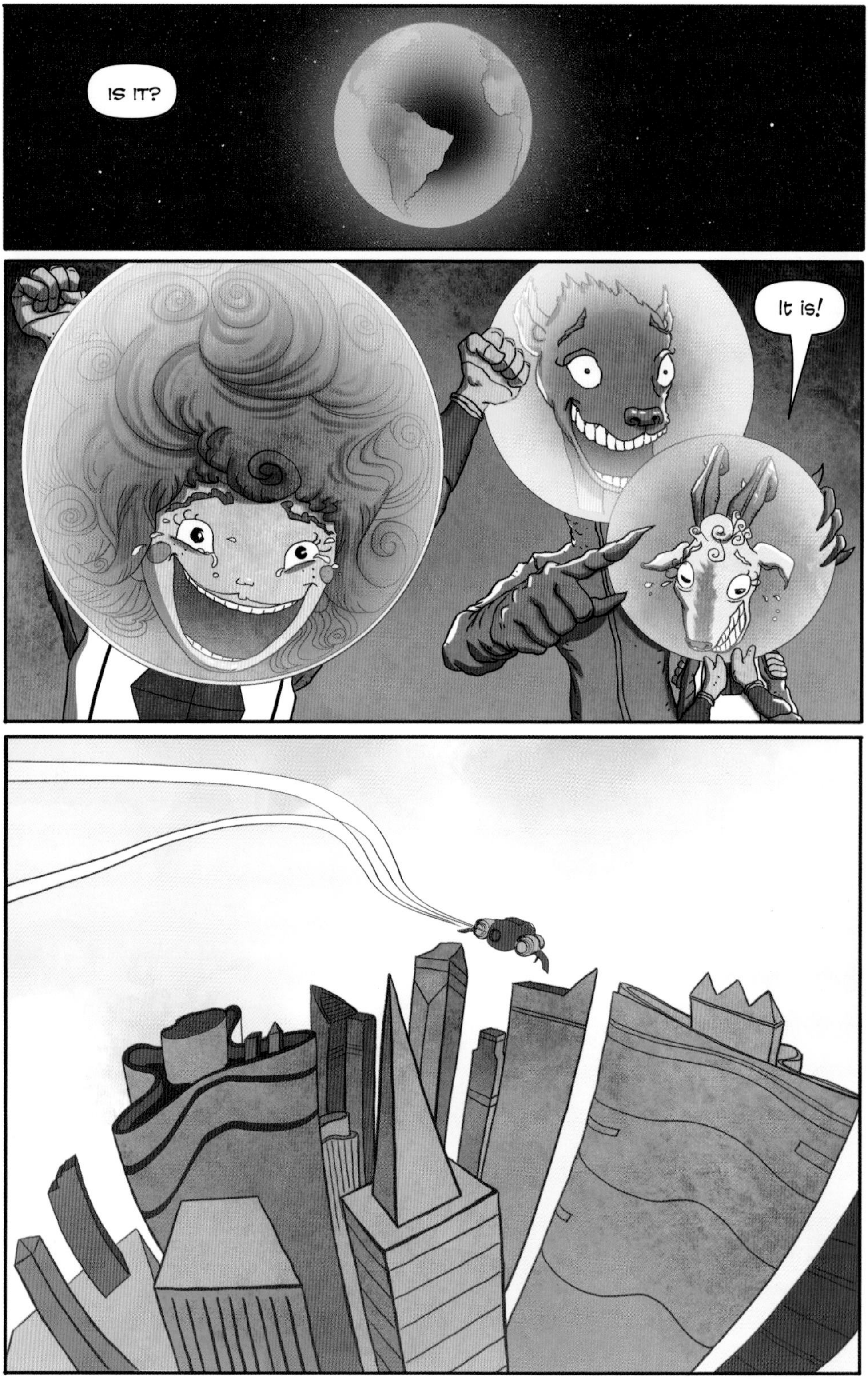
IS IT?
It is!

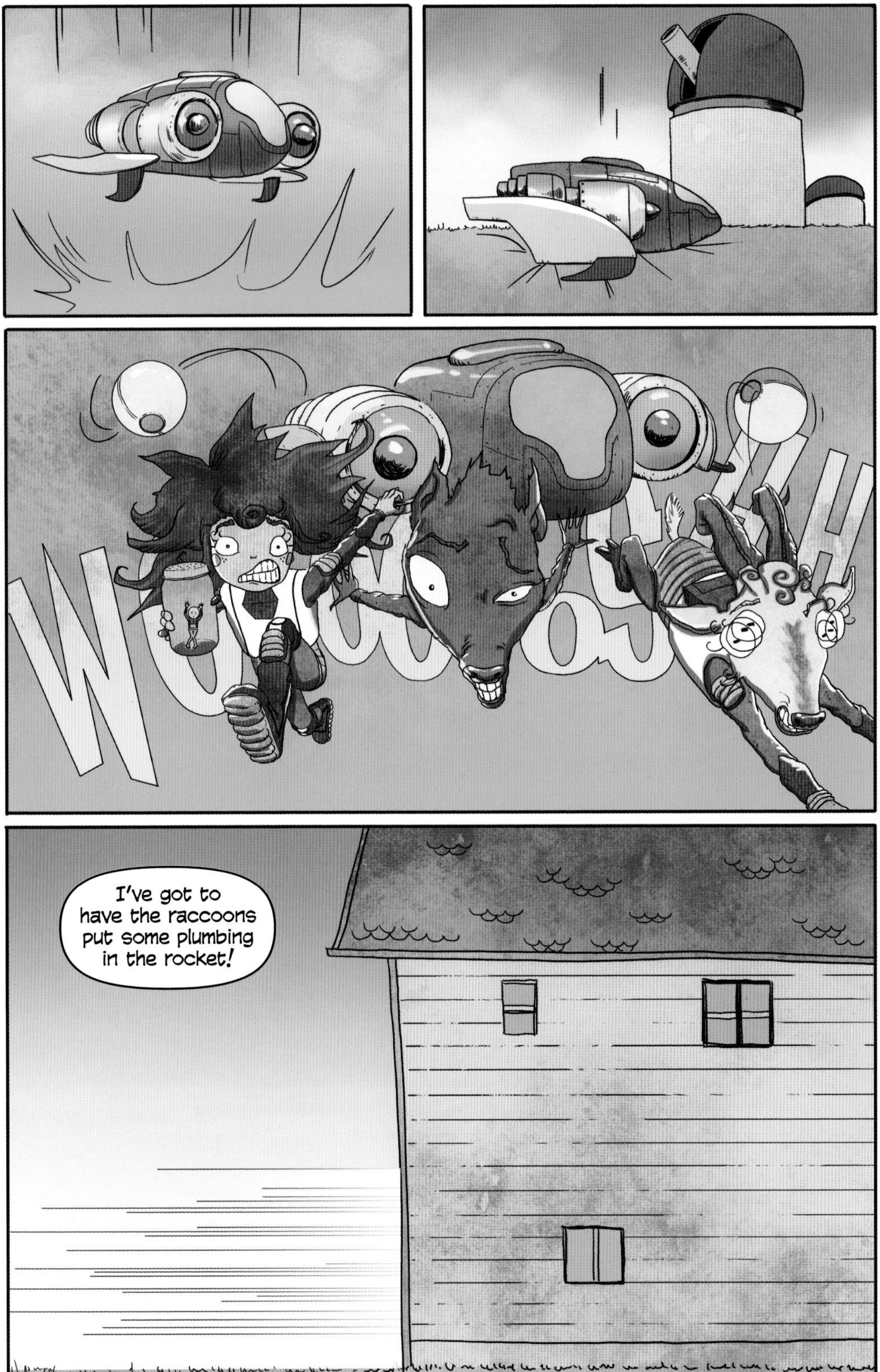
I've got to have the raccoons put some plumbing in the rocket!

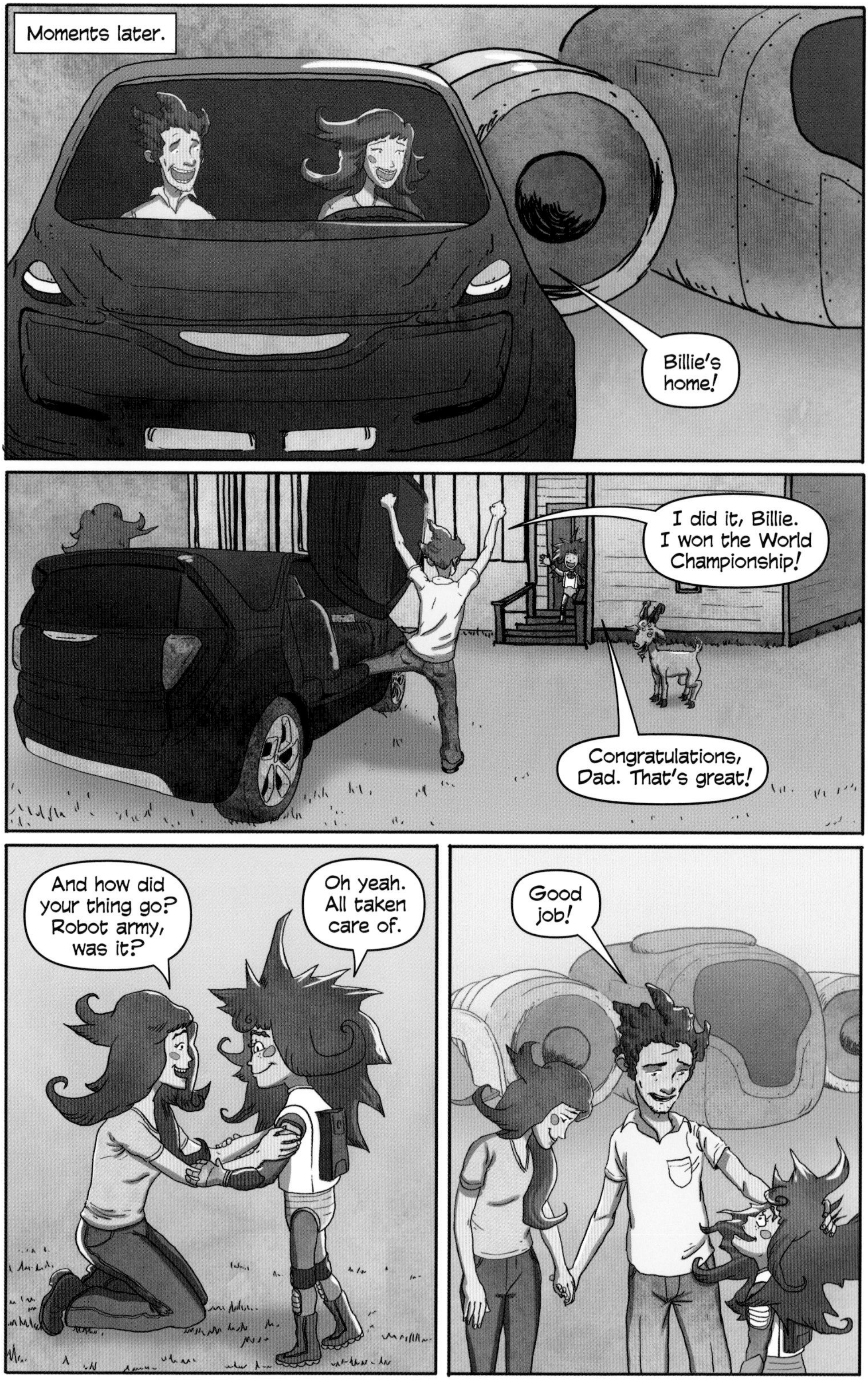

Moments later.
Billie's home!
I did it, Billie. I won the World Championship!
Congratulations, Dad. That's great!
And how did your thing go? Robot army, was it?
Oh yeah. All taken care of.
Good job!

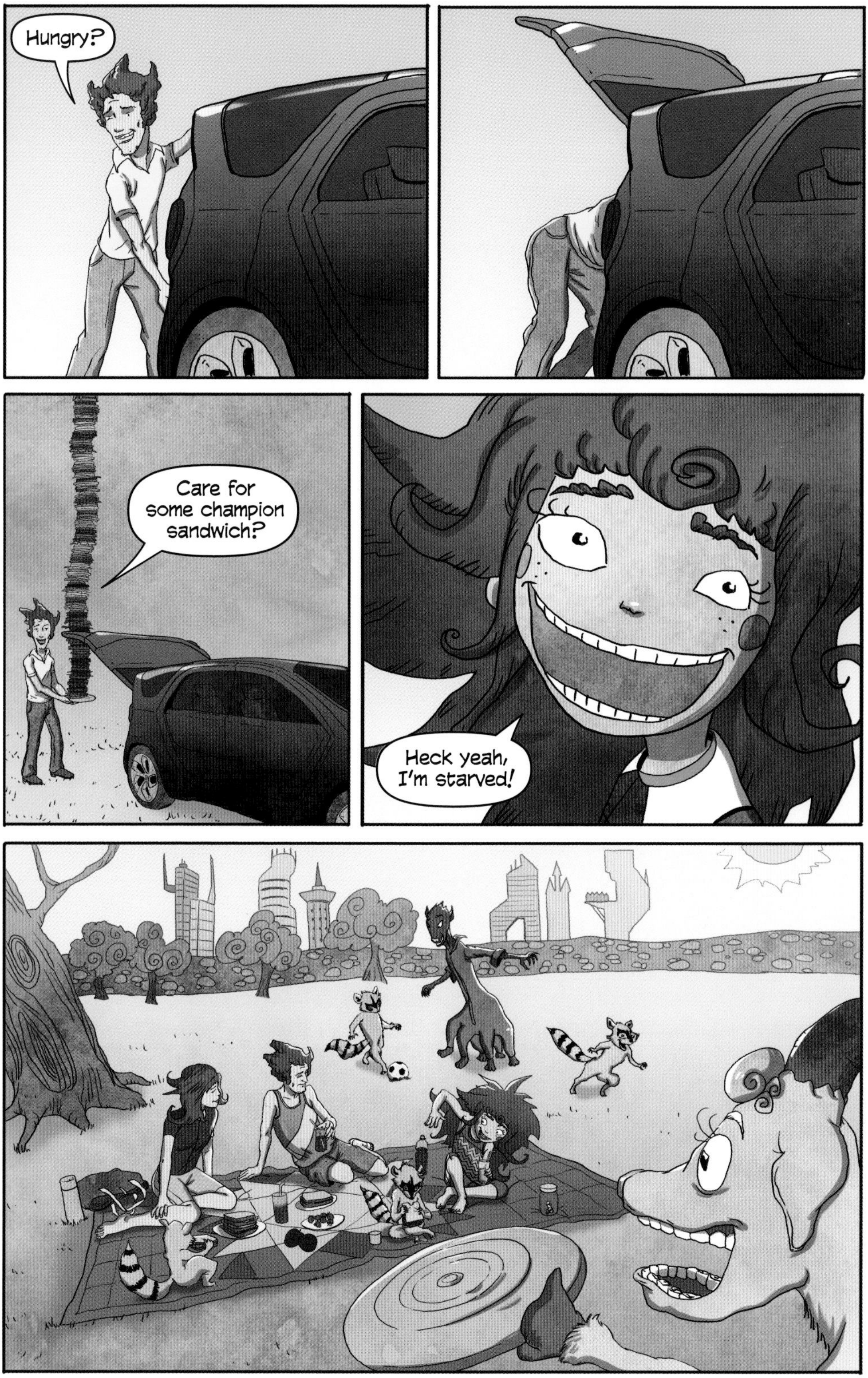
Hungry?
Care for some champion sandwich?
Heck yeah, I'm starved!

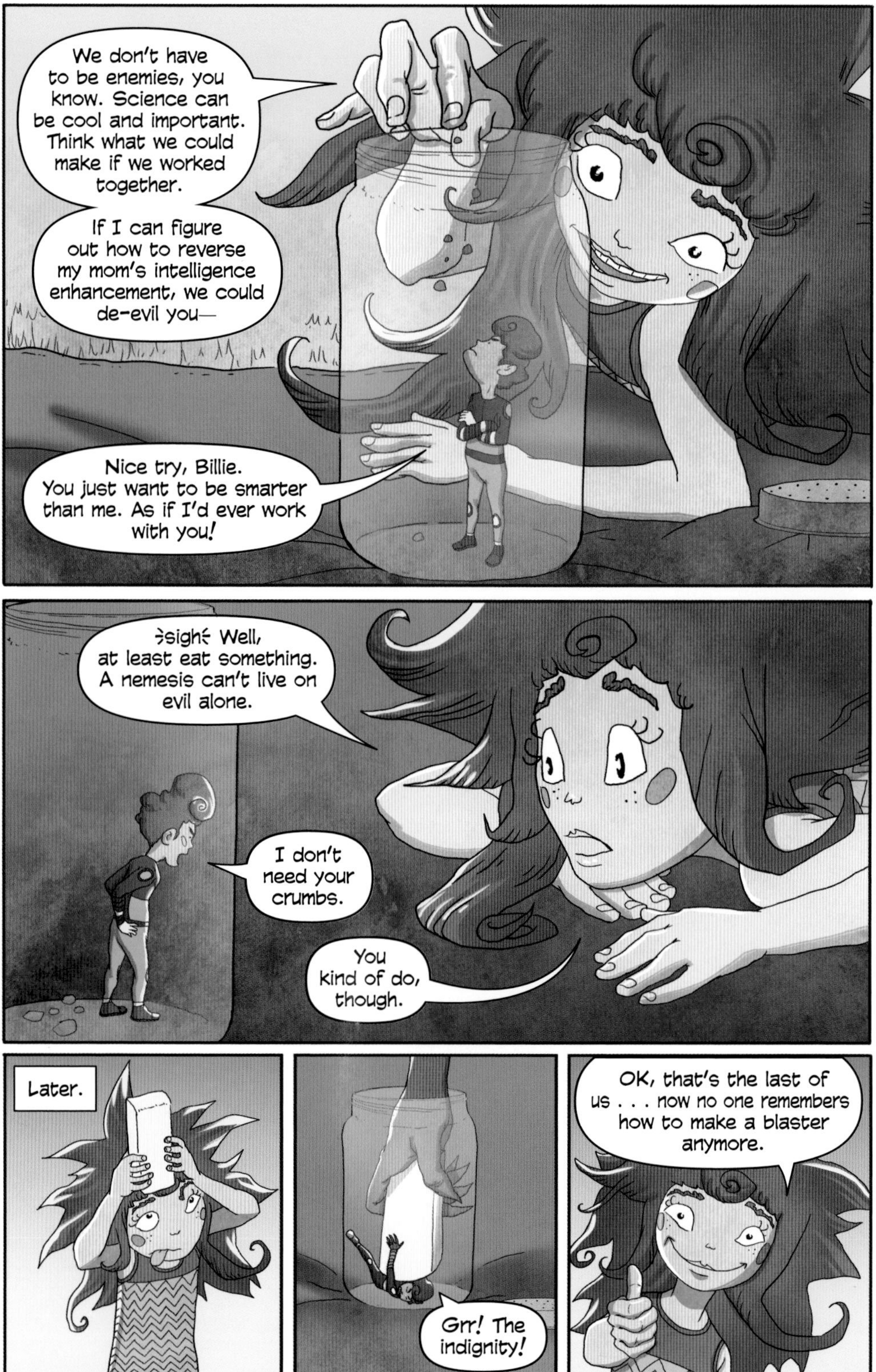
We don't have to be enemies, you know. Science can be cool and important. Think what we could make if we worked together.
If I can figure out how to reverse my mom's intelligence enhancement, we could de-evil you—
Nice try, Billie. You just want to be smarter than me. As if I'd ever work with you!
sigh Well, at least eat something. A nemesis can't live on evil alone.
I don't need your crumbs.
You kind of do, though.
Later.
Grr! The indignity!
OK, that's the last of us . . . now no one remembers how to make a blaster anymore.

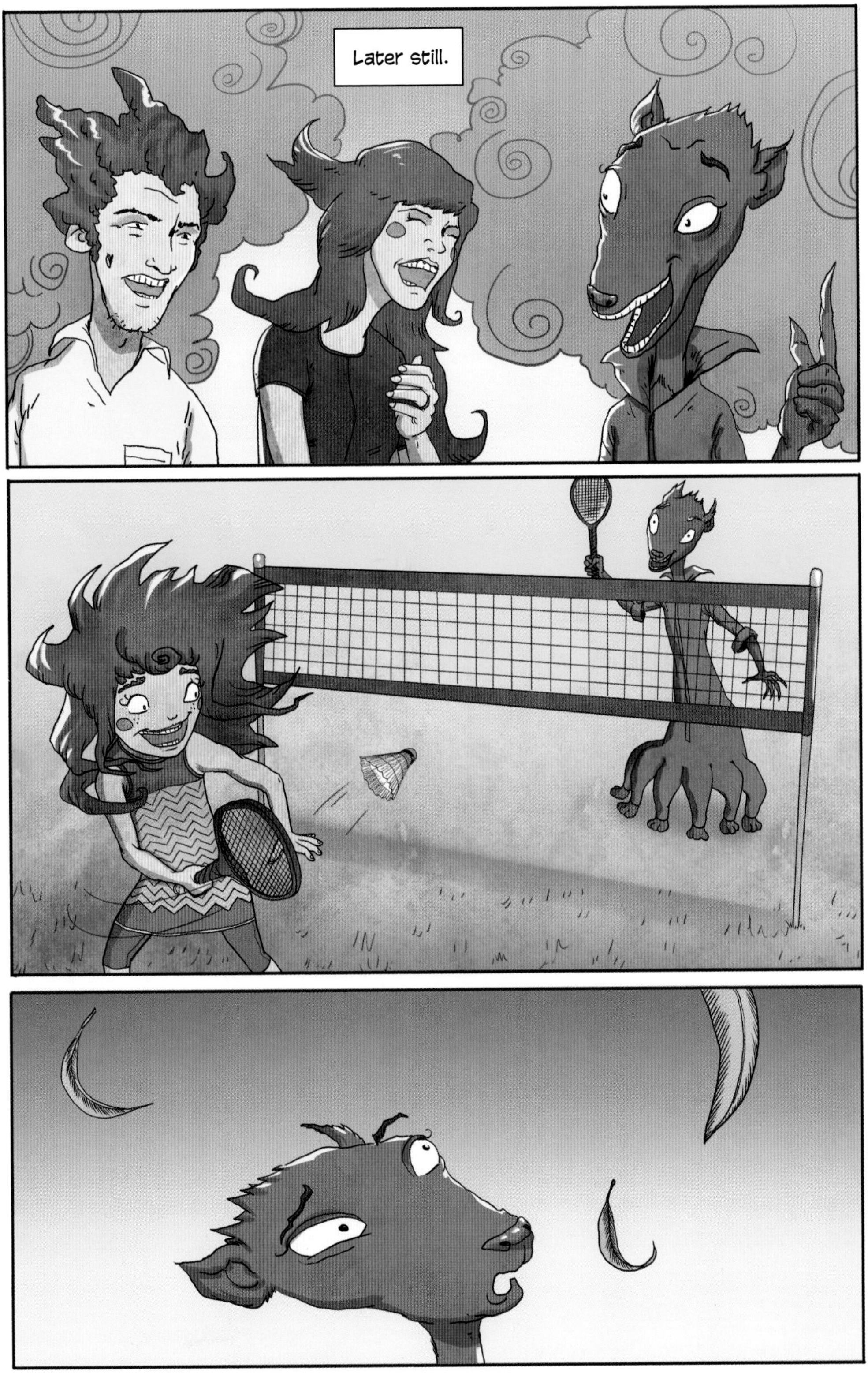
Later still.

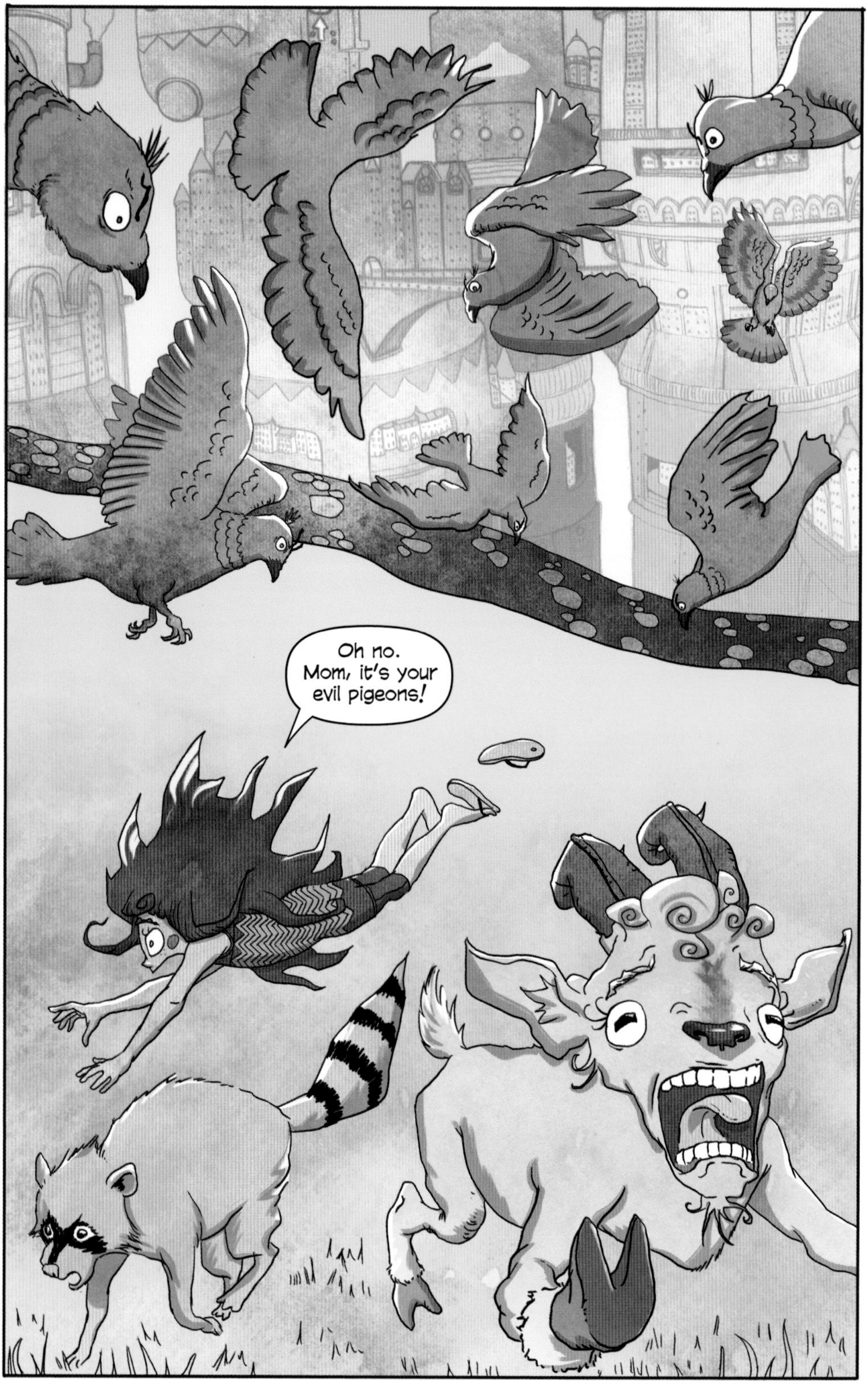
Oh no.
Mom, it's your
evil pigeons!

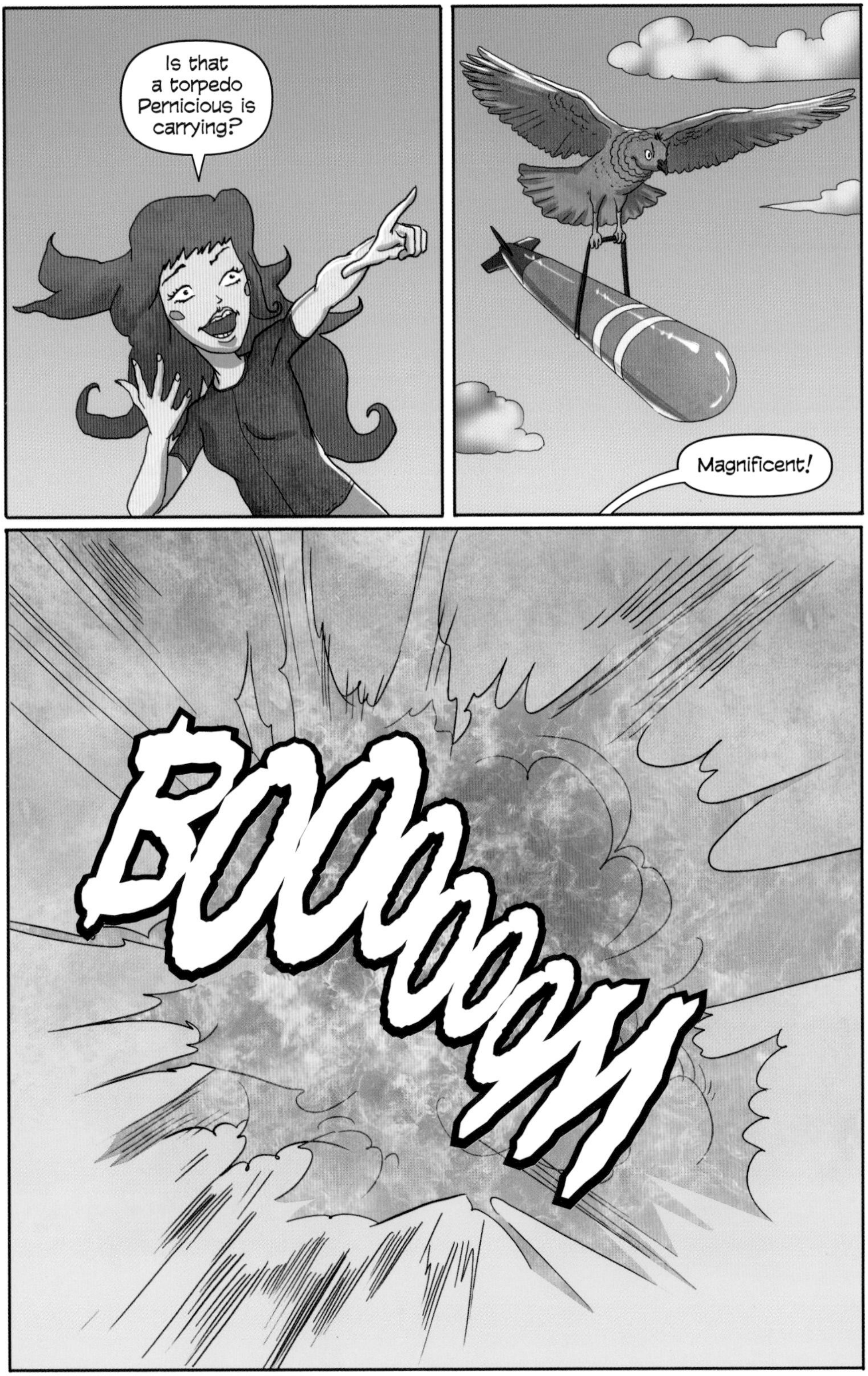
Is that a torpedo Pernicious is carrying?
Magnificent!
BOOOOOOM

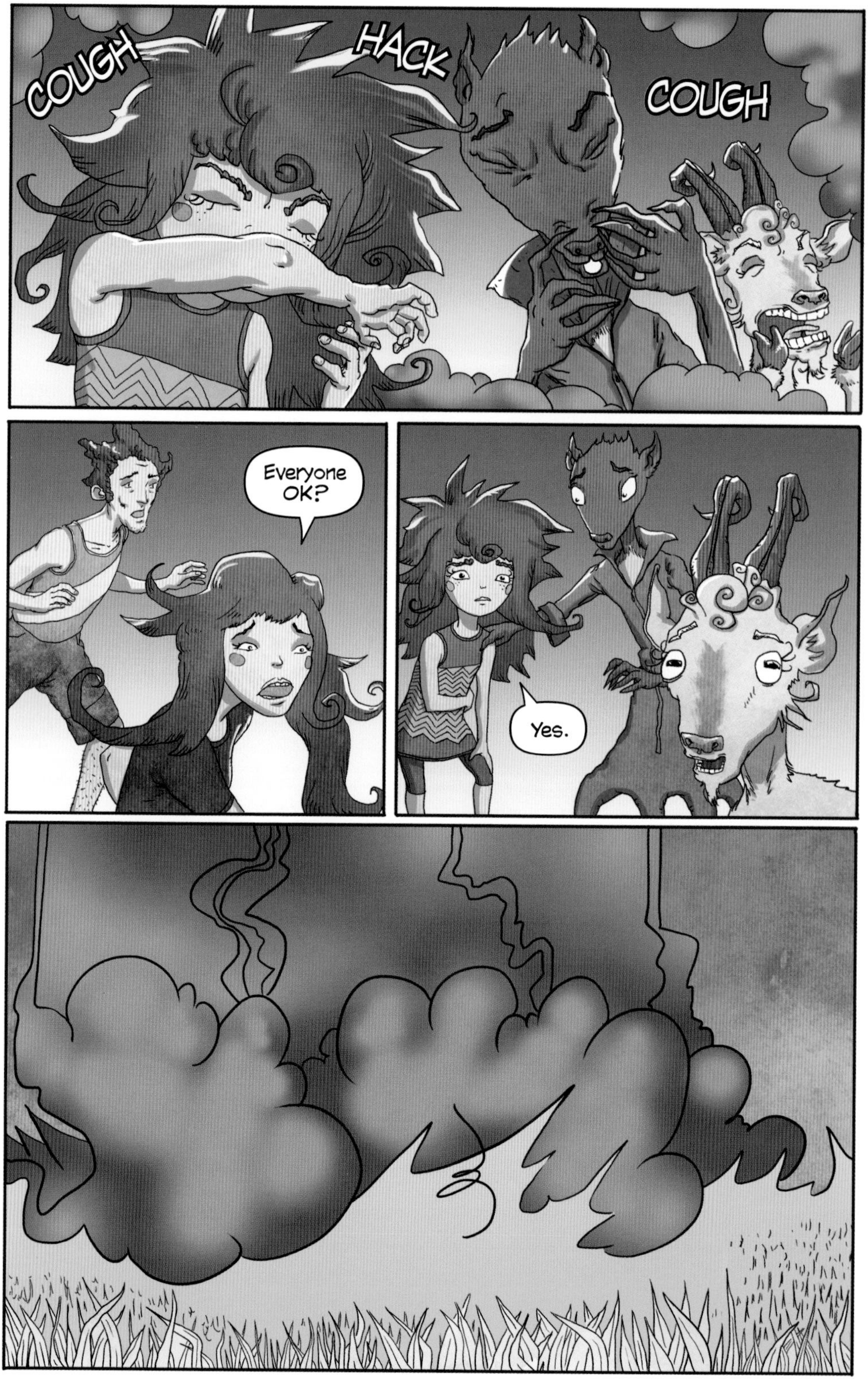
COUGH
HACK
COUGH
Everyone OK?
Yes.

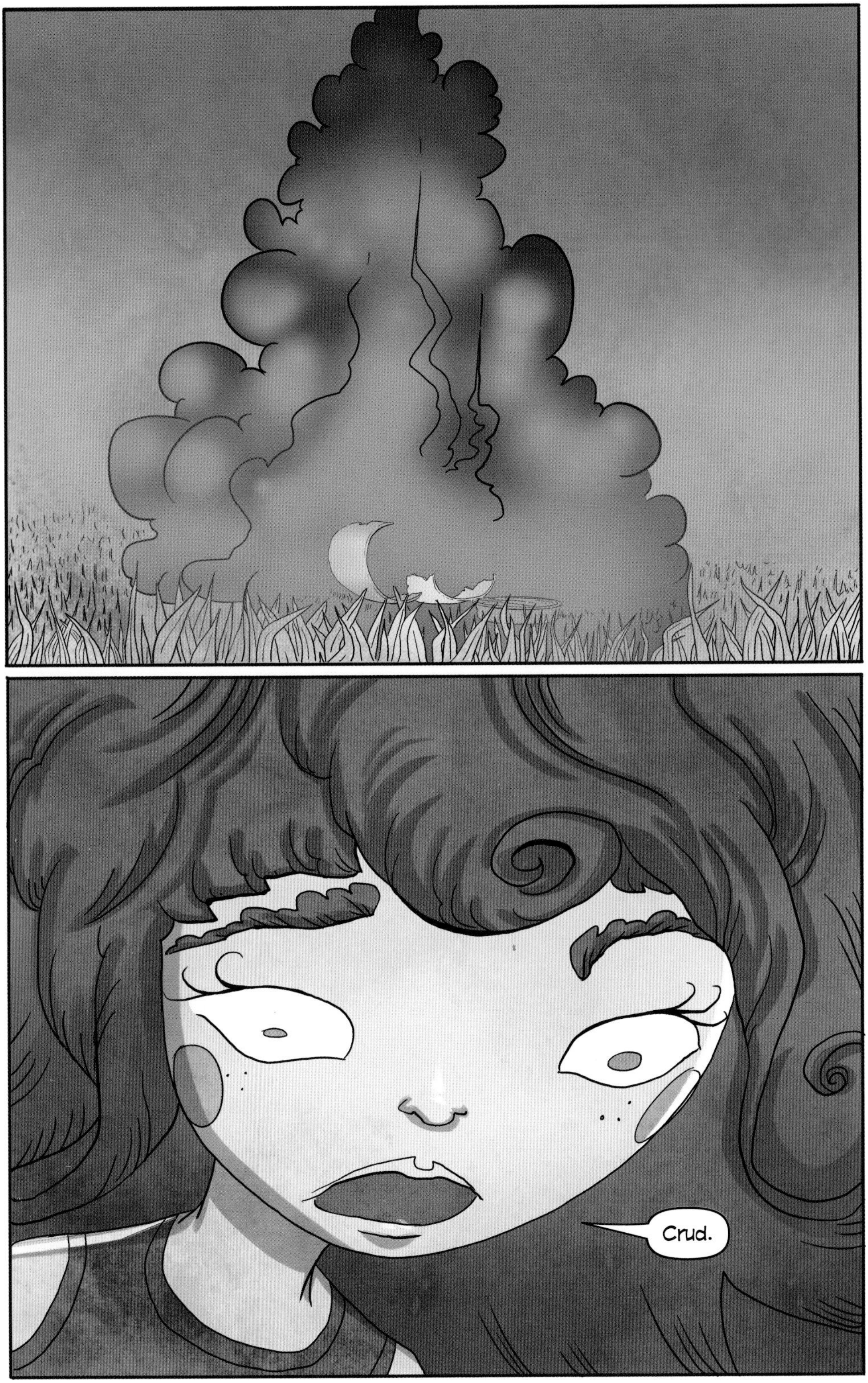
Crud.

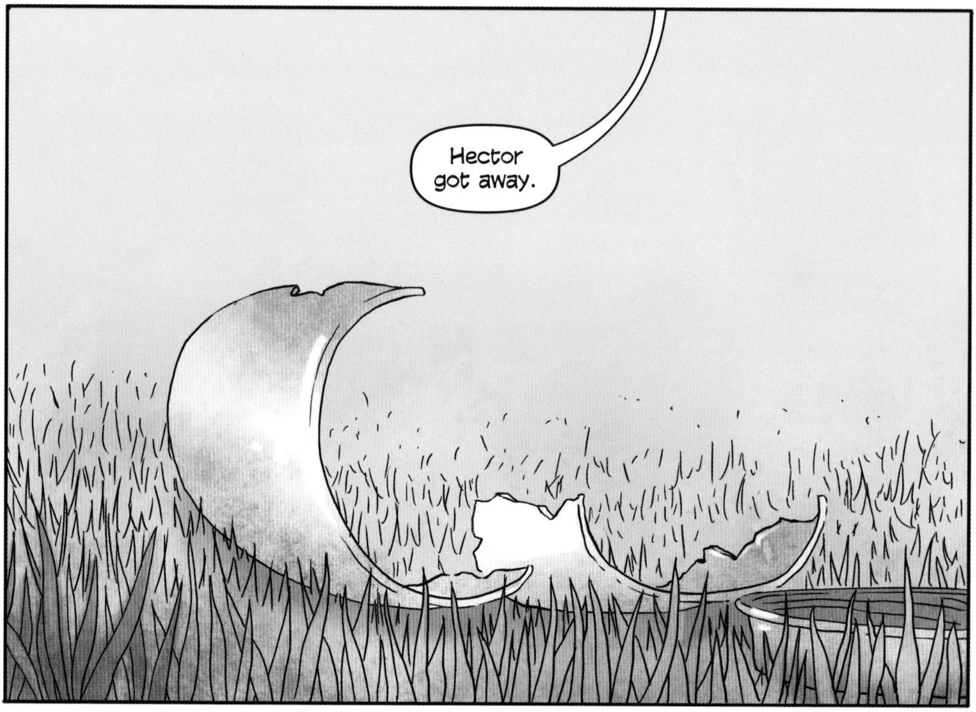
Hector
got away.

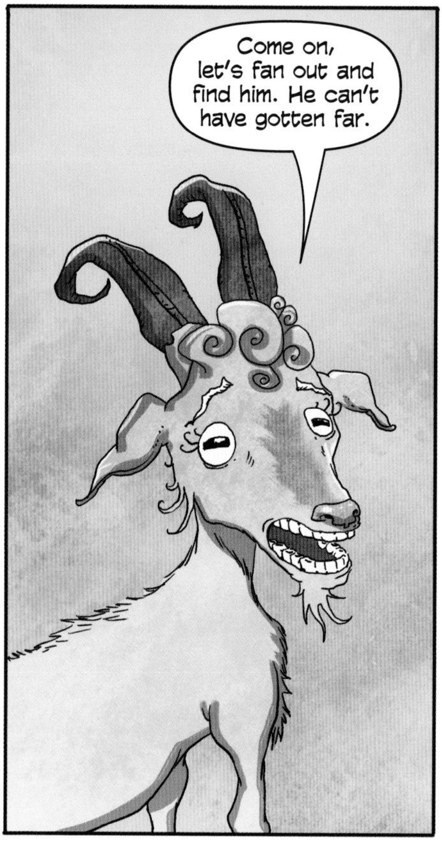
Come on,
let's fan out and
find him. He can't
have gotten far.

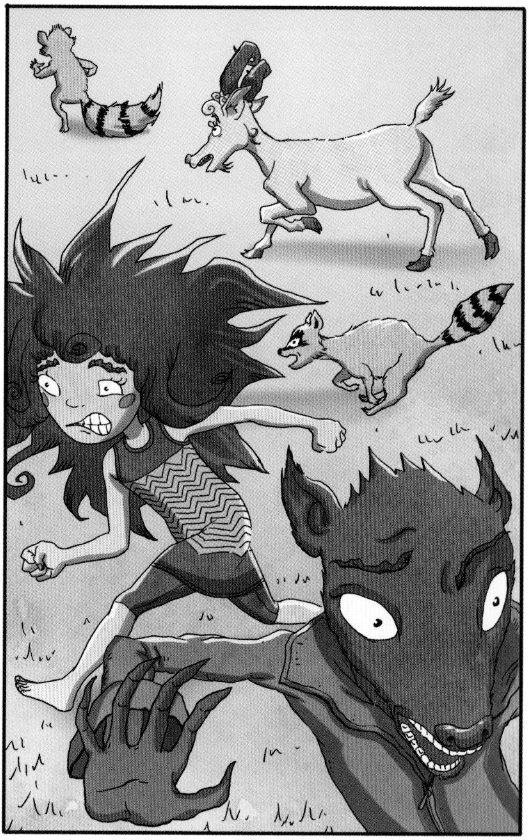

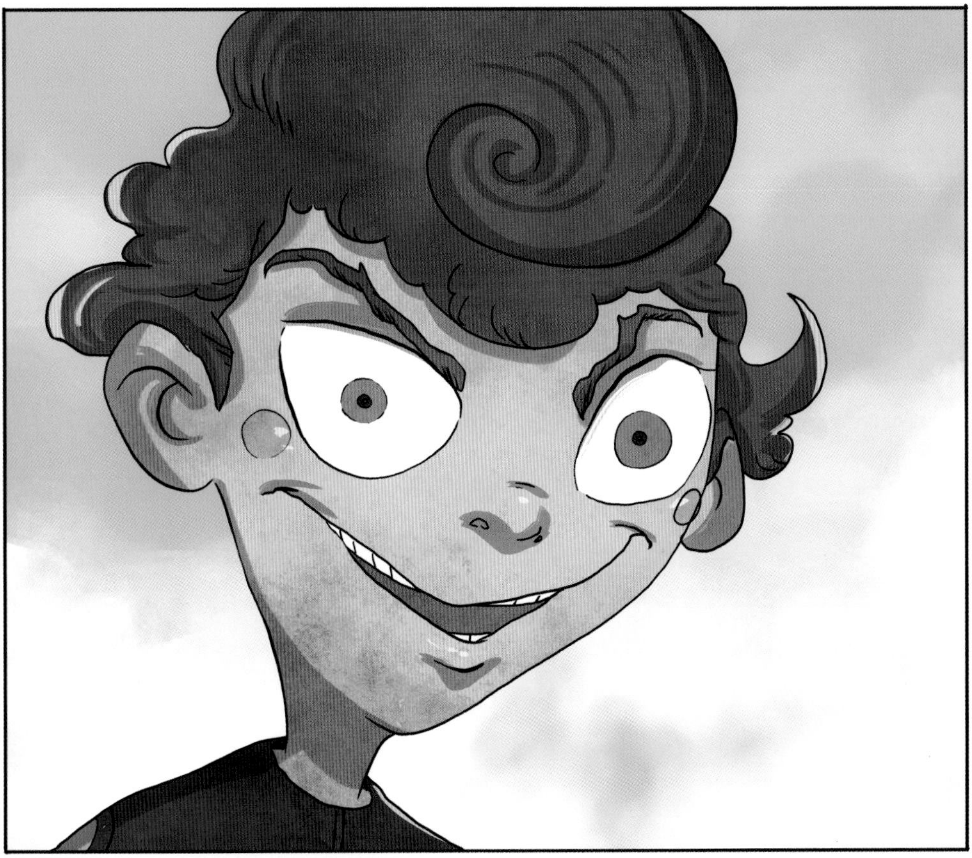

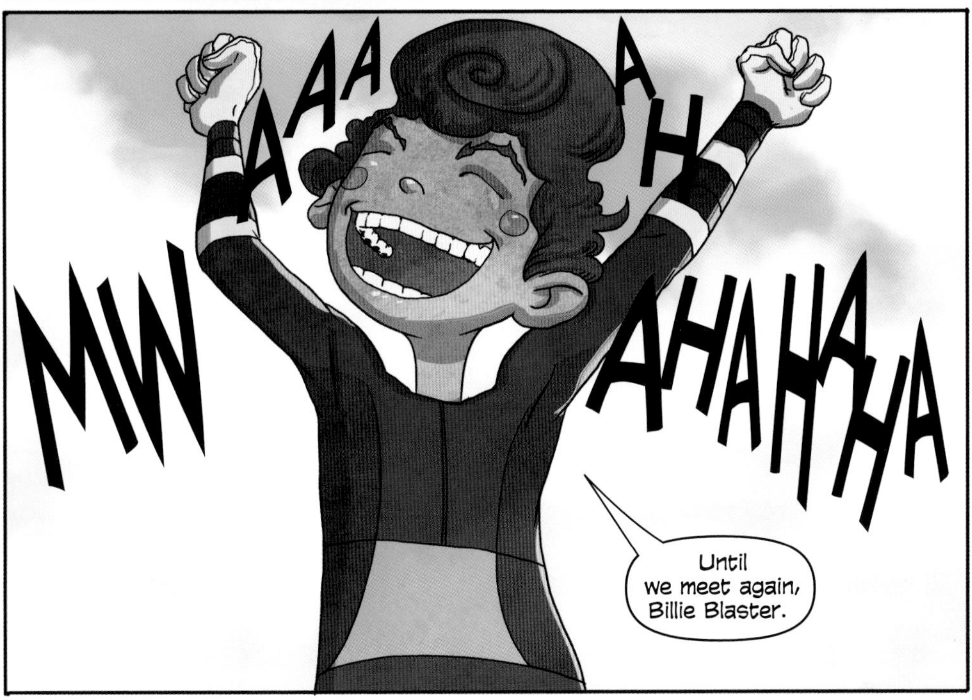
MWAAAAHAHAHAHAHA
Until we meet again, Billie Blaster.

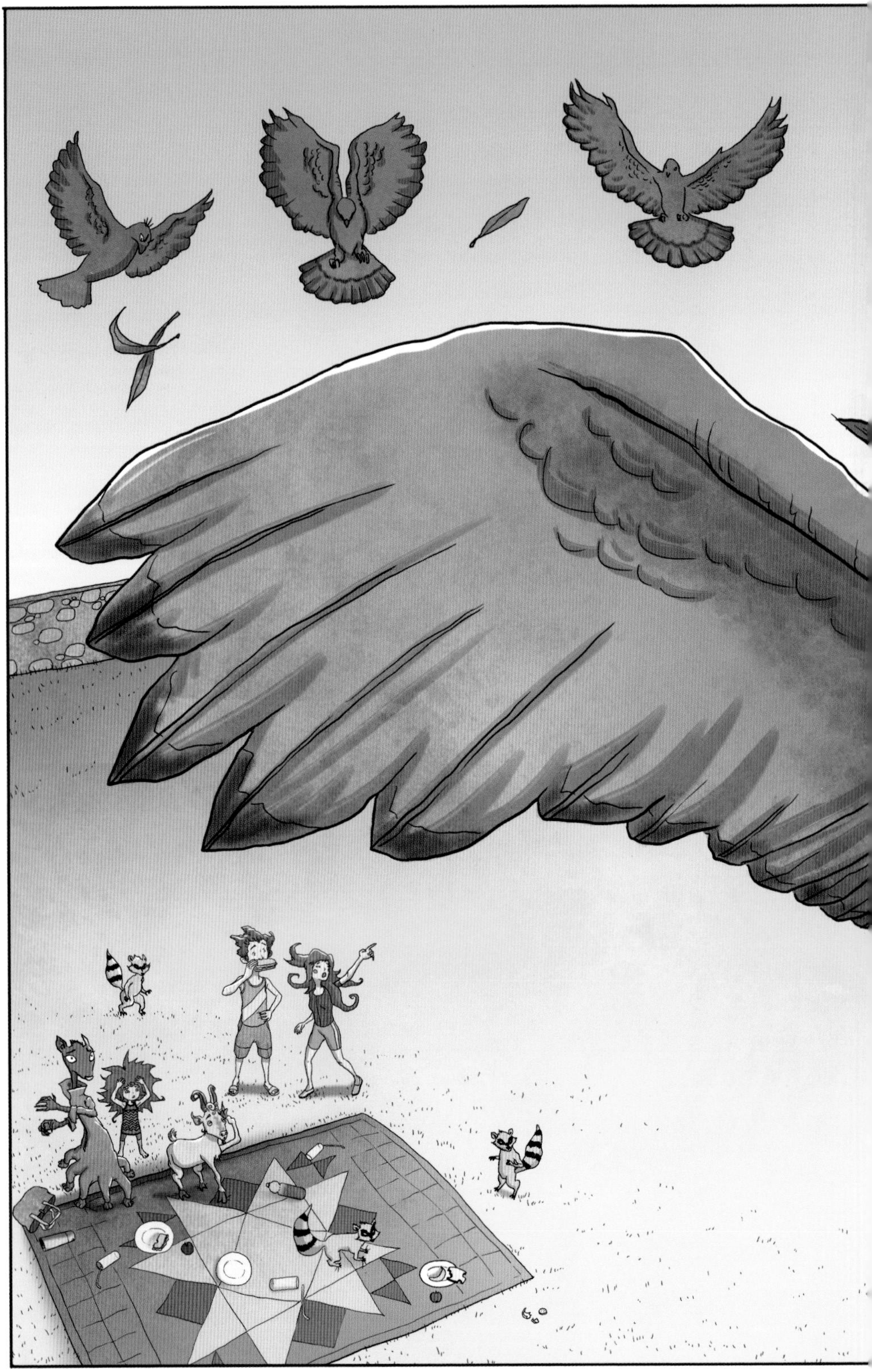

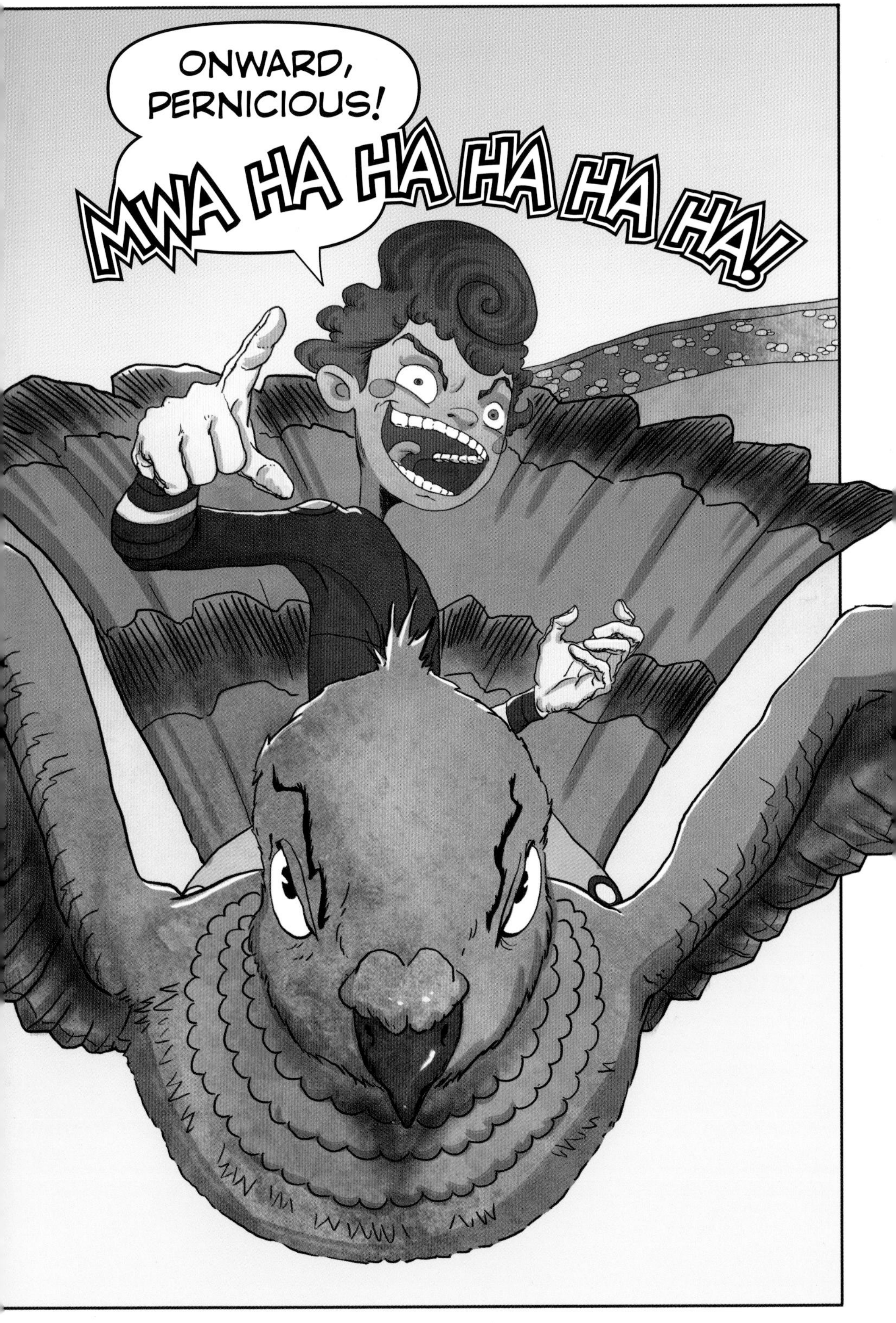
ONWARD, PERNICIOUS!
MWA HA HA HA HA HA HA!

ACKNOWLEDGMENTS

First and always: Immense gratitude to our agent, friend, confidant, and cheerleader, Jane Putch. Your enthusiasm is second to none, your support during the trials and frustrations of a creative career unwavering, and your humor and kindness so very appreciated over the many years that you've been our partner. There's no one else like you.

To the wonderful team at Abrams: Thank you so much for your hard work and dedication in helping us bring this book to life. Andrew Smith, we've had the pleasure of knowing you for over a decade now, and while we don't see you nearly often enough, we can wholeheartedly say that each and every time is an absolute joy, and too brief. (It is our sincere hope that creating Billie Blaster together will give us more occasions to see you!) To editor and organizer in chief, Maggie Lehrman: Thank you for steering the [space]ship so masterfully, and for all you've done to get this assembled and over the finish line. Every book (and especially every graphic novel) involves so much work and so many hands, and you've overseen all the moving parts so brilliantly, every step of the way. To Andrea Miller, art director extraordinaire: You were a delight to work (and chat!) with. And to colorist Nia Sahadewa: Thank you for knocking it out of the park.

Last but not least, we wanted to thank each other. Ha! Seriously though, some of the sillier parts of this story are straight out of the atmosphere of our home. Puns, dad jokes (and mom jokes), plentiful nonsense, and elastic-brained tangents of goofy references are a must around here. And though we do succumb to adulting when necessary (yawn/yuck!), we're overgrown kids much of the time. We're so lucky to get to dream up lap dinosaurs and toilet weasels for a living. Our hope is that we've given our daughter, Clementine, the solid foundation for a life full of creativity and laughter (and we're happy to say that it looks like we've succeeded).

Help Lucy Find the Words!

J	G	E	N	I	U	S	F	F	Q	Y	C	W	C	A	F	S	I
T	I	M	S	O	J	E	A	D	P	S	A	N	E	D	H	Y	P
O	N	I	B	P	K	J	Z	N	I	I	K	L	E	V	C	E	L
I	V	O	N	L	A	I	T	M	D	H	G	A	I	R	I	E	A
L	A	E	O	M	A	C	V	U	T	W	S	E	T	E	V	L	N
E	S	R	G	H	B	S	E	R	K	R	I	C	O	E	N	S	E
T	I	E	G	I	A	N	T	S	U	I	O	C	I	N	S	T	T
A	O	L	I	S	A	I	A	E	H	E	U	P	H	E	P	O	M
O	N	U	N	P	F	K	R	O	R	I	W	U	H	E	N	W	M
R	R	A	C	C	O	O	N	S	R	B	P	C	A	Y	E	C	M
D	W	E	A	S	E	L	J	C	T	E	M	P	E	R	O	R	E
N	E	M	E	S	I	S	J	J	K	O	O	R	O	B	O	T	N

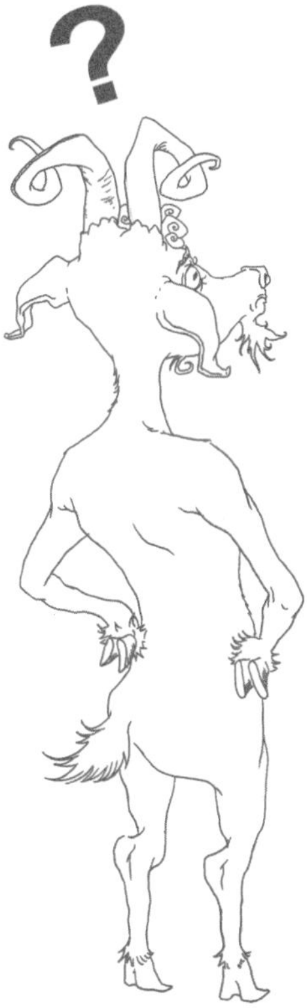

Find the following words in the puzzle.
Words are hidden → ↓ and ↘.

ALIEN
BLASTER
EMPEROR
EVIL
GENIUS
HAIR
INVASION
NEMESIS
NOGGIN
PIGEON
PLANET
RACCOONS
ROBOT
SANDWICH
SCIENCE
SKATES
SPACESHIP
TOILET
TROPHY
WEASEL

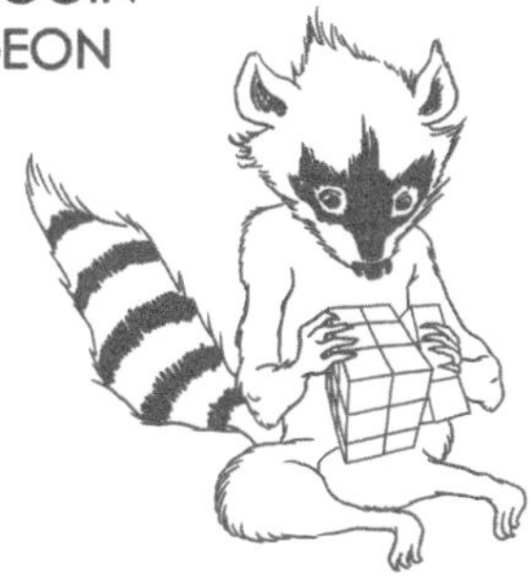